Gin Blanco has critics snared in her web!

Praise for Jennifer Estep's thrilling
Elemental Assassin series

TANGLED THREADS

"Interesting storylines, alluring world, and fascinating characters. That is what I've come to expect from Estep's series. . . . Easily the best of the series to date."

—Yummy Men and Kick Ass Chicks

"The story had me whooping with joy and screaming in outrage, just as all really good books always do."

—Literary Escapism

VENOM

"Estep has really hit her stride with this gritty and compelling series. . . . Brisk pacing and knife-edged danger make this an exciting page-turner."

—*RT Book Reviews* (Top Pick!)

"Gin is a compelling and complicated character whose story is only made better by the lovable band of merry misfits she calls her family. Definitely, by far, the best fantasy series I've read this year."

—Fresh Fiction

"Each book is just as solid and awesome as its earlier predecessors."

—Smokin' Hot Books

"Since the first book in the series, I have been entranced by Gin. . . . Every book has been jam-packed with action and mystery, and once I think it can't get any better, *Venom* comes along and proves me completely wrong."

—Literary Escapism

WEB OF LIES

"The second chapter of the series is just as hard-edged and compelling as the first. Gin Blanco is a fascinatingly pragmatic character, whose intricate layers are just beginning to unravel."

—*RT Book Reviews*

"A fantastic sequel in every respect. . . . Packed with pulse-pounding action and suspense, this urban fantasy truly delivers."

—*SciFiChick.com*

"With each Jennifer Estep book I read I'm more in awe of her writing. She always has fresh storylines with well-developed characters. . . . A must read."

—*Reading With Monie*

"One of the best urban fantasy series I've ever read. The action is off the charts, the passion is hot, and her cast of secondary characters is stellar. . . . If you haven't read this series, you are missing out on one heck of a good time!"

—*The Romance Dish*

SPIDER'S BITE

"When it comes to work, Estep's newest heroine is brutally efficient and very pragmatic, which gives the series plenty of bite. . . . Kudos to Estep for the knife-edged suspense!"

—*RT Book Reviews*

"The fast pace, clever dialogue, and intriguing heroine help make this new series launch one to watch."

—*Library Journal*

"Electrifying! Jennifer Estep really knows how to weave a fantasy tale that will keep you reading way past your bedtime."

—*Reading With Monie*

PREVIOUS BOOKS IN
THE ELEMENTAL ASSASSIN SERIES
BY JENNIFER ESTEP

Spider's Bite
Web of Lies
Venom
Tangled Threads
Spider's Revenge

Available from Pocket Books

BY A Thread

AN ELEMENTAL ASSASSIN BOOK

JENNIFER ESTEP

POCKET BOOKS

New York   London   Toronto   Sydney   New Delhi

Pocket Books
A Division of Simon & Schuster, Inc.
1230 Avenue of the Americas
New York, NY 10020

This book is a work of fiction. Names, characters, places, and incidents either are products of the author's imagination or are used fictitiously. Any resemblance to actual events or locales or persons, living or dead, is entirely coincidental.

First Pocket Books paperback edition March 2012

POCKET and colophon are registered trademarks of Simon & Schuster, Inc.

For information about special discounts for bulk purchases, please contact Simon & Schuster Special Sales at 1-866-506-1949 or business@simonandschuster.com.

The Simon & Schuster Speakers Bureau can bring authors to your live event. For more information or to book an event contact the Simon & Schuster Speakers Bureau at 1-866-248-3049 or visit our website at www.simonspeakers.com.

Manufactured in the United States of America

10 9 8 7 6 5 4

ISBN 978-1-4516-5176-8
ISBN 978-1-4516-5178-2 (ebook)

To my mom, my grandma, and Andre
for all their love and support over the years

ACKNOWLEDGMENTS

Once again, my heartfelt thanks goes out to all the folks who help turn my words into a book.

Thanks go to my agent, Annelise Robey, and editors, Megan McKeever and Lauren McKenna, for all their helpful advice, support, and encouragement.

Thanks to Tony Mauro for designing another terrific cover, and thanks to everyone at Pocket and Simon & Schuster for their work on the book and series.

And finally, a big thanks to all the readers. Knowing that folks read and enjoy my books is truly humbling, and I'm glad that you are all enjoying Gin and her adventures.

I appreciate you all more than you will ever know.

Happy reading!

* 1 *

"You need a vacation."

I looked up from the tomato I was slicing and stared across the counter at Finnegan Lane, my foster brother and partner in so many murderous schemes over the years.

"Vacation? I hardly ever take vacations," I said. "I have a barbecue restaurant to run, in case you've forgotten."

I gestured with the knife at the rest of the Pork Pit. Most people wouldn't consider the restaurant much to look at with its blue and pink vinyl booths and matching, peeling pig tracks on the floor that led to the men's and women's restrooms. The long counter that ran along the back wall was older than I was, as were most of the cups, dishes, plates, silverware, and stainless-steel appliances. But everything was neat, clean, and polished to a high gloss, from the tables and chairs to the framed, slightly bloody copy of *Where the Red Fern Grows* by Wilson Rawls that hung on the wall close to the battered, old-fashioned cash register. The Pork Pit might not be some fancy, highfalutin place, but it was my gin joint, my home, and I was damned proud of it. Always had been, always would be.

"A vacation," Finn repeated, as if I hadn't said a word. He was rather persistent that way. "Somewhere warm, somewhere sandy, somewhere where nobody knows your name, either as Gin Blanco or most especially as the Spider."

Finn's voice wasn't that loud, but when he said *the Spider*, the words echoed like gunshots through the storefront. The folks sitting at the tables behind Finn immediately froze, their thick, juicy barbecue beef and pork sandwiches halfway between their plates and lips. Conversation dried up like a shallow puddle in the desert, and everyone's eyes cut to me, wondering how I would react to the sound of *that* particular name.

My assassin name. The one I'd gone by for the last seventeen years, when I was out late at night killing people for money and eventually other, nobler reasons.

My hand tightened around the long, serrated tomato knife. Not for the first time, I wished I could use it to cut out Finn's tongue—or at least get him to think before he opened his mouth.

An elderly woman sitting two stools down from Finn noticed my death grip on the blade. Her face paled, and her hand clutched at the collar of her white silk blouse like she was about three seconds away from having a heart attack.

Sighing, I made myself relax and put the blade down on the counter. Fuck. I hated being notorious.

After a lifetime of being invisible, I was suddenly the most well-known person in Ashland. Several weeks ago, I'd done the unthinkable—I'd killed Mab Monroe, the Fire elemental who'd been the head of the city's underworld for years. Mab had murdered my mother and older sister when I was thirteen, and her death had been a long time coming, as far as I was concerned. I didn't know anyone who'd shed any real tears over the Fire elemental's messy demise.

But now, everyone wanted their pound of flesh—from *me*.

Mab's death had left a vacuum among Ashland's legit and not-so-legit power players, and they were all scrambling to stake their various claims, solidify their shady operations, and position themselves as the city's next top dog.

Some of them thought the best way to accomplish that last feat was by killing me.

Idiot after idiot had come to the Pork Pit in the last few weeks, either singly or in small groups, all with one thing on their minds—taking out the Spider. Most of the elementals came at me straight on, challenging me to duels and wanting to test their magic against my own Ice and Stone power. Everyone else, well, they were content to try to get the drop on me when I was either opening up or closing down the restaurant.

Whatever their method, it always ended the same way—with the challengers dead and me asking Sophia Deveraux to dispose of their bodies. I'd killed more people in the last month than I had in a year as the Spider. Even I was getting a little sick of the constant, not-so-surprise attacks and blood spatters on my hands, clothes, and shoes, but the stream of suicidal lowlifes showed no signs of slowing down anytime soon.

The old lady next to Finn sucked in a breath. I looked down and realized that I'd picked up the tomato knife again and was rubbing my thumb over the smooth, polished hilt. It wasn't as strong or sharp as the five silverstone knives that I had secreted on my body, but the serrated blade would do plenty of damage. Most things would, if you put enough force behind them, and being forceful was one of the many things I excelled at.

"What are you looking at?" I snapped.

The old lady's eyes widened. With a trembling hand, she reached into her purse, threw a twenty-dollar bill onto the counter, slid off her stool, and hightailed it out of the restaurant as fast as her square white heels would carry her.

"Another one bites the dust," Finn murmured, his green eyes bright and merry in his handsome face. He always loved my discomfort, even when he wasn't the cause of it.

I frowned and made a slashing gesture with the knife, but Finn just ignored my cold glare and threats of violence. Instead, he raised his coffee mug and gestured to a dwarf who was chopping long green ribs of celery to add to the macaroni salad she was mixing up.

"Sophia?" he asked. "Pretty please?"

Sophia Deveraux turned to stare at Finn. She was the head cook at the Pit, in addition to her side job of getting rid of any bodies I left in my wake as the Spider. I'd inherited the dwarf's dual services when I'd taken over the assassination business from Finn's father, Fletcher Lane. The old man had been an assassin known as the Tin Man, and he'd taught me everything he knew about how to help people quit breathing.

Sophia grunted and grabbed the pot of coffee that she always kept on for Finn, who usually dropped by the restaurant at least once a day. She topped off his cup, and the warm chicory fumes filled my nose, momentarily overpowering the cumin, red pepper, and other spices that flavored the air. The rich caffeine smell always reminded me of Fletcher, who'd drunk the same chicory brew. I breathed in, hoping that the comforting scent would help relax me, but it didn't—not tonight. Not for weeks now.

The Pork Pit might not be much to look at, but folks couldn't help but stare at Sophia. One by one, their eyes drifted from me over to her. It wasn't that she was a dwarf that drew people's gazes; it was because she was Goth—seriously Goth. Sophia wore heavy black boots and jeans, topped by a white T-shirt that featured a black scythe slashing across her chest. Grim Reaper, indeed. Her hair and eyes were black too, making her skin seem that much paler, despite the bright fuchsia lipstick she wore. The lipstick was the same color as the spiked silverstone collar that ringed her neck.

The good thing about standing next to Sophia was that it made everyone forget about me. After a few more seconds, the customers went back to their sandwiches, along with the baked beans, fried onion rings, and other hearty side dishes.

"Now, back to my vacation idea." Finn grinned, showing off his perfect white teeth. "Just think about it. You, Owen, me, and Bria, all happily ensconced in a swanky hotel by a beautiful beach. Bria in a bikini. You and Owen doing your own thing, Bria in a bikini. Did I mention Bria in a bikini?"

I rolled my eyes. "Geez. Have a little respect. That's my baby sister you're talking about."

Finn's grin widened. "I know."

Along with everything else that had gone down when I'd been waging my final battle against Mab, Finn had finally hooked up with my younger sister, Bria. I wasn't sure how serious the two of them were, but they'd been hot and heavy for weeks now and showed no signs of slowing down. I was happy for them—really, I was—but I could have done without Finn's giving me the play-by-play of their sex life on a regular basis. Hell, I didn't even talk about that stuff with Bria, and she was my sister. But that was part of the sordid charm of Finnegan Lane. He loved talking about women and their attributes just as much as he did sleeping with them.

Finn opened his mouth to cajole me some more, but I'd had enough—enough of the stares, enough of the whispers, enough of everyone wondering if I was going to kill them for setting foot inside my restaurant. I just wanted to be left alone by everyone right now, including Finn.

"I don't need a vacation," I growled, stomping away from him and the curious customers. "And that's final."

I grabbed a couple of trash bags, pushed through the swinging double doors, and walked through the back of the restaurant. I didn't stop until I opened another door and stepped outside into the alley that cut between the rows of buildings on the block.

It was after seven, and night had already fallen, wrapping the structures in thick, coal black shadows that stretched all the way up to the sky. Wispy clouds flitted by in front of the not-quite-full moon, rolling over the bright silver orb like waves crashing onto a sandy shore and then retreating back out to sea.

My eyes zoomed in on a crack in the alley wall across the way, a tiny sliver of space barely big enough for a child to fit into. My old hiding spot when I'd been living on the mean streets of Ashland back before Fletcher had taken me in. For a moment, I wished that I were still small enough to fit into the crack and hide from all my worries—at least for a little while.

I'd thought killing Mab would solve all my problems, but instead it had just created a whole host of new ones. Sure, business was better than ever at the Pork Pit, but only because people came to gawk at me. Everyone wondered if I was *really* the notorious assassin known as the Spider and if I'd *really* killed Mab Monroe like some folks claimed.

Then there were the people who actually *knew* I'd taken out the Fire elemental—people like Jonah McAllister. He'd been Mab's lawyer and one of her top lieutenants before her death, and he had a number of reasons to hate me, especially since I'd killed his son, Jake, last year. McAllister had even gone so far as to offer a price for my head, sending a variety of bounty hunters my way, but no one had been able to collect—yet.

To many, my taking out Mab had made me something of a folk hero, given all the people the Fire elemental had stepped on, hurt, tortured, and killed climbing her way to the top of the Ashland underworld. A few folks had even been bold enough to offer me an *atta girl* and other kind words upon her death. But to others, especially those who walked through the shady side of life, I represented nothing more than a fat payday or the means to make a name for themselves.

Either way, I was the center of attention these days— and I *hated* it.

I breathed in, enjoying the peace and quiet after the tight, nervous tension that permeated the restaurant. It was early April, and the nights were still cold and frosty, although the warm days whispered of spring. I heaved the trash bags into the closest Dumpster, but instead of going inside, I lingered in the alley outside the back of the restaurant.

I skimmed my fingers over the rough brick and reached out with my magic. As a Stone elemental, I could create, control, and manipulate the element in whatever form it took, from making bricks fly out of the wall in front of me to crumbling cobblestones to shattering the foundation of a house. I could even make my own skin as hard as marble, so that nothing could hurt me. I'd relied on that particular trick a lot these past few weeks.

My power also let me listen to the stone around me and all the emotional vibrations that it contained. People's actions, thoughts, and feelings sink into their surroundings over time, especially stone, as folks live, love, die, and more. Listening to the bricks that made up the

Pork Pit was one of my favorite things to do because the sound was almost always the same—one of low, slow contentment, just like the minds, hearts, and stomachs of all the folks who'd eaten in the restaurant. A good meal was one of the few things that could satisfy even the pickiest soul, and the Pit had served up its fair share of fine food over the years. I breathed in again, letting that soft sound fill me and soothe away all the stress of the day, all the stress, turmoil, and worry of the last few weeks.

Calmer, I dropped my hand and turned to go inside when the crackle of magic filled the air.

In addition to humans, dwarves, giants, and vampires, Ashland also had a substantial elemental population. Magic could take many forms, could manifest in all sorts of unusual ways, which meant that elementals in the city and beyond had everything from the ability to create balls of lightning in the palms of their hands to being able to control bodies of water. But to be considered a true elemental, you had to be gifted in one of the four main areas—Air, Fire, Ice, or Stone. I was the rarest of elementals in that I was able to tap into not one but two areas, Ice and Stone.

I narrowed my eyes and focused on the other person's magic, which felt like red-hot sparks landing on my skin. A Fire elemental, judging by the way the scars embedded in my palms began to itch and burn. The marks on both my hands were the same. A small circle surrounded by eight thin rays. A spider rune. The symbol for patience. Something that I was getting real short on these days.

I sighed and turned around. Sure enough, two guys stood in the alley behind me. One was a giant, judging by his seven-foot frame, while the other was human and an elemental. A ball of Fire flickered in the palm of his hand, gently bobbing up and down.

Ding, ding, Gin Blanco wins again.

"Let me guess," I drawled. "You're here to take out the notorious Spider."

The giant started to speak, but I held up my hand, cutting him off.

"I really don't care to listen to your blustering manifesto about what absolute badasses the two of you are and how you're going to make me beg for mercy by the time you're through with me," I said. "I just want to say this—do yourselves a favor. Walk away now, and I won't kill you."

"Did you hear that, Billy?" the Fire elemental cackled. "The Spider's going to go soft on us tonight. Lucky us."

Billy, the giant, cracked his knuckles together, a grin splitting his face. "She doesn't look so tough to me, Bobby."

I rolled my eyes. Most people might not know for sure that I was the Spider, but you'd think by now enough folks had disappeared in and around the Pork Pit for everyone else to realize that it might be a good idea to steer clear of me and my restaurant.

"Let's get her!" Bobby screamed.

The giant let out a loud whoop of agreement.

Apparently not.

They rushed me at the same time, and Bobby threw his elemental Fire at me. He was strong in his magic but, compared to the blazing inferno that I'd faced when I'd killed Mab, his power felt as weak as a candle flame. Still,

I ducked out of the way. I had no desire to have my hair singed off again this week.

I rolled to my left, came up on one knee, and grabbed the lid of one of the metal trash cans in the alley. I held the lid up over my head just in time for Billy to plant his massive fist into it. The sharp, ringing force of the giant's blow rocked me back for a moment. Billy raised his fist again, and I lashed out with my foot, driving my boot into his knee. Billy grunted and stumbled forward, one hand going to the alley floor, putting him down on my level.

I looked him in the eyes, smiled, and smashed the metal lid into his face as hard as I could.

It took several hard, sharp, ringing blows, but eventually blood started to pour out of Billy's broken, bulbous nose and the deep, jagged cuts that I opened up on his face. I hit him again with the trash can lid, driving the metal into his square chin, and the giant toppled over onto his back. His head cracked against the ground, and he let out a low groan. Down for the count already. Amateur.

Bobby looked stunned, just *stunned*, that I'd taken out his friend so easily. But his expression quickly changed to one of concern when I got to my feet and started walking toward him, holding the metal lid out in front of me like a shield. Bobby backpedaled, but he forgot to look behind him. He'd taken only two steps before he was pressed up against the side of one of the Dumpsters. Frantic, he snapped his fingers together over and over again, trying to push past his panic and summon up another ball of elemental Fire.

I didn't give him the chance.

Two seconds later, I slammed the metal lid into his face. I had to hit him only once before he crumpled to the ground.

When I was sure that neither man was going to get up anytime soon, I put the lid back on the trash can. The bloody dents in it matched the marks on all the other cans. More than one moron had jumped me in the alley this week. I eyed the two men, who were moaning, groaning, and trying to figure out how things had gone so wrong so quickly. I shook my head.

"Idiots," I muttered, and went back inside the restaurant.

A mirror with a cracked corner was mounted over one of the sinks in the back. I stopped there and washed the blood and grime of the fight off my hands, since I didn't want to make the customers any more scared of me than they already were. My hair had come loose while I'd been hitting the giant with the trash can lid, so I yanked the elastic band out and shoved my dark, chocolate brown locks back into a higher, tighter ponytail.

The *clink-clink* and *clatter-clatter* of silverware and dishes drifted through the swinging doors, along with the savory smells of grilled burgers and fries. Since it was creeping up on closing time, all of the waitstaff had already gone home for the evening, so I was alone in this part of the restaurant. Instead of going out into the storefront and getting back to work, I put my hands on the sink and leaned forward, staring at my reflection in the mirror.

Cold gray eyes, dark hair, pale skin. I looked the same as always, except for the blood spatters on my cheek from the fight and the purple smudges under my eyes. I wiped the blood off with a wet paper towel easily enough, but there was nothing I could do about the circles and the matching exhaustion that had crept over me these past few weeks.

All the stares, all the whispers, all the knock-down, drag-out fights. They'd all worn me down, until now I was just going through the motions. Hell, I hadn't even pulled out my silverstone knives tonight and permanently sliced up those bastards in the alley like I should have. Tangling with the Spider once was enough for most folks, but those morons would probably be stupid enough to make another run at me.

I let out a frustrated sigh. Weariness was a dangerous feeling, especially for an assassin. If I didn't do something about it, eventually I'd slip up and make a careless mistake. Then I'd wind up dead, my head served up on a silver platter to Jonah McAllister or whatever lowlife finally got the drop on me.

Much as I hated to admit it, Finn was right. I needed a vacation—from being the Spider.

I pushed through the double doors, stepping into the restaurant storefront. Once again, everyone froze at my appearance, as if they expected me to whip out a gun from underneath my blue work apron and start shooting. I ignored the curious, fearful, suspicious looks, went back over to the counter, grabbed my knife, and started slicing tomatoes again for the last of the day's sandwiches.

"Took you long enough," Finn said. "I was beginning to think you'd gotten lost back there."

"Not exactly. I had another pair of unexpected visitors I had to entertain."

He raised a questioning eyebrow. "Injured or dead?"

"Merely injured. What can I say? I was in a charitable mood tonight."

Finn arched his eyebrow a little higher at my sarcasm. Charity was one thing that assassins, even semiretired assassins like me, couldn't afford to have too much of. Especially not these days, when every wannabe hood in Ashland wanted a piece of me.

It took me the better part of a minute and two tomatoes to work up to my next words. Finn might be right, but I hated to let him know it. He tended to gloat about things like that.

"You know that vacation you were talking about?"

"Yes?" Finn asked, a sly, satisfied note creeping into his smooth voice.

I sighed, knowing that I was beaten. "When do we leave?"

✵ 2 ✵

Three days later, Thursday, I was cruising in a silver Aston Martin convertible, the top down and the wind whipping my hair into a hopelessly tangled mess.

And I wasn't alone.

My sister, Detective Bria Coolidge, belted out beach tune after classic beach tune at the top of her lungs as she steered the car down the narrow two-lane road. Her shaggy blond hair glistened like honey in the spring sun, and the warm rays had already brought out the pleasing pink in her cheeks. Oversize sunglasses hid her blue eyes from sight, and her lips were curved up into a smile.

"Come on, Gin," Bria wheedled. "Sing along with me. I know you know the songs."

I pulled down my own sunglasses and looked over the tops of the black lenses at her. "Sorry," I drawled. "Assassins don't sing—ever."

Bria snorted and turned up the radio.

It was just us girls in the convertible, which was reluctantly on loan from Finn. My foster brother collected cars like some people did glass figurines, and this convertible was the newest addition to his prized fleet.

"Try not to get blood on or in it, okay?" he'd grumbled this morning outside the Pork Pit. "In fact, don't even *think* about blood within a five-foot radius of my baby. No, wait. Better make that ten feet. Would twenty feet be asking too much?"

Bria leaned over and plucked the keys out of his hand. "Don't worry, babe. We'll take good care of it, I promise. I've already decided on a strict no-blood-and-bodies policy this weekend."

Finn scowled at her for making light of his fears, but his green eyes were soft and warm as he leaned forward to kiss her good-bye. Despite years of womanizing, he'd fallen hard for my sister—and she for him. They were a good fit. Bria's quiet, thoughtful nature balanced out Finn's boisterous antics, and he made her smile and laugh when she needed to the most.

"Well," he said, stepping away from the car. "You girls have fun."

"Don't worry," I said. "We will."

Finn eyed me. "You say that now, Gin, but let's face it: your idea of *fun* is different from most folks'. That's what worries me."

"I'm with Bria. No blood and bodies this weekend. I promised her. Cross my heart and hope to die."

I made the matching gesture over my chest, but Finn just snorted and shook his head in disbelief. Couldn't blame him for that. Trouble had a way of finding me whether I wanted it to or not.

That had been several hours ago, and now we were almost to our destination—Blue Marsh, a swanky beach town situated on an island on the Georgia–South Carolina line that was within spitting distance of Savannah.

It had been my idea to make the journey down here into a road trip with just the two of us, since Finn and Owen Grayson, my lover, were tied up until tomorrow. Finn was using his wiles as an investment banker to broker some huge, supersecret deal for Owen, who was one of the wealthiest and most powerful businessmen in Ashland. I didn't know the details, and I didn't really want to. Finn wasn't always legal and aboveboard in his methods, any more than I was in mine.

I was glad that the boys weren't with us because it gave me a chance to spend some quality time with my sister—something I thought we needed now more than ever. Even though Bria had been back in my life for several months, I couldn't help but stare at her whenever we were together, and not just because she was beautiful. So many bad things had happened to me over the years, to us, that some small part of me couldn't help wondering when it would all end. When I'd wake up from this wonderful dream I was having of Bria's being back in my life. Of our trying to be a family again, trying to be sisters again. Hell, just trying to be friends instead of strangers who shared the same magic and DNA—strangers who seemed to be growing further apart instead of closer together, no matter how hard I tried to make it otherwise.

The truth was that with Mab dead, my baby sister didn't need me to protect her anymore. The danger was over, the threats were past. Bria was to free to live her life on her own terms—with or without me in it. The idea that she might choose to do it without me scared me more than I ever would admit to anyone—even myself.

That's why this trip was so important to me and why I'd suggested that we come down a day early. I wanted to get to know Bria—the real Bria, the person she was when she wasn't out chasing bad guys, being threatened by Mab, or otherwise in danger.

I needed this weekend to work, to be fun and relaxing and carefree. I needed Bria to see that there was more to me than just being the Spider—that there was more to *us* besides banding together to fight a common enemy and being sisters in name only. I just hoped Bria felt the same way—that she realized there was something special between us. Something worth saving.

"What are you staring at?" Bria asked when the last song on the CD finally ended. "Do I have a bug in my teeth or something?"

"You," I said. "I'm staring at you because you look . . . happy."

I didn't think my sister had been happy since she'd come back to Ashland late last year. After Mab had killed our mother and older sister when we were kids, Bria and I had been separated, each of us thinking that the other was dead. I'd lived on the streets, while Bria had been adopted by a family in Savannah. But my mentor, Fletcher Lane, had managed to bring us together after his death. He'd sent me a photo of Bria, letting me know that she was alive, and he'd done the same to Bria by sending her a picture of one of the spider rune scars on my palms. We'd both started searching for each other as a result, but our reunion had been anything but smooth.

Bria was a cop, one of the few honest ones in Ashland, and she'd been determined to discover the Spider's real identity and bring her—me—to justice. When my sister had found out that her long-lost big sister, Genevieve Snow, had grown up to be a notorious assassin, well, let's just say it wasn't the best news she'd ever heard.

We'd been working on our relationship ever since. I'd thought we were making some real progress—until Mab had kidnapped Bria several weeks ago. The Fire elemental had figured out my connection to Bria, so she'd put a price on my sister's head to smoke me out. A bounty hunter named Ruth Gentry had eventually captured Bria and taken her to Mab.

The Fire elemental had wasted no time torturing my sister.

Mab had used her cruel magic to burn and blister Bria's delicate skin all the way down to the bone in places. Torture was something that the Fire elemental had excelled in. I knew from personal experience.

My eyes dropped to Bria's throat and the silverstone rune that she wore on a chain around her neck. A primrose, the symbol for beauty. I'd once had a necklace like hers, except mine had been shaped like a spider rune. The night that she murdered the rest of our family, Mab had duct-taped my spider rune between my hands, then used her Fire magic to superheat the metal until it had melted into my skin, forever marking me with two matching scars.

As if she could hear my thoughts, Bria reached down and fiddled with the two silverstone rings she wore on her left index finger. One of the bands featured small snowflakes, while ivy vines curled through the other, representing the runes that our mother, Eira, and older sister, Annabella, had worn. A snowflake for icy calm and an ivy vine for elegance.

A matching ring glinted on my right index finger, one that had a spider rune stamped into the middle of the band. Bria had had the rings made and had worn them for years as a reminder of our family. She'd given me the spider rune ring for Christmas. I wasn't much for jewelry, but I wore it every day, hoping that Bria would realize how much it—and she—meant to me.

"I am happy," Bria said, finally responding to me. "It's nice to come back for a visit, you know? Blue Marsh was my home for a long, long time. I miss a lot of things about it. The sand, the sun, the quiet. Especially the quiet."

There was no malice in her voice, no sarcasm or hidden meanness, but her words still pricked my heart. Sometimes, I wondered if Bria would have been better off not knowing that I was still alive. She'd suffered so much, been brutally tortured and almost killed because of me. Bria didn't talk much about what Mab had done to her, but I could see the shadowy horror of it in her eyes when her thoughts went back to that night, that long, dark night when she'd been at the Fire elemental's mercy.

I could also sense her disappointment in me—and her seething anger.

Oh, Bria tried to hide it, but the emotion was always there, simmering just below the calm mask that she presented to the world. I could see it glimmering in her eyes whenever she looked at me and in the way that she stiffened and her hands clenched whenever I was near her. Bria blamed me for Mab's torturing her, and part of her wanted to lash out at me, even hurt me the way that the Fire elemental had hurt her. I could tell that Bria was trying to get past her anger, trying just as hard as I was, but neither one of us seemed to know what to do or say to the other.

More than once, I'd thought about apologizing to my sister for who and what I was, for what she'd suffered because of me, but I knew it wouldn't do any good. Fletcher had always said that apologies were just empty words, and that actions were all that really mattered in the end. But try as I might, I couldn't think of what I could do or say to make things better between me and Bria, to bridge this chasm that still stretched between us.

"But mostly, I miss Callie," Bria continued.

The Callie in question was Callie Reyes, Bria's best friend since childhood. When Finn had first broached the idea of a vacation, Bria had immediately suggested Blue Marsh. Apparently, she'd been dying to come back and visit Callie ever since she'd left to go to Ashland. The last few days, Bria had talked nonstop about her friend and how much she was looking forward to seeing her again. The two of them had already made plans to spend some time together in between Callie's work schedule—plans that Bria didn't include me in. That had hurt more than I'd expected, but at this point, I'd do anything to make my sister happy—even let her spend our vacation with someone else.

"I can't wait to see Callie," Bria added. "And I can't believe she went and got engaged without me even meeting the guy first. She seems really crazy about him, but I need to check him out and make sure that he'll treat her right. My best friend can't just marry anybody, you know. Callie's always been there for me, especially when my parents died. I want to make sure that she's found the right guy."

"Of course you do," I said in a light tone, trying to match her mood. "I know how much you care about her, and I'm looking forward to meeting her. Maybe we can all go out for drinks one night and really get to know each other."

Silence. Once again, I felt that anger rolling off Bria—this time, for my trying to butt into her plans.

"Sure," Bria said, several seconds too late to be believable. "That sounds like fun."

An awkward silence filled the car, dimming the brightness of the day. Bria hit the replay button on the radio, but she didn't sing along this time. Instead, her hands tightened on the steering wheel, and she sped up, as if she now wanted the drive to be over with as soon as possible.

I sighed, put my head back on the seat, and closed my eyes, wishing the wind could whip my troubles away as easily as it tangled my hair.

An hour later, Bria crossed a bridge, turned off the road, and steered the car through an open iron gate that was set into the middle of a ten-foot-high, white stone wall. A gold plaque on one of the gateposts read *The Blue Sands est. 1899.*

We traveled along a curving driveway made of smooth white cobblestones for the better part of a mile. A lush eighteen-hole golf course spread out like an emerald carpet to the left, while the beachfront glinted like bronze diamonds to the right. Copses of peach, pecan, and palmetto trees broke up the flat horizon, although the thick, humid air shimmered in waves that seemed to match the steady rise and fall of the ocean.

The Blue Sands hotel was sandwiched in between the golf course and the beach. The structure soared an impressive thirty stories into the salty sea air, its white stone facade matching the outer wall and the cobblestones we'd just rolled over. Wrought-iron balconies curled around the various floors like ropes of metal ivy, while the roof was made out of red slate, completing the beautiful seaside vista.

I concentrated, reaching out with my magic and listening to the stone of the hotel. Sun-blasted, sand-crusted, and alcohol-soaked murmurs filled my mind, matching the thoughts and actions of the thousands of people who had stayed here over the years. This was a place where people came to take in the sun and sea air, with a bottle of coconut oil in one hand and a freshly made mojito in the other. The easy, breezy sounds weren't unlike the clogged contentment that rippled through the brick of the Pork Pit.

Bria parked the Aston Martin at the end of a long line of cars waiting to be whisked away by the scurrying valets, and we got out of the convertible. I pushed my sunglasses on top of my head and squinted against the sun's brilliance, my eyes moving over everyone and everything around us. The men in expensive polo shirts carrying heavy bags of golf clubs, hopping onto carts to be shuttled out to the back nine for their games. Their wives and girlfriends who were all tanned, trimmed, and toned to within an inch of their lives. The valets and bellmen in their white-linen jackets and pants hurrying to keep everyone happy and earn their tips for the day.

"We're staying here?" I asked. "This is a little more . . . visible than what I had in mind."

I might be on vacation, but that didn't mean that I could completely relax my guard. I'd killed plenty of people in Ashland and beyond, and I wouldn't put it past any of my enemies to try and track me down here. The Blue Sands wasn't exactly low-profile.

Bria shrugged. "Well, it was my idea to come down here for the weekend, and Finn asked me for hotel recommendations, since I grew up on the island. It's the fanciest hotel in Blue Marsh. You know how he is."

Finnegan Lane loved the finer things in life. Actually, *love* wasn't a strong enough word for his devotion to his own comfort and luxury—*obsessed* was more like it. My foster brother always had to have the best of everything, whether it was the latest Aston Martin car, a vintage wine, a decadent, outrageously expensive gourmet meal, or a slick new suit that fit him just so.

"The hotel has one of the best spas on the East Coast," Bria continued. "As soon as I told Finn that, he made the reservation."

"Of course he did," I muttered.

Finn's enjoyment of fine things extended to pampering himself as often as possible, and he was secure enough in his masculinity to indulge in everything from manicures to seaweed facials to full-body massages. Sometimes I thought Finn was more of a girl than I was.

A valet came over, took the convertible key from Bria, and opened the trunk for a bellman, who started putting our luggage onto a large brass cart. The bellman huffed a little when he lifted out my suitcase, and it thumped down onto the cart with an audible *clink-clink-clink*, like I'd filled it with loose change that was rattling around inside. His eyebrows drew together, and he looked at me, obviously wondering what I had in my suitcase that made it so heavy.

"My lucky golf clubs," I chirped in a bright voice. "Both sets. I like to be prepared."

I'd never played golf a day in my life, and I had no intention of starting while we were here. Although I wasn't above using one of the clubs to bludgeon someone to death, if the situation called for it.

The bellman shrugged and moved to get the next bag. Behind his back, Bria pulled down her sunglasses and narrowed her eyes at me in suspicion, but I just gave her a serene smile. If my sister thought that I would leave my silverstone knives and the other tools of my bloody, violent trade back home just because we'd come to the beach for a few days, well, she didn't know me at all.

The thought depressed me more than it should have.

Finn had put our suite for tonight in Bria's name, so she handled checking in while I kept an eye on our bags. Finally, twenty minutes later, the bellman grunted again as he heaved my suitcase onto the bed. Bria tipped him, and he left us alone, taking the cart and closing the door on his way out.

It might not have been my preferred choice for a hotel, but even I had to admit that Finn had booked us an impressive suite. Three lavish bedrooms all featured king-size beds, mounds of pillows, and flat-screen TVs, while the matching bathrooms contained oversize porcelain tubs that rested on real golden claw feet, along with white wicker baskets full of expensive soaps and flowery lotions. The bedrooms all connected to an enormous central living room with furniture done in shades of white, black, and gray, as well as a fully stocked kitchen and a wet bar that had almost as many different kinds of liquor as Northern Aggression, a nightclub that we frequented back in Ashland. Two French doors led out to a patio complete with furniture and that overlooked the ocean. Tomorrow, when the boys arrived, Finn had arranged for Owen and me to share a similar suite while he and Bria stayed in this one.

"Now what?" I asked, watching Bria while she riffled through the various room service and spa menus that had been propped up on the kitchen counter.

"What do you mean, 'Now what?'? Now we go out exploring. You know, see the sights, buy some souvenirs, things like that, before we go see Callie later this evening." Bria looked at me. "You have been on vacation before, haven't you, Gin?"

I shifted on my feet. "Sure I have. I went to Key West just last fall."

I didn't tell Bria that I'd spent most of my time down there reading, drinking, and brooding about a number of things, including Fletcher's murder and my strange relationship with Donovan Caine, a cop that I'd been involved with before he dumped me and left Ashland for good.

"Well?" she said, grabbing her purse off the sofa where she'd thrown it when we'd first come into the suite. "Are you ready?"

"You betcha."

Bria didn't seem to notice the sarcasm in my voice, and she turned toward the door so she didn't see the forced smile drop from my face. We'd just gotten here, but I could already tell that this was going to be a long, long weekend.

Watch out, tourists and locals alike. Gin Blanco is on the prowl.

One of the valets brought the car around, and we headed out. The resort hotel was close to one of the long, narrow bridges that connected the island and town of Blue Marsh to the outside world. Instead of crossing the bridge, Bria turned left and headed inland.

The farther we drove, the more the landscape shifted from smooth, sandy beaches to thick, swampy bogs choked with gray cypress trees full of thick wads of Spanish moss and neon green cattails that were taller than I was. But no matter the plant life that surrounded the soupy marshes, the still, shallow waters reflected back the brilliant blue sky overhead, until it seemed that the surface of the swamp was as bright and clear as the azure sky. Hence the name Blue Marsh, I guessed.

But the swampland was far from deserted. Through the twisted, gnarled trees, dozens of mansions could be seen clinging to what high ground there was, along with several themed shopping developments, coffee shops, and high-end restaurants. Looked like Blue Marsh was a bit of a Southern boomtown.

"It reminds me of Northtown," I said, watching something that looked like a gray-green log with eyes drift across a pond, disturbing the perfect reflection of the sky there. "But with gators."

Northtown was the rich, fancy, highfalutin part of Ashland where the city's power players—magical, social, monetary, and otherwise—lived on their immaculately landscaped estates. McMansions just like the ones I was looking at right now filled Northtown, along with sly, uppity folks who'd call you *sugar* to your face and then stab you in the back with their dessert forks the second they got the chance. I had no doubt that the people who lived in the mansions down here were just as dangerous. Geography might change from place to place, but human emotions and appetites rarely did.

Bria nodded. "Blue Marsh is definitely more of a resort town these days. Developers are buying up all the land, filling in the swamps as best they can, and pushing out the middle- and lower-class folks, making it too expensive for them to live here anymore even though they work in all the restaurants and hotels on the island. It's a shame, really. Every time I've talked to Callie, she's told me that it's only gotten worse since I've been gone."

"Ah, progress," I mocked, and we drove on.

Bria parked the car in one of the lots in the downtown district, and we spent the next two hours exploring the Southern coastal town. It was quite a bit warmer here than in the cool mountains of Ashland, and the oppressive humidity made the air thick and heavy, despite the steady breeze that blew in off the ocean. Shops, restaurants, and hotels filled the area, all facing the water to take advantage of the picturesque view and the strip of beach below.

We strolled along the cobblestone walkway that ran past the shops and cafés, ducking into the various storefronts and listening to the street musicians trying to impress passersby and pick up tips with their lively jazz tunes. In the distance, ships with glassed-in decks sailed up and down the waterfront, showing tourists all the sites worth seeing.

Shopping wasn't really my thing, but it seemed to make Bria happy, so I tagged along behind her, making the appropriate *oohing* and *aahing* noises when called upon. I even let her buy me a tacky T-shirt that said *I'm a real peach* above a picture of the fruit.

"Well," I said as we left the shop. "Finn will certainly get a kick out of the shirt."

Bria snickered. "I know."

She bought a few more things, including a massive T-shirt for Xavier, the giant who was her partner on the police force back in Ashland, and a much smaller one for Roslyn Phillips, his main squeeze. Then she stopped at a flower stand and picked out two bouquets of blue and white forget-me-nots.

"Who are those for?" I asked. "Callie?"

The smile faded from her face. "No, not Callie. You'll see."

We left the downtown district behind and walked through some of the island's historic gardens, passing more shops, restaurants, and museums along the way. Eventually we left the tourist sites behind and came to a wrought-iron gate that wrapped around a small cemetery. Magnolia, cypress, and palmetto trees had been planted around the gate, and their thick branches arced from one side of the square cemetery to the other, creating a canopy that blotted out the blazing sun and cloaked everything below in soft, sleepy shadows. The air was hushed and heavy inside the cemetery, and even the drone of the dragonflies seemed muted and far away.

Bria opened the gate, wincing at the loud creak it made, and stepped inside. I followed her. My sister walked slowly, her eyes fixed straight ahead. All around me, the granite gravestones whispered with low, mournful notes, echoing all the heart-wrenching sobs and quiet tears that folks had cried here for their lost loved ones. I heard the same hollow, empty sounds whenever I visited Blue Ridge Cemetery, where Fletcher and the rest of the Snow family were buried.

Bria finally stopped in front of a simple marker that spanned two graves. *Coolidge* flowed across the top of the gray stone in an elegant script, and a small heart had been carved in between the two names below. *Harry Coolidge. Beloved husband and father. Henrietta Coolidge. Beloved wife and mother.*

The marker gave the dates of their deaths, which had been a couple of years ago. Bria didn't talk about her adoptive parents much, but I knew that her dad, Harry, had been a police detective and her inspiration to become a cop as well. He'd died of a heart attack, while her mother, Henrietta, had been hit and killed by a drunk driver a year later. They'd been good people, and they'd loved Bria just as much as I did.

Bria knelt and picked a few dry, brittle leaves off the smooth grass before arranging the forget-me-nots on the two graves. White flowers for her mother, blue for her father—the colors made a pretty contrast against the lush greenery. She fussed with the stems and petals for several minutes, until they were arranged just so, while I stood still and silent behind her. These were her parents, this was her grief, and I didn't want to intrude.

Eventually, my baby sister wiped away the tears that had slid down her cheeks and got to her feet. She turned to face me, her blue eyes full of memories, love, and sorrow.

"I thought you might want to see their graves," Bria said in a quiet voice. "Besides, Callie's working right now, and I didn't want to come here alone."

I just nodded, not sure what I should say to Bria, not sure what I *could* say to make things better. The sharp edge of grief might dull with time, but it never truly went away. The cruel blade was always in your heart, just waiting to be twisted in again at a moment's notice and remind you of everything and everyone you'd lost. I knew that better than anyone.

Bria had done what she'd needed to do, so she headed toward the gate, her steps slow and her shoulders slumped. I stayed behind, giving her some space, and waited until she was out of earshot before I looked down at the two graves.

"Thank you for watching over her," I said in a soft voice. "For taking care of and protecting and loving her when she needed it the most."

I knew it was silly, but I said the words anyway. I didn't know if Harry and Henrietta Coolidge could hear me wherever they were, but they deserved my thanks, even if I was the only one who'd ever know that I'd given it to them.

"Gin?" Bria called out in a soft voice.

I turned and walked toward the cemetery gate, leaving the quiet shadows behind.

3

We walked to the convertible in silence, and Bria drove us back out toward the edge of the island. I'd thought we'd go straight to the hotel, but she surprised me by turning into a sandy lot that faced the ocean about a mile from the Blue Sands resort.

The unpaved lot fronted a restaurant made out of weathered boards. The wood might have been a soft blue at one time, but the wind had blasted it with so much sand over the years that the building was now a pale, washed-out gray. Several fiberglass picnic tables done in bright shades of electric blue squatted in the sand outside the ramshackle structure, while a neon sign the same color burned above the screen door. One by one, the letters lit up to form the restaurant's name—*The Sea Breeze*—before a tube lit up around them all, forming a clamshell.

I eyed the blue clamshell. The sign reminded me of the

heart-and-arrow rune that glowed outside Northern Aggression, my friend Roslyn's nightclub in Ashland.

"Does an elemental run this place?" I asked. "Because that's a rune if I ever saw one. That clamshell. It's a symbol for hidden treasure."

Dwarves, vampires, giants. Most magic types used a rune to identify themselves, their power, their business connections, and even their family alliances. Humans used runes too, but the practice seemed to be the most common among elementals.

For the first time since we'd left the cemetery, a smile creased Bria's face. "Nah, she's not an elemental, but Callie owns this place. The clamshell is her idea of a joke, of saying that her restaurant is a buried treasure just waiting to be discovered, like a pearl inside an oyster, although everyone on Blue Marsh already knows just how good the food is. C'mon, I told her that I'd swing by for dinner tonight, and I'm dying for some of her hush puppies. They're amazing."

My sister got out of the car, and I followed her. It was after six now, and the dinner rush was on. Lots of folks must have had the same opinion Bria did about the food because cars filled the sandy lot. I could see a dozen people eating outside at the picnic tables and even more crammed inside through the porthole-shaped windows. Waitresses bustled back and forth from the restaurant, through the rows of tables, and inside again, each one carrying white platters filled with shrimp as big as the palm of my hand and lobsters as long as my arm.

As much as I liked cooking, seafood wasn't really my thing. I supposed because shrimp and the like reminded me too much of the crawdads I used to catch as a kid in the creeks in the woods that surrounded Fletcher's house. Crawdads were slimy little suckers with sharp, nasty pinchers, and they'd made my fingers bleed more than once over the years. Deep-fried or not, I had no desire to stuff one into my mouth.

Bria wove through the crowd before pulling open the screen door and stepping inside the restaurant. I followed her and stood by the door a moment, taking in the scene before me.

The Sea Breeze was just what its name implied—a seaside joint with the island decor to match. Sand dollars, starfish, and spiked sea urchins preserved and mounted inside glass cases hung on the walls, along with thick fishing nets, spears, and even a few cracked oars. A wooden counter with polished brass railing ran along one wall, but what caught my eye was that a long, skinny boat had been placed on top of the counter, its hull sinking into the wood like it was bobbing along on top of the ocean. The boat then formed a bar where people could sit, eat, and drink. Clever. It matched the rest of the weathered interior and looked like something right out of *The Old Man and the Sea*, which was the latest book I was reading for a summer literature class that I planned on taking at Ashland Community College.

The inside of the restaurant was just as crowded as the outside, and we had to wait several minutes before two seats opened up at the end of the bar. The bartender came over, took our food orders, and mixed up a couple of drinks for us—a mojito for Bria and a gin and tonic with a twist of lime for me.

Bria put down her menu and looked at the bartender. "Tell Callie that Bria's finally here and to come say hi when she has a minute, okay?"

He nodded and pushed through a set of double doors, stepping into the back of the restaurant. Bria swiveled around on her stool so that she could look at all the folks enjoying their food. A smile curved her lips, and her blue eyes misted over with memories. It was obvious that she loved the restaurant and felt at home here.

I didn't begrudge Bria her trip down memory lane, but I couldn't help but be a little hurt by it. My sister had never looked so happy and relaxed at the Pork Pit—not once.

"Callie and I grew up together in Blue Marsh, and we were inseparable as kids," Bria said. "Her family's owned this restaurant for three generations now. I probably spent more time here as a kid and playing on the beach outside than I did at my own house. I think I told you about her once, about how you reminded me of her."

Bria had talked pretty much nonstop about Callie Reyes the last few days, ever since we'd decided to come here for a vacation. From everything Bria had said, I knew that Callie was more than just her friend, that Callie was like a sister to her—the sister I wasn't.

Callie was the one Bria had grown up with, the one she'd laughed and giggled and gossiped with. Callie was the one who'd held Bria when she'd cried over the deaths of her parents. Callie was the one who'd seen to the funeral arrangements and made sure that Bria was okay afterward. Callie was the one who'd always been around when I hadn't.

I respected Callie's role in my sister's life, was glad that she'd always been there for Bria, but part of me couldn't help but be jealous of the other woman as well. Of course, I couldn't tell Bria that, not without making things worse between us than they already were—especially not now when I was in the other woman's restaurant, in her gin joint.

"Of course, I remember," I said, my voice a little colder than I would have liked. "You told me all about how you lived in Savannah awhile before your foster parents moved out to Blue Marsh when you were ten. I remember everything you tell me about your life down here."

Bria eyed me, picking up on my hostile tone, but before she could call me on it, a waitress came over with our food—a steamy plate of shrimp scampi with a basket of deep-fried hush puppies for Bria and a Jamaican jerk chicken sandwich with thin, crispy sweet potato fries for me.

"Consider this meal on the house, Detective," a soft, feminine voice said. "Although maybe I should make you wash dishes for your dinner."

Bria's eyes lit up at the sound of the other woman's voice, and she swiveled back around on her stool. "Callie! It's so good to see you!"

Not just a waitress, then. Bria hopped off her stool, and the two women shared a long, tight hug. Callie drew back, holding Bria at arm's length, and I got my first good look at my sister's best friend.

Callie Reyes was a petite woman with a curvy body that looked strong and sexy at the same time. Her hair was pulled back into a sleek French braid and was such a dark brown that it almost looked black underneath the lights. Her skin had a lovely golden tint to it, while her gray-green eyes glittered with warmth, confidence, and intelligence. All put together, she was a beautiful woman, despite the simple white T-shirt and khaki cargo pants that she wore underneath a long blue work apron. I eyed the well-worn cotton. It could have been a twin to the aprons that I always wore at the Pork Pit, right down to the grease stains that covered the front of it.

Bria gave her friend a critical once-over, then sighed and shook her head. "You're just as gorgeous as ever."

Callie smiled and crossed her arms over her chest. "You're one to talk, blondie. I remember how crazy you used to make the boys back in high school and then in college too."

The two friends started talking, their words mixing and overlapping as they gossiped about all the boys they had dated and all the other people they knew in Blue Marsh and beyond. It only took a second for me to see just how much the two of them cared about each other, just how close they were. Hell, they even finished each other's sentences.

"Do you remember that time that the Loudon twins—" Callie started.

"Asked us to go to the senior prom with them?" Bria chimed in. "Of course! Best double date of my life, despite the fact that they wore those awful powder blue tuxedos."

They looked at each other, smiled, and laughed.

I sat on my stool feeling awkward and out of place. Three really was a crowd in this case.

"Wait a minute. Wait a *minute*. I almost forgot. Let me see that rock on your ring finger," Bria said, grabbing Callie's hand and holding it up to the light. "It's massive!"

Callie laughed and fluttered her fingers, making the not-so-small square-cut diamond on her left hand sparkle. "I told you that I've been busy since you left town. You were the first person I called after I got engaged last week."

"You know that I wouldn't have it any other way." Bria squeezed her friend's hand. "I'm so thrilled for you."

"Thanks. I've never been happier."

Callie finally noticed me watching them, and her eyes flicked from me to Bria and back again. "Hey, who's your friend?"

Friend? Bria and Callie talked all the time, from what my sister said. Surely, Bria had told her about me—right?

Bria hesitated. She sat back down on her stool to buy herself a few more seconds to answer, and I could almost see the wheels turning in her mind as she decided exactly what to say about me. "This is Gin, my . . . sister."

Callie frowned. "But I thought that all your family was dead. Your foster parents and your birth family."

Bria gave her a tight smile. "I did too, until a few months ago. Things have . . . changed since then."

Well, I supposed that was one way of putting it. I stared at Bria, but she wouldn't meet my eyes.

The seconds ticked by, with only the conversation of the other diners and the clatter of their dishes to fill in the silence. When it became obvious that Bria wasn't going to offer any more explanation about who I was and where I'd come from, Callie cleared her throat and held out her hand to me.

"Please forgive me for being rude and not introducing myself. Callie Reyes."

"Gin Blanco." I shook her hand. She had a strong grip, and her fingers were warm from the heat of the kitchen.

"Gin?" she asked.

I held up my gin and tonic and shook the glass, rattling the ice cubes and slice of lime inside. "Gin. Like the liquor."

"I see. So what do you do, Gin? Are you a cop like Bria is?"

Bria gasped and choked on the hush puppy that she'd just popped into her mouth. She made a few strangled sounds before she was able to swallow. Looked like my nighttime activities were something else Bria hadn't told her best friend about.

Callie frowned. "Are you okay? Do you need some water?"

"No, I'm fine," Bria wheezed, taking a sip of her mojito. "Just fine."

Her lips tightened, and she sat up straight on her stool, tension gathering in her shoulders. She didn't look at me, even though I was right next to her.

For the first time, I realized that my sister was actually embarrassed by me—ashamed, even. Well, not by *me* exactly, but by the fact that I was the Spider. That I was an assassin. That I'd killed as many people as she'd arrested as a cop. Sure, I still killed people, but usually only to protect my friends, family, or myself. I didn't slice and dice for money anymore. No, these days, the only jobs I occasionally took on were for good, decent folks who had problems that no one else could solve. With Mab's death,

I thought that Bria and I had finally moved beyond my bloody past.

Apparently not.

"Actually, I run a restaurant just like you do," I said, finally answering Callie's question. "The Pork Pit, serving up the best barbecue in Ashland."

The other woman grinned at me. "Well, it's not barbecue, but I hope that you'll find the food here to your liking."

My smile was as cold and brittle as hers was warm and friendly. "Oh, I always like to see what the competition's up to."

Callie knew a half-assed insult when she heard one, and the grin slowly faded from her face. I had to stop myself from wincing. I didn't often let my emotions get the best of me, but I sounded like a petty, jealous bitch, and I was acting like one too.

"Well, I hope you enjoy your meal," Callie said in a fainter voice. "I've got to get back to the kitchen. You know how it is. Bria, I'll be back just as soon as I get a break. Don't even think about leaving until we catch up on everything that you've been up to in Ashland—and I do mean *everything*."

Callie stared at me once more before turning, pushing through the swinging doors, and disappearing into the kitchen. As soon as she was out of sight, Bria glared at me.

"What is wrong with you?" she hissed. "That was my friend, my very best friend, and you were rude to her, Gin. Extremely rude. You know how much Callie means to me, how she's like a sister to me."

Yeah, the sweet, perfect sister that I'm not, I thought. *The sister that you wish I was.* But I didn't say the words or tell

Bria how much it hurt to see them together, how much it hurt to hear her defend Callie in a way that she had never defended me.

"Sorry," I muttered.

Bria glared at me another second before picking up her fork. Her hands tightened around the silverware as if she wanted to use it to stab me instead of her shrimp scampi. It took her a moment to unclench her fingers enough to start eating.

I just sighed, wondering if everyone had as much fun on vacation as we were having.

All around us, the other diners laughed and talked and joked over their meals, but Bria and I ate in silence, with only the scrape of our forks and knives on the plates to break the ugly, icy quiet between us.

At least the food was excellent, just like my sister had claimed it would be. The perfectly grilled Jamaican chicken had a wonderful jerk seasoning that was just the right blend of spicy and savory and was topped with a kiwi-mango salsa sweetened with honey. The poppyseed bun was homemade and still warm from the oven, while the sweet potato fries were crispy on the outside and soft on the inside. It was one of the best meals I'd ever had that I hadn't cooked myself.

Callie dropped by our end of the bar as often as she could, as well as moving through the whole restaurant, serving food, stopping at the tables to see if folks needed anything, and asking after the friends and families of her regulars. Not only was she beautiful and a great cook, but Callie Reyes knew how to work a crowd too. I could see why the Sea Breeze was such a success. Hidden treasure, indeed.

Not only was I jealous of Callie's relationship with Bria, but I also envied the easy camaraderie Callie had with her customers. If I tried to do the same thing at the Pork Pit, I'd wind up fighting for my life against whatever hoodlum had come by determined to take me out—after he'd eaten my barbecue, of course. No use dying on an empty stomach.

Eventually, the dinner crowd came and went, and the picnic tables outside were deserted for another evening. Only a few folks remained inside the restaurant, lingering over their food. Bria had ordered a slice of key lime pie for dessert, while I had a pineapple pudding that was just as good as everything else had been. I took another bite of the pudding, relishing the sweet tang of the pineapple in my mouth mixed with the creamy filling and graham cracker crust. Yep, I was definitely jealous now.

"Whew!" Callie said, plopping down on the stool on the other side of Bria. "I always forget how crazy things get in the spring. Won't be long now before the tourists start showing up, and we'll be slammed with customers all day long. It's a lot of work, but I would miss it."

She stared out at the restaurant, her eyes tracing over the furnishings like she was memorizing them, like they wouldn't be around for much longer.

"Why?" Bria asked, picking up on her friend's sad, wistful mood. "I know how much you love running the restaurant. You're not thinking about selling out, are you?"

Callie's eyes darkened. "Something like that, I guess you could say."

Bria started to ask her friend another question, but she never got the chance. The screen door banged open, and two men stepped into the restaurant. For a moment, it was like being back at the Pork Pit—everybody froze. The few diners, the two waitresses still on duty, the bartender, even Callie. They all stopped what they were doing to stare at the two men, and the mood immediately changed from one of easygoing dining to tight, nervous tension.

One of the men was a giant, topping out at seven feet tall. His skin, hair, and eyes were all the color of straight black coffee, and the loose white linen shirt and pants that he wore made him look even larger than he really was. The other guy was a much shorter human who was wearing a red shirt covered with green parrots over khaki cargo pants and plastic red flip-flops. His sandy blond hair, his sun-roasted complexion, and the small gold hoop glinting in his ear made him look like a wannabe pirate.

I might not be in Ashland anymore, but I recognized their type—low-level muscle that someone had dispatched to deal with a certain kind of problem. From the way Callie's face hardened at the sight of the two men, I was willing to bet she was that problem—and that things were about to get ugly.

✳ 4 ✳

Callie slid off her stool, squared her shoulders, and marched over to the two men. The shorter guy, the pirate, opened his mouth, but Callie snapped up her hand, cutting him off.

"I've told you before that you're not welcome here, Pete—and that I have absolutely no interest in selling out to your boss like everyone else on the island has already." Her voice was as cold and hard as mine had been earlier tonight. "Some of us happen to like Blue Marsh just the way it is."

Pete the pirate smiled at her, and I noticed that one of his teeth had a small diamond set into the middle of it. "Ah, now, I really hate to hear that, Ms. Reyes. Especially since you've been offered a very generous sum for your restaurant. Hasn't she, Trent?"

The giant, Trent, nodded back. His massive arms hung loose at his sides, and he was slowly flexing his long fingers like he was limbering up for a fight.

"You should sell now, while the offer is still on the table," Pete continued in a deceptively friendly voice. "Before your property is devalued. Hurricane season is about to start up again. Not to mention all the other accidents that could happen in the meantime. A grease fire in the kitchen, an electrical short, vandalism. It wouldn't take much to wipe this place completely off the map, if you know what I mean."

Wow. I think anyone who'd ever watched a bad mob movie knew exactly what he meant. Those were some clichéd and not-so-veiled threats if ever I'd heard them. It didn't look like the bad guys in Blue Marsh were any more creative than the ones in Ashland.

Bria slid off her stool. Her danger radar was pinging just as mine was, and she walked over to stand beside Callie. I got up as well, but I stayed at my spot by the bar. I'd come to Blue Marsh to get away from these kinds of confrontations for the weekend—not make a whole new bunch of enemies down here. Besides, this was Bria's city, not mine. She knew the lay of the land and the players better than I did. I'd let her take the lead—for now.

Pete leered at Bria and me behind her, before turning his attention back to Callie. "Who are your friends? The rest of Charlie's Angels?" he snickered.

"Only if I get to be Farrah Fawcett," Bria said in a sweet, syrupy tone. "Pete Procter. Long time, no see. Last I heard, you were awaiting trial on some small-time, check-cashing scheme."

He looked at her a little more closely, really studying her face. It took him a moment, but his pale blue eyes narrowed in recognition. "Detective Coolidge. I heard that you'd left Blue Marsh for greener pastures."

"Well, I'm back, and I think that you should leave—right now," Bria said. "Before you annoy my friend any more than you already have."

"Yeah?" Pete asked, his voice taking on a low, ugly tone. "And who's going to kick me out? You, Detective? I don't think so. Not anymore. Things have changed in Blue Marsh since you've been gone—a lot of things."

Bria's hand dropped to her waist, but her fingers came up empty. Normally, her gold detective's badge would be clipped to her leather belt, along with the holster that held her gun. But we were on vacation, and Bria had left both of those items back in Ashland.

Pete realized that she wasn't armed, and his smile widened, making his diamond-embedded tooth twinkle like a tiny star in his mouth. "I always wondered what it'd be like to bang a haughty bitch like you. Looks like tonight is my lucky night."

"If you even think about touching her, I will make it so that you never bang anything again," I drawled. "Not even in your dreams."

I might be on vacation, might be trying to keep a low profile, but nobody threatened my sister—nobody.

Pete looked over at me, his gaze taking in my sneakers, khakis, and long-sleeved T-shirt. He snorted, dismissing me as unimportant, and turned his attention back to Bria.

Trent kept staring at me, though, his dark eyes never leaving mine. He'd heard the cold promise in my voice and realized that I was just as dangerous as I claimed to be. Looked like the giant was a little smarter than his buddy was. I hoped he was smart enough to walk away and drag Pete along with him. I wasn't eager to get involved in things, but I would if necessary to protect Bria, myself, and even Callie. Despite my jealousy, I didn't want to see the other woman hurt, but that was clearly something Pete and Trent thought was on the menu tonight.

Pete pushed past Bria and Callie and ambled over to the bar with its sunken-boat top and polished brass railing. The bartender had planted himself at the far end of the long counter, next to the doors that led into the back of the restaurant. He stood there with the two waitresses, their faces tight, all of them clearly wishing that they were somewhere else. The diners remained frozen in their seats, forks and glasses halfway to their lips, scarcely daring to breathe, much less eat what remained of their food before it got cold.

Pete reached behind the bar, grabbed a bottle of gin, and ambled back over to Callie. He unscrewed the top and took a long, healthy swallow of the shimmering liquid before wiping off his mouth with the back of his hand. Classy. He grinned at Callie, then whipped around and threw the bottle as hard as he could. It smashed into the mirror and the glass shelves behind the bar and exploded, causing several more bottles to fall off and break. Alcohol fumes filled the air, smelling as harsh and caustic as gasoline.

Callie flinched, and Bria put a comforting hand on her friend's arm. I eased over so that I was standing in between Callie and Trent, despite the fact that I was sighing on the inside. Pete and Trent were determined to make trouble, which meant that my break from being the Spider was going to be officially over in another minute, two tops. Vacation or not, low profile or not, I couldn't just stand by and watch two guys trash someone else's restaurant—especially not when that restaurant belonged to Bria's best friend.

"I think that it's time you realized just how serious we are, Ms. Reyes," Pete said when the crackling tinkles of breaking glass had finally stopped. "And just how eager our boss is to buy your restaurant, no matter what shape it—or you—are in. I thought you got the message six weeks ago when you had that accident. You know, the one where you fell against the bar and broke your arm? You were lucky it was just a hairline fracture and not something more serious—and that you didn't hit that pretty face of yours on the way down."

Callie flinched again, but she stood her ground in front of Pete. My eyes narrowed. So they'd roughed up Callie once already. Why? What was so important about her restaurant? And who wanted it so badly that they'd beat her up to get it?

"Callie?" Bria asked in a surprised voice that clearly said she didn't know anything about her friend's so-called accident.

"It was nothing," Callie replied in a tight tone. "I slipped, that's all."

"Sure," Pete said in an easy voice. "She slipped—with a little help from me. And she's right. That was nothing then. But I think it's going to be quite a bit more serious than that now just to make sure our boss's wishes are coming through loud and clear."

He went back to the bar, grabbed another bottle of liquor, and drew back his arm, ready to send it flying—right into Callie's face this time. Callie gasped, and Bria grabbed her friend so she could push Callie behind her.

"Hey now," I said, stepping in front of both of them and holding up my arms like I was going to surrender. "We don't want any trouble."

My move made Pete hesitate for just a second, but that was all the time I needed to grab a bowl of peanuts off the bar and fling it at him. Of course, the bowl and peanuts didn't do any real damage, but they still made Pete curse and stagger back, which bought me enough time to turn my attention to the real threat here—Trent, the giant, who was already reaching for me.

I pivoted and lashed out with my foot, driving my sneaker as hard as I could into the giant's right knee. Trent grunted and hunched over, his leg twisting at an awkward angle, but he didn't go down. So I stepped forward and slammed my fist into his face. It was like hitting a concrete block, and I felt the jarring impact all the way up to my shoulder, but I managed to put enough force into the blow to make Trent list even farther to one side, like a sailboat about to tip over. Even as his head turned in my direction, I grabbed a wooden chair, hoisted it up, and brought it down on his back. The giant finally lost his balance. His temple clipped the edge of a table before smacking onto the floor, and he let out his first real groan of pain.

Bria grabbed Callie and pulled her back against the wall and out of my way, while Pete stood in front of the bar, his mouth open in surprise.

The chair had splintered on impact, and I snatched up one of the thick round legs from the floor. Before Trent could even think about defending himself, I crawled onto his back and hooked the chair leg underneath his thick neck. Then I leaned back as far as I could, grinding the wood into his throat and cutting off his air. The giant flailed around on his hands and knees, trying to buck me off like he was a wild bronco that I was riding, but I dug my knees into his ribs, tightened my grip on the chair leg, and hung on. Thirty seconds later, he slumped to the floor, unconscious.

I tossed the chair leg away, got to my feet, and turned to his friend.

Pete's mouth fell open a little more when he realized that Trent was out of the fight already, but he wasted no time smashing the bottle that he was still holding against the bar. The liquor that had been inside splashed everywhere, adding even more harsh fumes to the mix, while the handle broke off in his hand. The jagged edges glinted like razor-sharp diamonds.

I'd thought—even hoped—that Pete might hightail it out the door once his buddy was down, so that I could at least try to keep the violence to a minimum. But I could tell by the anger flashing in his eyes that he just wasn't that smart.

"You stupid, bitch," he growled. "Don't you know who we work for? Not that it matters now, because I'm going to cut you to pieces for messing with Trent."

I shook my sleeve, and a silverstone knife slid into my left hand. The weapon was one of five that I normally carried on me. Two up my sleeves, two in the sides of my boots, one against the small of my back. Since we were on vacation and I was wearing sneakers, I'd left the two in my boots in my suitcase at the hotel. But the other three knives were locked and loaded in their appropriate slots, so to speak, even though I knew it would take only one to deal with the likes of Pete Procter.

"Did you say cut you? Why, I'd be happy to oblige," I drawled again.

It was one thing to try to keep the violence to a minimum, but I wasn't about to let some lowlife hood come at me with a broken bottle and not fight back. Especially not when he could easily turn his attention to Bria if I didn't take him down.

My hand tightened on the knife, and I could feel the small spider rune stamped into the hilt pressing against the larger, matching scar on my palm. Owen had made this set of knives for me as a Christmas present, and he'd put my rune, my mark, on all the weapons. They were the best blades I'd ever had, and I had no qualms about using one to whittle Pete down to size.

Pete's eyes widened, but he didn't back down, even though he'd just watched me take out his giant friend. Dumbass. He lurched forward, swiping at me with the broken bottle. I easily sidestepped him again and again and again. I could have kept this dance up all night long.

"Stand still," he growled.

"Why, whatever you say, sugar."

The next time he came at me, I stepped into his body, already turning, turning, turning. I put my back to his chest, grabbed the arm with the broken bottle, and used his own momentum to neatly flip him over my shoulder. Pete slammed into the floor, the bottle sliding out of his fingers and tinkling across the floor. He blinked and started to get up, so I punched him in the face, cutting off that idea. But Pete kept flailing around, his right hand reaching, reaching, reaching for his broken bottle, so I drove my silverstone knife all the way through his palm, pinning it to the floorboard underneath.

For a moment, silence filled the restaurant—complete, utter silence.

Then Pete started screaming, and he didn't stop. I let him blubber on for about thirty seconds before I yanked the knife out of his palm and used the hilt to clip him in the temple. He immediately went slack and still, although blood continued to pour out of his wounded hand. The steady stream soaked into weathered wood, covering it like a fresh, glossy coat of crimson varnish.

I got to my feet and realized that everyone was staring at me—again. Just like they had for weeks now at the Pork Pit. Eyes wide, nostrils flared, fear tightening their faces. This time, I couldn't help the tired sigh that escaped my lips.

So much for my vacation.

Once I made sure that Pete and Trent were out cold, I headed over to the bar where Callie was now slumped on a stool and took a seat beside her. The other diners had paid up and left as soon as the fight was over, and the two waitresses had scurried out the door as well. That left me, Bria, Callie, and the bartender in the restaurant, along with the still-unconscious goons.

"Do you want me to call him before I leave?" the bartender asked.

Callie stared at the two men, the shattered shelves, and the mess of broken bottles, glass, and liquor behind the bar. She bit her lip, then nodded. "He'll hear about it one way or another. Besides, this is his beat now, remember? So go ahead and call it in."

"Who are you talking about?" Bria asked.

"My fiancé," she said. "He's a cop just like you, Bria. I told you about him, remember? Don't worry. He'll take care of those two. They won't bother me again. At least not for tonight."

She murmured the last few words in a sad, defeated voice, but Bria and I still heard them. The bartender moved to the other end of the counter, picked up a phone there, and made his call. As soon as he was out of earshot, Bria turned to me.

"I thought you left your knives at home!" she hissed.

I just looked at her.

Bria threw her hands up in the air. "I can't take you anywhere, can I?" she muttered, and started pacing back and forth in front of the bar.

"What knives? What's Bria talking about? Who the hell *are* you?" Callie asked. "And where did you learn how to fight like that?"

"Let's just say that I'm in the . . . security business," I said.

Callie's brows drew together in confusion. "But I thought you ran a barbecue restaurant. What would you know about security?"

"Oh, you'd be surprised the things I know about," I

said. "I like to read and . . . study up on various topics in my spare time. I take a lot of classes at the local community college up in Ashland."

Bria groaned and started massaging her temples, like my words had just given her the mother of all migraines. I wasn't feeling too great about things myself. We hadn't even been gone from home a day, and I'd already gotten into a bar fight. Not exactly how I wanted to start my vacation, especially when I'd promised Bria that there wouldn't be any blood this weekend.

Even worse was the fact that it wasn't just any fight with any goons. From the way Pete had talked, these two had someone backing them, someone rich and powerful, which meant there would most likely be repercussions from our brawl. How bad those repercussions would be remained to be seen, but I wanted to know exactly whom I was dealing with so I could take the appropriate steps to protect all of us.

So I ignored my baby sister's less-than-gracious response to my whopping whale of a tale and focused on Callie. "Now, why don't you tell us who these guys work for and what they really wanted, other than to mess up your restaurant and scare the shit out of you. Because from what Pete said, it's not the first time that they've come in here and threatened you, is it?"

Uncertainty filled the other woman's eyes, and she turned to Bria, asking her a silent question.

Bria sighed and nodded. "Go ahead, Callie. You can trust her. Gin's . . . used to situations like this."

I raised an eyebrow at the sarcasm in her voice. Bria snorted and started pacing again.

Callie looked back and forth between the two of us for several seconds before shaking her head and starting her story. "There's this guy named Dekes who wants to buy my restaurant. Pete and Trent work for him, along with several other men. Giants, mostly, private bodyguards, that sort of thing."

I nodded. I knew exactly the type of muscle she was talking about. Lots of giants in Ashland and beyond hired themselves out as bodyguards to rich folks, since it paid so well. Of course, for those rich folks who dabbled in things that weren't quite legal, the giants acted more as enforcers than bodyguards, which was exactly what I was willing to bet Trent was.

"Anyway, Pete, Trent, and the others have been coming in for a couple of months now, offering me more and more money every time if I'll close down the restaurant and sell out to their boss. Lately, they've gone from being pleasant to what you saw tonight. Tough. Threatening. Violent."

"And your arm?" I asked in a quiet voice.

Callie sighed. "It was something of an accident. I told Pete to leave, and he shoved past me to get to the bar. I stumbled and hit my arm."

"But Pete didn't exactly apologize, now, did he?" I asked.

Callie didn't say anything.

"Wait a second," Bria said. "Did you say Dekes? As in Randall Dekes?"

Callie nodded. Bria cursed and quickened her pacing, moving from one end of the bar to the other with sharp, precise movements.

"I take it you've heard of him?" I asked my sister.

She nodded. "Unfortunately. He's a real estate mogul and developer who's had a home here for more than a century. Remember all the mansions and shopping centers that we drove by today? Dekes built all of those."

"He's practically bought up the whole island," Callie added in a soft voice. "He plans to build a big resort complex on Blue Marsh—a casino, golf courses, spas, restaurants, the whole nine yards. It'll put everything else on the island to shame and probably out of business as well. There were a few initial holdouts like me, but everyone else has sold out to him already."

"Why?" Bria asked. "Because of the money he was offering for their property?"

Callie nodded. "That and the fact that there have been some . . . accidents. Vandalism, mostly. Another business owner was beaten up pretty badly one night when his store was robbed."

Accidents. Right.

"Where is Dekes going to build this resort?" I asked.

"He's adding it on to the Blue Sands hotel." Callie held her hands out wide. A brittle smile tightened her face. "According to the plans that I've seen, we're sitting in the middle of the main floor of his casino. He's supposed to break ground on construction in two weeks, but he's having a press conference tomorrow at the Blue Sands to formally announce the project. He owns the hotel, and his mansion adjoins the grounds."

Bria let out another curse, one that was longer and louder than all the ones she'd muttered so far. I eyed her. My sister wasn't much for swearing, not like I was, and it took a lot to get her riled up. Usually, only Finn could ruffle her feathers like this.

"There's more, isn't there?" I asked her.

There always was in situations like this one.

"Real estate isn't all that Dekes is into," Bria said. "I started investigating him just before I left to go back to Ashland. Extortion, intimidation, gambling, prostitution, murder. He's got quite a racket going, and his hands are in practically every legal and illegal business on the island. And it's not just here. He has interests up and down the East Coast, from the Outer Banks of North Carolina all the way south to Key West."

"In other words, Randall Dekes is the Mab Monroe of Blue Marsh," I said.

Bria nodded. "Only he hides it a lot better than she did. He's buddy-buddy with all the local politicians, gives money to the fire and police departments, sponsors kids' sports teams, things like that. He's a very slick salesman that way. He also happens to be a very old and very powerful vampire. Some folks say that he has elemental magic too, although I don't know if that's true or not."

Despite all the popular myths and stories out there, vampires were born, not made, just like everyone else was. They had heartbeats, breathed air, and could walk around in the sun just as easily as I could. Vamps could wear as much silver as they wanted, and garlic didn't do any more than give them bad breath or the occasional case of indigestion.

Just about the only myth that was true when it came to vampires was that they all needed blood to live, in addition to more mundane food. To them, sucking down a pint of O-positive was just like regular humans chowing down on a steak. Animal blood would do in a pinch, but most vamps preferred people blood, and there were dedicated vampire blood banks that paid folks very well to come by and donate as often as they could. The blood banks then turned around and distributed all those precious pints like cartons of milk, with a slight markup, of course.

The twist was that vampires got more than just nutrition from blood, depending on whose platelets they were dining on. Regular old human blood was enough to give most vampires enhanced senses, extra strength, and lightning-fast reflexes. It was when they drank from other magic users that things got really interesting.

A vampire who chugged down the blood of a dwarf or giant would take on characteristics of those races and become just as strong as dwarves and giants naturally were—at least until the blood cycled out of the vamp's system like food moving through a human's body. Vampires who drank blood from elementals got the ability to use that person's power, whether it was Air, Fire, Ice, Stone, or one of the offshoots of those areas, like electricity, acid, water, or metal. And of course some vamps were elementals themselves—they had the inherent magic flowing through their veins already, just like Bria and I did.

Whether he had elemental magic himself or stole it from his victims, Randall Dekes sounded like a very dangerous man.

"You know, Dekes has offered me far more than what the Sea Breeze is worth," Callie said, interrupting my thoughts. "He's even promised me a job heading up one of the new restaurants in the resort complex."

"So what's the problem?" I asked.

She looked at Bria. "There was a fire about a week ago at an ice-cream shop not too far from here. Remember Stu Alexander?"

Bria nodded. "He used to give us free chocolate-dipped cones sometimes when we went into his shop. He was such a sweet old man. I remember he sent flowers to my parents' funerals, even though he didn't know them or me very well."

"Well, he was killed in the fire. Burned alive inside his own store. Stu Alexander, who never hurt anyone in his entire life. I still can't quite believe it." Callie wrapped her arms around herself, but she couldn't completely hide her shiver. "The cops are still trying to determine whether it was an accident."

"But you don't think it was an accident," I said.

Callie stared at the floor. "I went into the shop the day before the fire to pick up an ice-cream cake for one of the waitresses' birthdays. Stu told me that Dekes and some of his men had been by the shop that morning. That Dekes said it was his last chance to sell out or else. Stu loved his store just as much as I do the Sea Breeze. It was his whole life. He said he'd told Dekes that he was never going to sell, no matter how much money the vampire offered him. Stu even bragged about how he got his gun out from behind the counter and got Dekes and his men to leave. But the next day, Stu was dead."

She shivered again. "Of course, I told the police what Stu told me, but they say they can't do anything without proof. Stu was the last holdout besides me."

This wasn't the first time I'd encountered a situation like this. Not too long ago, I'd helped out Warren Fox, an old friend of Fletcher's. A coal tycoon named Tobias Dawson had secretly discovered diamonds on Warren's land and had done everything he could to get his hands on them, even sending someone to rape and kill Warren's granddaughter, Violet. I'd stopped Dawson, though— one of my growing number of pro bono deeds as the Spider.

"Why didn't you tell me about all of this?" Bria asked. "I could have helped you before it got this far."

Callie shrugged. "Whenever I've called lately, you've always sounded busy, distracted, worried. It seemed like you were having enough problems of your own in Ashland, and I didn't want to bother you with mine."

Bria's gaze cut to me, and I knew what she was thinking. That maybe if she hadn't been so busy looking for her long-lost big sister, Genevieve Snow, looking for the Spider, looking for me, maybe Callie would have told her about Dekes. Then maybe Bria could have figured out a way to help her friend before now—and maybe even saved an old man from being murdered. Bria didn't say anything, but I could see the guilt glimmering in her eyes—along with that anger again.

Anger at me and the fact that I hadn't come straight out and told Bria who I really was when she'd come back to Ashland. Anger that I'd let Mab capture her. Anger that the Fire elemental had tortured her, despite my promises to keep that from ever happening. I didn't think Bria was wrong to blame me. I'd failed to protect her when it mattered most, something that would always haunt me.

Mab Monroe might be dead, but I wondered if things would ever really be right between me and my sister. If the Fire elemental and the two divergent paths that she had put me and Bria on, the things that she'd done to us, would ever really be forgotten—or forgiven.

But that was a worry for another day. Right now, the question was what to do about Randall Dekes. Was taking down Dekes the smart thing to do? I had few doubts it was the right thing, given everything that Callie had said and what I'd witnessed here in the restaurant tonight.

But I'd come to Blue Marsh to get away from my troubles as the Spider, not throw myself knives-first into someone else's problem, especially someone that I didn't have any real connection to. Callie was Bria's friend, not mine. But that was the catch—Bria loved Callie like a sister, and I loved Bria. I'd do anything for my sister, including protect her friend the best way that I knew how.

I hadn't known Stu Alexander, but I could keep Callie from ending up like him. I could keep Bria from crying over her best friend's grave like she had her parents' earlier today. I could do at least that much for my sister. I didn't know if it would make up for everything she'd suffered because of me, but all I could do was keep trying—and hope that it counted for something with Bria in the end.

"What if I told you that I could help you with Dekes?" I asked Callie. "That I could get him to leave you alone—for good?"

Bria sighed, knowing what was coming next. "Gin . . ."

She didn't get to finish her thought. The screen door creaked open, and quick footsteps sounded, hurrying across the wooden floor.

"Callie!" a worried voice called out. "Are you okay?"

This time, I was the one who froze—shocked into absolute stillness just like everyone else had been earlier. I couldn't have been more surprised, more stunned, than if the ground had opened up at my feet and Mab had crawled out of her grave right in front of me.

I'd never thought I'd hear the light, quick tread of his footsteps again. I'd never thought I'd hear that low, sexy, slightly raspy voice again. I'd never thought I'd see him again, not after everything that had happened, not after the bitter way that things had ended between us.

Not after he'd walked away from me without so much as a backward glance.

For a moment, I sat there, still frozen, wondering if I was just imagining things, if my mind was playing tricks on me—cruel, cruel tricks.

"Callie?" he asked again, drawing closer. "Why aren't there any customers? Where's the rest of the staff? And who are these women?"

I breathed in, and his familiar scent filled my nose—that sharp, clean scent that always made me think of soap. And I knew that I wasn't wrong or mistaken or just imagining things.

I drew in a breath and slowly swiveled around on my stool.

Detective Donovan Caine stood behind me.

❖ 5 ❖

The last time I'd seen Donovan Caine had been when he'd dumped me at the Pork Pit, ending our brief but intense affair. That had been several months ago, but he still looked the same as I remembered—the same as I'd pictured him in my mind more than once on a late, lonely night, wondering where he was and what he was doing. Whom he might be with.

His black hair was cropped close, looking as dark as midnight above his smoky, topaz-colored eyes. He had a strong chin and smooth bronze skin that hinted at his Hispanic heritage. Donovan topped out at just over six feet, and the blue suit he wore showed just how lean and muscled his body was. He wasn't wearing a tie, and his white button-down shirt was open at the throat. His hair was also standing straight up, like he'd been running his hands through it.

Still, despite his rumpled appearance, he looked . . . calmer, happier, and more at peace than I'd ever seen him.

Donovan stared at Callie, making sure that she was all right, before turning his attention to Bria, then me. He started to look back at Callie but did a double take instead, his golden gaze locking with my gray one.

In that moment, I remembered how he'd felt pressed up against me, how he'd whispered my name over and over again, how he'd made me feel—and then how he'd walked away without giving me a chance. Without giving *us* a chance. My heart constricted in my chest, squeezing in on itself, but I couldn't tell whether it was with longing or anger.

His eyes widened, his mouth fell open, and all the color drained out of his face. "Gin? Gin Blanco?"

I tried to smile, but I couldn't quite make my lips turn up. "The one and the same. Hello, Donovan. You're looking well."

Donovan blinked several times, as if I were a ghost and he could somehow banish my image just by staring right through me. When that didn't work, his gaze went to Pete and Trent, who were still out cold on the floor.

"Your work, I assume?" he said, leaning over and checking each man's neck for a pulse.

"Of course."

"I'm surprised they're not dead," he muttered, and straightened back up.

I suppose I could have told him that I hadn't come here looking for trouble. That I was trying to relax this weekend, not carve up bad guys for kicks. That they'd started it, not me, and that they were damn lucky I hadn't finished it—permanently. But the fact that one of the first things out of his mouth was an insult after all this time made my hackles rise.

I grinned, baring my teeth at him. "What can I say? I've mellowed since the last time we spoke, Detective."

Donovan looked at me, I looked at him, and Callie and Bria stared at both of us, wondering what the hell was going on. Nobody spoke for several seconds.

Finally, Bria cleared her throat, stepped forward, and held out her hand. "I'm Detective Bria Coolidge."

"Detective Donovan Caine," he murmured, shaking her hand.

Bria nodded, like the name actually meant something to her. "I took your job in the Ashland Police Department, and you took mine in Savannah. We never met in person, but we spoke on the phone a few times, working out the details of the switch."

"Of course," Donovan said, recognition filling his face. "I remember you now. I did work in Savannah for a while before transferring out here to Blue Marsh."

This time, I was the one who blinked in surprise. When Donovan had left Ashland, he'd made it perfectly clear that he wanted to disappear and never see me again. So I'd tried not to think too much about where he'd gone, and I hadn't tried to find him, although Finn had volunteered to hunt him down and kneecap him for hurting me. Turns out, the detective had been closer than I realized this whole time. He'd taken Bria's place down here to get away from me, his troublesome assassin lover, and she'd assumed his job up in Ashland to try to find me, her long-lost sister. Ah, the irony. Kicking me in the teeth just as usual.

"You're a detective, and you're here with Gin?" Donovan asked, a suspicious note creeping into his voice.

Bria's face tightened. She realized what he was really asking just like I did—if Bria knew I was the Spider.

Her eyes frosted over, and she put on her hard, flat cop face. "Of course. Gin's my sister. We were just telling Callie about Gin's . . ."

"Security business," I finished in a helpful tone.

Bria gave me a look that said it would be a very good idea for me to shut the hell up right now. "Yes, her *security business*, when you arrived, Detective."

Donovan let out a harsh, bitter laugh, something he'd done more than once when I was around. Even now, after all these months, the dark, caustic sound still felt like a knife twisting in my stomach.

"Donovan?" Callie asked, laying her hand on his arm. "Are you okay?"

He turned to her. "I'm sorry. It's just been a long day, and I was so worried when I got the call about the fight here. Are you all right? Did anyone hurt you?"

"I'm fine, really. Gin made sure that those men didn't harm me or anyone else."

Donovan didn't look at me. "I'm glad."

Callie wrapped her arms around Donovan. The two of them shared a soft, gentle kiss; then he pulled her into a tight embrace, sliding his arms across her back and burying his face in her neck. The diamond ring on Callie's finger winked at me like a cold, mocking eye, and I finally put two and two together. Took me long enough.

Callie had mentioned that her fiancé was a cop and had asked the bartender to call him. I'd just never expected it to be *my* cop. Or my ex-cop. Or whatever the hell Donovan Caine was to me now.

Callie was Donovan's fiancée. The thought rattled around inside my head, echoing over and over again. Of course she was. If I'd thought the irony of the situation had merely been kicking me before, it was now laying a full-body smackdown on me, concentrating on my bruised ego and battered pride—and maybe my wounded heart too.

I felt as though a giant had just sucker punched me, but I kept my face cold, smooth, remote, and impassive. Hiding my true feelings was one of the first things Fletcher had taught me when he'd started training me to be an assassin—even if I wasn't quite sure what those feelings were right now. Anger, longing, regret, attraction. They were all a big jumbled mess inside me, tiny barbed threads that pulled my emotions first one way, then the other, until everything was twisted, tangled, and snarled beyond all comprehension.

Donovan and Callie broke apart, although he kept one arm around her waist, holding her close to his side, something he'd never done with me—not even once. He hadn't been able to get away from me fast enough whenever we were together.

"You want to tell me what happened?" Donovan asked in a quiet voice, finally looking at me. "And why you're in Blue Marsh?"

"Bria and I are here on vacation," I said in an even tone. "Her idea. We drove down from Ashland earlier today. Callie and Bria are old friends, and Bria wanted to stop and catch up with her. We were finishing our dinner when those two clowns showed up and started threatening Callie. Things were getting ugly, so I made sure the good girl won, just like I always do. End of story."

"You should have seen her, Donovan," Callie said, a bit of awe creeping into her voice. "It was amazing the way that she took those two guys down all by herself. Especially that giant."

"I just bet it was," he muttered.

"I told them about Stu's murder and Randall Dekes and how the vampire's been pressuring me to sell my restaurant to him." Callie hesitated. "Right before you showed up, Gin was telling me that maybe she could figure out a way to get Dekes to stop harassing us. To get him to leave us alone—for good."

Donovan's face hardened, and his golden eyes sparked with anger. "Absolutely not," he growled. "I told you. I'll handle Dekes. I'll get him to back off. What happened to Stu won't happen to you. I promise you that."

Callie frowned at her fiancé, obviously wondering at his sudden show of temper. "You've said yourself that Dekes thinks that he's above the law. That he gives too much money to too many people for anyone to want to rock the boat. So far, you've been right. The cops haven't even questioned him about Stu's death. So if Gin can help, then why not let her?"

"Because I don't exactly do things by the book or even by the law," I said. "And you know how Donovan is—he's such a stickler for the rules."

Donovan opened his mouth to say something, probably to call me out for mocking him, when Pete let out a low groan on the floor. A few seconds later, Trent rolled over onto his side and started to come to as well. Bria helped Donovan prop them both up in chairs and handcuff them; then Donovan called some of his fellow boys in blue to come haul them off to the nearest jail.

Bria and Donovan moved to the other end of the bar, talking to each other cop-to-cop, while Callie grabbed a broom from the corner and started sweeping up all the broken glass. That left me to lean against the bar and keep an eye on the bad guys.

After staring at me for the better part of two minutes, his face red with rage, Pete finally opened his mouth. But before he could speak, I casually palmed one of my silverstone knives and started flipping it end over end in my hand.

"Yeah, yeah," I said. "I know exactly what you're going to say. I'm a bitch, this isn't over, and I'll be seeing you again real soon. If I had a dollar for every time I'd heard that, I'd be even richer than I already am."

Pete kept glaring at me, so I leaned forward so that my face was level with his.

"Trust me, dude," I said, letting him see the cold violence that always lurked just below the surface of my wintry eyes. "You do not know who you are messing with, and you do not want to find out. Do yourself a favor. When your boss Dekes springs you from the pokey, tell him that Callie Reyes is off-limits and to find somewhere else to build his fancy resort—or he will be sorry that he didn't. You got that?"

"Yeah," Pete muttered. "I got it."

Maybe I was still feeling tired, maybe I wanted to limit the mess I made down here, or maybe I was still hoping to salvage some part of my much-needed vacation, but I was giving Pete and his boss a chance to walk away before things got any bloodier. I doubted that either one of them would take me up on my generosity, though. Still, it was more than I normally would have done. If they persisted with things, well, what happened would be on them, not me.

The po-po arrived soon after that, their blue and white lights flashing in the parking lot and casting garish shadows into the restaurant. Bria stayed inside to say her good-byes to Callie, but I followed Donovan outside and watched him and two other cops load Pete and Trent into the back of a squad car. The two cops got into the front of the vehicle and pulled out of the lot.

"How long will it take Dekes to bail them out?" I asked Donovan.

He watched the blue and white lights fade away. "Not long enough."

"That's what I thought."

We didn't speak for a minute. A breeze blew in from off the ocean, plastering Donovan's suit to his side and outlining his firm body. He stared out into the semidarkness as though the night held all the answers to his questions. I could have told him not to bother, that the shadows only whispered of lies, when they bothered to speak at all, but he wouldn't have listened to me. He never had. Not before. Not about anything that had really mattered.

Still, I'd felt something for him once and I hoped that he had for me. I owed him something for that, even if I knew that he would probably reject me just the way he always did.

"You know, my offer still stands," I finally said.

"And what offer is that?"

I didn't know if it was intentional or not, but his voice dropped to a low, husky whisper, and his eyes glimmered like pure gold in his strong face. I realized that we were alone for the first time all night—and I wasn't sure how I felt about that.

I wasn't good with feelings. I never had been, and everything that I'd seen and done as the Spider had only made me guard my heart that much more carefully. The more you cared about someone, the more and the easier they could hurt you, whether it was with words, actions, or the lack thereof. But I'd thought that Donovan had potential, that *we* had potential, so I'd opened myself up to him, or at least tried to. But he'd turned his back on me and walked away with no hesitation and seemingly no regrets. Donovan's leaving had hurt me far more than I'd let on to anyone—even Owen.

"To help Callie with Randall Dekes. To get him to back off—or else."

"I thought you were retired."

The old, sharp accusation flared in Donovan's voice, and it surprised me how much it still stung to realize just how little he thought of me.

I shrugged. "Assassins don't ever really retire. But eventually, some of us decide to use our particular skill set for things besides killing people for money. Better things. That's what I'm doing these days."

"Really? Is that what you did to Mab Monroe?" Donovan asked. "I heard, you know. About an assassin named the Spider killing Mab a few weeks ago in Ashland. Was that one of your better deeds?"

"No," I said. "Mab was personal, and the bitch got exactly what was coming to her."

Donovan shook his head and let out another laugh—that hard, caustic, bitter laugh that felt like acid eating away at me. After a moment, he looked at me again, his face remote, his eyes cold.

"Stay away from me, and stay the hell away from Callie. I'll keep her safe from Dekes. I don't need your help, Gin," Donovan snarled. "I didn't back in Ashland, and I certainly don't now. Got it?"

"Yeah," I said. "I got it."

Donovan glared at me another second before he stalked into the restaurant, turning his back on me—again.

Bria came outside a few minutes later, and we drove back to the Blue Sands hotel in silence. It was still early, not quite nine o'clock, but we both went through the motions of getting ready for bed. Pulling robes and pajamas out of our suitcases. Laying out clothes for tomorrow. Showering.

Eventually, I wound up on the patio, staring out at the endless black sea from three stories up. A light, steady breeze blew in off the ocean, carrying the tang of salt and sand with it. It was full dark now, but the night was warm, pleasantly so, and the humidity felt like a welcoming hug instead of the hot, suffocating embrace of earlier in the day. The silvery moon was as big and bright as I'd ever seen it, and the stars burned with pure, white light, like they were seconds away from falling from the sky. All around me, the stone of the hotel drowsily whispered of another day of fun in the sun and the promise of more of the same tomorrow.

But the revelry wasn't over for everyone. Down below, tiki torches blazed around an enormous, palm-tree-shaped swimming pool. Palm trees were a common rune in these parts, being the symbol for coastal beauty, and the elaborate shape of the pool was in keeping with that theme. More than a few folks had decided to go for a late swim, relax in the lounge chairs, or down some more daiquiris from the bamboo-and-grass-covered bar nearby. Couples swayed to cheerful calypso music on a patio on the far side of the pool. Beyond that, a few bonfires flickered on the beach, the folks milling around them backlit by the orange flames.

Bare feet whispered on the patio behind me, and Bria came up to lean next to me on the wrought-iron railing. We watched the swimmers, dancers, and drinkers until the song ended and the live band decided to take a brief break.

"So what's the deal with you and Donovan Caine?" Bria finally asked.

I sighed. Bria was a cop, a good one, and she could be just as tough and tenacious as me when she set her mind to it. I'd known that the questions about Donovan were coming—I just hadn't figured out what the answers were to them yet.

"We used to have . . . a thing."

"A 'thing'?"

I sighed again, a little deeper and a little longer this time. "I've told you about Alexis James, the Air elemental who killed Fletcher and framed me for a murder I didn't commit?"

Bria nodded.

"Well, Donovan was a detective with the Ashland Police Department back then. He got caught up in the conspiracy and found out that I was the Spider. But one of his superiors was working for Alexis, so we joined forces to take them both down. Later, he helped me out a bit with Tobias Dawson when Dawson was threatening Warren and Violet Fox. Along the way, Donovan and I slept together a few times."

"Until . . ."

"Until Donovan decided that he couldn't be the kind of man he wanted to be and still be with me at the same time. Basically, his chose his morals and his sense of right and wrong over me, the evil assassin who'd seduced him."

Bria winced. "Ouch."

"Yeah, ouch."

We lapsed into silence, listening to the laughter and splashes that floated up from the pool and the lively, pulsing beat of the calypso music as the band members returned from their break and picked up their instruments again.

"So what are you going to do now? About Donovan," Bria asked.

I shrugged. "Donovan made it perfectly clear when he left Ashland that he didn't want me, that he didn't want anything to do with me, and he did the same thing again tonight at the restaurant. We've both moved on. He has Callie, and I have Owen. Donovan also made it clear that he didn't want my particular brand of help in dealing with Randall Dekes."

"Can't blame him for that, can you? He is a cop, after all. He's supposed to follow the rules. Asking you to assassinate Dekes would not be following the rules."

I looked at her. "Yeah, but you're a cop too, and here we are."

Bria shifted on her feet. "That's different. You're my sister."

I didn't say anything because we both knew that it wasn't different, not really. In her own way, Bria had just as tough a time accepting my being the Spider as Donovan had. She was just trying harder than he had to get past her aversion to my bloody, violent profession because we were family and I'd ultimately rescued her from Mab. Bria thought she owed me something for those things. She didn't realize that I would have saved her whether we had a relationship or not, whether she wanted me in her life or not—whether she hated me or not.

But running into Donovan and seeing the old, familiar disgust in his eyes made me wonder when Bria would quit trying. When she'd just give up on me. Donovan had, and my sister was the same kind of good, honest cop that he was. It wasn't too much of a stretch to think that someday she'd make the same choice as Donovan. That someday she'd tell me she'd had enough, leave me behind, and never look back. Now that Mab was dead, she was free to do it anytime she wanted.

I'd had plenty of pain in my life already, but I knew that if Bria turned her back on me like Donovan had, the tiny scrap of my heart I'd been able to salvage from my ugly childhood would break—and it would never, ever mend.

All I'd wanted had been a simple, fun, carefree vacation, a weekend when I could relax from being the Spider and finally try and connect with my sister. But now I was right back in the middle of another messy situation whether I wanted to be or not. I might not love Callie like Bria did, but I just couldn't stand by and do nothing either—not when I knew a good, decent person was being threatened and in very real danger of being murdered—burned to death, even. Fletcher had taught me better than that, even if I *was* an assassin.

"And how do you feel about Donovan now?" Bria asked in a soft voice.

I shrugged again. "You know I'm not good with feelings."

My sister raised her eyebrows at that particular understatement. She turned to face me and crossed her arms over her chest, her eyes level with mine. Waiting, just waiting. I knew she wouldn't leave without an answer.

"Donovan is a smart, strong, capable, attractive man," I finally said. "That's what drew me to him in the first place."

"But?"

"But I love Owen," I said in a firm voice. "Owen Grayson is one of the best things that's ever happened to me. I'm not going to forget that—ever—and I'm certainly not going to do anything to mess up our relationship."

I meant every word that I said. Seeing Donovan again had only made me appreciate Owen that much more because Owen did the one thing that Donovan never had and never would—he accepted me for who and what I was. My bloody past as the Spider didn't bother Owen because he'd gone through the same things that I had—losing his parents, living on the streets, trying to protect his younger sister, Eva. And he'd done some of the same things that I had—including killing people who threatened him or Eva. Owen hadn't necessarily done all those dark things for money, not like I had as an assassin, but he understood them and me all the same. That's why I loved him.

Bria nodded. "Good. Because Callie's my best friend, and she wouldn't get engaged to someone if she didn't love him with all her heart. I don't want her to get hurt by being in the middle of you and Donovan and your . . . 'thing.'"

"Don't worry," I said. "She won't get hurt. Not by me. But Randall Dekes is another matter, and we both know it."

"I talked to Donovan in the restaurant," Bria said. "He's been investigating Stu Alexander's death, trying to find some way to connect it to Dekes and put the vampire in jail where he belongs. But he keeps running into problems with his superiors, who are getting heat from their superiors, because the vamp is so chummy with all the muckety-mucks on the island."

I snorted. "Well, that's all well and good, but what's Donovan going to do, exactly? Go out to Dekes's fancy house and threaten to arrest him? Please. Dekes will laugh in his face. Or worse, he'll keep Donovan there long enough for some of his goons to go out and hurt Callie. Is that what you want?"

"Of course not," Bria snapped. "But you can't just go around killing everyone you don't like, Gin. There wouldn't be anyone left in the entire city of Ashland if you did that."

I thought about telling her that I was getting tired of killing people all the time back home, that I'd come down here this weekend to get away from all of that, but I kept my mouth shut. She wouldn't believe me. Not tonight. And I didn't think that she really wanted to anyway. She couldn't do that and hold on to her anger at me at the same time.

"Donovan and I deal with rich sleazeballs like Dekes all the time," Bria continued. "Donovan will handle him."

"Like you handled Elliot Slater when Mab sent him to your house to murder you?"

Bria flinched, and old memories darkened her eyes.

"Because the way I remember it, you were gutshot, and Slater was about a minute away from beating you to death when I showed up and took out his men instead."

It was a low, vicious blow, reminding Bria of how Slater had almost killed her, of how he *would* have killed her if Finn and I hadn't intervened, but it was a necessary evil. I didn't want Bria to make another tear-filled trip to the cemetery to bury her best friend, but that's what would happen if Dekes was as determined to get his hands on Callie's restaurant as I thought he was.

Bria pushed away from the railing and straightened up. The anger in her gaze glittered as brightly as the stars above.

"I told Callie I would come by the restaurant for brunch in the morning," she said in a low voice. "That

I'd help her and Donovan find some way to deal with Dekes."

My eyes narrowed. "You didn't mention that before."

"You didn't ask."

We glared at each other, neither of us willing to compromise or admit that the other might have a valid point. Maybe, just maybe, Bria and Donovan could get Dekes to back off, at least for a little while. But what would happen when Bria went back to Ashland? What would happen when Donovan was called away on a case? Callie would be alone and vulnerable at the restaurant. A moment of opportunity, a locked door, a few matches, a little gasoline, and Bria's friend would be just as crispy and deep-fried as the food she served up. That's how I'd play things, if I were Dekes, along with planning a convenient alibi for myself. Hell, it sounded like the vamp was so connected and so powerful that he wouldn't even have to go to the trouble of doing that.

But I couldn't make Bria understand that, any more than I'd been able to make Donovan realize the same thing back in Ashland. Maybe they didn't want to understand. Hell, maybe they just *couldn't* understand. Despite everything they'd seen on the job, Donovan and Bria still wanted to believe in the good in people, whereas my faith in the inherent decency of others had been shattered a long time ago. Maybe they were right and I was wrong, but I couldn't let go of my cynicism, any more than they could relinquish their hope.

Stalemate, once again.

"I'm going to bed," Bria muttered. "You coming?"

"In a little while."

Bria stalked back inside the suite without another word. I heard her moving around, switching off lights, turning down the covers, and even brushing her teeth before shutting the bedroom door behind her, but I made no move to follow her. Better to let her cool off.

Instead, I stayed outside for a long time, listening to the endless ebb and flow of the ocean and wishing the soft waves could carry my worries and fears out to sea with them, never to be heard from again.

❋ 7 ❋

Eventually, the lights around the pool dimmed, the band packed up their instruments, and the bar closed down. The swimmers, dancers, and other stragglers went back inside the hotel to finish their nights with a shower, a fresh drink, and perhaps a quick fuck or two in their soft, comfortable beds.

I stepped back inside the suite, closing and locking the glass doors behind me. Before I went to bed, I walked through the suite, familiarizing myself with the locations of everything from the light switches to the coffee tables to the butcher's block full of knives on the kitchen counter.

Given what had happened earlier at the Sea Breeze, there were things I would do now if I were Randall Dekes, things that were best taken care of in the dark of the night, and I wanted to be prepared just in case the vampire or his men decided to act accordingly. Paranoid?

Perhaps. But I hadn't lived this long by not being ready for the bad guys when they decided to come calling.

The last thing I did was open the front door and ease my head outside. There was no one in the long, wide hallway, although someone had left a large brass luggage cart next to the elevator. I stepped out and studied the wall that fronted the suite. The Blue Sands was made out of solid white stone, but instead of plastering over the stacks of bricks, the designers had left many of the interior walls rough and exposed, giving the hotel an elegant but sturdy air.

I leaned forward and ran my fingers across the rough stone, listening once again to the sunbaked murmurs and whispers of the waves. Then I reached for my Stone magic. For a moment, I relished the cool flow of magic running through my veins before focusing and pushing the power up into my hand. A silver light flickered on the end of my index finger, hissing like a small blowtorch. I used the magic to trace a series of runes into the stone around the door. Small, tight, spiral curls—the symbol for protection. The curls shimmered with the silver glow of my magic before sinking into the stone wall and disappearing from sight.

In addition to using runes to identify themselves and their interests, elementals could also imbue the symbols with magic, get that power to spark to life, and make the runes perform certain functions. Elemental magic was great for creating everything from bombs to magical trip wires to alarms. Now, if someone tried to force his way inside the suite tonight, my magic would trigger the hidden runes, and the stones would shriek out a warning to me—one that would be loud enough to wake me from the deepest, deadest sleep.

Satisfied, I went back into the suite and shut and locked the door behind me. Then I crawled into bed, closed my eyes, and waited for the dreams to come.

Ever since Fletcher's murder several months ago, I'd been plagued by vivid, vivid dreams—nightmares, really. But the twisted thing was that the images that haunted me weren't really dreams at all, but instead flashes of my past, memories I desperately wanted to forget.

Mostly, the memories had to do with all the horrible things that had happened the night Mab had murdered my mother and older sister. Watching them die, reliving the Fire elemental's torture, hearing Bria scream, lashing out with my Ice and Stone magic, collapsing our mansion, thinking that I'd accidentally killed Bria with my power, that she'd been crushed to death by the falling stones of our house.

But ever since I'd killed Mab, the dreams had changed, offering me other glimpses into my past, letting me remember other horrors I'd endured, other trials I'd faced by design, chance, choice, or something else. Like tonight . . .

"I don't understand," I said. *"Why did we come all the way out here?"*

Here *was deep in the forests high above Ashland, since the city was located in the woodsy corner of the world where Tennessee, Virginia, and North Carolina met in the Appalachian Mountains. Early this morning, Fletcher had roused me out of bed, handed me a backpack of supplies, ushered me out to the car, and started driving north. I'd fallen asleep and had only woken up when Fletcher stopped the car at the base of what he called Bone Mountain, a large, ominous-looking peak whose craggy ridges seemed to stretch all the way up to the gray clouds that darkened the sky. That had been several hours ago, and we'd been hiking up the mountain ever since.*

I had no idea where we were or how far we'd come, but I didn't mind the long trek. I enjoyed walking through the forest, listening to the sound of the wind whistling through the trees and watching rabbits and chipmunks dart through the thick underbrush. Most of all, I liked being with Fletcher, just the two of us, without Finn lurking around, glaring at me and making snide comments whenever he thought his dad wouldn't hear him. Finn didn't like me much, and the feeling was definitely mutual. I thought he was a spoiled brat who took his father for granted.

Fletcher looked at me. His green eyes were as bright as the leaves on the spring trees, while his walnut-colored hair blended in with the rest of the landscape, despite the silver threads that glinted here and there in his thick locks. He wore his usual blue work clothes, along with a pair of sturdy boots, and carried a backpack that was even bigger and heavier than mine.

"I told you. We're looking for wild strawberries. Ain't nothing better than wild strawberry preserves on a hot buttermilk biscuit. I'll get Jo-Jo to teach you how to make them both."

He swung the tin pail he'd brought along, as if to confirm his story. "Come on. It's not too much farther now to the strawberry patch."

He set off through the trees, and I fell in step behind him, taking care to watch where I was going so I wouldn't trip on a rock or put my foot in a hole hidden by leaves.

I'd been living with Fletcher for several months now, and he often brought me into the forest to look for herbs, pick berries, or skin the bark off trees. Fletcher had lived in the mountains all his life, and he had a keen interest in natural folk remedies, like putting honey on burns or making natural teas and salves from barks and berries to fight colds and coughs. The last time we'd gone hiking, he'd shown me how to use a spiderweb to pack a wound and slow the bleeding in case I didn't have anything else on hand to use as a bandage.

It was a neat idea, but one I doubted I'd ever use. Even though Fletcher was training me to be an assassin like he was, I didn't think I'd ever be that *desperate. Besides, most folks that Fletcher got paid to kill lived in big fancy mansions in Northtown, not out in the woods. Anyway, I was going to be a good assassin, just as good as Fletcher was as the Tin Man. I wasn't ever going to be taken by surprise or put in a situation I couldn't handle. It was a vow I'd made to myself after my family had been murdered. I was always going to be in control from now on, and Fletcher was going to teach me how. That was the whole reason I wanted to be an assassin in the first place—so that no one would ever be able to hurt me again.*

We kept walking, winding our way up the mountain. Eventually, we came to a fork in the trail. Fletcher pointed to the path that veered off to the right.

"The strawberry patch is about a mile up that way. You can't miss it. Why don't you go on ahead? This old man has to answer the call of mother nature. Too much coffee this morn-

ing." Fletcher gave me a sheepish grin. "I'll catch up to you in a few minutes."

"Okay."

Fletcher moved off into the trees, and I turned and started walking up the trail, enjoying the shades of green, brown, and gray that streaked the landscape. Still, despite the peace and quiet, something about our hike was bothering me, some nagging little thing that I couldn't put my finger on. I kept thinking about the dented tin pail swinging from Fletcher's brown, speckled hand. It took me ten minutes of walking, but eventually I realized what was wrong.

"But it's too early for strawberries," I said to the trees around me. "It's only April. Strawberries aren't really in season until the summer, May at the very earliest, especially the ones out here in the wild."

I frowned, wondering why Fletcher would bring me up here to pick strawberries that weren't even ripe yet. Then I realized something else—I hadn't heard a whisper of movement behind me. No branches cracking, no twigs snapping, no leaves crunching underfoot. I hadn't been walking all that fast, and Fletcher should have caught up to me by now. So where was he? Could he have gotten into some sort of trouble? Maybe stumbled and twisted his ankle? But if he'd done that, then why wasn't he calling out for me? For help. Why did it seem like I was here on the mountain by myself now?

Panic filled me then, and I turned and ran back down the trail the way I'd come.

"Fletcher!" I yelled in between breaths. "Fletcher!"

He didn't answer me.

I made it all the way back down to the fork where we'd split up, but there was no sign of him, his tin pail, or his backpack. It was like he'd never even been here to start with. My head whipped left, then right, then left again—and that's when I saw the note.

A white piece of paper had been tacked to one of the trees right by the trail, with the name GIN written on it in big black block letters. The panic pulsing through my body slowly turned to fear, and a sick, sick feeling filled my stomach. Somehow, I knew what the note was going to say even before I yanked it off the tree and opened it with trembling hands.

"I'm sorry," the note said in Fletcher's distinctive handwriting. "This isn't working out. I can't have you hanging around anymore. You're on your own now. Fletcher."

That was it. There was nothing else. Just a few simple sentences to explain the fact that Fletcher had dumped me out here in the middle of nowhere. I felt like a puppy someone had left in a cardboard box by the side of the road—alone, abandoned, unwanted. But mostly, I didn't understand why. Why bring me all the way out here when just kicking me out of the house and telling me to stay away from the Pork Pit would have been so much simpler?

I couldn't help but wonder what I'd done that was so wrong. What had been so horrible about having me around that the old man had gone to such extreme lengths to get rid of me?

"Fletcher?" I whispered, panic filling me once again. "Fletcher! Where are you? Come back! Please!"

But he didn't answer me. He was already gone, leaving me alone on the mountain, all alone—

The sharp shriek of magic snapped me out of my dream. It took me half a second to realize what the sound was—the spiral protection runes in the stone of the outer wall of the suite surging to life and warning me that someone was trying to get inside.

I glanced at the clock by the bed: 11:33. They'd shown up sooner than I'd expected them to. I would have waited until much closer to dawn myself. Harder for people to rouse themselves from sleep then.

I pulled a silverstone knife from under my pillow, got up off the bed, and nestled it against the small of my back. Then I grabbed two more weapons off the night-stand, enjoying the cold, comforting feel of the blades in my hands before sliding one of the knives up my sleeve. I'd been wearing a long robe when I'd been out on the patio, talking to Bria; but after my sister had gone to bed, I'd changed into my usual ensemble of black jeans and a long-sleeved black T-shirt. I'd gone to sleep with my boots on, with my final two knives resting in the side of either shoe.

I'd wanted to be prepared in case Dekes decided to send me a message for roughing up his two goons, and it looked like the vampire's men were knocking on my door. The poor bastards should have walked away when they'd had the chance—because I wasn't giving them a second one.

I eased out of my bedroom and tiptoed across the dark suite, using the mental map that I'd made earlier to skirt around the couches, tables, and other furniture. I stepped up to the door, careful to keep away from the glass peephole so that whoever was lurking around outside wouldn't realize I was awake and already waiting for them.

I looked across the suite at the closed door that led to Bria's bedroom. As an elemental, she'd be able to hear the stone's cries too, although they wouldn't resonate as loudly with her, since she had Ice magic and not Stone like I did. I waited a moment, wondering whether she'd heard my alarm and would come out and investigate, but her door remained closed. Looked like I'd have to deal with our visitors myself. Not a problem.

I blocked out the stone's wails, put my ear close to the door, and listened. Right next to me, the brass doorknob softly turned and rattled.

"Sorry," someone muttered on the other side of the door. "Wrong key. It's this one, I think. The third time's the charm, right?"

So he'd tried two wrong keys already, and that's what had triggered the protection runes in the stone. Sloppy, sloppy, sloppy. If he'd used the right key the first time, he might have avoided tripping my silent alarm.

"You'd better do more than think," a familiar voice growled. "That bitch skewered my hand like it was a fucking kebab, and I plan on doing the same to her—and worse."

So Pete Procter, the guy I'd stabbed earlier at the Sea Breeze, was outside, along with his friend with the keys. But neither one of them were elementals, otherwise they would have heard my alarm and realized they were walking into a trap. Too bad for them.

"And Ron, one of the night clerks, told me that sweet little blond piece of ass is in there with her too," Pete continued. "We'll have fun taking turns with her. Maybe both of them, all of us, at the same time. There'll be enough for everyone."

Pete laughed at his ugly promise, and I heard a few more sly chuckles chime in with his. Make that more than one friend outside. I smiled in the darkness like an animal baring its fangs. Good. I'd hate to get out of bed just for Pete.

"There," the second guy said. "I told you I had the right key. Get ready."

A soft *snick* sounded as the door unlocked. I eased away from it and stepped behind a fake palm tree in a brass pot in the front corner of the suite.

The door opened a crack, and a pair of bolt cutters slid through the narrow space and caught on the security chain. From my hiding spot, I saw a hand squeeze down on the cutters, which easily sliced through the flimsy metal. Trent, the giant, I thought. He'd have the strength to use the cutters with one hand, and he was probably as pissed at me as Pete was for busting him up earlier. That made at least three guys outside. I wondered how many more Dekes had sent, or if they'd decided to do this on their lonesome. Didn't much matter. They were all getting dead.

"Quiet now," Pete whispered. "I don't want those bitches to know what hit them. Maybe if we're lucky, we'll still catch them in bed and make it that much easier for us. We'll do the two of them tonight, then go out to the restaurant tomorrow and do the same thing to Reyes."

More dark chuckles filled the air, but they weren't nearly as black as the cold rage that slowly seeped into my body. It was one thing to threaten me—that was part of my job description as the Spider. But nobody—*nobody*—came after my baby sister and lived to tell about it. Randall Dekes and his men had just made this fight very, very personal.

The door whispered opened, and light spilled in from the hallway outside. I stayed where I was, hidden behind the potted palm, and let my eyes adjust to the growing brightness. The door opened all the way, and Pete stepped inside the suite. He had on the same garish shirt he'd worn earlier at the Sea Breeze, and his right hand was heavily bandaged where I'd rammed my knife through his palm. That wouldn't be the only cut he got tonight—not by a long shot.

Another guy, a short human, slipped in behind him holding a large ring of keys that went *jingle-jingle-jingle* together.

"Quiet!" Pete hissed.

The guy stuffed the keys into his pants pocket. He wore the white linen uniform I'd noticed on the valets earlier, which meant that he worked here at the Blue Sands. Of course he did. Callie had said that Dekes owned the hotel. No doubt the vamp had several folks on staff he could call on for occasions just like this one.

A giant I didn't recognize crept in behind the valet, and Trent, the giant I'd beaten down before at the restaurant, brought up the rear. The four men eased down the three stone steps into the living room, and there was a whispered conversation as they debated which of the bedrooms to search first.

I stayed where I was, waiting to see if anyone else would follow the men inside, but no one else appeared, and I didn't hear any soft scuffles of footsteps on the carpet or see any shadows in the hall. Four of them, one of me. Bad odds for them.

The worst fucking odds of their lives.

"There's no way they're getting past us," Pete whispered. "Charlie, turn on the lights so we can see what the fuck we're doing."

Charlie, the valet with the key ring, trotted back up the steps and obligingly flipped the switch on the far wall. The second the lights came on, I stepped out from behind the potted tree and kicked the door shut behind me. Didn't want to be a bad guest and wake the neighbors with the screams that were sure to come.

The door thumped into place, making Charlie, the guy closest to me, whirl around in surprise.

"What the hell—"

That's all he got out before my knife rammed into his heart, and a crimson stain blossomed like a tropical flower on his white shirt. Charlie was dead before I yanked out the blade and let his body thump to the floor. For a second, the other three men looked at me, eyes wide, mouths open, as if they couldn't believe that I was up, ready, and waiting for them.

"Get that bitch!" Pete screamed, all pretense of being quiet and sneaky gone. "Now!"

And the fight was on.

Pete rushed at me first. I waited until he was on the stairs, then stepped forward and slammed my fist into his face. He stumbled back, falling off the stairs and hitting a wooden coffee table before rolling off the side and landing on his ass. Before I could follow and finish him off, the two giants came at me.

Swing-swing-swing.

Trent and the other giant worked in tandem, leaping up the steps and lashing out with their fists, trying to pin me against the door, where they could take their time beating me to death. But I slid to one side and scooted back behind the potted tree. The second giant reached through the leaves, trying to grab hold of me, but I ducked around the other side.

Swipe-swipe-swipe.

The giant didn't even get a chance to untangle himself from the tree before I palmed another knife and started in on him. He was half turned toward me, so I couldn't slam my blades into his heart and put him down immediately the way I wanted to, but I cut up the right side of his thick, muscular chest like I was butterflying a slab of meat. The giant screamed and staggered back, but I kept right on going with him, opening his stomach from one side to the other, blood and intestines spilling across the white marble floor. The giant screamed again, his feet going out from under him, and slumped to the floor. I drove my knife into his throat, cutting off his hoarse cries of pain, before yanking it back out. He toppled over and joined the valet on the floor, both of them dead.

Trent stared at me, his eyes flicking around the room as if he was considering whether he wanted to fight or run. He should have run.

I started toward the giant, not giving him the chance to decide. Trent turned and headed for the door, but he'd forgotten that the dead valet was lying on the floor behind him. Trent stumbled over the other man, and his head cracked against the closed door. That was all the opening I needed to ram both of my silverstone knives into his back. One blade slipped between his ribs, ripping into his lung, while the other plunged into his heart. Trent screamed once and wobbled back and forth for a moment, his brain struggling to catch up with his fatal injuries. When that happened, the giant crumpled to the floor. I pulled my knives out of his back, knowing that he'd be dead soon enough.

And then there was one.

I turned around and headed toward the last man breathing. Pete scrambled up to his feet, reached around to the small of his back, and came up with a gun. He smiled and leveled the weapon at me. I was too far away to get to him before he pulled the trigger, and we both knew it. I reached for my Stone magic, ready to push the power out into my skin, head, hair, and eyes, ready to turn my body into a hard, impenetrable shell—

A wolf whistle sounded. Pete whirled around at the sound, and a bright, bluish white ball of Ice magic slammed into his chest, knocking him all the way across the room. His body hit the far wall and slid off. He didn't get up after that.

I walked over to where he'd fallen. Jagged shards of elemental Ice stuck out of Pete's torso, making it look like a dozen skewers had been driven into his chest. And he thought that I'd shish-kebabed him earlier with my knife. He'd been dead before he'd hit the wall, and his eyes were still open wide with shocked disbelief and agonizing pain.

I turned to look at my sister. Bria stood in the open doorway of her bedroom, her hand outstretched, the cold glow of her Ice magic still coating her fingers. She was a strong elemental in her own right, and she'd had more than enough power to take out Pete with that one blast.

"Nice," I said. "Very nice."

Bria dropped her hand, and the cool caress of her Ice magic faded away. "Well, I couldn't very well let him shoot you, now, could I?"

I shrugged. "I thought you might, after the fight we had earlier."

Something like hurt flickered in Bria's blue eyes, but I didn't have time to think about how much I'd pissed her off again. Instead, I went up the steps and cracked open the door, listening. The suites were spaced pretty far apart, but I'd kicked the door shut, and the men had let out a couple of screams before I'd killed them. Slamming doors weren't uncommon in hotels, but yelps of pain were another matter.

But the walls must have been thicker than I thought, because I didn't hear any movement out in the hall. No whispers, no running footsteps, no other doors opening or slamming, nothing. No one seemed to have heard the commotion at all, or if they had, they just didn't care what it was. Good. That meant we had some time to clean up the scene and get the hell out of here. I didn't know how many more men Dekes might have in the hotel, either on the staff or his own goons, but Bria and I had definitely worn out our welcome. Best to get while the getting was good.

I closed the door and locked it again.

"Sorry I wasn't more help. I had earplugs in, or I would have heard your elemental alarm and woken up sooner," Bria said, moving around the room and staring at the dead men. "Who are these guys?"

"Some of Randall Dekes's men. Remember Pete and Trent from the restaurant?"

Bria looked at the bodies, and her face tightened with recognition. "They didn't stay in jail very long, did they? They must have come looking for us as soon as they made bail. But how did they know where to find us?"

"Callie said that Dekes has his hands in everything in Blue Marsh, remember?" I said. "Besides, Pete recognized you at the restaurant, and we checked into the hotel under your name. So it was just a matter of Dekes finding which hotel you were staying at and then sending in Pete and his boys to do their thing. The fact that we were here at the Blue Sands just made it that much easier, since Dekes owns the hotel."

"Yeah, but why come after us?"

I shrugged again. "Any number of reasons. Maybe word got back to Dekes that you were a cop, and he didn't want you sniffing around while he tries to take over Callie's restaurant. More likely, though, he knew his boys got their asses handed to them earlier, and he told them to get their payback—or else. You know how it works. If you or your men show any sign of weakness or incompetence, the other sharks smell the blood in the water and start circling around. Dekes can't afford to show any chinks in his organization, not now when he's so close to building his new casino. And from what I heard him say before he came into the suite, Pete was exactly the kind of guy who would relish hurting two women, whether it was on Dekes's orders or just his own sick idea."

Bria surveyed the blood and bodies that littered the once-pristine suite. After a moment, she sighed and shook her head.

"Now what?" she asked. "Because these dead guys aren't just going to disappear. Not with Sophia back in Ashland. And we can't just leave them here. Like you said, the room's in my name. Besides, we both know that you aren't going to call the cops and explain all this to them."

I pretended I didn't hear the chastising tone in her voice and stood there, thinking, my eyes flicking around the room just as Bria's had a moment before. Finally, my gaze lit on the patio doors, and an idea popped into my head.

"Uh-oh," Bria muttered. "I know *that* look. You've thought of something. The question now is exactly how bad is it, and do I really want to know about it?"

"Don't worry, baby sister. It's nothing too dark or sinister—this time. We're going to get rid of these bodies easy peesy."

Her eyes narrowed with suspicion. "And how the hell are we going to do that?"

I smiled at her. "We're going to dump the bastards in the pool."

¶

Bria changed into jeans, sneakers, and a T-shirt and packed up our things. My clothes were dark enough to hide the blood that had spattered onto them, so I got to work. The first thing I did was go out into the hallway, grab the luggage cart that had been left by the elevator, and roll it into the suite. Then I stripped off the linen jacket the valet was wearing and wrestled his body onto the cart. I put him on the bottom and piled Pete on top of him, to hide the valet's wounds. As a final touch, I threw the valet's jacket over Pete to cover up his injuries as best I could.

"Are you sure this is going to work?" Bria asked, eyeing the haphazard way I'd stacked the bodies on the cart. "They're going to get rug burn from their hands and feet dragging off the side like that."

"Well, they're dead, so I doubt it will bother them," I replied. "Now let's roll them onto the elevator."

Bria helped me push the cart out of the suite and down to the end of the hall. I stabbed the button for the elevator. Since we were on the third floor, we didn't have to wait too long for it to arrive. Given the late hour, the car was empty. Even if someone had been inside, I was going to cheerfully say my friends had had too much to drink and that Bria and I were taking them to their room. Not the best excuse I'd come up with, but I didn't have time to be more creative or clever.

For once, my luck held, and we made it down to the ground floor without seeing anyone. Given the fact that the hotel didn't have any security cameras in the hallways, elevators, or common areas, I didn't have to worry about a guard spotting us on a screen somewhere and coming to see what we were up to.

I stepped outside and checked to make sure no one was using the pool, but the area was deserted. Even the bonfires had burned out on the beach. I craned my neck up, looking at the many stories above me, but I didn't see anyone else out on their patio. The night was as still, dark, and quiet as it was going to get.

"Still clear inside," Bria murmured from her spot in the doorway, looking back into the hotel. "But are you sure you want to do this? Someone's bound to hear the noise."

"I doubt that, given how many folks I saw sucking down mai tais earlier. They're either in their rooms sleeping off their buzz or holding on tight to their honeys right now. Even if they do hear something, they'll probably just think it's some late-night skinny-dippers out having a little fun. Besides, I don't see how we have much of a choice,"

I said. "As you pointed out, Sophia isn't here to clean up the mess like she usually is, and we can't exactly leave the bodies in the room with your name on the bill. So let's go. Heave-ho. These guys aren't getting any warmer."

Bria sighed with either resignation or agreement. I couldn't tell which exactly, and I wasn't sure I wanted to know.

We pushed the cart out onto the patio and up to the edge of the pool. Thankfully, the wheels didn't squeak. We started with Pete, since he was on top. Bria grabbed his legs while I took hold of his shoulders.

"One, two, three," I whispered.

Together we rolled his body off the valet's and into the deep end of the pool. Bria was right—the splash was louder than I'd thought it would be, but there was nothing I could do about that now. We quickly pushed the valet into the pool as well before shoving the cart back toward the door. Ten . . . twenty . . . thirty . . . I counted off the seconds in my head as we worked. It took us ninety seconds to dump the bodies and make it back to the door. But no lights snapped on around the pool and no one came outside to investigate, so I figured we were safe enough to do the same thing to the other two goons.

Only one giant would fit on the cart at a time, so we had to make two more trips. One by one, we hefted their bodies onto the luggage cart, took it downstairs, and dumped the giants into the pool, trying to make as little noise as possible. By the time we finished, the four bodies looked like overgrown lily pads bobbing up and down in the pool, and the shimmering blue water had turned a muddy pink from the blood still oozing out of the men's wounds. It wasn't the best or most discreet body dump I'd ever done, but hopefully no one would notice the dead men until morning. I planned for us to be long gone by then.

"Now," I said, pushing the cart away from the pool for the last time. "Let's go upstairs and tackle the room."

The suite was equipped with everything, and the kitchen was fully stocked right down to a box of rubber gloves and a wide assortment of cleaning supplies under the sink, probably so the maids wouldn't have to push their carts into the room and disturb the guests any more than necessary. I grabbed a pair of gloves, a bucket, some rags, and a bottle of bleach.

Since I'd killed three of the men right inside the door, most of the blood was limited to the marble floor there. The stone had already taken on a darker, more somber sound as the blood had started to dry on top of it. I splashed bleach over the whole area and wiped it down three times, while Bria straightened up the rest of the room, making sure she cleaned up all the melted traces of her elemental Ice blast. I also wiped down the luggage cart with bleach and cleaned our fingerprints off the brass rails.

It was after one in the morning when we finished. I stepped back and surveyed the suite with a critical eye. The area wasn't as pristine and spotless as it would have been if Sophia had been here and used her Air elemental magic to sandblast the blood into nothingness, but the bleach would muddle whatever evidence it didn't outright destroy. This wasn't the first murder scene I'd cleaned up on my own, and it wouldn't be the last.

Besides, nobody but Randall Dekes knew that the men had been sent to our suite in the first place. He couldn't exactly complain to the cops that we'd gotten away with murder, not without implicating himself. Despite how rich and powerful Dekes was, I doubted that even he would want to deal with the hassle of four dead bodies, how they'd gotten that way, and where they'd come from. When the cops got around to questioning him, the vampire would probably claim he'd never set eyes on any of the men before—even if everyone already knew they worked for him.

Blue Marsh might be hundreds of miles away from Ashland, but sociopathic assholes were the same no matter where you went.

I stuffed the gloves, rags, and empty bottle of bleach I'd used into a plastic bag and shoved the whole thing into my suitcase to dispose of at another, safer location. I also stopped long enough to put a fleece jacket on over my T-shirt, hiding the bleach stains on my dark clothes. Then Bria and I locked the suite and left. On our way to the elevator, we left the luggage cart in the hallway where I'd first found it.

Checking out of the hotel was a calculated risk. When the bodies were found, the cops would be sure to look at the guest list and who had left when. Our departing this late at night might draw some unwanted attention, but I wasn't overly concerned. I could always manufacture some reason for why we'd had to leave in the middle of the night—an illness, a family emergency, a problem at the Pork Pit. Besides, I doubted the cops would look too hard at us. After all, we were two women. How could we possibly have had the brawn and brains to kill four men and dispose of their bodies in the pool? And the fact was that we simply couldn't stay here where we'd be sitting ducks for more of Dekes's men—or the vampire himself.

We made it down to the registration desk without any problems. I stepped up to deal with the paperwork while Bria got the night bellman to load our luggage onto another cart—one that hadn't been used to haul around dead bodies. The clerk behind the counter was a college girl who looked barely old enough to drink.

"Are you arriving or departing?" she asked in a voice that was way too perky for this late at night.

"Checking out," I said, matching her chipper tone. "The hospitality wasn't quite what I had in mind."

I'd thought there might be a few more of Dekes's men waiting in the lobby to help Pete just in case we got past him, but the area was as quiet and empty as the pool on the back side of the hotel had been. That didn't mean I didn't keep an eye out, though, as I stepped outside at the front of the building. Behind me, Bria pushed along the cart that held our luggage. The valet on night duty was slumped over a podium, his white linen jacket draped over his shoulders like a blanket. He jerked awake at the sound of our footsteps and the wheels of the cart roll-ing across the cobblestones. I palmed one of my silver-stone knives, just in case he was part of Dekes's crew, recognized us, and decided to do something stupid like scream.

But the valet just blinked at us with sleep-crusted eyes. He didn't know who we were, and he didn't care. He started to get up, but I marched over and scanned the rows of keys on the metal rack behind him. It didn't take long for me to spot a solid gold key ring shaped like a dollar sign. The dollar sign wasn't a rune in this case, not really, but it was still one of Finn's favorite symbols.

"No worries," I said in a bright tone, plucking Finn's keys off the board. "We've got it. We're in a bit of a hurry, so just tell me where the garage is."

The valet started to protest, but the hundred bucks I slipped him was more than enough for him to jerk his thumb over his shoulder. He'd already gone back to his half doze before we'd rounded the side of the building. The dark opening of the garage waited up ahead.

"Careful now," I told Bria in a low voice. "Let me go first. Dekes might still have a guy or two down here, waiting in a car to drive Pete and the others back to whatever hole they crawled out of."

Bria nodded, leaving the luggage cart at the entrance, and I stepped in front of her. Together, we eased into the parking garage. All around me, the concrete let out low, uneasy mutters. Even here at an upscale hotel, the stone resonated with sharp notes of fear, worry, and paranoia. Not surprising. Most people didn't like parking garages, since they were great places to get mugged—or dead.

But no one was lurking behind the thick concrete posts or in the midnight shadows that filled in the spaces between the rows of luxury cars. That didn't mean we didn't run into trouble, though.

Because Finn's convertible was a mess.

The windshield had been hit in at least three places with a baseball bat or tire iron, and deep, jagged cracks crisscrossed the glass like the thick, silvery threads of a spider's web. The side mirrors had been knocked off, the radio had been busted, and the leather seats had been ripped to ribbons. Dents covered the car's hood, while scrapes sliced down the sides where someone had used his key on the slick silver paint.

Looked like someone had told Pete what car we were driving, and the four dead men had decided to bust it up for fun before they came up to the suite and did the same to us.

Bria let out a low whistle. "Finn is going to freak when he sees this."

Freak was an understatement. I could already hear Finn bitching about how he'd lent us his brand-new baby, and we'd gotten it busted up in less than twenty-four hours. Although that was something of a record, even for me.

"Well," I said. "At least they didn't slash the tires too. Let's go."

I retrieved the cart and threw our luggage in the back-seat before shoving the now-empty cart over into one corner of the garage. Then I helped Bria brush the broken bits of glass, metal, and plastic out of the front seats as best we could. Five minutes later, Bria drove the convertible through the open iron gate at the edge of the hotel grounds and stopped just outside it.

"Where to?" she asked.

"The Sea Breeze."

Bria looked at me, her eyes full of worry. "You think that Dekes sent some men there too?"

"Probably not, given what I heard Pete say outside the

room about going after Callie tomorrow, but there's only one way to be sure."

Bria put her foot down on the gas, and we left the Blue Sands hotel behind, with even more trouble probably waiting on the road in front of us.

Bria steered the convertible toward Callie's restaurant. We were the only car on the road, and only the steady *whoosh-whoosh-whoosh* of the tires on the pavement broke the silence. The night was dark and eerily quiet. Trees crowded up to the very edge of the narrow, two-lane road and then arched and twisted over it, blocking out everything but a small strip of stars overhead. Thin black tendrils of weeping willows waved back and forth like skeleton fingers in the constant breeze, while the swamp grass and cattails undulated in perfect time below next to the rippling surface of the water. Every once in a while, the convertible's cracked headlights would catch an animal hiding in the marshes on either side of the road, and its eyes would flash like fiery rubies before we zoomed past.

It seemed to take forever, but it was only a few minutes later when we pulled into the sandy lot that fronted the Sea Breeze. The weathered structure was dark inside and locked up tight for the night, although a lone streetlight burned at the edge of the road. Mosquitoes and other bugs buzzed around the harsh glare, their moving mass of bodies throwing twisted shadows across the landscape.

"Looks like Dekes and his men decided to leave the restaurant alone—at least for tonight," Bria said.

"Or maybe they just went straight to the source," I replied. "Where's Callie's house? Does she live alone?"

"No, she's not alone. She's already moved in with Donovan. Callie said that she didn't want to try to move and plan a wedding at the same time." Bria paused. "They're getting married this summer."

My heart twinged with old, familiar, bitter hurts, but I kept my face smooth. "Good. She'll be safe enough with Donovan tonight, but we'll drive by there anyway and make sure. Dekes probably sent his men after us to show Callie exactly what would happen to her if she doesn't sell out to him. Bodies tend to motivate people far more than threats do. Maybe he thought she needed some more encouragement besides Stu Alexander. We'll come back out to the restaurant tomorrow and talk to Callie about what to do next, about how we can stop Dekes for good."

Bria shook her head. "What you really mean is that you're going to pump Callie for information about how you can get close enough to Dekes to kill him. I don't know why it surprises me anymore, but it still does."

I stared at her. "Dekes sent his men to rape and murder us tonight, just because we dared to stand up to his goons. That's plenty enough reason for me to kill him, but what makes you think that he won't do the same to Callie? Or worse? His men certainly wanted to have a go at her. We're just minor annoyances, tourists passing through who were tougher than they looked. Callie is the one that Dekes really needs to get rid of in order to build his seaside casino. People are more vicious about money than any other thing, and it sounds like the vamp has already sunk quite a bit of dough into his project. He's not going to let one woman stand in the way of it, no matter what he has to do or how ugly things get. If Dekes is the kind of man that I think he is, then he likes ugly—revels in it, even, like a hog in slop."

Bria didn't like it, but she couldn't argue with my logic. My sister might not be as far gone into the shady side of life as I was, but she'd seen her share of bad things as a cop, and she'd dealt with a lot of scumbags, especially since coming back to Ashland.

"Fine," she muttered. "We'll come out here for brunch in the morning and talk to Callie like I planned. But that's hours away. So what do you want to do after we check on Callie's house? If you're right, Dekes can track us to any hotel that we might stay at here on the island, and I don't think you want to ask Donovan if you can sleep on his couch."

"One step ahead of you, baby sister. One step ahead." I pulled my cell phone out of my jeans pocket and scrolled through the screens until I found what I was looking for. "Do you know where 213 Mockingbird Drive is?"

"Yeah. Why?"

"Because that's where we're going to stay tonight," I said. "I took the precaution of renting a beach house under another name just in case we ran into trouble down here."

Bria shook her head. "You can't do anything like a normal person, can you? Not even relax enough to go on vacation for one measly weekend."

The cold reproach in her voice made me shift in my seat. "I like to be prepared. There's nothing wrong with that."

Bria snorted, but she made a U-turn in the parking lot and headed back the way we'd come. Callie had given my sister Donovan's address before we'd left the Sea Breeze earlier tonight, and we pulled up to the detective's house a few minutes later.

It was a two-story ranch house made out of gray brick with a wide, flat yard surrounded by a matching gray wooden fence. It was an anonymous suburban home in a nice middle-class neighborhood. No lights were on inside the house. A few televisions flickered through the windows of some of the other homes on the block, but everything else was dark and quiet. Dekes's men hadn't come here, which meant that Donovan and Callie were safe and snug inside his house—and probably in bed together for the night.

Even though there was nothing particularly special about it, I couldn't quit staring at the detective's house. It was a perfect, modest home and just the sort of place that I could see Donovan settling down and being happy in. Kissing his wife good-bye in the morning, coming home to her at night, mowing the yard on Saturdays, playing football with the kids on Sundays. Yes, that's exactly the kind of life I could picture the detective having—with Callie.

"Well, you were right," Bria murmured. "Dekes sent his men after us instead of them. Do you want me to knock on the door and let them know what's going on?"

"Nah. It looks like they're asleep for the night," I said, my voice thick and husky with emotions that I didn't want to think too much about right now. "Let's not wake them. There will be plenty of time to talk tomorrow."

Bria drove away from the curb. Try as I might, I couldn't help but look back a final time before we turned onto the main road and Donovan's house disappeared from sight.

We passed the Blue Sands hotel again with its gleaming white stone and perfectly landscaped grounds. Bria kept right on going, steering the car all the way to the other side of the island before eventually veering onto a wide, smooth road. We drove through a ritzy subdivision, although the houses were so large and spaced so far apart that *subdivision* didn't adequately describe the upscale community.

A few minutes later, we came to the end of the road and stopped in front of a three-story beach house that was half a mile away from its closest neighbor.

"Two-thirteen Mockingbird Drive," Bria said.

"Wait here," I told her, and got out of the car.

I'd rented the beach house a few days ago under the name Aurora Metis, which was an alias of mine, and had arranged to have it stocked with some staple foods, fresh linens, and all the other essentials that someone might need for a long weekend at the beach. Given how many people were gunning for me back in Ashland, it hadn't been out of the realm of possibility that some of them might follow me to Blue Marsh, and I'd wanted a safe house to retreat to in case that happened.

The key was right where the realtor had e-mailed that it would be, under a small gray stone statue shaped like a lighthouse that perched on the front porch. An obvious hiding place, if you asked me, but I wasn't going to be too critical, not after everything that had happened tonight. Even if I hadn't been able to find the key, all I would have had to do to get inside was use my elemental magic to create a couple of Ice picks and jimmy one of the locks.

I used the key to open the front door and slipped inside the beach house. I walked through the interior, a silverstone knife in either hand, and peered into all the rooms, corners, and closets. Everything was clean and spotless, just as the realtor had promised me it would be. We'd be safe enough here for the night, but I still took my usual precautions, familiarizing myself with the location of the light switches and furniture and taking the time to trace more spiral protection runes into the various stone walls that made up the house.

When I was finished, I stepped through the door that led to the three-car garage, crossed the concrete, and opened the outer door so Bria could drive the convertible inside, where it would be hidden from sight.

"Now what?" she said, climbing out of the car.

"Now we go inside, get cleaned up, and get some sleep. Tomorrow's going to be another long day." I looked at the ruined convertible. "And one of us needs to call Finn and explain what happened to his car."

Bria gave me a knowing, sarcastic, slightly evil smile. "Oh, that pleasure is all yours, big sister."

We turned on a few low lights and hauled our suitcases inside. The beach house was equipped with a stone fireplace in the main room, and I rummaged through the kitchen drawers until I found a pack of matches. It was too warm for a fire, but then again, the added heat wasn't really my intention—destroying evidence was. I grabbed the plastic bag of bloody rags and the empty bottle of bleach and stuffed them inside the grate, along with a few pieces of newspaper and kindling from a nearby brass basket. Bria went into the back of the house to take a shower, and I sat there on one of the couches and watched the evidence of my latest crime crackle and burn while I dialed Finn.

"Hello, sexy. I knew that you couldn't get through the night without me," Finn's smug, slightly sleepy voice filled my ear. "So why don't you tell me what you're wearing?"

I rolled my eyes. Apparently, my foster brother hadn't bothered to check his caller ID before he'd picked up the phone. I wondered if this was how he answered all his late-night calls, or if he'd actually been expecting to hear from Bria. I really hoped it was the second one.

"What am I wearing? Why, right now it would be the blood of two giants, among other naughty unmentionables," I purred. "What does that do for you, sexy?"

Silence.

Then Finn cleared his throat. "Uh, Gin? Did you dial my number by mistake? Shouldn't you be cooing these sweet, sweet nothings into Owen's ear instead of mine?"

"No mistake," I chirped in a bright voice. "I just thought I'd call you and tell you that there's been a slight change of plans. Bria and I aren't staying at the Blue Sands hotel anymore."

"Why not?" he asked in a sharp voice.

It was amazing just how much suspicion and accusation Finn could put into two simple words. Then again, he knew me all too well. And really, suspicion and accusation were always warranted whenever the Spider was around.

"Let's just say that we had some unwanted visitors tonight—the kind who were intent on making sure we didn't live to see the dawn. Of course, that didn't work out so well for them."

More silence.

"What the hell did you do?" he finally asked. "And more importantly, is my car still in one piece?"

"Well," I said. "I suppose that depends on your definition of *in one piece*."

Finn just groaned.

❖ 10 ❖

I filled Finn in on what had happened. He agreed to call Owen so they could get an early start, drive down to Blue Marsh, and meet Bria and me for brunch at the Sea Breeze at ten. I also asked Finn to dig up everything that he could on Randall Dekes. I wanted to know exactly whom and what I was dealing with before the vampire sent more men after us—or decided to make an appearance himself.

I hung up with Finn and took a long, hot shower, washing away the stench of bleach that clung to my hands and scrubbing the blood out from underneath my fingernails. When I was done, I changed into a pair of loose cotton pajamas and brushed out my wet hair. Bria had already gone to bed, and I added my bloody clothes to hers, which were already burning in the fireplace. I should have crawled into bed and tried to sleep, but instead, I curled up on a couch in front of one of the sliding glass doors that overlooked the endless ocean.

Restless, I picked up my cell phone and hit one of the numbers in the speed dial. He picked up on the third ring.

"Hello?" Owen Grayson's deep voice rumbled through the receiver.

"Hi, it's Gin," I said, even though he knew my voice as well as I did his.

"Hey." Warmth immediately filled his tone. "How are you? I just got done talking to Finn. He told me that you and Bria had a run-in with some local muscle earlier."

"You might say that."

I told Owen what had taken place tonight, starting with Pete and Trent showing up at Callie's restaurant and threatening her and ending with Bria and me dumping the four men's bodies into the palm-tree-shaped pool at the Blue Sands hotel.

Owen chuckled at that. "You know, you're going to give the pool boy a heart attack in the morning when he goes out to clean the filters."

I joined in his laughter. "I know."

We fell silent, but it wasn't an awkward, uncomfortable pause. It was one of the many things I loved about Owen. He didn't rush to fill in the empty spaces but was content to just let them—and me—be when I needed him to.

"So why did you really call?" Owen finally asked in a soft voice. "I can tell that there's something else going on besides Bria's friend being threatened. I can hear it in your voice. Something's bothering you."

Owen and I had only been together for a few months, but he could read me better than almost anyone else could, even Finn sometimes. I'd told Owen everything—except for the fact that I'd also run into Donovan tonight.

I was still trying to figure out how I felt about seeing the detective again. Oh, I didn't love him, not like I did Owen, but Donovan and I had shared something once upon a time, even if it had been only for a little while. It was hard to ignore the echoes of the old feelings and memories in my heart, even though I knew that what I felt for Owen was much, much deeper and that he was far more important to me than Donovan had ever been.

"I called because I wanted to hear your voice," I murmured. "I needed to hear it. Being on vacation is . . . harder than I thought it would be."

"How so?"

I rubbed the spider rune scar on first one palm, then the other, struggling to put my feelings into words. "Because I don't seem to be very good at it. We haven't even been gone a day, and it feels like I'm right back where I started. Like I never even left Ashland and the bad guys behind. I was looking forward to relaxing. And I tried today—I really did. I let Bria drag me around all afternoon, and I even *oohed* and *aahed* over tacky T-shirts and cheap seashell necklaces just like you're supposed to when you're on vacation. Can you believe that? I don't think I've ever *oohed* and *aahed* in my entire life."

Owen laughed again.

"What? It's not funny," I grumbled. "It's downright embarrassing."

"Ah, don't worry about it." I could hear the smile in his voice through the phone. "This too shall pass."

"I know, I know. It's just a long weekend, and I'll make the best of it. But then there's Bria," I said, finally focusing on what was really bothering me.

"What about Bria?"

I sighed. "She loves it down here, Owen. She absolutely loves it. You should have seen her face today. Other than the visit to the cemetery, she was so happy, especially when we first walked into the Sea Breeze and she saw Callie again. I keep forgetting that this was her home for so many years, that she had friends and a job and a life down here. Part of me wonders if she regrets leaving all of that behind to move to Ashland. To find me. Because, let's face it, things haven't exactly been easy for either one of us these last few months."

"Just give it some time," Owen said. "Bria's only been back in your life for a few months. The two of you are still getting to know each other. There's bound to be an adjustment period as you both figure out what kind of relationship you can and want to have, especially now that Mab isn't around to constantly be a threat to both of you."

"Yeah, but so far, I don't think that Bria likes what she sees very much. I wanted this vacation to be stress- and bad-guy-free so we could finally have a chance to connect with each other, but it looks like it's going to be anything but that."

We fell silent again. Outside, the waves continued to crash into the shore, while the moon slowly sank toward the ocean, making the frothing water glimmer with a pale, ghostly light.

"You know, if I left now, I could be down there just after sunrise," Owen murmured in a low, sexy tone. "You, me, a deserted beach. The possibilities are endless."

Liquid heat flooded my veins as I pictured the two of us rolling around in the sand together, the sea spraying over us as we made love, Owen's hands moving up and down my body, even as mine did the same to his. "Mmm. Tempting. Very tempting."

"But?"

"But you'd have a hell of a time dragging Finn out of bed tonight. He tends to whine whenever his precious sleep is interrupted. I already woke him up once. I wouldn't want you to have to listen to him bitch for the next several hours."

Owen laughed again. "It would be worth it for you, Gin. Besides, I'm sure I could find some duct tape somewhere here in the house. A couple of pieces of that would take care of even Finn's whining."

I smiled. Whether we were having a simple conversation about nothing important or discussing something as deep and convoluted as my feelings toward my sister, Owen always knew exactly what to say to make me feel better.

"I don't know," I drawled. "Finn's got an awfully big mouth. I don't think that just one roll of duct tape would do it."

Owen laughed again.

We flirted with and teased each other for a few more minutes before the conversation wound down. We paused again, and I thought once more about telling Owen about Donovan and how the detective had suddenly reappeared in my life. But that would lead to another conversation about my gnarled, knotted feelings, and I felt like I'd already exposed enough of my doubts, insecurities, and vulnerabilities to Owen. I'd never considered myself a coward, but I just didn't have the balls to get into my history with Donovan. Not tonight.

"I love you," Owen finally said.

"I love you too," I whispered back, and hung up.

I put the phone down on one of the coffee tables, but instead of going to bed like I should have, I sat there in the dark and stared out at the ocean, wondering what new troubles the sunrise would bring with it.

The rest of the night passed uneventfully, and Friday morning dawned clear, bright, and hot. By the time Bria and I left the rented beach house to drive over to the Sea Breeze, the temperature had already climbed into the lower eighties, and the stifling humidity made it seem ten degrees warmer than that. I spotted a few people moving in and around the other houses farther down the street as folks gathered up their chairs, blankets, umbrellas, coolers, and sunscreen for a day at the beach, but nobody showed any interest in us that they shouldn't have.

As powerful and connected as Dekes was, he and his men hadn't tracked us from the hotel last night. I hadn't expected them to, given my alias, but it was nice to know that we were in the clear—at least for now. I had no doubt that the bodies in the hotel pool had been found by this point. I didn't know exactly how Dekes would react to the death of his men, whether he would rage and scream or quietly, coldly plot out his payback, but I'd have my guard up, just like I always did.

Bria and I got into Finn's busted-up convertible and headed for the Sea Breeze. I thought that the car might get a few strange looks with its cracked windshield, ripped seats, and dented hood, but Bria parked it in a far corner of the lot next to a few junked pickup trucks, and it blended right in.

Apparently Callie's restaurant served up an even better brunch than they did supper because the lot was even fuller than it had been last night, with several cars double-parked and others lining either side of the road. All the seats at the picnic tables were already taken, so we once again headed inside to wait for a table.

"Do you think that Finn and Owen are already here?" Bria asked, standing on her tiptoes and looking over the crowd.

I opened my mouth to answer her when a large, familiar body sidled up next to me.

"Why, hello, gorgeous," a low, sexy voice rumbled in my ear. "Can I interest you in a walk on the beach?"

Smiling, I turned around to find Owen standing behind me. Finn was there too, but I only had eyes for my lover.

Owen was on the tall side, topping out at about six foot one, with a strong, sturdy body that had hard, sleek muscles in all the right places. His hair was black, and the sunbeams streaming in through the porthole windows made the hidden blue highlights in his thick locks shimmer. The midnight color of his hair set off his pale skin and his piercing violet eyes. His nose was a little crooked, the result of having been broken long ago, and a thin white scar slashed down his chin, but I thought that the small imperfections only added to his rough, rugged appeal. He'd dressed down today in a pair of khakis and a short-sleeved black polo shirt that showed just how wide and strong his chest was, and I thought he was the most handsome man in the room. Hell, in the whole South.

I wrapped my arms around Owen's neck and drew his mouth down for a kiss. I'd meant for it to be a quick caress of my lips on his, but Owen coaxed my mouth open, his tongue stroking against mine, his hands kneading my back, and liquid heat pooled in my stomach. It was several seconds before I pulled back, breathless, aching, and yearning for something else besides breakfast. Something that would be even more delicious and far more satisfying.

"You know, that walk on the beach is sounding better and better all the time," Owen murmured, his eyes glinting with the same heat that thumped through my veins.

"Later," I promised. "We've got work to do this morning, remember? Finn, did you bring the information that I asked you to? Finn?"

He was too busy bending Bria over backward and planting a sound, lingering kiss on her to answer. It took them even longer to come up for air than it had Owen and me, and by the time Finn set Bria back up on her feet, most of the people in the restaurant were staring at them. A few of the wives were even poking their husbands in the chests, muttering about how *they* never got kissed like *that* anymore.

Finn grinned, gave an elaborate flourish with his hand, and dipped into a low bow before straightening up and addressing the entire restaurant. "And that, ladies and gentlemen, is how it is *done.*"

A couple of the older women broke out into enthusiastic applause, and Finn winked at them all in turn. A furious blush flooded Bria's cheeks at the unexpected, unwanted attention, but her blue eyes were sparkling.

Whatever his faults might be, Finn made my sister happy, and that was all I really cared about, even if I'd wanted to keep a lower profile this morning.

We got a booth in the back and sat down, with Finn and Owen sliding into the opposite side from Bria and me. Finn was carrying a silverstone briefcase, but he didn't open it and put it on the table. He didn't need to. I knew what was inside already—all the information he'd been able to dig up on Dekes in the last few hours. In addition to his prowess as an investment banker, Finn also dabbled in information trading. Well, perhaps *dabbled* wasn't the right word when you had an extensive network of spies and snitches in Ashland and beyond like he did. Either way, there were few things he liked better than unearthing other people's deepest, darkest secrets, whether it was for cold, hard cash or just his own personal amusement.

There would be plenty of time to sort through the files later. Right now, I was determined to enjoy a meal with some of the people I cared about the most. I was still on vacation, and I was determined to act like it—at least for the next hour or so.

We ordered enough food for an army, and the four us of laughed and talked and joked while we waited for everything to arrive, like we were out on a casual double date instead of getting ready to consider what to do about Dekes. Or maybe this was just our own sort of date, plotting against the bad guys while we chowed down.

Thirty minutes later, Callie came over to our booth with several platters of steaming food balanced on her forearms, with two more waitresses trailing along behind her carrying even more dishes.

Stacks of thick Belgian waffles drizzled with peach syrup, piles of fresh-cooked bacon, sizzling sausage, golden hash browns, deep-fried cinnamon rolls drizzled with sweet icing, toasted pineapple muffins slathered with whipped cream cheese, iced glasses full of mango mimosas. I breathed in, relishing the smells of the sticky waffles, flaky muffins, and hearty meats. They mixed together with all the other mouthwatering flavors in the air, creating a cloud of succulent aroma over the table.

"It all looks wonderful," Bria said. "Thanks, Callie."

The other woman nodded. "Sure. It's my pleasure. I hope you guys enjoy it."

She smiled, but the tight expression didn't really lift her lips. Callie looked like she hadn't slept well last night. Purple smudges had gathered in the corners of her eyes, streaking out across her skin like a football player's greasepaint, and her whole body was tight and rigid. Even her blue work apron and the casual white T-shirt and khakis she had on underneath seemed stiff and starched with tension.

"What's wrong?" Bria asked, picking up on her friend's dark mood.

"Four bodies were found floating in the pool at the Blue Sands hotel this morning," Callie said in a soft voice. "It's the talk of the whole island."

Yeah, I'd figured it would be, and coming into the restaurant had only confirmed my suspicion. I'd heard more than a few folks around us say words like *dead bodies* and *murdered* and *pool* since we'd been sitting in our booth. Not too hard to figure out what everyone was buzzing about.

"The Blue Sands happens to be the same hotel where you told me that you had booked a suite," Callie continued. "One of the men was Pete Procter, and another was his buddy, Trent. I'm sure you remember them. They're the two guys who came into the restaurant last night and threatened me. The same two guys that your sister . . . dealt with."

Callie looked at me, and I met her gaze head-on. If she hadn't figured out by now that there was more to me than met the eye, well, she hadn't been paying attention. Callie didn't strike me as the kind of woman who missed much. She'd already put most of it together, and all she needed now was confirmation from us. How she would react when Bria told her what had happened was what was going to be interesting.

Bria hesitated. "Come back later when you get a break, okay? There are some things that we need to talk about, including what happened to those two guys. In private."

Callie stared at me another second before dropping her gaze and nodding at Bria. "Sure. Just as soon as I get a chance."

She turned, threaded her way through the packed tables, and headed back into the kitchen to start on her next order, with the waitresses trailing along behind her. Nobody at our booth spoke for a moment.

"Well, that was rather awkward," Finn said.

None of us answered him.

But Finn being Finn, he ignored the silence, smiled, and picked up one of the platters of food. "But on to more important matters. Who wants waffles?"

We spent the next hour eating. The food was just as delicious as it had been the night before. The waffles were light and fluffy, the peach syrup was sweet without being too sugary, and the mango mimosas packed just enough of a champagne punch to make you think about lazing away the rest of the day in a chair out on the beach.

Finally, though, the food was finished, the platters were cleared away, and it was just the four of us at the table once more, which meant that vacation time was over—for now.

"All right," I said. "Lay it out for us, Finn."

"Why, I thought you'd never ask," he drawled.

Finn put his silverstone briefcase on the table, popped it open, and pulled out a thick manila folder. He flipped it open, turned it around, and scooted the file over to me and Bria.

"Randall Michael Dekes," Finn said. "Vampire, real estate mogul, and all-around bloodsucking bad guy. Exact age and magical abilities unknown, but he's rumored to be more than three hundred and exceptionally powerful, with lots of elemental magic to spare."

Finn had included a color head-and-shoulders portrait of Dekes that looked like it was taken off some corporate website. I picked it up so I could study it a little closer. Randall Dekes had sable brown hair, a thick, bristling mustache, and pale green eyes. His dazzling white teeth made his skin seem even tanner than it was, and he wore a fancy gray suit that even Finn would be envious of. A diamond shaped like a miniature palm tree winked in the middle of the solid gray tie that trailed down his chest. Overall, he reminded me of an old-fashioned movie star, a Clark Gable type playing the part of a tropical island lord—dark, strong, sleek, and handsome.

And dangerous. Dekes was smiling in the photo, but the expression didn't reach his eyes. Instead, he stared at the camera in a way that was mocking, smirking, and predatory all at the same time, like he knew some great secret that no one else did. His lips were curled back far enough to show the glittering edges of his pearl-white fangs, like he was considering sinking them into whoever was holding the camera and wondering whether the resulting bloodstains would be worth running his expensive suit for. Oh yes, definitely dangerous—and arrogant too.

"Over his three hundred and some years, Dekes has built up a vast real estate empire concentrated primarily on coastal properties in the Carolinas, Georgia, and down into Florida, with a few recent purchases in the Bahamas as well," Finn continued. "On the surface, he's a well-respected, legitimate businessman who's responsible for some of the most successful developments on the East Coast. Casinos, hotels, restaurants, golf courses, luxury spas, shopping centers. If it's on the waterfront and it's a smashing success, then Dekes probably had a hand in creating it."

Bria looked up from the pages she'd been reading. "And below the surface?"

Finn shrugged. "He does whatever it takes to buy up the land that he wants to develop, usually for a fraction of its value. Threats, intimidations, bribes. In the last year, Dekes and the men he employs have been linked to half a dozen beatings and even more arson investigations related to property owners who didn't want to sell out to him. Interestingly enough, the beating victims survived. The arson ones didn't. Like I said, I don't know what kind of magic Dekes does or doesn't have, but he enjoys playing with fire, whether it's elemental power or the old-fashioned kind that you get with matches and gasoline."

I put the portrait of Dekes down on the table and sorted through several other pictures that Finn had included in the folder. Instead of being more images of the vampire, these photos showed the burned-out, smoldering remains of various homes, businesses, and other assorted properties. Blackened bodies could be seen in all the photos, gnarled, twisted, and burned, the victims' mouths open in silent screams.

The photos reminded me of how Mab had used her elemental Fire magic to reduce my mother and sister to nothing more than ashy husks. For a moment, I was back there in our burning mansion that night, my own screams ringing in my ears, the harsh, acrid smell of seared flesh filling my nose, the sickening stench overpowering everything else—

A waitress dropped a fork on the floor in front of our booth, and the harsh, reverberating *clang-clang-clang* snapped me out of my memories. I sighed. Mab might be dead, but I wondered if I'd ever be able to truly overcome what she'd done to my family. But this wasn't about me—it was about helping Callie—so I pushed away my troubling thoughts and kept studying the photos.

It didn't take me long to realize that Dekes didn't just limit his cruelty to the property owners who wouldn't sell out to him. Many of the bodies in the photos were too small to be adults, and a few were obviously the remains of animals, their silverstone collars still glinting around their charred necks. Men, women, kids, pets. Dekes and his men had killed them all indiscriminately. In a way, that made the vamp worse than me. I might have murdered people for money, but I'd never killed a kid, cat, dog, or some other poor, pitiful, defenseless creature who couldn't fight back. Those were the rules Fletcher had instilled in me, the code that I still followed to this day. Dekes didn't appear to have even that much decency—or mercy.

I wondered if the vampire sank his fangs into his victims and drained them dry before he murdered them, or if he'd simply locked them in their own houses and businesses alive before he burned the buildings down around them. Either one would be a horrible, horrible way to die.

"So he's got a pattern," Owen murmured. "He starts out with threats, then moves on to beatings. If that doesn't convince you to sell your property to him, then Dekes and his men torch your home or place of business—with you locked inside it. Then he buys up the property for a song after the fact, if he just didn't get you to sign it over to him before he killed you anyway."

Finn made a shooting motion at Owen with his finger and thumb. "Bingo."

"And now he wants Callie's restaurant," I said. "What did you find out about the casino that Dekes is planning on building on the island?"

"It's going to be a big, big deal," Finn said. "Every kind of game that you could want to play, along with Vegas-style shows, dancing, liquor, five-star restaurants, high-end shops, even a set of stables so they can have live horse races and polo matches on the grounds. You've got to hand it to the guy—he definitely thinks on a grand scale."

"But can't he just build the casino somewhere else on the island," Bria asked, "since he owns so much other land here already?"

Finn shook his head. "Nope, like you said, Blue Marsh is an island, which means that it has a finite amount of space. Sure, Dekes owns most of that space, but there are a few other movers and shakers on the island that even he couldn't piss off without some serious reprisals. He just doesn't have enough parcels of land strung together to build the kind of casino that he wants. At least, not without the land that the Sea Breeze sits on. And we all know that it would be far easier for him to go after Callie than the island's other power players."

I stared out at the framed seashells on the walls, the old, tattered fishing nets strung between them, the brass railing and the sunken boat that make up the bar. Despite my jealousy of Callie's easy friendship with Bria, I was big enough to admit that her restaurant was something special, something worth saving. More than that, it was Callie's home just like the Pork Pit was mine.

I might be on vacation, might have wanted to leave all the blood, bodies, and violence back in Ashland for the weekend, but I wasn't going to stand by and let some vampire thug take Callie's restaurant away from her, not when I could do something to help her. Not when I knew just how much she and this place meant to Bria.

Besides, Randall Dekes had either ordered or approved of his men raping and murdering Bria and me last night. The bastard was going to pay for that alone—even if I was supposed to be on vacation.

"Dekes is a cocky bastard too," Finn added. "Apparently, he's having a press conference late this afternoon out on the south lawn of his estate to formally announce the construction of the casino—even though he doesn't have the last piece of land that he needs to start breaking ground. Here's another interesting tidbit: the press conference was supposed to take place on the patio around the pool at the Blue Sands hotel, but the location was changed due to some unforeseen circumstances."

I snorted. "You mean the four bodies I left floating in the water there."

Finn just grinned at me.

"He's holding a press conference? Really?" I asked. "Is that all that bad guys know how to do? Hold press conferences and parties?"

"Why do you say that?" Bria asked.

"Do you know how many people that I've killed before, during, and after press conferences? It's laughable, really. You basically stand up in front of everyone and brag about how rich and powerful you are. It's like an open invitation to an assassin like me. *Come on down, take a free shot at me, and have a drink while you're at it.* I don't imagine Dekes's event will be any different. The only question is how easy it will be to get in. Right, Finn?"

He shot me a grumpy look. "Despite what you think, I'm not a magician, you know. I can't just conjure up invitations out of thin air, especially since we're not in Ashland anymore."

I raised an eyebrow at him.

"Okay, okay," Finn grumbled. "So I *might* have started working on getting us invites as soon as I found out about the press conference. I don't think it will be too hard, since Dekes has basically invited everyone who's anyone on the island. I actually do business with some folks who are friendly with Dekes, so the four of us can get in that way. Friends of a friend and whatnot."

"No," I said. "The three of you can get in that way. I'm thinking about taking another approach. Just in case things get a little messy with Dekes."

"And what would that be?" Owen asked.

I smiled at him. "The great thing about throwing a press conference to announce your new multimillion-dollar casino is that you have to actually invite the press. The bad guys have to have someone to crow to about their accomplishments. So I'll go in as a reporter. That should be an easy, plausible way to get a few minutes alone with Dekes. You can create some quick credentials for me, can't you, Finn?"

"Sure," Finn grumbled again. "I might as well wave my magic wand and do that too while I'm at it."

"Oh, quit bitching," I said. "You know you love little challenges like this. Schmoozing invitations and creating fake documents gets your blood pumping and makes you feel all clever and larcenous."

He shot me a sour look.

"Anyway, I think it's a good plan," I said.

Owen reached over and took my hand in his. "But what about—"

He stopped in midsentence. He blinked for a few seconds before his violet eyes narrowed, his mouth flattened out into a hard, thin line, and his hand tightened on mine. I turned to see what he was glaring at—and spotted Donovan Caine standing in the door of the restaurant.

❖ 11 ❖

"What the hell is he doing here?" Owen asked in a flat voice.

Finn leaned to one side so he could see what Owen was looking at. His eyes widened when he caught sight of the detective, and he sent me a questioning glance, which I ignored, since I was focused on Owen right now.

"He's Callie's fiancé," I replied in a low tone. "He showed up here at the restaurant last night after I dealt with the two guys who were threatening her."

"And you just forgot to mention that before now?" Owen asked, his eyes narrowed in thought.

I shifted on my side of the booth. I couldn't exactly tell Owen that I didn't know what to make of Donovan being back in my life any more than he did. The detective noticed Owen glaring at him and did a double take as well, as surprised by his appearance as Owen had been by his. The two men stared at each other for several seconds before Donovan squared his shoulders and headed in our direction.

"Incoming," Finn muttered, letting out a low whistle and then a crashing sound under his breath, like a bomb was about to drop down and explode on our heads.

I kicked him under the table, trying to get him to shut the hell up. This was going to be bad enough without him making wisecracks. Finn winced, gave me a dirty look, and leaned down to massage his bruised shin.

Donovan stepped up to the booth. He nodded at Bria and Finn, then turned to look at me and finally Owen.

"Owen."

"Donovan."

The detective's gaze fell to the table and Owen's hand, which was still resting on top of mine. Donovan's face tightened, and his lips turned down the slightest bit. I had no idea why. *He*'d left *me*, after all, come down here and gotten engaged to another woman in the space of a few months. So why did he look so pissed that Owen was holding my hand? And why did his expression make me feel just a little bit smug inside?

"I hear that congratulations are in order," Owen finally said. "On your *engagement*."

He put a little extra emphasis on the last word, but Donovan just nodded, not rising to the bait.

"They are. Callie's a really special woman. I'm lucky to have her in my life."

"You were lucky to have Gin in your life too, but you managed to fuck that up," Owen said in a mild tone. "Callie seems like a nice lady. Let's hope that history doesn't repeat itself—for her sake."

He gave Donovan a smirking, mocking smile, which caused the detective's hands to tighten into fists and his whole body to swell up with tension. Donovan looked like he was another quip away from challenging Owen to a showdown out in the parking lot—or just reaching across the table and throttling Owen where he sat.

I tightened my grip on Owen's hand. We had too much to do today for my current lover and past one to get into a petty fistfight in a restaurant full of people, despite the fact that part of me thought it would be pretty damn entertaining to watch. I might be the toughest assassin around, but the idea of two men brawling over me had a certain sexy appeal—especially since I knew that Owen would wipe the floor with Donovan. Oh, the detective would put up a good struggle, but Owen would fight dirty to win—just like I would.

Owen turned away from Donovan, dismissing him as unimportant, and laced his fingers through mine. I raised my eyebrows at the macho show, but Owen just grinned at me.

Donovan stood there staring at our linked fingers for a moment, that tight expression still on his face, before he shook his head. "What are the four of you doing here? And don't tell me that you came just to get brunch."

"Callie is my best friend," Bria said in a quiet voice. "We're here to help her, Donovan."

The detective's features darkened with anger. "I told Gin last night that I didn't need or want her help. I'll handle Dekes, and I'll do so through legal means. That's all there is to it."

Bria looked at him, then over at me. I could see the struggle in her blue eyes. Part of her agreed with Donovan that it would be best to handle Dekes through the law. That's what they were supposed to do, that's what the two of them had sworn to do as cops. But the other part of her remembered Mab and all the awful things the Fire elemental had done to us over the years—things that there was only one kind of justice for.

"It doesn't seem to me that legal means will work with Dekes," Bria said in a careful tone. "Not after what happened to me and Gin last night."

Donovan frowned. For a moment, a spark of concern shimmered in his golden eyes, but it was gone so quickly that I thought I'd only imagined it.

"You mean those four bodies found at the Blue Sands hotel? I got called out there bright and early this morning to work the case. Imagine my surprise when the coroner told me how they'd all been stabbed to death." The sarcasm in his voice was thicker than a steak. Now, the only thing I saw in his gaze was anger.

Finn held up his hand like a student patiently waiting for the teacher to call on him. Donovan looked at him, and my foster brother smiled.

"Let's go into the back of the restaurant," Finn suggested in a cheery voice. "Too many eyes and ears out here for this kind of discussion."

He was right. The brunch crowd had thinned out considerably, but more than a few folks stared in our direction, wondering who we were and why there was so much tension among the five of us.

"Fine," Donovan muttered. "Follow me."

We slid out of the booth. Brunch was my treat, so I left more than enough money on the table to cover our food and give the waitresses a generous tip. Then the four of us followed Donovan into the back of the restaurant. I didn't look at Owen as we wound our way through the tables, but I could feel my lover's eyes on me. He might have seemed nonchalant with Donovan, but I knew that Owen was pissed and probably a little hurt that I hadn't mentioned the detective to him last night when I'd called.

I sighed. I'd never claimed to be good at this relationship stuff, and once again, it seemed I'd made a mess of things without even trying.

The doors next to the bar led into the restaurant's kitchen. My eyes scanned the stainless-steel appliances, the pots of coffee brewing on their burners, the white order tickets tacked up over a series of stoves that lined the back wall. Even though it was a relatively small space, everything was neat and clean just like it was at the Pork Pit. I approved.

Callie stood in the middle of the kitchen, pouring thick, creamy batter into a series of waffle makers, calling out orders and instructions to the other cooks, and handing finished plates of food to the waitresses standing by. She had a smile on her face as she talked and laughed with her staff, and it was easy to tell that she was the heart and soul of the kitchen. That the food she served up at the Sea Breeze had a little bit of her love and joy in every single bite.

Callie looked over her shoulder at the sound of the doors swinging open, probably expecting another waitress to come hurrying through with a new order, and her eyes lit up when she realized that it was Donovan instead. She finished the latest waffle she was making, slid it on a plate, and passed it off to another chef to be topped with fresh peaches, honey, and whipped cream. Then she hurried over to Donovan, stood on her tiptoes, and kissed the detective's stubbled cheek. The food wasn't the only thing that Callie loved—she cared about Donovan too.

My heart twinged again, and a sort of wistful sadness filled me. I didn't want the detective for myself, but I didn't know that I wanted to see his obvious happiness either, especially when I'd been the cause of so much unhappiness in his life.

Donovan smiled down at his fiancée. Then his gaze cut to me, and his face iced over once again. He took a step back from Callie.

"Can you take a break and go into your office for a few minutes?" Donovan asked in a low voice. "Gin and her friends have some things that they'd like to talk to you about. Things that we all need to talk about."

Callie stared at me, then back at her fiancé, clearly wondering what was going on between us. Damned if I knew.

"Sure. This way."

We left the kitchen and stepped through another door into a small office in the very back of the restaurant. A desk, a computer, a phone, a couple of printers, piles of paper and invoices everywhere. It was your typical small-business office with a typical jumbled mess. Callie took the seat behind the desk, Donovan perched on the edge of it, and the rest of us crowded inside the cramped space.

Finn closed the door behind him so we wouldn't be overheard.

"What's going on?" Callie asked, looking at Bria. "You said earlier you wanted to talk."

Bria nodded and drew in a breath. "We need to discuss what we're going to do about Randall Dekes and the threats he's made against you."

Callie shook her head, causing her dark ponytail to swish against her shoulders. "I've told you before, Bria, that there's nothing for you to do. Dekes is my problem, not yours. Sooner or later, Donovan will find something to connect him to Stu's death, and the vampire will be put in jail where he belongs."

"Maybe, but it won't stick. Not for long. And he won't find it before Dekes kills you," I said in a soft voice. "The vamp's already made the decision to do that."

Callie flinched, like I'd hauled off and slapped her. After a moment, she forced out a weak laugh. "What? That's crazy."

She tried to make her voice sound strong, confident, sure, but I could hear the doubt in her tone. She'd heard the shocked, horrified whispers of how Dekes had gotten the other people on the island to sell out to him already, and she'd been threatened by his goons herself. Not to mention what the vamp and his men had done to the old man at the ice-cream shop a few days ago. Callie sat there, chewing on her lip and tapping her fingers on top of the papers scattered across her desk.

"How do you know that Dekes plans to murder me?" she finally asked.

"Because Gin's an assassin," Donovan said in a cold, flat voice. "She kills people."

My hands curled into fists at his sneering, superior tone, and for a moment, I thought about punching him in the face. I'd hoped to avoid telling Callie exactly who I was and what I did, if only for Bria's sake. Not many people could be friends with an assassin—or friends with the sister of one. I might be jealous of Callie, but I didn't want to come between the two women. I loved Bria too much to be that petty. But I should have known that Donovan would tell his fiancée all about me and what I did late at night—and pass the same old judgments on me here that he had back in Ashland.

Callie's face paled, and she looked at me with wide, fearful eyes. She might have guessed that I had something to do with the dead men in the pool, but it was another thing to have her worst suspicions confirmed.

She turned to Bria. "An assassin? Your sister's an assassin?" her voice dropped to a whisper.

My sister shifted on her feet, not quite meeting Callie's shocked stare. "Yes, Gin's an assassin."

"I go by the name the Spider," I said, trying to spare Bria from having to explain anything else about me and further alienate her friend. "Perhaps you've heard of me."

I'd meant the words as a joke, but Callie's face paled a little more, the golden glow completely washing out of her skin.

"The Spider? The assassin who killed that Fire elemental up in Ashland?" Callie looked at Donovan. "The assassin that you couldn't stop obsessing about a few weeks ago? The one that you tried so hard to find out if she was dead or alive?"

My breath caught in my throat, but I kept my features blank. Donovan had actually been concerned about me? Now? After all this time? I didn't know what to make of that—or that news of my taking down Mab had made its way this far south. That last point was particularly troublesome, to say the least.

Callie gazed at me, then at Donovan, who was doing his very best not to look at me. I could almost see the proverbial lightbulb snap on over her head.

"It's her, isn't it?" Callie said, a note of accusation and worry creeping into her voice. "Gin's the reason you left Ashland. The woman that you were . . . involved with. The one who made you doubt yourself and what you were doing by being a good cop in such a corrupt city."

I glanced at Donovan, who still wouldn't look at me. I hadn't thought that I'd made any kind of dent in his moral righteousness, but apparently I had, if the detective had brought his emotional baggage into his relationship with Callie.

"Awkward," Finn said in a singsong voice.

This time, Bria kicked him in the shin. Finn winced and bent down to rub his leg.

I cleared my throat. "Anyway, Donovan is right. I'm an assassin. I used to kill people for money—"

"A *lot* of money," Finn interrupted in a dreamy voice. "Stacks of it, actually. Do the job, get paid, walk away. Those were the good ole days, if you ask me. These freebie jobs have zero profit margin."

Bria drew her leg back for another kick, but Finn held

up his hands and backed away from her as far as he could in the tiny office.

"Like I said, I used to kill people for money, but these days I run more of a pro bono business," I said. "I help folks with certain . . . problems that they and the law can't or don't know how to handle."

"Problems like Randall Dekes," Callie said.

"Problems exactly like Randall Dekes."

She stared at me, her gray-green eyes dark with suspicion, hurt, and a touch of fear. I wondered if the last emotion was because I was the Spider or the fact that she knew that I used to fuck her fiancé. "And why in the world would you want to help me? I certainly can't pay you much. I can't pay you anything, really. The wedding—"

She stopped, realizing how ironic it was to mention her impending wedding to her fiancé's ex-lover. But I'd give Callie her props because she sucked in another breath and finished her thought. "The wedding has taken up most of my savings, along with some repairs and renovations that I've recently made to the restaurant. So I ask again—why would you want to help me?"

"Because you're Bria's best friend. She loves you, and I'd do anything for my sister," I answered honestly. "And because you don't deserve what Dekes has in store for you. You just want to run your restaurant, cook your food, and see to your customers. Nothing else. You never wanted any trouble, but it has come looking for you these past few months. Believe me, I can relate to that—more than you know. That's why I'd help you. That's enough for me. Let it be enough for you too."

Callie shook her head. "But you're still talking about killing someone, just because I asked you to."

I grinned at her. "Sweetheart, you don't even have to ask. Not after last night."

"That's the second time someone's said something about last night," Donovan said. "What the hell happened? And how did it end with me fishing four bodies out of the pool at the Blue Sands?"

"Dekes sent some of his men to the hotel suite where Bria and I were staying," I said. "They were planning to rape and murder us. That's when I heard them talking about Callie as well—about how they were planning to do the same thing to her after they got done with me and Bria."

Finn pointedly cleared his throat.

"And they also busted up Finn's car along the way," I added.

"Bastards," my foster brother muttered. "You never, *ever* key an Aston Martin, much less crack the windshield or rip up the seats. They deserved to be gutted like fish for that alone."

Callie's eyes widened at the venom in his voice, and she stared at him like he'd just grown another head. Finn smiled at her, following it up with a sexy wink. Bria kicked him again just for that.

Donovan's eyes narrowed to slits. "I thought as much. I knew it was you as soon as I heard that they'd been stabbed to death."

I could have pointed out that Bria had actually killed Pete Procter with her Ice magic, but I knew it wouldn't make a difference to Donovan.

"Guilty as charged," I quipped. "Just like old times, right?"

Donovan gave me a disgusted look then—the same disappointed, disheartened, utterly disgusted look that he had dozens of times before. The look that said that he couldn't believe he hadn't shot me when he'd had the chance, the first night we'd met at the Ashland Opera House. The look that said he couldn't believe he'd ever let himself get close to me. The look that said I wasn't worth one single shred of his time, attention, consideration, or sympathy.

My heart twinged again, but this time it was more from anger than some deep, dark, hidden longing.

"Look," I snapped. "I didn't come down here looking for trouble, but whether you like it or not, Bria and I are in this thing with Callie now. We've embarrassed the vampire twice and killed four of his men. From what little I know about him, Dekes doesn't seem like the kind of guy to let things like that slide. He can't—not and be the badass everyone claims he is. And he still needs the land that the Sea Breeze sits on to build his casino. He's not just going to forget about that either, no matter how much you might want him to."

Donovan couldn't argue with my logic, but he couldn't bring himself to agree with me either. I knew that Donovan's morals meant more to him than I ever had, but I wondered how he felt now that Callie's life was the one in danger. Because Callie was everything I was not—good, sweet, innocent. Would Donovan bend his morals to let me save her? Or would he refuse, foolishly try to go after Dekes through legal methods, and get them both killed in the process?

"Why don't we let Callie decide?" I asked. "Since it's her life on the line."

We all looked at Callie. Some of the color had returned to her face, but confusion, surprise, and hurt still filled her eyes. She kept staring at Donovan like she'd never seen him before. I wondered if it was because she'd just found out that he'd slept with an assassin or because he hadn't told her who I really was last night. Looked like Donovan wasn't any better at this relationship stuff than I was.

"I'm not sure," Callie finally said in a hesitant tone. "I know that Dekes is a horrible person, that he's hurt people, that he killed Stu Alexander or had it done, but we're sitting here talking about *murdering* him. As much as I love the Sea Breeze, it's not worth his life."

"Well, Dekes thinks that it is definitely worth *your* life," I said. "And *I'm* the one talking about murdering someone. Everyone else is just an innocent bystander."

"I'd go with cheerleaders myself," Finn said in a help-ful voice.

This time, Bria shoved her elbow into his side. Finn winced and shuffled a little closer to Owen, who gave him an amused look.

"I can't let you do that, Gin," Donovan said in a low voice. "I can't let you go after Dekes. You know that."

The anger that had been simmering in my stomach turned into a slow boil, and I glared at him. "You aren't *letting* me do anything, Detective. Not one damn thing. I'm a big girl, and I make my own decisions, remember? And I've decided I'm going to crash Dekes's press confer-ence this afternoon. That's all there is to it."

"If you go after him, I'll arrest you," Donovan snapped. "I won't be part of your murdering him. I won't let you get it away with it again. Not here. This is my town, Gin. Not yours. You can either play by my rules or you can get the hell off my island."

I opened my mouth to snap back that I'd like to see him try to fucking arrest me, when Callie got to her feet and held up her hands.

"Please, enough, stop. Both of you. I . . . appreciate what you're trying to do, Gin," she said. "What you're offering to do for me. But I'm not any more comfortable with this than Donovan is, especially since you're talking about murdering Dekes like it's something casual that you do every day of the week."

Callie's statement was far closer to the truth than she knew, given how many thugs I'd taken out in Ashland over the past few weeks and all the others that would be waiting for me when I went back home. Vacation or no vacation, things in the Ashland underworld were by no means settled. It made me tired just thinking about how many more hoods I'd have to take out before the others got the message to leave me the hell alone—if they ever did.

But more than that, I sensed that same kind of bone-tired weariness in Callie. She'd been fighting Dekes for months now, and the struggle had taken its toll on her. Oh, she seemed happy enough on the surface, cooking in her restaurant, laughing and joking with her staff and customers, but tension radiated off her like lightning from a storm cloud. Even now, in the privacy of her own office, her petite body was ramrod straight, and her troubled eyes kept drifting toward the door, as if she expected more of Dekes's men to barge in at any second just because we were talking about the vamp. I was willing to bet that today wasn't the first morning that Callie had woken up with tired smudges under her eyes and knots in her stomach—but it could be the very last, if I had my way with Dekes this afternoon.

"I understand," I said in a gentler voice. "So how about we compromise? Instead of doing what I usually do, I'll *strongly suggest* that Dekes leave you alone. We'll leave it up to the vampire what happens from there. What he does from then on and all the consequences are on him, okay? Can you live with that?"

Callie nodded with obvious relief, but the tension didn't leave Donovan's rough features. The detective knew me far better than his fiancée did. He knew exactly what I'd do if the vampire failed to heed my advice: that I'd stick my knives in Dekes and walk away before the vamp's body even hit the floor. And the worst part for Donovan was that he also realized there wasn't a damn thing he could do about it. Not really. Oh, I imagined he could warn Dekes, but all that would do was make it harder for me to get to the vampire and delay the inevitable. And really, all Donovan's talk about stopping me was just that— talk. Just like it had been back in Ashland. The detective wanted Callie to be safe, and deep down he was happy to let me be the one to get my hands dirty instead of him.

Good thing I liked playing in the muck.

✸ 12 ✸

There was nothing else to say, so Owen, Finn, Bria, and I left Callie and Donovan in the office. The four of us walked back through the kitchen and the front of the restaurant before stepping outside into the afternoon sun. The day was even hotter and more humid than the previous one had been.

"I think that went rather well," Finn said in a cheery voice. "All things considered."

I looked at Bria. "Do you want to slap him or shall I?"

Bria held out her hand in a go-ahead motion. "The pleasure is all yours."

Finn winced and ducked behind Owen. "Quick! Let's make a break for it!"

Owen laughed. "You're on your own, buddy. Let me know how that turns out for you."

Finn huffed, but he didn't step out from behind Owen.

Most of the brunch crowd had already gone, leaving only a few cars parked in front of the restaurant—including Finn's smashed-up convertible. He walked over to his beloved Aston Martin and examined it from every angle before he turned to look at me.

"Now I'm doubly glad you killed those black-hearted sons of bitches," he muttered. "Look what they did to my car, my beautiful, beautiful car. If they were here, I'd shoot out their kneecaps myself."

I rolled my eyes. "It's just a car, Finn. It's not like you don't have a dozen others back home in the parking garage of your apartment building."

He sniffed. "Yes, but those are back home, and we're *here*. And this model was destined to be a classic. Now it's just another piece of junk."

He stuck out his lip, pouted, and then kicked the tire the way that a little boy would.

I looked at Bria. "How do you put up with him?"

Bria started to open her mouth, but Finn piped up instead.

"She puts up with me because I happen to be rich, handsome, charming, a witty conversationalist, and exceptionally talented in bed," he smirked. "Flexible too."

I groaned. "I did not need to hear those last two."

Finn just grinned. Nothing restored his good mood more than needling someone else, and I was happy to take one for the team, since it was my fault that his car had gotten trashed in the first place.

Finn pulled out his cell phone and arranged for a tow truck service to haul his convertible to a garage to get the dents beaten out of it and have the windshield and seats replaced. Then the four of us got into Finn's Cadillac Escalade, which he and Owen had driven down to Blue Marsh this morning. We stopped to pick up some groceries and other supplies, and an hour later, we were back in the beach house I'd rented.

Finn walked through the house before stepping back into the living room. He sniffed his displeasure. "I *suppose* that it will *do*. But it's not nearly as nice as staying at the Blue Sands would have been. There's no pool, no bar, and most importantly, no gorgeous blonde to give me a full-body massage." He grinned at Bria. "Unless you want to volunteer for that last particular duty."

Bria snorted, but I could see the heat glittering in her eyes. Finn might drive her crazy with his motormouth and excessive ego, but she couldn't keep her hands off him any more than I could keep mine off Owen.

"Homework first, children, and then you can play," I drawled. "Finn still has to secure our invitations to Dekes's press conference and whip up some fake credentials for me, remember?"

"And it won't take me more than an hour to do all that," Finn said. "Besides, I'd much rather play first and do homework later. That's always so much more fun."

He leaned in close and whispered something in Bria's ear. She blushed, then let out a small, slightly embarrassed giggle. Finn gave me a triumphant look, his green eyes sly and bright in his ruddy face. He grabbed Bria's hand, and the two of them disappeared down the hall without a backward glance. A few seconds later, more giggles filled the air, along with the sound of a door slamming shut.

That left me alone in the living room with Owen. He hadn't said much in Callie's office or on the ride over to the beach house, but he'd been staring at me with a dark, guarded expression ever since Donovan had shown up at the Sea Breeze.

"How about we take that walk on the beach now?" he suggested. "And give Finn and Bria some privacy."

I nodded. Owen didn't say anything else, but I had some explaining to do, and we both knew it.

I grabbed a couple of large blankets and a blue-and-white-striped beach umbrella from one of the downstairs closets. Owen took the umbrella from me, hoisting the white metal pole up on his shoulder like it weighed nothing. I took a moment to admire the ripple of his muscles under his shirt. Unlike the other wealthy businessmen in Ashland, Owen came by his sculptured physique the old-fashioned way—through hard physical labor. He'd spent years working as a blacksmith while he built up his own business empire, and he still made weapons and iron sculptures in the forge in the back of his house.

Once our supplies were gathered, we set out. We were on the far side of the island from the hotel, and according to Bria, this was the quiet part of Blue Marsh. The local folks rented out their fancy beach houses for exorbitant fees and went somewhere cooler for the summer, while the tourists moved in to get away from the problems that plagued them back home. For a few days, anyway. Too bad it wasn't working out that way for me.

It was still early in the season, and we passed only one other person—a woman playing with a small, sand-colored corgi along the water's edge. Owen and I wandered about a mile from the house, stopping when we came to a small curve in the beach. The ocean rushed back into a hidden cove that slithered inward like a fat snake trying to wiggle its way inland. A small ridge of glossy black rocks ran along the back of the cove, separating it from the rest of the island. Beyond the rocks, I could see the cypress trees and tall, waving cattails of the island's boggy marshes.

Off to my right, the ridge rose to a sharp, jagged peak, and a small lighthouse clung to the edge of the rocks there. The lighthouse had been black at one time, with thin white stripes running down its sides, although all the paint had long since faded to various shades of gray. From the way the structure was boarded up, it had been abandoned long ago and left to someday fall into the ever-encroaching sea.

We strolled into the cove. The ridge of rocks and the lighthouse provided a bit of shade, making the air seem a bit cooler back here, and the waves muted to more of a misty, refreshing spray. I spread out the blankets while Owen planted the umbrella in the sand, then opened it. I pulled off my sneakers and socks, sat down on the edge of one of the blankets, hugged my knees to my chest, and dug my bare toes into the warm, crusty golden sand. Owen plopped down beside me, kicking off his own shoes and socks, and leaned back on his elbows. We sat there and watched the water foam and froth for several minutes.

"So," Owen finally said. "Donovan Caine."

"Yeah, Donovan."

A few seagulls and terns with fluffy white feathers circled overhead, although the constant rush of the ocean mostly drowned out their hoarse, hungry cries.

"I had no idea that he was in Blue Marsh," I said. "When Donovan left Ashland, he didn't tell me where he was going, and I didn't try to find him. You know that."

Owen nodded.

I drew in a breath. Now came the hard part. "I know that I should have told you last night that I'd seen him again, that he was Callie's fiancé. But I wasn't sure how to tell you. I was still trying to figure out how I felt about seeing him again."

"And have you? Figured out how you feel about him?"

I shrugged. "Nothing's changed between us. I still kill people, and he still hates me for it. Same old, same old."

"Yes," Owen agreed. "Same old, same old. Right down to the way that he looks at you."

I frowned. "What do you mean?"

He sighed. "Donovan might be engaged to Callie, might have put a ring on her finger and promised to love her forever—hell, he might even *really* love her forever. But he was looking at you the whole time that we were in her office."

I thought that Donovan had done a rather splendid job of not looking at me at all, but I didn't say anything.

"He still wants you," Owen said in a hard, blunt tone. "Even now he's thinking about making a play for you, but I'll be damned if he's going to have you."

I raised an eyebrow. "Is that jealousy I hear?"

"You're damn right I'm jealous," Owen growled. "Because I saw how you used to look at *him*, and he didn't even realize it. But more than that, I saw how much it hurt you when Donovan turned his back on you when he realized that you'd survived the collapse of Tobias Dawson's coal mine."

I couldn't help but flinch. Things had not gone well when I'd tried to kill Dawson at a party that Mab had thrown. The dwarf had gotten the drop on me instead and knocked me out. I'd woken up in one of Dawson's coal mines—the one with all the diamonds in it that ran right under Warren Fox's land. Using my Ice and Stone magic, I'd caved in the mine—hell, the whole damn mountain—on top of Dawson and his men, killing them.

After that, I'd managed to crawl and claw my way out of the collapsed mine with a little bit of skill and a whole lot of luck. When I'd finally made it back to civilization, I'd expected Donovan to be, well, happy to see me. Or at least fucking *relieved* that I'd survived. Instead, the detective had seemed disgusted and disappointed, like things would have been so much easier for him if I'd been buried under that mountain forever and wasn't around to tempt him anymore. Donovan had even gone so far as to turn his back on me, instead of trying to help me and see that I got the medical attention that I needed. The detective's open, curt dismissal had cut me deeper than I liked to admit. Even today, I could still feel the faint sting of it. That had been the beginning of the end of Donovan and me, even if I hadn't realized it at the time.

"Not one of my finest moments, I admit," I joked, trying to lighten the mood. "I excel at killing men, not so much at picking the right ones to date. At least, I didn't until I met you."

Owen smiled a little at that, but his face soon turned serious once more.

"You don't even see it, do you?" he asked. "How similar you are to Callie."

I frowned. "What do you mean? I'm nothing like Callie."

He shook his head. "Sure you are. Think about it. You're both beautiful, strong, smart women. You both have dark hair and pale eyes. You both run these cool, quirky restaurants and are great cooks. Hell, she even wears blue aprons just like you do at the Pork Pit. It's a little eerie if you ask me."

I didn't know what to make of his words. Bria had told me once that I reminded her of Callie, but I hadn't thought much about how alike we were. I wondered if Donovan had noticed it—if it was what had drawn him to Callie in the first place. I didn't know whether to be flattered or weirded out.

"Donovan had you, and he was a fool to leave town, to leave *you*," Owen said. "Now, he's trying to replace you with Callie. That's *his* business. But I don't want you to make the same mistake with him twice, especially when I know that he'd only hurt you again. I love you too much for that, Gin. I do now, and I always will."

The raw sincerity burning in his violet eyes made my heart quiver in a way that nothing else ever had—especially not Donovan. I leaned forward and cupped my hands around Owen's rough, rugged face.

"I love you, Owen. I want to be with *you*—not Donovan. You've got nothing to worry about. Donovan is my past. I can't change that or the old memories that he stirs up in me, but you're my present—my today, my tomorrow, my future. You always will be."

Owen stared at me, his eyes searching mine as if he could somehow see past the cold, indifferent mask that I usually presented to the world and peer into my very soul. I let him look a second longer, then leaned forward and pressed my lips to his. I'd meant the kiss to be brief and gentle, but it turned into far more than that. Donovan's reappearance had shaken us both up a little more than either one of us would have liked to admit.

Owen's solid arms snaked around me, pulling me down onto the blanket next to him. He plundered my mouth like a pirate searching for buried treasure, his tongue teasing, retreating, and diving against mine again and again. Hot, demanding need pulsed through my body with every sure, quick stroke, and I ran my hands over the strong, chiseled planes of his face, skimming my fingers over the scar under his chin, his slightly crooked nose, and the faint lines that fanned out from the corners of his eyes. All the little imperfections that somehow made him so irresistible to me.

Finally, we broke apart, both of us panting and aching for more—so much more.

"You're mine," Owen said in a fierce whisper, the heat in his eyes as bright as the scorching sun. "Not his. *Mine.* Only mine. Always mine."

"I'm yours," I agreed, then pushed him over onto his back. "But don't you forget that you're *mine* too. Only mine. Always mine."

Owen growled and pulled my head down for another hard, almost brutal kiss. He wound his fingers through my hair, holding me just where he wanted to. I let him take control, let him lose himself in the emotions that were urging him on, urging both of us on.

Owen stripped off my clothes even as I wrestled with his, making sure to grab a condom out of his wallet so we would have even more protection besides the little white pills that I took. Soon, there was nothing between us. The warmth of the sun beat down, searing us through the shade of the umbrella, but it was nothing compared to the fire that burned between us.

Owen trailed kisses down my neck, stopping here and there to bite me gently, then a little harder, then a little harder still. I dug my hands into his shoulders, kneading his muscles, urging him on. His head dipped lower, and his tongue swirled lazily around my nipple before he nipped it with his teeth. Pleasure spiked through me at the sensation.

"Do you like that?" he rasped.

"I love everything that you do to me," I whispered back. "I love the way you make me feel."

Owen smiled. "Good answer. Because things are about to get a whole lot better."

He slipped a finger inside me, then another, pumping them back and forth, in and out, in and out, in a steady, furious rhythm. He leaned forward, his tongue flicking against first one nipple, then another, his faint, bristly stubble scraping against my skin, making me that much more sensitive to his touch.

"Hey now," I said, panting, my nails digging into his shoulders. "Don't think that you're going to have all the fun today."

A wicked smile curved Owen's lips, and he moved down my body and bent his head. His tongue flicked against my outer folds and then slid in deeper, then deeper, then deeper still, as if he could lick his way to the very center of me.

I arched and arched my back as if that would relieve the delicious pressure building and building inside me. But every time I was ready to go over the edge, Owen would bring me back down just a little, just enough to ratchet up my need that much more. His rich, wonderful smell filled my nose, the one that always made me think of metal, until I was dizzy with it—and dizzy with the sensation of being loved by him.

Just when I thought I was going to scream from the pleasure of it all, Owen raised his head and kissed his way back up my body. I reached up for his head, but he pinned my arms to the blanket and stared down at me.

"You're beautiful," he said in a hoarse voice. "So strong and beautiful."

"So are you."

Then he leaned forward and captured my mouth with his again.

I squirmed against him and opened my legs, wet and aching for him. Owen braced his weight on his elbows and rested his hard cock against me. He surged his hips forward the tiniest bit, rubbing against me, but not sliding inside. Not yet. Teasing me instead. I groaned. Above me, Owen did the same, but he didn't stop his game.

Finally, I couldn't take it anymore. I slid my hands out of his hold and rolled him over onto his back, my hand moving down to capture his stiff erection.

I did the same thing to him that he'd done to me. Licking, stroking, and caressing his thick length until his hands clenched the blanket. But Owen didn't let me play for long. He reached for the condom and put it on, then pulled me up so that I was sitting on his lap. Every part of my body was aching for him, and my legs locked around his waist.

"Mine," Owen whispered a final time before sliding deep inside me.

I moaned at the length of him finally filling me after so much teasing. Back and forth we moved together, thrusting against each other, our lips and hands building the pressure, the desire, the need, that much more.

I'd been right back at the restaurant—it was deliciously good and oh, so satisfying.

All around us in the cove, the water sprayed and frothed and foamed, but we were already lost in another sort of undertow, swept away until there was nothing left but the climax that drowned us both.

☀ 13 ☀

"Wow," I whispered when we were through. "I'll have to make you jealous more often."

Owen grinned. "It does have its perks."

I settled my head on his chest, and we lay on the blankets in silence, listening to the rush of the water in and out of the cove and watching the black shadows of the seagulls and terns streak across the sand like skittering spiders.

Owen and I lazed around for the better part of an hour before reluctantly pulling on our clothes and walking back to the beach house. I would have loved to spend the rest of the day with him, but Callie was still in trouble, and I had an appointment with Dekes that just wouldn't wait.

Using his seemingly endless network of business connections, clients, spies, and snitches, Finn had managed to score himself, Bria, and Owen invites to Dekes's press conference just like he said he would. The four of us regrouped in the living room that afternoon to go over some final details.

I looked at the laminated press card, the photo ID, and the other phony credentials that Finn had created for me. "So my name is Carmen Cole, and I write for some newspaper up in New York. Don't you think that's a little out there? A reporter coming all this way just to talk to Dekes about his casino?"

Finn shrugged. "Not really. According to the guest list, there are reporters from a variety of publications and states coming in for the party. I figured that was the easiest thing to do, since I have a subscription to the financial section of that newspaper and can give you some details about what it covers and how. Simpler is better, remember? That's what Dad always used to say."

That had been one of many pearls of wisdom Fletcher had given us over the years and one that I'd taken to heart today. The plan was straightforward. Using the fake credentials that Finn had created for me, I was going to pretend I was writing a business story on Dekes's new casino and its potential economic impact on Blue Marsh. When the time was right, I'd approach Dekes and ask him for a private interview. Powerful or not, I imagined that he'd be happy to suck up to a lowly reporter if he thought it would get him some good press.

Once I was alone with Dekes, I'd make my move and *strongly suggest* that he leave Callie alone. Depending on what the vampire did then, I'd either walk out of his office and rejoin the press conference or sneak out the back covered with blood.

I was good with either option.

"Now, on to more important matters," Finn said, striking a dramatic pose. "How do I look?"

Finn loved dressing up, and he had more high-end suits hanging in his closet than most people had white cotton socks stuffed into their chests of drawers. But he'd gone all out this afternoon. Finn sported a fitted white linen suit that showed off the muscular lines of his body. His shirt was black, and so were his shoes, which were so slick and glossy that I could see my reflection in them. A white Panama hat with a slim black ribbon around the brim perched on top of his carefully styled, walnut-colored locks. Finn had spent more time on his hair than Bria and I had—combined.

"A Panama hat? Really?" Owen asked, raising an eyebrow.

Finn grinned. "When in Rome."

In contrast to Finn, Owen wore a simple navy suit with a sky blue shirt and tie and a pair of black wingtips. He looked every inch the strong, shrewd, powerful businessman that he was. To me, there was nothing sexier than a man in a well-tailored suit, and I found myself wanting to slip off Owen's jacket and slide my fingers down his chest before undressing the rest of him. Mmm.

"Well, I don't know about you three, but I feel ridiculous in this dress," Bria muttered.

A long, slinky gown clung to my sister's body, showing off her killer curves. Black and white orchids covered the dress, creating an interesting geometric pattern, and small black sequins gleamed on the garment's spaghetti straps, bringing out the exquisite paleness of Bria's skin. Her blond hair just brushed her shoulders, the ends curling around the primrose rune that rested in the hollow of her throat. Smoky black shadow and liner rimmed her blue eyes, adding to her beauty, while strappy black stiletto heels gave her an extra three inches of height.

"I can't believe that I let you talk me into wearing this," she said, glaring at Finn. "Much less buy it in the first place."

Heat sparked in his bright green eyes. "Don't worry, cupcake. You won't be wearing it long, if I have my way."

Bria's eyes narrowed, but her red lips curved up into a knowing, satisfied smile.

"It's just too bad that Gin doesn't look as smashing as you do," Finn lamented. "Really, Gin, could you have put on something any more boring?"

Since I was going in as a journalist, I'd opted for a more serious, professional look—a body-hugging black camisole over matching black pants. My dark brown hair was pulled back into a ponytail, and I'd gone dark and smoky on the makeup, just like Bria. Unlike her open-toed stilettos, I had on a pair of ankle-high boots, with two of my silverstone knives already tucked inside them. Some pens, a notepad, and a small digital voice recorder were nestled inside the purse I was carrying, adding to the journalist facade.

For the final touch, I'd slipped on a fitted black jacket. But it wasn't just any jacket—this one was lined with silverstone. The magical metal commanded a high price due to its ability to absorb and store all forms of magic. No matter what power they possessed—Air, Fire, Ice, or Stone—many elementals had rings, necklaces, watches, and other pieces of jewelry made out of the metal. The bits and pieces of silverstone looked innocent enough glinting on fingers, necks, and wrists, but really, they gave folks a bonus boost of magic in case they needed it—like for a duel.

That's how elementals fought, by dueling each other, by testing their magic against another person's. Only the strong survived an elemental duel, and the result for the loser was never a good one. Suffocated by a lack of Air, fried to a crisp by Fire, an Ice knife slammed into your throat, your heart turned to Stone in your own chest. Not exactly peaceful or painless ways to die, given how cruelly creative elementals could be with their powers.

I had my own piece of silverstone jewelry, thanks to Bria—the spider rune ring that I wore on my right index finger. The metal hummed with my stored Ice magic and felt like a cold thread wrapped around my skin. The ring and the extra bit of power it contained was what had helped me kill Mab.

In addition to absorbing and storing magic, silverstone also had the added benefit of being tougher than Kevlar. Whenever I was out working as the Spider, I usually wore a vest made out of the metal, since silverstone was great for stopping bullets, knives, and other weapons. But since I couldn't go into Dekes's press conference looking like an assassin, I'd opted for the suit jacket instead. It wasn't as thick and heavy as one of my normal vests would have been, but there was enough silverstone sewn into the lining to give me a fighting chance against any bullets or blasts of magic that might come my way. Plus, the jacket let me stuff two more knives up my sleeves, while another one rested against the small of my back as usual.

That last knife felt as cold as the spider rune ring on my finger, since the blade contained my Ice magic—something else that had come out of my final fight with Mab. My body had burst into icy silver flames when I'd been dueling the Fire elemental, and the silverstone knife, along with the others I'd been carrying, had absorbed quite a bit of my magic. I'd never before used the power in this particular knife, the one that I'd killed Mab with, but it comforted me to know that it was there, just in case I needed it.

As for the icy flames, it was a trick that I hadn't done since then, although I'd tried a time or two to get my fists to ignite just to see if I could. So far, I hadn't had any luck. Then again, I hadn't been as desperate as I had been fighting Mab. I imagined that had quite a bit to do with my cold spontaneous combustion that night.

"Are you sure that you want to do this, Gin? Take on Dekes?" Bria asked, staring at me. "I know that you came to Blue Marsh to get away from all the thugs in Ashland who are after you right now. And Callie's my friend, not yours. I should be the one to help her, not you."

"I know," I said. "But you're my sister."

Bria stood there, like she was expecting me to say something else. But in my mind, I'd given her reason enough for putting myself in danger again. Yeah, maybe I was a coldhearted assassin, but I'd do anything for the people that I loved. Cheat, lie, steal, even kill for them. I'd done it before when I was battling Mab, and I would gladly do it again. I might be in a different city, but the rules of the game were still the same—and it was a game that I was determined to win.

"If we're all ready," I said, "let's go pay Randall Dekes a visit that he won't soon forget."

An hour later, a taxi dropped me off at the entrance to Dekes's island estate. It was just before five now, and the press conference was ramping up, judging by the people I saw streaming into the house.

"Right here is fine," I told the driver, slipping him a nice tip and climbing out of the backseat.

The taxi drove off, but I stayed where I was, looking at everything from the spikes on the open iron gate to the thick stone wall topped with razor wire to the armed giants that I could see walking along the manicured grounds in a specific, timed pattern. Dekes might be throwing open his doors for his press conference, but he was still being careful about things.

Just not careful enough, since the Spider was here.

I walked up the smooth cobblestone driveway, moving faster than the line of limos and news vans that crept up toward the front door. I'd been in and around many mansions, but Dekes's sprawling villa was impressive, even by Ashland standards. With its white stone, wrought-iron railings, and red slate roof, the multistory building looked like a slightly smaller but more elegant version of the Blue Sands hotel. According to the information that Finn had dug up, Dekes had built his home back in 1889, ten years before he'd started construction on the hotel.

I reached the top of the driveway and paused a moment, reaching out with my magic and listening to the stone of the mansion above me. Low, pain-filled mutters drifted down to me, along with a faint ripping sensation that made it seem like something was biting into the stone again and again and slowly tearing it apart from the inside out. It was a dark, ugly sound, one filled with sly menace and deadly intent. Despite its pristine appearance, Randall Dekes had done some violent things in his mansion over the years—some very violent, very bloody things. No surprise there.

The stones' mutters grew louder as I flashed my press credentials at the giants working the front door and stepped inside the mansion, but I pushed the sound to the back of my mind. The stones' warning wasn't unexpected or unwelcome, but I'd see for myself exactly what kind of man Dekes was soon enough.

The inside of the mansion was just as perfect, polished, and lavish as the outside. Crystal chandeliers, antique furniture, expensive paintings, exquisite statues, delicate carvings. Dekes had the very best of everything, just like I'd thought he would, and he seemed to embrace the location of his island home. Many of the furnishings were suggestive of the beach or sea, from the paintings of famous shipwrecks to the gold doubloons that glimmered in glass cases on the walls.

I followed the flow of traffic deeper into the mansion, stepped through a wide archway, and found myself back outside. The south lawn was dominated by an enormous pool that had the same distinctive palm tree shape as the one at the Blue Sands hotel. According to Finn, Dekes used the palm tree as his own personal rune, since so many of his business interests were located on the coast. A variety of colorful orchids and roses floated in the pool, their sweet scents mixing with the spicy colognes and cloying perfumes of the businessmen and businesswomen in attendance, along with the sweat of the news crews hauling around their cameras and other equipment.

I could also see the Blue Sands hotel from here, glimmering like an oversize opal in the distance. The back nine of the hotel's golf course ran right up to the edge of Dekes's property, which was cordoned off by a low stone wall. With a pair of binoculars, you'd be able to clearly see the hotel pool and the beach with its sunbathing beauties beyond. I imagined Dekes was the kind of man who enjoyed looking out over his little empire.

Roughly two hundred people were gathered around the pool already, while dozens more giant waiters moved through the crowd bearing trays of food and neon-colored drinks topped with tiny umbrellas and skewers of fresh lemons, limes, oranges, and pineapples. Despite the fact that this was officially a press conference, Dekes was still offering refreshments. Why, how very considerate of him. Or perhaps boozy journalists just led to more flattering coverage.

I grabbed a glass of gin mixed with grapefruit juice from one of the waiters and strolled around the pool, looking for my friends and enemy for the afternoon.

Owen, Finn, and Bria stood in a ring of people, sipping champagne. As usual, my foster brother was in the middle of the group, regaling the onlookers with one bawdy, boisterous story after another. Bria slouched next to him, looking a little bored, while Owen stood next to her, scanning the crowd just like I was.

Our eyes met, violet on gray. Heat shimmered in Owen's gaze, along with concern. Despite my breezy assurances to

Callie that I could handle Dekes, Owen and I both knew how dangerous the vampire was. You didn't amass as big a fortune and survive in the underworld as long as Dekes had without having a few aces up your sleeve. As always, my lover's worry touched me, as did his willingness to let me do what needed to be done. Donovan had never looked at me the way Owen did, and he certainly would never understand me like Owen did. After our confrontation in Callie's office, I knew that more than ever.

I winked at Owen, telling him that I was ready for whatever might come up, and moved on.

Besides the pool, the other thing that caught my eye was a scale model of what the casino would look like when it was built, complete with trees, sand, and even real water in the pseudo swimming pools and fake ocean. The far side of the miniature landscape started with the Blue Sands hotel and showed how the original structure would stretch out and eventually meld into the new casino, just about where the Sea Breeze stood. Shots of the proposed interiors stood on easels behind the model, showing just how lavish the new, improved resort would be.

Callie had been right—her restaurant was in the middle of the main gaming hall, which meant that Dekes couldn't build his casino without her land. That knowledge only made me more determined to get the vampire to back off—or else.

Finally, I spotted the man of the hour himself—Randall Dekes. The vampire was just as handsome in real life as he was in the headshot Finn had shown me. His sable brown hair and matching mustache gleamed in the sunlight, his skin just a shade lighter, while laugh lines crept out from the corners of his pale green eyes. His trim body was further set off by a smoke gray suit, and a large palm-tree-shaped diamond glimmered in the middle of his matching silk tie. He was easily one of the most striking men here. I wasn't the only one who thought so, judging from the longing looks that the other women and even a few men shot his way.

But what the photo hadn't quite captured was the constant crackle of magic that emanated off Dekes. I stood there, sipped my fruity gin, and tried to puzzle out what kind of power it was. Even when they weren't actively using their power, many elementals constantly gave off waves of magic, like heat radiating from the sun even when it was behind the clouds. Since I was an elemental too, I could sense that excess energy. Most of the sensations followed a pattern. Magic from a Fire elemental would feel hot, like sparks or fiery needles stabbing at my skin, while power from an Ice elemental would be cold, like snowflakes swirling through the sky. An Air elemental's power might feel thick and stuffy like fog creeping over the landscape, while a Stone elemental's magic could seem as hard as a concrete shell covering his or her body.

The sensation rolling off the vampire slid across my skin like water, but I couldn't quite figure out which specific elemental area Dekes was gifted in—Air, Fire, Ice, or Stone. Somehow, the magic trickling off him felt like all of those things at once. Hot and cold, soft and hard.

I frowned. Everyone knew that Dekes was a vampire, but Finn hadn't been able to determine whether he had any elemental magic as well. The vampire might have the power flowing through his veins as an elemental himself or he might simply be absorbing it from the blood of his victims. Either way, what worried me was how strong the sensation was. Unless I was seriously mistaken, Dekes had just as much elemental juice as Mab had had, which meant that I had to be even more careful with him than I'd originally planned to be.

As I watched the vampire, a tall, slender woman stepped out of the crowd and headed toward Dekes. She pressed a kiss to his cheek, then looped her arm through his. I recognized her from another photo that had been in Finn's file. Vanessa Suarez, the vampire's wife. Finn hadn't spent as much time looking into her background, but he'd learned that she came from a prominent Fire elemental family in Charleston, South Carolina. Her father had gotten involved in one of Dekes's real estate deals, and she'd married the vampire about a year ago. Finn didn't know whether the marriage was a love match, a political alliance, or something else, but it didn't much matter. If she got in my way, then I'd deal with her the same way that I would her husband—in a brutal, bloody, permanent fashion.

Vanessa was as beautiful as Dekes was handsome, with cinnamon-colored skin and ink black hair and eyes. She was a bit overdressed for a press conference, but her black evening gown hugged her body in all the right places, and a wide choker embedded with diamonds and pearls gleamed around her slender neck. For some reason, the necklace reminded me of one of the collars that Sophia wore. Matching cuffs that were just as wide adorned Vanessa's wrists.

I eyed the jewelry. Even with all the other, more subtle and understated jewels being worn by the various men and women, I could still hear the gemstones' whispers. But instead of proudly murmuring of their own beauty like the others were, Vanessa's diamonds and pearls wailed with high-pitched, angry, hurt notes—almost like they were screaming. Interesting—and more than a little disturbing.

But what really intrigued me was that I didn't feel any sort of magic emanating from Vanessa. No flickers, no flares, no fiery waves. From Finn's file, I knew she was a Fire elemental, purportedly a very strong one. Perhaps her power was self-contained, like mine. As long as I didn't actively use my Ice and Stone magic, other elementals couldn't sense my power, something that had gotten me out of more than one jam.

Vanessa whispered something in Dekes's ear. The vampire nodded, and the two of them headed over to the wooden podium and microphone that had been erected beside the casino model. Dekes stepped behind the podium, while Vanessa remained off to one side.

"Ladies and gentlemen," Dekes said into the microphone. "We're ready to get started."

It took a few moments for the crowd to quiet down. I slipped into the ranks of the other reporters and pulled out my digital recorder, pen, and notepad, pretending to be just another journalist here to cover the press conference.

"Thank you all for coming," Dekes said, giving the crowd a winning smile. "As you know, I asked you here today to formally announce construction on my new casino, the biggest project that this island has ever seen . . ."

The next hour dragged by. Eventually, after a series of speeches by Dekes, the mayor, and all the other muckety-mucks talking about how wonderful the new casino would be, the press conference wound down. Dekes stepped away from the podium, with Vanessa still by his side. He took questions from the various reporters and did a few TV interviews before shaking hands with all the businesspeople in attendance.

I kept an eye on the couple and drifted in and out of groups of people for about half an hour, waiting for the perfect moment to strike. Finally, Dekes's latest round of fawning well-wishers left, and I sidled up to him before anyone else could get their hooks into him.

"Mr. Dekes," I said, giving him a dazzling smile and holding out my hand. "Carmen Cole. Congratulations on your new casino development."

"Why, thank you," Dekes said. "I'm most honored by your presence."

His voice was low and smoky, with a throaty, seductive rasp, and it matched his sleek, dark good looks perfectly. The vamp took my hand in his and lifted it to his lips for a chaste kiss. His thumb stroked the inside of my wrist, right where my pulse was, even though his wife was standing beside him. I'd thought that Dekes's green gaze might trail down to my breasts, but he kept his eyes on mine. Still, despite his polite smile, I could see the sharp, sudden hunger in his face.

Perhaps this would be easier than I'd thought. I'd be happy to offer Dekes the chance for a quick, clandestine fuck if it meant that I could get him alone. The bastard would still be trying to get his dick out of his pants while I had one of my knives pressed against his throat.

"Tell me," Dekes said. "What do you like best about my new casino?"

"Well, there are many things to admire about the construction, but my favorite is the way it will so elegantly blend in with the existing Blue Sands hotel. It looks like you're going to make good use of the surrounding landscape. And of course, the overall structure of the casino itself. It's going to have beautiful architectural lines."

Landscaping and architecture weren't exactly my areas of expertise, but I'd taken enough classes in enough subjects at Ashland Community College that I could bullshit about almost anything and make it sound somewhat plausible and intelligent.

My answer must have pleased Dekes because his smile widened, showing me a hint of the fangs in his mouth. I decided to press my advantage. The sooner I got Dekes alone, the sooner I could tell the vampire what was what— and figure out if I needed to put him down for good.

"Actually, I was wondering if I might have a few moments of your time," I said. "So I can conduct a private interview one-on-one and let my readers discover the real man behind the curtain, so to speak."

Vanessa stiffened at my words, but Dekes didn't notice. Or if he did, he just didn't care.

"Of course," the vampire murmured. "There are a few folks that I need to say hello to first, but I'd be happy to give you a private interview. Why don't you meet me by the door in, say, fifteen minutes? We can go inside and get out of the heat for a while."

I smiled. "It's a date."

Dekes returned my smile with an even wider one of his own. "Indeed. Now, please excuse me. In the meantime, I'm sure that my lovely wife will be more than happy to talk to you about the interior of the casino, since she's the decorator for the project. Vanessa, please keep this lovely lady entertained for a few minutes while I see to our other guests."

Vanessa pinched her lips together into something that was supposed to resemble a smile. "Of course. It will be my pleasure. It always is."

Dekes pressed a kiss to his wife's cheek before moving off into the crowd. The two of us stood there and watched him move from group to group, shaking one hand after another.

"He's certainly charming," I murmured. "Much more charming than I expected him to be."

Vanessa stared at me, her black eyes cold in her face. "Do yourself a favor. Stay away from my husband."

"Or what?" I asked, immediately rising to the rancor in her voice. "You'll get your giant guards to throw me out? I doubt that your husband will let that happen, since he's so eager to . . . talk to me."

Anger and disgust tightened her beautiful features. "You have no clue what you're getting yourself into if you go off with my husband for a *private chat*. Don't say that I didn't warn you."

She turned on her stiletto and stalked off. I watched her weave in and out of the crowd, barely stopping to acknowledge the people who tried to talk to her. Her reaction wasn't unexpected. I'd played the part of the saucy seductress more than once to get close to a target, and more than once, I'd been confronted by angry wives and girlfriends who wanted me to stay away from their men. Or else.

Still, I'd seen something lurking in the depths of Vanessa's gaze, burning there along with the faintest flicker of her Fire magic—fear. Not for herself, her relationship to Dekes, or whatever threat that I might pose to her.

No, unless I was mistaken, Vanessa's fear had been for me—and I had no idea why.

✶14✶

I shook off my concerns about Vanessa and wandered back over to the model of the casino. A few minutes later, Owen sidled up beside me. He stood with his back to the model, staring out into the crowd. I leaned over, pretending to peer at some detail in the miniature landscape and scribbling nonsense notes on the pad that I'd pulled out of my bag.

"I take it that you set up your meeting with Dekes?" Owen asked, raising his champagne glass to his lips to mask the fact that he was talking to me.

"I'm meeting him in a few minutes," I murmured. "After that, I imagine that he'll take me to his office or somewhere else private so that we can have a little chat."

"Be careful," Owen whispered. "I didn't like the way he was looking at you."

"What is it with you and the looks this weekend?" I teased, trying to make a joke.

I could see only the side of his face, but the hard set of his mouth told me he didn't think it was funny at all.

I sighed. "Okay, so tell me. How was Dekes looking at me?"

Owen frowned. "Like you were on the dinner menu, and he was the only one who knew it."

His words echoed what I'd felt when I'd looked into Vanessa's eyes a few minutes ago. I didn't have precognition, and I couldn't see the future, not like my Air elemental friend Jo-Jo Deveraux, but something wasn't right. Oh, the stones of the mansion whispered to me of all the violent things Dekes had done here over the years, but there was more to it than that. I just couldn't put my finger on exactly what that mysterious *it* might be.

For a moment, I thought about calling the whole thing off. Just walking away, leaving the mansion, and pretending I'd never heard of Randall Dekes. It would definitely be the safer option, at least until I could gather some more intel on the vampire and his magic, whatever it might be. Fletcher had always told me to trust my instincts, and mine were warning me away from Dekes like red lights flashing at a train crossing. Get on the tracks to try and beat the train, and you were going to get splattered.

But I couldn't cut and run. Not when Callie was counting on me to get Dekes to leave her alone, even if she wouldn't admit it to herself—or Donovan. I couldn't abandon Bria's friend any more than I could any of the other people who'd asked me for help over the last few months. Warren and Violet Fox, Roslyn Phillips, Vinnie and Natasha Volga.

Like it or not, I'd changed, and I wasn't the cold-blooded assassin I used to be. Bit by bit, piece by piece, my heart had slowly thawed, until now I was just as determined to help people as I was to kill them—even if one almost always seemed to follow the other these days.

Dekes finished his latest round of handshaking and started scanning the lawn, no doubt looking for me. The vampire's eyes settled on me, and he smiled, showing me the white glint of his fangs once more. Dekes raised his eyebrows and pointed to the house, indicating that he was ready for our meeting. I held up my index finger, telling him I'd be there in a minute, just as soon as I finished looking over the casino model and writing down a few more notes.

"All right," I murmured to Owen, tucking my pad back into my bag. "I'm going in. Keep an eye out. If something goes wrong, you, Finn, and Bria get out of here. I'll find a way to slip out, make it back to the beach house, and meet up with you."

"I don't want to leave you alone here, Gin," Owen murmured.

"I know," I said in a soft voice. "I know that you want to come with me and protect me more than anything else. And that's why I love you. But I've got work to do. That's the other thing I love about you—you let me do what needs to be done to help other people."

Owen's broad shoulders tightened with tension, but after a moment, he let out a small sigh and nodded his head. I brought my hand down, brushing my fingers against Owen's. He reached out and caught my hand in his for a second before letting go.

"Be careful," he whispered.

I smiled, even though he couldn't see it with his back turned to me. "Always."

I left Owen's side and strolled over to Dekes. The vampire held out his arm to me, and I looped my hand over the crook of his elbow. Once again, I felt that crackle of elemental power in the air around him. I half expected to get a jolt when I touched him, just like I had a few months ago when I'd taken on Elektra LaFleur, an assassin who'd had electrical elemental magic. But my fingers settled against his arm, and all I felt was the rich, expensive fabric of Dekes's suit.

Still, the feel of his magic—whatever the hell it was—brushed against my skin and clung there like a spider's sticky web. It wasn't an uncomfortable feeling, not exactly, not like Mab's Fire power had always been with its hot, sharp, pricking sensation, but it was enough to make me even more cautious around the vampire.

"Are you ready for our interview?" Dekes said.

"Of course. Thank you for making time for me."

The vampire smiled, showing me a little more of the two fangs in his mouth and the hunger burning in his eyes. "Anything for a beautiful woman."

Dekes led me inside, then up two staircases to the third floor of the mansion. To my surprise and frustration, two giant guards separated themselves from the crowd outside and trailed after us. I'd hoped to shove Dekes into the first dark, secluded corner that we came to and tell him what was what, but that wasn't going to happen with his two goons a mere three steps behind us and even more guards roaming through the hallways. I could take out the giants easily enough, but add Dekes and his mysterious elemental magic to the mix, and the situation could quickly spin out of my control. So I decided to wait and see how this farce played out. Sooner or later, Dekes would have to send his men away—unless he liked to fuck in front of an audience. Maybe he did. Stranger things had happened to me as the Spider. If it came to that, well, I'd think of something. I always did.

While we walked, Dekes chatted about various pieces of art that we passed. Paintings, statues, carvings. Most of the items were things you'd find in the home of any wealthy businessman. But the deeper we moved into the mansion, the more I noticed other things—quirky things, odd things, even downright bizarre things. A marble chess set sitting on a table between two empty chairs. Cases full of guns, knives, swords, and other weapons. Miniature airplanes dangling from the ceiling on thin strands of fishing line. A row of lockets, each one open to show the faded locks of hair curled inside. Even a display of antique dolls in frilly dresses. Their open, empty, staring glass eyes seemed to follow me as we strolled past them.

Dekes also seemed to have a fascination with pirates and shipwrecks. Gold coins, silver goblets, jewel-crusted daggers, and more glittered in glass cases, along with small, perfect models of the ships that the plunder had supposedly come from.

All of the items were clean, polished, and in mint condition, even the dolls. If Finn had been here, he would have been salivating, especially over the gold and the jewels. But Dekes just strolled by all the finery, barely pausing to glance at it before moving on to the next room, the next case, and the next treasure that it contained. He had all these fine things, exquisite things, but it seemed like the vamp had long ago lost interest in them, as if knowing that he possessed them was enough, and he had no further need to admire or even look at them ever again.

"Your home is lovely," I said. "You seem to be quite the collector—of all sorts of unusual things."

"Mmm. Yes, I suppose you could say that I'm a collector. Some would call my tastes eclectic, but if I see something that I want, then I go after it," Dekes murmured. "No matter what it is and what it takes to acquire it. The biggest, the best, the most expensive, the most delicate, the macabre, and the unusual. It fascinates me, the things people hold dear, the things that they value."

"And what's your favorite thing to collect? Paintings? Sculptures? Antiques?"

He smiled, and for a moment, I felt a surge of elemental magic roll off him. "Nothing so mundane as that. I simply enjoy surrounding myself with beautiful, powerful women."

I wondered at his odd answer, but I kept the conversation going, mindful of the two giants still watching me. "It seems to me like you already have one of those. Your wife is quite stunning."

Most men would have bragged long and hard and loud if they'd had a beauty like Vanessa on their arm and in their bed, but Dekes waved a hand, dismissing my comment. "My wife has her uses. That's why I married her. But I find the old saying to be true—variety really is the spice of life. I tend to live for the moment and all the pleasures that can be had in it."

His words were meant to be seductive, the kind of sly double-talk that rich men indulged in with women they thought were beneath them but wanted to fuck anyway. Still, something in the vampire's tone worried me. There was a smugness in his voice, a note of sly triumph, like he knew something that I didn't. It worried me—and I didn't like to be worried.

Finally, we reached a pair of double doors at the end of a long hallway. By this point, we were in an entirely separate wing from the pool where the press conference had been held. Except for the two giants trailing us, I couldn't have asked for a more perfect spot to have my chat with Dekes. We were far enough away from the south lawn that no one would hear the giants or the vampire scream if I decided to kill them. But instead of making me feel better, the deserted location ratcheted up my tension.

In my experience, nothing was ever this easy. I could almost see a giant cartoon anchor hovering in the air over my head. I just didn't know when it was going to drop on me—and how bad the damage would be when it did.

"And now, another one of my pride and joys," Dekes said in a vaguely bored voice.

He threw open the double doors, stepped inside, and turned around, his hands spread out wide, inviting me to follow him inside. By this point, it felt like the giants were hemming me in instead of just protecting their boss. Since I didn't have another option, I walked forward.

We stood in a massive library, which was just as rich, lavish, and immaculate as the rest of the mansion. Dark, glossy wooden shelves stretched from the floor to the ceiling, with ladders on rollers attached to the sides so that folks could have access to the books on the top shelves. A stone fireplace took up the middle of the back wall, while several chairs, a table, a rolltop desk, and a green leather sofa perched in front of it. Titles by classic American authors like Edgar Allan Poe and Mark Twain filled the shelves closest to me, the gold and silver foil on the spines gleaming like the pirate doubloons that I'd seen in other parts of the mansion. A pair of French doors set into the far wall led out to a wide patio. Next to the doors, a wet bar was stuffed into the back corner of the library, and a crystal goblet had already been set out, probably on Dekes's orders so that he could have a nightcap or two after his press conference was over with. I wondered if the vampire preferred blood or liquor to help him relax. I was betting blood.

"A library," I said. "How charming."

"It's more than merely *charming*," Dekes said. "I have several valuable first editions in here, and the temperature is climate-controlled to keep them in pristine condition, given the wretched humidity on this island. One of the joys of being a vampire is the long life span. Books that I bought for a pittance a hundred years ago are quite valuable today."

Vampires could live a long, long time, just like dwarves. Five hundred years wasn't an uncommon age for both of those races to reach, while giants and elementals only tended to reach the one hundred fifty mark or so. Finn had estimated Dekes to be at least three hundred, which meant that he'd reached middle age in vampire years.

Some folks even speculated that vampires could live indefinitely, as long as they had a steady supply of blood and took care of their bodies by exercising, eating right, and whatnot. But I'd never heard of a vamp making it much past five hundred. The longer folks lived, the more enemies they tended to make, and the greater the chance was of one of those enemies hiring someone like me to step in and cut a vamp's life short.

Dekes walked over to the fireplace. I trailed along behind him, with the giants bringing up the rear. My eyes scanned the library for cameras, phones, and anything that looked like a panic button that the vampire might reach out and press when I made my move. Two giants at my back were two too many, and I didn't want him summoning even more of his men in here.

"Actually, I have a confession to make. I brought you here because I was told that you like books," Dekes said, turning to face me.

I looked at him, wariness slowly creeping up my spine like a cold finger. "How could you possibly know that?"

"An old friend of mine told me how very fond you are of reading."

Suspicion surged through me at his easy tone, but I forced myself to play along and ask the obvious question. "And what friend would that be?"

Dekes's smile widened. "Why, Jonah McAllister, of course. He's told me quite a bit about you, Ms. Blanco. Tell me, do you care if I call you Gin?"

* 15 *

Fuck. Randall Dekes knew exactly who I was—which meant that things were about to get seriously ugly. I wasn't just going to have a chat with the vampire and warn him to leave Callie alone. Not anymore. Now only one of us would be leaving this room alive, and I was determined that it was going to be me.

I thought about immediately launching into full-scale attack mode but quickly discarded that idea—at least until I was out of reach of the two giants looming behind me. It wouldn't do to let them latch onto me, not when I still didn't know what kind of elemental magic Dekes had and what he planned to do to me with it. I had no doubt that Dekes would kill his own men if it meant taking me down with them.

No, the vampire was the real threat here, and I needed to deal with him first. So instead of reaching for one of my knives and charging at my enemies, I walked over, put my purse up on the mantel so both my hands would be free, and leaned against the fireplace, affecting a nonchalant air. The whole time, though, I was calculating speed, distances, and angles and wondering how much of his weird elemental magic Dekes might blast me with before I put him down for good.

"So you know my real name. Bravo for you. I assume that Jonah told you about my alter ego as well?"

"That you're really the assassin the Spider? Oh yes. Jonah and I had quite a fascinating conversation about you—and the fact that you killed his son, Jake. Jonah was very upset about that. Still is, as a matter of fact."

I'd killed Jake McAllister during a party at Mab's house, leaving his body in one of the Fire elemental's bathtubs. Jake had tried to rob the Pork Pit, in addition to wanting to rape and murder me, but I showed Jake just what a fatal mistake he'd made by taking me on—just as I was going to show Dekes.

But instead of backing up or moving away from me, Dekes gave me a smug, satisfied, slightly maniacal smile the Cheshire cat would have been envious of. The vampire didn't seem concerned at all that he was in the same room with a notorious assassin. My worry cranked up another notch. Dekes didn't strike me as the kind of man to lay his cards on the table without first being absolutely sure that he had the winning hand.

"Tell me, is my good friend Jonah here at the press conference?" I asked, matching Dekes's calm with a bored, indifferent mask. "Because I'd love to personally thank him for introducing us, so to speak."

"Sadly, no. Jonah couldn't make it," Dekes said. "But

we had an interesting conversation on the phone this morning. It was something of a fluke, really. I was dealing with other things, namely the discovery of the bodies of several men I employ that were found floating in the pool of the Blue Sands hotel. It was doubly embarrassing for me, since not only did my men die rather brutal deaths but I'd originally planned to have my press conference there, as I own the hotel. Naturally, I had to change the location. Bodies in the pool are not good for business."

"No," I agreed. "They never are."

"I've known Jonah a long time, and he's handling some of the paperwork regarding my new casino. He called me this morning, and naturally I mentioned the unfortunate incident at the hotel and how I'd sent my men out to deal with what seemed to be a very small, easily solvable problem, but that they'd ended up dead instead."

The pleasant smile never left the vampire's face, but his green eyes were just as cold and hard as mine were now. "I lamented to Jonah that my men couldn't do something as simple as handle two female tourists, much less the restaurant owner that they were trying to help. You can imagine my surprise when he asked me what the two tourists looked like—and if my men had been stabbed to death. When I told him that, yes, my men had indeed been stabbed to death, that's when he mentioned your name. We had quite a long talk about you, Gin. Jonah was even kind enough to text me a photo of you, along with those of your friends."

Damn and double damn. I'd thought that maybe getting out of Ashland for a few days might change my perpetual bad luck, but the bitch was out in full force tonight and ready to fuck me over once again.

Since there was no point in hiding why I was really here any longer, I palmed one of my silverstone knives and held it up so that Dekes could see it.

"Well, since you know I'm the Spider, surely you realize why I came here this evening."

Dekes made that arrogant, dismissive wave with his hand again. "I assume it had something to do with Callie Reyes. From what my sources have been able to dig up, she's good friends with your . . . sister, is it? Detective Coolidge? I believe I saw the detective by the pool. A beautiful woman, your sister."

My hand tightened around the knife. If this bastard thought he was getting anywhere near Bria, then he obviously hadn't listened closely enough to McAllister. I might not like the smarmy lawyer, but I knew enough about him to realize that he'd tell Dekes every little detail he knew about me, including how I'd killed Mab. So why wasn't Dekes worried I'd do the same to him? I didn't know what game he was playing, but I had a feeling that I'd already lost. The only question now was how high the price was going to be.

"But as beautiful as your sister might be, she's just not as special as you are, now, is she, Gin?"

"Special?" I asked. "What the hell are you talking about?"

I didn't care what he thought was so damn special about me, but I asked the question because it let me slide another step in the vamp's direction. I'd been easing closer and closer to him as we'd talked, and now I was only about fifteen feet from him. As soon as I got within arm's reach, I was lunging forward and taking him out with my knives, magic, or both if necessary. The two giants stood off to my left, their gazes fixed on me. They'd noticed the steps I'd taken, but they'd made no move to counter them, not even to unbutton their suit jackets and reach for the guns they were probably wearing. Apparently they thought their boss could handle me all by himself. A troubling thought, and I started to wonder just how badly I'd underestimated the vampire.

Dekes's eyes gleamed in his face, and I felt like a mouse staring into the face of a very large, very hungry cat. "You see, what really intrigued me about you, Gin, and the reason I let you and your friends slip into my press conference is your elemental power—and the fact that you have both Ice and Stone magic. At least, that's what Jonah claimed on the phone. I couldn't quite believe it myself. It's an exceptionally rare gift, being able to tap into two elemental areas like that. I've certainly never met anyone with a dual gift before—and I've had quite a bit of experience with elementals over the years."

I opened my mouth to say something, anything, to keep him talking so I could creep even closer to him, but Dekes beat me to the punch.

"Bring them in!" the vampire called out in a loud voice.

Footsteps sounded in the hall, and a third giant stepped into the library, dragging Vanessa into the room. The other woman gave me a look that was a mixture of anger, disgust, and pity. A second later, two more giants entered the library—also dragging Vanessa inside.

I blinked, staring at the limp figure that hung in between the last two giants and wondering if I was seeing double. No, wait, that wasn't Vanessa. The woman, who looked to be unconscious, had the same black hair and beautiful skin that Vanessa did, indicating that they were related, but her features were younger, softer, smoother. She also wore an elegant black evening gown, but the fabric didn't hide how painfully thin she was. I could see the bones in her chest all the way across the room. But the strange thing was that she had on the same diamond and pearl jewelry that Vanessa did—a wide choker around her neck and matching cuffs on either wrist. Two more giants stepped into the library and shut the double doors behind them.

Now there was a total of seven giants in the room, along with me, Dekes, and the two women. Not great odds, but I'd survived worse.

"I'm not sure if you realize it or not, but my lovely wife, Vanessa, has a younger sister, Victoria."

Dekes nodded at the giants, who dragged the two women over to where we stood. The giants dumped the still-unconscious Victoria onto the green leather sofa while Vanessa broke free of the man holding her, rushed forward, and dropped to her knees beside the couch, cradling her sister's head in her hands. Anguish filled Vanessa's face as she looked at her sister, an anguish that I knew all too well. I'd felt the same thing the night Bria had been kidnapped and taken to Mab. Fear, rage, and utter, humiliating helplessness that I'd failed to protect my sister.

Earlier at the press conference, Vanessa hadn't been warning me away from her husband because she thought I might steal him from her—she'd been trying to save my life. I'd just been too smug and arrogant about my own prowess as the Spider to realize it. *Never believe your own reputation.* Fletcher had told me that more than once, but that's just what I'd done tonight, thinking that Dekes would be an easy mark for an assassin like me.

I wondered if it would be the last mistake I ever made.

"Darling," Dekes said in a soft voice. "Let's show Gin just how good I am to you and your dear sister."

Vanessa's back stiffened, and her whole body trembled with fear, rage, or perhaps both. For a moment, I thought she wasn't going to do what he said, but she slowly pushed herself to her feet and turned to face me. With shaking hands, Vanessa yanked the jeweled cuffs off her arms, unsnapped the choker from around her neck, and let them all drop to the floor.

Bite marks covered her neck and wrists—deep, vicious, ugly bite marks.

The skin around Vanessa's wrists was mottled, purple, and broken from the wounds, and the same marks ringed her neck like the choker she'd just torn off. Most of the marks looked fresh, but I could see the gleam of old white scars and newer pink puckered ones here and there—so many fucking scars. I couldn't tell how many times Dekes had bitten her or for how long, but my stomach recoiled at the sight, and the spider rune scars embedded in my own palms began to itch and burn with old memories. I knew what it was like to be marked like that, to be branded, to be tortured. I'd only endured it once, but Vanessa had been subjected to it over and over and over again, ever since she'd been married to Dekes—perhaps even longer.

Now I knew why the diamonds and pearls had whispered and wailed with anger, pain, and fear instead of their own sparkling beauty. The jewels were echoing Vanessa's own feelings of being trapped in her marriage to Dekes, of being used so cruelly by the vampire.

"I said that Vanessa has her uses, and she does. The Fire magic flowing through her veins is quite powerful and quite delicious, Her sister, though not as strong, is gifted in Air magic," Dekes said in a calm voice, as if he were talking about a gourmet meal he'd just ordered for dinner. "Rather like red and white wine, both cleanse and refresh the palate in their own unique way."

Vanessa shuddered and looked away from her husband, but I kept my eyes on Dekes, once again wondering what game he was playing at and how I could beat him at it—and cut his fucking throat.

"Until recently, I had a third beauty in my elemental stable, an older woman with Ice magic. But alas, she wasn't quite strong enough to handle the wear and tear of being one of my most prized possessions." Dekes gave me a thin, disappointed smile.

"Mona killed herself," Vanessa snapped, her voice breaking on the words. "To get away from *you*. I only wish that I was strong enough to do the same."

"But you aren't that strong, are you, darling?" Dekes said. "You're too worried about your sister's safety to do anything that foolish. And more's the pity for Victoria. We both know that she's growing anemic. She barely wakes up long enough to eat anymore. Soon she won't be of any use to me."

Back at the Sea Breeze this morning when Finn had been telling me about Dekes, I'd thought that the vampire was just another businessman bad guy, a bullying thug with too much money who thought he was entitled to whatever he wanted.

Now I knew what a sick, sick bastard he really was.

"Let me guess. Vanessa and Victoria aren't the first women you've done this to, are they?" I asked. "How many women have you *collected* over the years? How many have you killed? And for what, their blood?"

"Hardly," Dekes sniffed. "This is about so much more than mere blood, Gin. This is about power—elemental power. You asked me before what my favorite thing was to collect. Well, this is it."

That cold finger of dread started crawling up my spine again. Dekes held up his hand, and elemental Fire sparked and crackled on his fingertips, glowing like red-hot matches. I tensed and reached for my own Stone magic, ready to use it to turn my skin into a hard, impenetrable shell. But instead of throwing the Fire at me, the vampire casually tossed the flames into the fireplace, causing the logs inside to ignite. He stared at the flames a moment before holding up his hand again. This time, a blast of Air roared through the room, swirled into the fireplace, and snuffed out the burning logs.

Now I knew why the crackle of elemental magic around Dekes felt like Air, Fire, Ice, and Stone all at the same time—because that's what it was. The blood that he'd drunk from various elementals had all mixed together in his veins, letting him tap into all four areas. He'd mentioned a woman with Ice magic, and I had no doubt that there'd been one with Stone power just like my own before her—and countless others over the years. All trapped here in Dekes's odd gilded cage and forced to feed him their blood one way or another until he sucked them dry or they killed themselves to be free of him.

"So you don't have any actual elemental power of your own," I said. "You just take it from the women that you force to give you their blood. You know what, Dekes? For all your money and knickknacks, you're nothing but a common thief."

"Yes, and it's a system that I've perfected over the years, if I do say so myself. And now I've decided to add you to my collection," Dekes said. "You should be honored."

I raised an eyebrow. "Really? You really think that I'm just going to lie down for you?"

Dekes gestured at his men, who'd spread out in the library like a group of NFL linebackers, putting themselves between me and the doors. "Of course not. That's why I brought in reinforcements."

I laughed in his face. For the first time, annoyance flared in the vamp's eyes, and his whole body bristled with indignation, including his mustache. He didn't like being laughed at—nobody did—but in his case, it was probably the first time that it had happened in a hundred years.

"In case you didn't hear, in case your buddy Jonah didn't tell you, I killed *Mab fucking Monroe*, who was rumored to be the strongest elemental born in the last five hundred years," I growled. "Do you really think that you and your giants are going to put me down? Dream on, you sick son of a bitch."

Dekes glared at me another second before making a visible effort to rein in his temper. "You will do exactly what I say," he said in a soft voice. "You will lay down the knife in your hand and all the others that you have on you, and then you will bare your neck to me."

"Or else what?" I asked, even though I had a pretty good idea what the *or else* was going to be.

Dekes stared at me. "Or else I will drain every single drop of blood out of sweet Victoria while Vanessa watches. Then I'll go do the same to your sister, Bria. Jonah told me about her too, and all that lovely Ice magic she has."

Yeah, I'd thought it would be something like that. I wasn't too worried about Bria. My sister was just as tough as I was, with her own Ice magic to fall back on. She could handle getting away from Dekes's goons with no problem, and she'd have Finn and Owen to help her. Sooner or later, the three of them would realize that things had gone to hell in a handbasket and find a way to escape from the mansion. They wouldn't like it, but they'd leave me behind, hole up at the beach house, and wait for me to appear.

Now the question was how I was going to get myself out of here.

Vanessa looked at me, pleading at me with her dark eyes, begging me to do what Dekes wanted to save her sister. I'd never killed kids or pets as an assassin, and I didn't want to be the cause of an innocent woman's death now either, but I'd do what I had to in order to survive. And right now, that meant playing along with Dekes until I could get close enough to him to strike—or escape. As badly as the situation had deteriorated, I'd be good with either one of those at this point.

I didn't want to leave Vanessa and Victoria behind, didn't want them to suffer anymore at the vamp's hands, but I couldn't get all three of us out of here, not with Victoria unconscious and Dekes and his giants watching my every move. It was a calculated gamble, but I didn't think the vamp would actually kill either of the two women—not as long as they still had elemental magic he could feast on. He was too greedy that way to back up his threat. No, he was just trying to use them to subdue me, and I'd be damned if I let that happen.

"Fine," I snarled, playing along and pretending I was already beaten. "You may have the winning hand right now, but I'll tell you the same thing I told your man Pete before I dumped his body in the pool. You have no idea who you're messing with."

"Oh, I think I do," Dekes said. "So get rid of your weapons—now. All of them."

I put the silverstone knife I was holding on top of the stone mantel that jutted out from the fireplace, then pulled out the four others I had hidden on my body and placed them there as well. I made my movements slow and exaggerated so the giants wouldn't have an excuse to rush me en masse and also to give myself a few more seconds to think.

I had two choices. I could reach for my Stone magic, use it to harden my skin, smash through one of the French doors, and run like hell. It was the safer option, even though there was no guarantee of success. And of course, I'd have to leave Vanessa and Victoria behind to face Dekes's wrath. Or I could wait for Dekes to move within arm's reach, grab him, blast him with all the Ice magic that I had, and hope that it was enough to cut through his own stolen power and turn him into a Popsicle. A much bigger gamble, since I'd still have the giants to deal with, but the reward was much greater: kill the vampire now and hopefully save the two women from this house of horrors.

Run or fight, run or fight.

I decided to fight.

I put the last of my knives onto the mantel and waited for Dekes to move into range.

"How nice," Dekes said, walking over and picking up one of the blades. "A matching set. I'll have to add these to my weapons collection."

He sidled even closer to me. I reached for my Ice magic and waited—just waited for him to take a few more steps in my direction.

"I collect weapons, you know," Dekes said, not seeming to realize the danger he was in. "I'm sure you saw some of them earlier during our tour. I especially like small guns, dart guns. Like this one."

And that's when the vamp whirled around and shot me.

Too late, I heard something mechanical snap and saw the glint of metal appear in Dekes's left hand. In addition to the elemental power that he stole from his victims, their blood also gave Dekes something else, something that blood gave so many vamps—unbelievably fast reflexes. He already had his gun up and pointed at me before I realized what was happening, and I didn't even have time to create an Ice shield to block his attack or use my Stone magic to harden my skin before he pulled the trigger and a small dart stung my neck. I cursed and yanked it out, but it was already too late. Even as I tried to summon up enough of my Ice magic to blast Dekes to hell, I could feel my limbs going numb.

I only managed to take one step toward the vampire before my legs went out from under me. My last thought before I thumped to the floor was that I'd made the wrong choice, picked the wrong magic—and now I was going to pay for it.

* 16 *

My arms and legs went dead—absolutely, immediately cold, numb, and dead—but my mind remained strangely clear, and I didn't lose consciousness. No, I was painfully aware of lying there on the library floor, wanting to kill Randall Dekes more than anything else and not being able to do it. I couldn't get any part of my body to work, not so much as a finger to twitch, much less point my hands at Dekes and blast him with my Ice magic.

"Prop her up in one of the chairs, and tie her there nice and tight," Dekes said somewhere above my head. "I don't want any surprises. Quickly now, before the drug wears off."

Hands lifted me up and maneuvered me into a chair in front of the fireplace. One of the giants hurried over to the wet bar and reached down for something hidden on one of the shelves there. He came up with a coil of rope, the kind of thick, heavy, almost unbreakable rope that you'd find on a sailboat, the kind of rope that would be a bitch to slice through, even if I'd still had one of my silverstone knives on me. Not that I could have used them, given how numb my fingers were right now.

The giant stepped forward and quickly tied me down to the chair, looping the rope over my chest, arms, and legs until I was trussed up tighter than a Thanksgiving turkey.

Never let yourself be immobilized by the enemy. Fletcher had told me that over and over again, but here I was, tied down to a chair and about to be tortured for the second time in my life. Fuck.

I managed to loll my head to one side to look at Vanessa, but the Fire elemental lowered her eyes. She didn't want to meet my gaze. Couldn't blame her for that. I wouldn't want to watch what was about to happen next either—especially since there was nothing I could do to stop it. Not one damn thing. For a moment, I wished for the blindfold Mab had used when she'd tortured me by melting my spider rune necklace into my palms. At least then I wouldn't have to see Dekes bite me. But I wasn't that scared thirteen-year-old girl anymore. I was older and stronger, if not exactly wiser. Either way, I'd face my enemy head-on.

Dekes walked around so that he was beside me and leaned forward over the chair, so close I could feel his hot breath brush against my cheek and smell his spicy aftershave. The floral scent made me want to gag.

"Don't worry, Gin," Dekes purred in my ear. "I just gave you a muscle relaxant to make you a little more pliable so my men could get you into the chair right where you needed to be. The effects won't last more than another minute. You should already start feeling some sensation returning to your arms and legs, while your mind remains completely unaffected. You see, I want you to know exactly what's happening to you. I want you to feel every last bit of it. I wouldn't have any fun otherwise."

He was right. The absolute numbness was already starting to fade, replaced by small, painful tingles. I concentrated and was able to move my fingers, but I knew that it wasn't going to be enough, that I wasn't going to recover quickly enough to escape what the vampire had in mind.

Dekes reached down and tilted my head to one side, exposing my throat to him. I couldn't help but look up into his face. Lust blazed in Dekes's green eyes, and his tongue eagerly darted out to moisten his lips underneath his bristling mustache. The vampire smiled a final time, letting me see just how long, sharp, and deadly his fangs were.

Then the bastard sank them into my neck.

There are some folks who think that being bitten by a vampire is sexy.

Some people like that first pop of pain, the dizzying rush of their blood leaving their own body, the weak, languid feeling of having someone else steal away part of them. Some folks even get a high off those kinds of feelings, a heady, electric charge that seems to make it all worthwhile.

I am not one of those people.

Being bitten by a vampire is like being stabbed in

the neck with a dagger—two of them at the same time. Dekes's bite was hard, brutal, merciless, and vicious, just like he was. I screamed as he drove his fangs deep into my neck, and I screamed again as he started to suck out my blood in long, agonizing spurts. The last of the numbness from the drug immediately vanished, replaced by pure, pulsing pain. It felt like there was a giant fist wrapped around my neck that was just *squeezing* and *squeezing* and *squeezing* the blood and everything else out of me. The magic, the power, the life.

Some vamps are skilled enough to make their bites feel like minor annoyances, like a veteran nurse knowing exactly how to slip an IV needle into a patient's hand to minimize that initial prick of pain.

Dekes was not one of those vamps. He didn't want to minimize my pain or discomfort—he wanted the elemental power in my blood, and he wanted to brutalize me while he took it. The only one getting any pleasure out of this was him, and I could feel his erection pressing against my thigh as he leaned over me. Sick, sadistic bastard. It wouldn't surprise me at all if he was one of the vamps who got a power boost off sex just like he did from drinking blood.

The hot stench of my own coppery blood filled my nose, overpowering everything else. Sweat slickened my hands, my whole body trembled, and white starbursts exploded in my eyes. And still, Dekes kept sucking out my blood. *Squeeze, squeeze, squeeze.*

As an assassin, I'd suffered just about every injury big and small that a person could experience over the years. I'd been stabbed, shot, beaten, burned, electrocuted, blasted with elemental magic, and buried alive too many times to count. But this was a different kind of agony altogether because not only was Dekes hurting me, he was also taking a piece of me with him at the same time—the elemental magic that was as much a part of who and what I was as the spider runes branded into my palms.

My hands were tied down to the chair arms so I couldn't see the scars, but I could feel the silverstone—and the magical metal seemed to be wriggling around like hot worms underneath my skin. I blocked out the agony of the vampire's bite and concentrated on that strange sensation—and I realized that I could feel my scars burning, burning, burning with the cold power of my Ice and Stone magic, until it seemed like the silverstone was soaking up just as much of my power as Dekes was. I didn't know if I was consciously doing it or some self-preservation switch had been flipped in the back of my brain, but somehow I was directing my magic into the silverstone that had been melted into my flesh, storing the power there and trying to keep as much of it away from the vampire for as long as possible.

Maybe the blood loss was making me hallucinate already, but it almost seemed like I could feel the silverstone scars stubbornly holding on to my power even as Dekes tried to pull it out of my neck. It felt as if I was playing a bizarre tug-of-war with my own magic deep inside my veins. Every time Dekes sucked at my neck, I could feel the scars yanking back, trying to keep my elemental power inside my own body where it belonged instead of flowing through my blood and out into the vamp's greedy mouth. Too bad I didn't know what—if any—good it would do me. I might be an elemental, but there was only so much blood that I could lose and still live.

Finally, just when I thought I couldn't stand another second of the vamp's fucking fangs in my neck without going absolutely crazy, Dekes lifted his head and stared at me. I'd thought that his eyes had gleamed like a cat's before, but now they blazed like two emerald suns in his tan features. It was eerie, sickening, and disconcerting, looking into the vamp's face and seeing my own Ice and Stone power reflected in his gaze. A small, dazed part of me wondered if my eyes ever burned that brightly when I reached for my elemental magic.

Jo-Jo always claimed that I was one of the strongest elementals she'd ever met, and I'd managed to go toe-to-toe with Mab and survive. But the amount of magic that I sensed in the vamp right now was just staggering—and it was supposed to be *mine*. It *was* mine, until the bastard had taken it away from me.

"The power," Dekes murmured in a low, reverent whisper, his words slurring like he was drunk on wine. "I never dreamed of such raw *power*."

Then the bastard bit me again, driving his fangs into my right shoulder and snapping my collarbone. I screamed again, although the sound came out as a hoarse rasp, since I was already so weak from the blood loss.

I didn't know how many people Dekes had fed off during his three hundred–plus years on this earth, how many women he had used for their blood and elemental magic, how many times he had brutalized them until their bodies and power wore out and they simply had nothing more to give him. The vampire had no doubt left hundreds of dead women in his wake, thinking no more of them than humans did of the food they consumed on a daily basis.

But apparently Dekes had never encountered anyone with as much power as I had because the vampire fell into a feeding frenzy, like a shark frantically thrashing around in a sea full of chum, trying to snap up every single bloody, bony scrap that he could. The vamp bit me over and over and over again all across my neck and shoulders, his fangs tearing and ripping and slicing into my flesh as if he couldn't get enough of my blood, as if he couldn't ever get enough of the Ice and Stone magic flowing through my veins.

"Stop! Stop it, Randall! You're taking too much! You're going to kill her!"

I was dimly aware of Vanessa screaming at the vampire and clawing at him with her hands, trying to pull him off me, but I knew that it was no use. Dekes was high on my elemental power, as high as a junkie on any drug could be, and he wasn't coming down until there wasn't a single drop of blood or magic left in me.

The bastard was going to drain me dry—and there was nothing I could do to stop him.

For a moment, I sank into the cold, lethargic blackness that was slowly clouding my vision, my body, my mind. It would be so easy to let go, to let myself drown in the darkness where there was no more pain, no more torture, no more anything . . .

Fuck that, I growled at myself. Gin Blanco never gave up—not now, not ever.

I'd found my way out of a collapsed coal mine, I'd been electrocuted by LaFleur—hell, I'd even killed Mab fucking Monroe against all the odds. I'd survived all those things, and I'd come out stronger each time. Not to mention Bria, Finn, the Deveraux sisters, and Owen. I had them to live for now, and I wasn't going to let some psychotic, power-hungry vamp be the end of me.

Think, Gin. Think.

I struggled to push away the numbing blackness from my mind and focus. My situation wasn't good. I was tied down, immobilized, and bleeding from the deep, vicious bites that Dekes had inflicted on my neck and shoulders. Even if I were free, there was no way I could have fought my way past the vampire and the giants in the room. Not now, when I was so weak and injured and when Dekes had already stolen so much of my Ice and Stone magic.

Desperately, my gaze zoomed around the library, looking for something, anything, that would help me out of this mess. That would at least make Dekes stop biting me and give me a chance to fucking regroup. But there was nothing. Just books and giants and Vanessa screaming and Victoria lying limp on the couch . . .

My eyes focused on the other woman's unconscious body, and a plan popped into my head. I couldn't fight my way out of here, but maybe I didn't have to. All I needed was a little bit of magic, but that was another problem. There was no way that I could reach for my own power, not with Dekes sucking it out of me as fast as he could—but maybe I didn't have to do that either.

I looked down at the spider rune ring on my right index finger—the one that contained my Ice magic. I didn't know if my crazy plan would work, but it was the only chance I had left.

I pushed the pain of Dekes biting me, of his teeth tearing into my neck, to the very back of my mind, surrounded it with imaginary stone walls, and locked it away where it wouldn't distract me. Then I reached for the Ice magic stored in my ring.

Normally when I used my Ice magic, I pushed it outward, releasing the power through my hands and using it to create lockpicks, knives, and other shapes. But this time, I forced the magic inward, coating my own heart with elemental Ice and then letting the magic spread to my lungs and the rest of my internal organs before carefully pushing it out toward my skin.

Thump . . . thump . . . thump . . .

My heart slowed, and my breathing stuttered, as my lungs frosted over. For a moment, I wondered if I'd miscalculated, if I was actually killing myself with my own magic instead of saving my ass. But I'd subconsciously used my Ice magic to preserve my body once before when I'd jumped into the Aneirin River in the winter, and I was hoping the same thing would happen here. I *needed* that to happen, or I was as good as dead. Besides, Jo-Jo had always said that my elemental magic was part of me and that it was mine to command however I wished—not the other way around.

I hoped the dwarf was right, because I was about to bet my life on her wisdom.

When I pulled enough Ice magic into my body to make myself completely cold and numb, I rasped out a great shuddering, agonizing cry, arching and thrashing against the ropes as much and as violently as I could. They didn't call them death throes for nothing.

The sudden bucking motion surprised Dekes enough to get him to stop biting me and lift his head. I kept up with my twitching and thrashing, and the vampire took a step back, wondering what the hell was going on. His eyes were even brighter than before, and once more, I could see my own power burning in his gaze. The sight made me angry—so fucking *angry*—and even more determined to get out of this alive. Randall Dekes would not be the death of me. *He would not.*

I kept up my fake death throes for another ten seconds before closing my eyes, slumping forward in the chair as much as I could, given the ropes that held me tight, and letting my body go completely slack.

Nobody moved, nobody spoke. All I could hear was Dekes's ragged breathing as the vampire struggled to come down from the magical high he was riding on.

"Check her," the vamp finally ordered.

Clothing whispered together, and soft footsteps crept toward me. A second later, I felt Vanessa's slender fingers skim my throat, trying to find a spot that was free of blood where she could check for a pulse.

Thump . . . thump . . . thump . . .

By this point, my heart was barely beating, and my lungs struggled to function against the Ice that was weighing them down, but I was still breathing. The question now was whether Vanessa would notice or if the little trick with my Ice magic would fool her.

The other woman's fingers finally pressed against my cold skin, causing more blood to trickle out of the bite marks on my neck. I sat there, holding my breath, limp and still, and waited. Ten seconds passed . . . twenty . . . thirty . . . forty-five . . . sixty . . . My lungs started to burn from the lack of oxygen, but still I didn't breathe. Sixty-five . . . seventy . . .

"You killed her," Vanessa said, dropping her fingers from my neck. "Her skin's already getting cold."

"Are you sure?" Dekes asked.

"I think I know what a dead woman looks and feels like," Vanessa muttered. "Given how many of them you've made me watch you murder in here. I warned you that you were taking too much blood from her, but you didn't listen. You've got no one to blame but yourself, Randall."

I drew in a shallow breath, to ease the ache in my lungs. I didn't know if the Fire elemental really thought I was dead or if she was just saying that to convince Dekes. Didn't much matter. What was important now was what he decided to do with my body—and whether I had the strength to somehow slip out of the mansion before the vamp or anyone else realized that I was just faking.

More footsteps whispered on the carpet, and I got the sense that Dekes was pacing back and forth in front me. I stayed exactly where I was, slumped forward and doing my best to remain completely still. I'd seen more than enough bodies in my time to mimic the loose slackness of death. Yeah, maybe playing dead wasn't my finest, most inspired, or deadliest moment as the Spider, but Fletcher had always told me that there was no shame in it if it got you out of a bad situation—like the one I was in right now.

The vampire's hand touched my neck, but instead of checking for a pulse, he started stroking my wounded flesh, dragging his fingers through the sticky blood that coated my skin and clothes. For a moment, I wondered what the hell he was doing, but then he drew his fingers away and I heard a low sucking sound, followed by a long, satisfied sigh.

The bastard—the bastard was actually *licking* my blood off his fingers, like I was a piece of fried chicken that he'd been snacking on and he just couldn't resist getting that last bit of greasy goodness off his hands and into his hungry mouth. The thought made my stomach roil, despite the elemental Ice that still coated my internal organs.

"Such a waste," Dekes said, swiping his fingers across my neck and licking them clean again. "She was even stronger than Jonah thought. I could have fed off her Ice and Stone magic for *years*, and no one would have been able to stand against me. No one would have dared to. And I was so looking forward to taking Gin's power for a test drive. Perhaps even using it against Callie Reyes, since she's been so reluctant to accept my offer for her restaurant."

"Why?" Vanessa snapped. "Have you grown tired already of using my Fire magic to burn people to death?"

"Something like that," Dekes replied in a mild tone. "After a while, it's all the same. The tears, the screams, the flames. You know how I hate to be bored."

I thought of the photos that I'd seen of the vamp's arson victims. So Dekes drank Vanessa's blood and then used the Fire magic he absorbed from her to toast the people who tried to stand up to him, victimizing everyone but himself in the process. He was a fucking sociopath if I'd ever met one.

At that moment, I wanted nothing more than to turn my head, bite off his fucking fingers, and spit them back in his face, but I concentrated on the Ice magic in my ring, using it to make my skin even cooler, as though the chill of death were already settling into my corpse just as Vanessa had claimed it was.

"Very well," Dekes said. "Since she's of no further use to me, take the bitch's body out on the west balcony and dump it into the marsh. Maybe the gators will have some interest in her rotting corpse."

❖ 17 ❖

Dekes left the library, ordering five of his men to take Vanessa and Victoria back to their room and lock them away for the evening before returning to their regular posts. I had no idea if the vampire would feed from the other women tonight, but there was nothing I could do to help or save them.

First I had to save myself.

The footsteps faded away, leaving me alone in the library with the last two giants. If I hadn't been tied down and lost so much blood already, I might have leaped out of the chair, grabbed my silverstone knives from the mantel, and had at the two men. But I was in no shape to do that or anything else, so I kept my eyes closed and my body slack.

"What a mess," one of the giants muttered. "There's blood everywhere—her neck, her chest, I think it's even in her hair. I don't want to touch her."

"Yeah," the other one replied. "Dekes tore her up good, didn't he? She must have been really strong. I've never seen him act like that with any other elemental, not even Vanessa when she first came here."

"Well, it doesn't matter now because she's dead," the giant said. "So let's dump her body and be done with it."

The two men got to work. One of them opened a drawer, probably in the desk that I'd noticed earlier, and drew out something with a distinctive crinkly sound. A garbage bag, I thought. The bastards were going to wrap me in a plastic garbage bag so I wouldn't drip too much blood onto Dekes's pricey Persian rugs and hardwood floors as they carried me to my final destination. The vamp wouldn't want me to ruin any part of his house or his precious collections.

"Put the bag on the floor," one of them said, confirming my suspicions.

More crinkles whispered, along with the sounds of someone smoothing something down. Then one of the giants cut through the ropes that held me to the chair. Since I was leaning forward, I slid off the seat and thumped to the floor, my arms and legs sprawled at awkward angles. I didn't dare move. Not yet.

I felt hands on my side, turning me over onto my back. One of the giants drew the plastic bag across my chest. By this point, I'd exhausted the Ice magic that had been stored in my spider rune ring, but the giants didn't notice that my skin wasn't quite as cold as before. They wrapped me up in the garbage bag. Then one of the men picked me up and threw me over his shoulder as if I were Cleopatra in a carpet being taken to see Caesar.

"I'll send in Sean to clean up the blood on the chair and rugs," the first giant said. "Let's go."

The two men left the library. I swayed back and forth on the giant's shoulder as they walked through the house. I didn't hear anyone else moving around in this part of the mansion besides them, so I cracked my eyes open. But since all I could really see was the floor sliding by and my blood dripping small teardrop-shaped tracks onto it, I shut them again.

Finally, the giants stepped out onto a balcony. I couldn't tell exactly where we were in the mansion, but I got the impression it was the far side of the house, the one that faced the marsh instead of the golf course. The air was cooler here, and I could smell the whiff of decay that went with the still water and rotting logs. The sun had set while I'd been inside the library, and darkness had already covered the land.

"Grab her feet and we'll heave her out as far as we can," one of the giants said. "You know how Dekes hates it when the gators crawl up on the lawn and start chewing on their legs."

The giant who'd been carrying me dumped me on the stone patio, making even more pain shoot through my body, and I stifled a groan. Then he grabbed my shoulders while the other man's hands clamped around my ankles. Together, they lifted me up and shuffled forward.

"One . . . two . . . three!"

They swung me back and forth a couple of times before letting go and flinging me out into the darkness as far and high as their enormous strength would let them. I felt my body rise up in an arc and quickly plummet.

My final thought before I hit the water was that I'd done this very same thing to Dekes's men just last night.

Ah, irony. Going to be the death of me one day.

Maybe even tonight.

The murky, brackish water closed over me, warm, slimy, and disgusting, but I didn't try to kick my way to the surface. Dekes's men might still be out on the balcony, watching to make sure that I sank. Instead, I focused on getting one hand, then the other, free of the garbage bag and unwinding the whole thing from around my body. It wouldn't do to get away from the vampire only to drown in the swamp outside his mansion.

While I worked on the bag, I counted off the seconds in my head. Ten . . . twenty . . . thirty . . . forty-five . . . At the minute mark, the last of the plastic slipped off my legs, my head broke free of the water, and I blinked, trying to get my bearings in the semidarkness.

There wasn't any current in the marsh, but my struggles with the garbage bag had carried me out of the pool of light from the balcony that had arced out onto the landscape below. I remained still and quiet, doing just enough to keep my head above the surface of the water.

"She's gone," the voice of one of the giants floated down to me. "The gators will find her on the bottom soon enough. Let's go back inside."

A few seconds later, a door slammed somewhere far above my head. The giants thought I was dead, just like their boss did. Good. Now all that was left was to make sure the marsh and blood loss didn't finish the job that the vampire had started.

I stayed in the water, too tired and exhausted from Dekes's attack to even think about lifting my arms and swimming to shore. Eventually, though, I spotted a ridge of land a little higher than the bog that surrounded me, and I forced myself to thrash toward it. My arms and legs felt as numb and dead as lead weights strapped to my body, not because I'd used my Ice magic on myself, but because there just wasn't that much blood left in them. Somehow, I splashed and flailed around and finally managed to heave my chest up out of the water.

I lay there, my face in the mud, panting from the effort of doing something so small. My neck and shoulders pulsed with pain with every breath that I took, ribbons of red-hot agony winding tighter and tighter around my upper body and strangling me from the inside out. But this time, instead of pushing the hurt away, I embraced it. As long as I was in pain, I was still alive and not sliding into the cold, cold oblivion that was the alternative.

I put one hand in front of the other, weakly kicking my legs, digging my fingers into the slippery mud, and slowly pulling myself up the bank until I was back on semisolid ground again. Still panting, I rolled over onto my back and forced myself to sit up. The moon and stars were out in full force tonight, their pale light streaming in through the thick canopy of twisted trees that surrounded me. The silvery glow matched the starbursts erupting in my eyes.

I don't know how long it took for me to crawl over to the closest tree, wrap my hands around the rough bark, and pull myself to my feet. I stood there for several minutes, resting my forehead against the trunk and trying to keep the world from spinning around and the flashing starbursts to a minimum. Then I pushed away from the tree and forced myself to start walking.

Well, I don't know if I'd really call it *walking*. I stumbled from one tree trunk to the next, weaving worse than a drunken frat boy, with no idea of where I was, where I was going, and not really caring about either one at the moment. I had a much more important mission right now—stopping the rest of my blood from leaking out of my body.

Dekes had made some nasty wounds with his fangs, including one in my right shoulder that went all the way down to my collarbone. I could feel the broken edges of the bone scraping against each other and threatening to break through the tight skin that was stretched over their now awkward alignment. I could barely raise my right arm so I couldn't set the bone, not by myself, but the bite marks needed to be covered up at the very least so that what was left of my blood would have a chance to clot. It was just dumb, blind luck that the vampire hadn't hit my carotid artery when he'd launched into his feeding frenzy. Otherwise, I would have bled out back in the library.

I stooped down, dug my fingers into the mud at my feet, and plastered some of that on my wounds, but more of it seemed to slide off than actually stick to my skin. Ditto for the grass and moss that I tried next. So I got to my feet and trudged on. I don't know how long I stumbled through the swamp, teetering and tottering from one slippery step to the next, but finally, I came across something that could help me—a spider's web.

I walked right into the web, not even realizing it was there until I felt it stick to my skin. I blinked and lurched back, wondering if I'd stumbled into some sort of trap, perhaps an elemental trip wire or an elaborate snare that a hunter had made with fishing line. It took me a moment to spot the silken strands clinging to my bloody chest and realize what they were.

Despite the fact that the Spider was my assassin name and my own personal rune, I'd never really studied up on the critters themselves. I didn't know what kind of spider had made the web, but it stretched from one tree to the next like a thick hammock that had been turned on its side. The moonlight slipped in through the cracks in the leaves above, making the individual threads glimmer like spun silver and showing off the web's intricate pattern.

For a moment, the scene blurred, and I was back in the sunlit forests of Ashland, patiently listening as Fletcher explained another one of his folksy mountain remedies to me—the one I'd thought I'd never, ever use. But once again, the old man's teachings were going to save me—or at least help me save myself.

"Fletcher," I whispered.

The old man's name seemed to echo through the trees, melting the happy illusion in my head and snapping me back to the here and now and the danger that I was in. Still, for the first time all night, a smile spread across my bloody face.

It was a shame to destroy something so delicate and beautiful as the web, but I did it anyway, just as I had so many other horrible, hurtful things over the years. I grabbed gobs and gobs of the silken strands and started packing them into the wounds on my neck and shoulders as best I could, given the fact that I could really only use my left arm. The threads stuck to my skin like glue.

When I packed the wounds with the last of the web, I managed to shrug out of my suit jacket, put it over the whole sticky mess, and loop the sleeves around my neck like a scarf, since I didn't have the strength to try and actually tie them together. It wasn't the best bandage I'd ever made, but hopefully it would keep me from losing any more blood.

My mission complete, I drew in a breath and headed deeper into the marsh.

I don't know how long I walked, just plodding through the swamp. Mud, water, grass, more mud. They all merged together into a seemingly endless landscape, each one sucking at my feet and threatening to pull me down with every step I took. Half the time I would think that I'd finally found some dry land to walk on, only to find myself up to my knees in water two seconds later.

But the worst part was the mosquitoes. Drawn to the scent of my blood, the insects buzzed around my head in a thick, suffocating cloud, their high-pitched whines echoing in my ears like a hundred tiny chain saws and making me grind my teeth together. I had to squint my eyes and hold my left hand up over my nose and mouth to keep from swallowing gobs of them. Ugh.

Every once in a while, I would see the golden glow of lights through the trees from one of the mansions that backed up against the marsh, but I didn't dare try to find my way over to any of them. For all I knew, I'd been walking in circles this whole time and the lights I noticed belonged to Dekes's mansion—or one of his buddies'. Even if they didn't, I wasn't going to take that kind of chance, especially when I looked like something the Swamp Thing would be afraid of.

There would be too many awkward questions to answer and too much risk of word getting back to Dekes that a wounded woman had stumbled out of the marsh. No, the best thing to do was to keep wading through the swamp. It had to end sometime, and then I'd get my bearings and figure out where I was and how to get back to the beach house.

I only hoped that Finn, Bria, and Owen had realized the danger they were in and had managed to get away from the mansion before Dekes had sent his giants to round them up. I couldn't let myself think they hadn't or I didn't know how I'd be able to keep going. Especially now that I knew exactly what Dekes would do to Bria if he ever got his hands on her.

My stomach roiled again at the memory of the vampire sinking his teeth into me, but I swallowed down the bitter bile that rose up in my throat and kept walking. I stepped onto what looked like more solid ground, only to feel my feet slide out from under me in the hidden bog. I stumbled forward and fell to my hands and knees in the water, with even more mud and muck squishing between my fingers. I weakly thrashed around for a few seconds before managing to get to my feet. I raised up my head and peered into the darkness, wondering what was next, what other new obstacle I would have to face.

And that's when I saw the gator.

I'd been so intent on putting one foot in front of the other that I hadn't realized I'd come to the edge of a small pond hidden in the larger marsh. I was on one side of the pond, and the gator was on the other, with only a few feet of murky water separating us.

It was a big sucker, at least seven feet long, and its eyes glimmered like ghostly marbles in the moonlight. Its gnarled, bumpy body looked like a rotten log resting in the grass, but the distinctive curve of its long snout gave away the illusion. I couldn't see its teeth, but I knew that they were there, resting inside those powerful, massive jaws. If I'd thought that being bitten by Dekes had been agonizing, it would be nothing compared to being attacked by a gator. The creature would latch onto me, drag me into the water, and drown me before gobbling up my bloody remains at its leisure.

The gator stared at me, and I glared right back at it. Sometime during the long night, the pain pounding through my body had turned to rage—rage at Dekes and what he'd done to me, what the vamp had done to Vanessa, Victoria, and who knew how many other women over the years, what he still might do to Bria and maybe even Callie if I didn't stop him. The rage coated my heart much like my Ice magic had earlier tonight. The cold, dark emotion and even uglier, blacker thoughts of revenge were the only things that were keeping me upright at this point.

"Fuck off, sugar, or I'll make a pair of shoes out of you," I growled.

Yeah, I knew it was nothing but talk. All of my silverstone knives were back on Dekes's mantel, and I didn't see so much as a sturdy stick I could use to fend off the gator—much less stab it to death. Besides, it wasn't like I had the strength to do that anyway. But Dekes had already sunk his teeth into me tonight, and I'd be damned if anything else would.

Maybe the gator had already eaten. Maybe it realized that I wouldn't go down without a fight. Or maybe it recognized the dangerous predator in me just as I did in it, but the creature stared at me another second—and then it slipped into the water and swam off in the other direction.

Well, well, well. It looked like luck, that capricious bitch, wasn't quite done with me yet. I didn't know whether to smile or cry.

I kept walking, with only the soft, silvery glimmer of the moon and stars to light my way. Eventually, I stepped out from behind a tree—and walked right into a low rock wall.

Surprised, I staggered back, wondering what I was imagining now, but after a moment, I realized that the wall was as real as I was. No, that wasn't quite right. It wasn't a man-made wall but a natural stone formation. Something about it seemed vaguely familiar, although I was too exhausted to figure out exactly what it was. I was too weak to try to climb over the rocks, so I put one hand on the rough wall and hurried along it as fast as I could. It didn't take me long to reach the other side of the rocks and stumble forward, determined to keep on going no matter what.

But instead of more muck, my muddy, battered boots sank into a thin crust of sand. That was enough to rouse me out of the dazed, dreamlike state that I'd fallen into and make my heart quicken with excitement. Sand meant that I wasn't too far away from the beach. Which beach and on what side of the island, I didn't know, but at least the sand would make the walking easier. I kept going and realized that there was a darker shadow up ahead, pooling on the ground like black ink. I looked up, searching for the source of it.

The moonlight outlined the lighthouse perched on the rocks above my head.

I blinked again, and the rest of the landscape snapped into focus. Sandy beach, frothing water, a few seagulls and terns circling overhead in the night sky.

Somehow, I'd made it from Dekes's estate through the marsh, across the island, and into the cove where Owen and I had made love yesterday. Now that I knew where the hell I was, all that was left to do was walk the short distance to the beach house. Finn, Bria, and Owen were sure to be waiting there for me by now. I didn't want to think about what might have happened to them if they weren't there, if they hadn't been able to get away from Dekes's men after all.

But there was only one way to find out and to let them know what had happened to me, so I drew in a breath and started the final leg of my journey.

✴ 18 ✴

It took me far longer than it should have to walk through the cove, trudge down to the shore, and reach the beach house, but eventually I stumbled up the steps onto the back patio. I leaned against the side of the house for a moment, resting; then I raised my hand and banged as loudly as I could on the sliding glass door.

I don't know how long I stood there, but the world went fuzzy again. Suddenly, a face loomed up on the other side of the glass—a pale face framed by black hair.

I blinked, wondering if I was imagining things for the third time. "Sophia?" I mumbled. "What are you doing here?"

The dwarf's black eyes widened at the sight of me, and she hurried away from the door.

"Wait," I said in an even weaker voice, my legs already slipping out from under me. "Come back."

I landed hard on my ass on the deck and flopped over onto my side, like a fish tossed into the bottom of a boat. The wood still felt warm from the day's sun under my cold, aching cheek, and I felt myself relaxing. I was going to lie here just for a second, I promised myself. Just for a second and then I'd get back up and pound on the glass until somebody let me into the house.

But the weariness crept up on me before I knew it, and my eyes slid shut.

The blackness wasn't as soothing as it should have been. For one thing, I kept hearing people talk, men and women chattering on and on like a flock of seagulls, each one crying out, one right after another.

"She just walked up to the house?"

"Look at her neck."

"Her collarbone's broken, and she's lost a lot of blood."

"This is all my fault. Callie's my friend. I should have found another way to help her."

"I'm going to kill that bastard Dekes for this."

Not if I get to him first, I thought, but I didn't have the strength to voice my dark, violent promise. *Not if I get to him first.*

Eventually the voices quieted down, but that's when the needles started. Thousands and thousands of them pricking my skin like tiny, invisible red-hot pokers. For a moment I thought that Dekes had somehow found me, that the vampire had bitten me again, but this pain felt different. Duller, calmer, soothing even. In fact, the needles almost seemed to make me feel . . . better.

"There you go, darling," a low, sweet voice whispered in my ear. "Just relax, and I'll take care of you, just the way that I always do."

Something about that voice soothed me, made me feel I was safe, at least for the moment. So I let go and spiraled down into the darkness once more.

Slowly, the needles faded away, and the still, quiet blackness returned. But before long, colors and sounds began to flicker in my mind, and I started dreaming. At least, I thought that I was dreaming . . .

I'd been in the woods for an hour—what seemed like the longest hour of my life. After I'd read Fletcher's note, I'd curled up at the base of a maple tree, hugged my knees to my chest, and tried to hold back the hot, scalding tears and deep, aching hurt I felt at the fact that the old man had abandoned me. That he'd brought me out here on a ruse and dumped me in the middle of the forest instead of at least having the decency to face me at the Pork Pit and tell me to get the hell out of his restaurant and life—forever.

I would have gone quietly, if only he'd asked me to. I would have done anything Fletcher had wanted me to—that's how important he'd become to me over these last few months. I'd thought Fletcher had cared about me, that maybe he'd even started to love me, just a little bit, like I had him. But instead, he'd left me here miles from anyone or anything. And why? I just didn't understand why.

More tears slid down my cheeks, and Fletcher's voice whispered in my mind, despite my efforts to block him out. Tears are a waste of time, energy, and resources. That was one of the very first things that Fletcher had ever said to me.

I let out a cold, bitter laugh, startling the mockingbirds that had gathered in the limbs above my head and making them fly away. I'd thought that saying was so clever, that Fletcher was so smart and wise, but now I knew the truth— and just how mistaken about him I'd been.

The more I sat there and thought about Fletcher, the more my hurt and bewilderment turned to bitterness—and determination too. So the old man had left me out here in the middle of nowhere. So what? I'd find my way off this mountain. We'd driven up here in a car, which meant that there was a road somewhere within walking distance. It might take me a while, but I'd find it, and I'd hitchhike back to Ashland and live on the streets again. No matter what, I'd survive, just like I had when my family was murdered. I'd done it once, I could do it again.

Furious now, I swiped away the last of my tears and unzipped the backpack that Fletcher had so casually given me this morning. A compass, a bottle of water, a pack of matches. There wasn't much in the backpack, but then again, Fletcher never brought much with him when we came out into the woods. He actually enjoyed living off the land, as he called it, and he'd taught me how to do the same. So I wasn't too worried about the lack of supplies.

I might have just been tossed aside like trash, but I wasn't going to give up. I didn't need Fletcher, and I didn't need him to care about me—not anymore. That's what I told myself over and over, even if the little voice in the back of my head whispered that it wasn't true.

I took a long swig from the bottle of water, then stuffed it and the matches back inside the pack and zipped up the whole thing. I got to my feet and slung the straps over my shoulders, adjusting the pack so that it rested comfortably on my back. Then, with the compass in one hand, I started walking.

Since I was so close to the top of the mountain, I decided to walk the rest of the way up to get my bearings. Maybe I'd even be able to spot the road from the summit. It was worth a shot.

It took me an hour to break free of the last of the trees and reach the peak of Bone Mountain. I stepped out onto the rocky ridge and stared at the sweeping vista before me. Trees in various shades of brown and green stretched out as far as I could see, the new buds on their blossoming branches soaring up like they were growing into the clouds overhead. The wind whipped my brown hair into a tangled mess, and I could smell the cool scent of rain in it.

Just below me, the earth fell away in a series of jagged gray ridges that arched and curved like a person's spine. I wondered if that was how the mountain had gotten its name. Fletcher would have known but of course he wasn't around for me to ask. Still, it was a beautiful scene, despite the hurt I'd experienced to get here.

I stood there for a long time, my eyes scanning the horizon. I couldn't see any sort of road from up here, but I thought I recognized some of the ridges and rock formations across the way—places that Fletcher had taken me to on other hikes— and I knew I could get back to Ashland. It might take a while, but I'd make it back there eventually.

I felt better now, calmer, and more in control. Fletcher might have abandoned me, but I still had myself to rely on. Genevieve Snow and Gin Blanco rolled into one. Maybe I'd even invent a new name for myself, instead of using the one Fletcher had given me. The thought made me laugh again but without as much bitterness as before.

We'd left Ashland and driven north this morning, so I made sure to use my compass and orient myself south before walking back into the forest and starting the long trek down the mountain. An hour into my journey, the sky darkened, lightning flashed, and rain started to fall down in sheets. I found a small cave to hole up in. It reminded me of the crack in the wall behind the Pork Pit that I slipped into whenever I wanted some time to myself. The cave was dark and damp, but not unpleasantly so, especially given the soft murmur of the rocks around me. The stones whispered of the rain and wind and all the other spring storms that had swept down the mountain this year. The sound soothed me.

I wasn't afraid. There was nothing out here but me and the weather and the animals. It was people that you had to watch out for, anyway—people like Fletcher who could really hurt you, deep down in your heart where it mattered most. But even he was gone now, which meant that there was nothing to fear. Not anymore.

I went to sleep, and by the time I woke up, the rain had stopped. I wasn't sure how much time had passed, maybe an hour or two, but I got to my feet, left the cave, and started walking down the mountain again, using my compass as a guide.

The sun had just started to set when I reached the bottom. I'd been able to see the gray sliver of the road for some time now, and I quickened my pace, hoping that I could catch a ride back to the city before night fell. I stepped out of the last tangle of trees—and realized that he was there, waiting for me by the side of the road right where we'd parked this morning. I stopped cold.

"Fletcher?" I asked in an uncertain voice. "What are you doing here?"

He was sitting on the hood of the car, his back flat against the windshield, whittling a block of wood with the small knife that he always favored. Judging from the pile of shavings on the metal next to him, he'd been here the whole time that I'd been up on the mountain.

The old man raised his head at the sound of my voice and smiled. "Why, I've been waiting for you, Gin."

I approached him warily. "Waiting for me? Why? You left me up on the mountain, remember?"

He nodded. "I did, and I'm sorry about that, but it was a necessary evil."

My eyes narrowed. "What kind of necessary evil?"

Instead of answering me, Fletcher put his knife and block of wood aside. He swung his legs over the side of the car, hopped off the hood, and walked over to stand in front of me. His green eyes swept over my face and body. When he realized that I was just fine, his smile got a little wider.

"I left you on the mountain and pretended to abandon you because it was part of your assassin training," he said in a quiet voice. "To help you get over your fear. It's the one thing that can kill an assassin quicker than anything else. If you're afraid, you can't act. And if you can't act, you can't strike back at your enemy—much less hope to survive."

I frowned, puzzled. "Fear? What fear? I'm not afraid. I'm not afraid of anything."

"Yes you are," he said in a kind voice. "You never let me out of your sight at the Pork Pit or when we're at home either. You're always watching me, always following me. And if I'm *not around, then you do the same thing to Jo-Jo and Sophia or even Finn.*"

It was true. Even though I tried not to, I trailed after Fletcher like a lost puppy, and I had to make myself not panic whenever he was out late on one of his jobs. Even when I was at school, I was counting down the minutes until I could see him and even Finn again and make sure they were okay. That they hadn't left or been taken from me like my family had. I hadn't thought Fletcher had noticed, but I should have realized that he had. The old man noticed everything.

"*I wanted you to realize that you didn't need me or Jo-Jo or any of the others. That you were strong enough to rely on yourself, Gin. That you were strong enough to survive on your own, no matter what happened.*"

I frowned, more confusion filling my body. "I don't understand. So this was all just a test? Of what? How much you could hurt me?"

Fletcher shook his head. "I know I hurt you when you thought that I abandoned you up there on the mountain. I'm sorry for that, but it was something you had to learn, something you had to face down. You never talk about your family or where you came from, but I know things didn't end well for you—or them. But you kept on going despite all that, and I wanted to remind you that you could do it again. Today, tomorrow, and any time that you needed to—no matter what. Do you understand?"

Maybe it was crazy, but I did understand. I'd lost my old family, and I'd tried to use Fletcher and the others as a substitute. But I'd held on to them too tightly and had been too afraid they'd be taken away from me like my mother and sisters. Fletcher had wanted me to see that it didn't matter where I was or whom I was with, as long as I kept fighting—and that's exactly what I'd done today.

"So does this mean that I can come back home to the Pork Pit with you?" I asked in a soft voice, trying to keep the hope out of my face.

"There was never any question of that," Fletcher said in a gruff tone. "I was going to give you until sunset, and then I was going to come and get you if you couldn't or wouldn't find your way down the mountain. I already love you like you're my own daughter, Gin. Nothing will ever change that. But assassinating people is a dangerous business, no matter if you're doing it for money or love or something else. I'm not always going to be around to protect or help you. Even if I were, we're not always going to agree on how to do things. In the end, you have only yourself to depend on. It's up to you to make sure that you're strong enough to handle the hurts and disappointments that come your way—no matter what they are."

I stood there and thought about the old man's words. After a few moments, I nodded, telling him that I agreed with him and that all was forgiven, if not forgotten.

Fletcher smiled again. "Now that you've conquered your fear, you're ready for the next step. But that's a talk that can wait for another day. Right now, I'm ready to go home. Are you?"

I nodded again.

The old man held out his arms. I hesitated, then stepped into his warm embrace . . .

My eyes fluttered open. For a moment, I was back there in the woods, safe in the old man's strong arms, but the ghostly warmth of his embrace faded all too quickly, the way the best dreams, the best memories, always do. I focused on the beige ceiling above my head, wondering where I was, since the ones in Fletcher's house were all white. It took me several seconds to realize I was back in the beach house in Blue Marsh. I vaguely remembered knocking on the back door, but what happened after that was just a blur of color, light, and noise.

A faint fluttering sound caught my attention, and I turned my head to the right without thinking. I winced and tensed up, waiting for the pain of Dekes's bites to shoot through my neck and shoulders, along with the agony of my broken collarbone, but the sharp, stabbing sensations didn't come. A second later, I realized why.

A dwarf sat beside my bed, flipping through a thick beauty magazine, looking just as polished and put together as the cover model. Her white-blond hair was arranged in a series of perfect curls on top of her head, and her makeup looked just as soft, fresh, and pretty as if she'd applied it a moment ago. She wore a pale pink sundress that looked like it was her Sunday best, and a string of pearls dangled from her neck. Her feet were bare like always, although hot-pink polish gleamed on her toenails.

She must have sensed me watching her because she looked up from her magazine. Her eyes were clear—colorless, really—except for the pinpricks of black in the centers of her irises. A smile spread across her middle-aged face, causing laugh lines to crease in the corners of her eyes and mouth.

"Welcome back to the land of the living, darling," Jo-Jo said.

❖ 19 ❖

I frowned and sat up in bed. "Jo-Jo? What are you doing here?"

Jolene "Jo-Jo" Deveraux put her beauty magazine down on the nightstand beside her elbow. "Why, patching you up, of course."

I shook my head. "But I don't understand. Why aren't you home in Ashland at your salon?"

Jo-Jo owned one of the busiest beauty salons in the city. She jokingly referred to herself as a *drama mama* because she made a very, very good living gussying up women of all shapes, sizes, and ages for everything from beauty pageants to weddings to fancy dinners with their rich husbands.

One of the reasons Jo-Jo's salon was so popular was that she used her Air elemental magic to augment the more standard waxing, plucking, teasing, curling, perming, dyeing, tanning, and other beauty treatments she offered. Letting an Air elemental blast your skin with a pure oxygen facial was a great way to keep Father Time at bay, although some people took it too far, getting so many facials that their skin took on a tight, slick, sandblasted look. Jonah McAllister was infamous for having a face that was smoother than a twenty-year-old's, despite being in his sixties with a thick coif of silver hair.

My thoughts darkened at the thought of the smug, smarmy lawyer and how he'd managed to fuck me over from hundreds of miles away. I was going to have to do something about McAllister when I got back to Ashland—something bloody, violent, and permanent. Despite the fact that I'd killed Mab, McAllister was still determined to be the death of me. Last night the lawyer had almost succeeded in taking me down by proxy by siccing Dekes on me. Oh, yes. McAllister was definitely on my to-do list now.

"Correction, I *was* in Ashland," Jo-Jo said, answering my question. "But Finn called me and Sophia early yesterday morning talking about some sort of trouble you'd run into down here and how you were probably going to need my services before it all was said and done."

So Finn had phoned Jo-Jo even before he and Owen had left Ashland. Well, that explained why the dwarf was here. I didn't mind Finn calling in reinforcements, though. I'd needed them.

"So Sophia and I loaded up the convertible, dropped Rosco off with Eva and Violet, and came on down," Jo-Jo added. "Eva's staying with Violet at Warren's house, and the girls were more than happy to watch Rosco for a few days."

Rosco was Jo-Jo's tubby basset hound and quite possibly the laziest dog on the planet. He wouldn't even get out of his wicker basket in the corner of the salon unless there was food in the offing or a chance of getting his fat tummy rubbed. No doubt Eva Grayson and her best friend, Violet Fox, would spoil the dog even more than Jo-Jo already did.

"Once Rosco was taken care of, Sophia and I drove down lickety-split, since I had a feeling that you'd need me," Jo-Jo continued.

In addition to being able to heal others, Jo-Jo also had a bit of precognition. Her Air magic let her hear all the whispers on the wind, all the possibilities and hints of things that might come to pass, just like my Stone magic muttered to me of all the things that had already come to be, all the ways and all the places that people had hurt the others around them.

"Good thing too, since you showed up this morning looking like death warmed over. But I took care of that."

The dwarf reached over and patted my hand. Along with dolling up the folks who came into her salon, Jo-Jo also happened to be one of the best healers around. I'd lost count of the number of times she'd patched me up when I'd shown up at her house late at night, covered with blood and bruises from my latest job as the Spider.

The needles that I'd sensed when I'd been weaving in and out of consciousness hadn't been Dekes at all—the pricking sensation had been Jo-Jo using her magic on me. The dwarf could tap into and control all the natural gases in the air the way that I could the stone around me. That's how Air elementals healed others—by grabbing hold of the oxygen in the atmosphere and forcing it to circulate through wounds, cleaning out the cuts and scrapes, and making the molecules mend together all the rips, tears, and holes in someone's skin—in *my* skin.

I reached up and touched my right shoulder; my collarbone was completely mended, the broken bones fused together and in their appropriate places once more. I'd expected nothing less, but still, something felt slightly off, like I wasn't completely healed, although I knew that Jo-Jo wouldn't have stopped using her Air magic on me until I was fully well again.

Thinking about the dwarf's magic made me reach for my own power, and it was then that I realized what was wrong with me, what was missing—my magic.

I was always aware of my Ice and Stone magic, of the elemental power flowing through my veins, the way that a giant or dwarf would subconsciously sense their own inherent strength or humans would their fingers and toes. But now, that hidden force wasn't there anymore. It was like a piece of my heart had been cut out and all that was left was an empty, aching chasm inside my chest. In a way, I felt as cold, numb, and dead inside as I had in the library last night after Dekes had shot me with that tranquilizer dart.

"It's gone," I whispered, looking at Jo-Jo. "My magic's gone."

The dwarf shook her head. "Not gone, darling. Not entirely. Your gas tank's just running a little low right now. That's what happens when a vampire sucks so much blood out of you. Reach for your power, really concentrate, and you'll see what I mean."

I did as she said. It took a moment, but I realized Jo-Jo was right. My magic was still there, that cool power deep down in the very center of my being—but there was just barely any of it to work with. I reached for my power. A few silvery sparks of magic flickered in my hand, centered over the spider rune scar in my palm, but that was it. There was no bright glow, no cold crystals, and no other indication that I had any kind of real elemental power at all. I grabbed my magic again, and the same thing happened. After a moment, I let go of my power completely. I didn't want to waste what little I had left.

"A vampire sucking out someone's magic is one of the few things that even I can't heal," Jo-Jo said. "I'm sorry, Gin. I wish I could fix it for you like I did everything else."

I shrugged, struggling not to let her see just how upset I was, how hollow and empty I felt without my magic. "You did the best you could. It's not your fault. Believe me, I'm plenty grateful for everything you did heal."

I hesitated. "But how long will it take? For my magic to come back? Will it even . . . come back?"

Jo-Jo reached over and clasped my hand. "Of course it will come back. No matter what, your magic is a part of you, Gin. It comes from *you*, not anyone else. Never doubt that."

Her words made some of the tightness in my chest ease.

"As for exactly when it will come back . . ." This time, Jo-Jo shrugged. "It's hard to say. It will probably take a few days, at the very least."

My stomach clenched. "That long?"

Jo-Jo nodded. "You're a strong elemental, Gin, with a lot of raw power, but Dekes took almost everything you had last night. Your blood, your magic, and almost your life. Your neck was the worse mess that I've seen a vampire make in a long time."

My fingers eased over to my neck, but the skin there was smooth and unbroken, and I knew there wouldn't be any marks of Dekes's vicious attack on me—not on the outside, anyway. But the vamp had hurt me more than I would have liked to admit, making me feel something that I didn't often experience—fear.

The image of him rose up in my mind, his eyes glowing with my Ice and Stone magic, my blood smeared all over his lips, his fangs gleaming like crimson-coated daggers in his mouth. Phantom pain lanced through my neck, and my whole body tightened, as if the vamp were here and getting ready to sink his teeth into me again.

"Do you want to talk about it?" Jo-Jo asked in a soft voice.

Despite how tightly I held on to my emotions, the dwarf could always sense when I was struggling with something—that's how well she knew me.

I shifted on the bed. "The bastard gnawed on my neck like a dog chewing a bone. He hurt me, Jo-Jo. More than I thought he would, more than I thought he *could*. I didn't think there was anyone as powerful as Mab, but Dekes showed me just how wrong I was last night. I stupidly thought I could go in and take care of him as easily as I did his men at the hotel, but he almost killed me instead. Hell, he *would* have killed me if I hadn't managed to play dead. It was just dumb luck on my part that I got away from him."

"Your fight with Mab was a long time coming," Jo-Jo said, her clear eyes locking with my gray ones. "You've focused so much energy on her these past few months that you've turned a blind eye to everything else. The fact is that there are people out there who are just as dangerous as Mab ever was, some of them with magic, and some of them without. The Fire elemental dying at your hands doesn't change that."

"So what do I do about it?" I asked, feeling just as lost as if I were still plodding through the dark marsh.

Jo-Jo smiled and patted my hand. "You do what you always do, darling. You keep going and fighting and struggling—and then you take the bastard down any way you can."

The dwarf got up and started moving around the room, humming under her breath as she gathered up some clean towels and clothes so I could take a shower and wash the rest of the stink of the long night off me. I sat there on the bed and watched her work, turning over her words in my mind.

Jo-Jo was right. I'd been so focused on Mab that I'd forgotten that someone didn't have to be an elemental to be dangerous—and that a vampire could kill me as easily as anyone else could. Whether I liked it or not, Dekes had almost done the deed so many others had tried to do and failed. But even worse, the vampire had scared me. I'd accepted that Mab would probably get the best of me, but I hadn't thought Dekes would be such a threat, that he could come so close to killing me. The vampire had proved to me just how wrong I'd been. Sure, I'd had something of a deadline, given Callie's situation, but I'd been stupid, arrogant, and sloppy even to waltz into his mansion without more information, especially about what kind of elemental magic he did or didn't have, and I'd almost paid the ultimate price for my foolishness.

But if there was one thing I was good at, it was learning from my mistakes. Yes, Dekes had gotten the best of me last night, but I was still alive, still breathing, which meant I still had another chance to take the vamp down.

Jo-Jo might have healed my wounds from Dekes's gruesome bites, but the horror that I'd endured at the vampire's hands had still scarred me. The vicious brutality of his attack had left its own grooves and nicks on my black heart, right alongside the ones that Mab, LaFleur, Elliot Slater, and so many others had before.

But I'd repaid those marks in spades to the people who'd caused them—and I was going to do the same thing to Dekes very, very soon.

I got out of bed, took a shower, and put on some clean clothes. I still felt a little tired, the way I always did whenever Jo-Jo used her Air magic to bring me back from the brink of death. It would take my mind a few hours to play catch-up and realize that my body was whole and well once more. Normally, I would have gone back to bed for a few more hours, but I couldn't rest today.

Not while Callie was still in danger. Not while Vanessa and her sister were still being held hostage at the vampire's mansion. Not while Randall Dekes was still breathing. I'd rest after the vamp was dead.

It was going to be sooner than he'd ever fucking dreamed.

It was noon now, and the others were waiting in the downstairs living room, staring out at the ocean without really seeing the waves or the bright, sunny beauty of the day. They all jumped to their feet when I came into the room, and Owen immediately wrapped his arms around me, holding me tight. I buried my face in his neck and breathed in, letting his scent fill my nose.

"I was so worried about you," he whispered.

"I know. I'm sorry."

I didn't tell him that something like this wouldn't happen again because we both knew it would. Like it or not, violence was a part of my life. It had been ever since I was thirteen, and it wouldn't stop now just because Mab was dead. But I was the Spider, and Fletcher had trained me to face whatever the world threw my way. He'd made me strong enough to do it time and time again, to take my licks and come back even tougher and more determined than before. I wasn't about to disappoint the old man now, even if he was dead and gone.

I pulled back, stood on my tiptoes, and gently kissed Owen. He returned my kiss, drew back, and rested his forehead against mine—just holding me like I was holding him. I closed my eyes and concentrated on the feel of his body against mine, letting his warmth spill into the cold, dark places in my heart and mute the horrors I'd faced last night. And then I sighed with relief, with love, with everything I felt for him but always had so much trouble putting into words.

"I know," he whispered again. "Me too."

I could have spent the rest of the day in Owen's strong, comforting embrace, but as tempting as that was, it wouldn't solve the problem of how to kill Dekes. Like it or not, it was time for me to put on my game face again.

So I opened my eyes and pressed another kiss to Owen's lips before slipping out of his arms and heading into the kitchen.

I pulled open the refrigerator door and eyed all the vittles inside that we'd brought home from the grocery store yesterday, before moving over and doing the same thing to the cabinets. Once I'd taken stock of everything, I started grabbing the items I wanted. Buttermilk, flour, cornmeal, chicken, olive oil, shortening, salad fixings, and more soon crowded onto the kitchen counters.

"You're not seriously going to cook now, are you?" Bria asked, eyeing the boxes and bottles that I'd lined up in neat rows. "Shouldn't you still be resting?"

"I think I've rested enough," I said. "Besides, I'm starving. Being drained by a vamp will do that to a girl."

My sister didn't smile at my gallows humor, but she did step into the kitchen and start rifling through the drawers, looking for dishes, glasses, silverware, and more. Finn, Owen, Sophia, and Jo-Jo settled themselves around the long, square table in the dining room that branched off the kitchen.

I washed my hands and got to work. First I added a generous dash of salt and black pepper to the flour that I'd poured into a small, shallow dish. Then I cleaned and soaked the chicken in a bowl full of buttermilk before dredging it in the flour mixture. A few seconds later, the first piece sizzled when I put it in the skillet full of olive oil that I'd heated on the stove. More pieces joined that first one, until the smell of meat filled the kitchen. Once I got all the chicken in the skillet, I took the rest of the buttermilk that was left in the carton and mixed it with the remaining cornmeal, forming a thick, creamy batter, while a black cast-iron skillet went into the preheated oven so that the shortening I'd coated it with would melt.

Cooking was one of my passions in life, and it never failed to make me feel better, even if I'd almost had my neck chewed off by a vamp last night. The familiar motions of mixing and stirring soothed me, as did the aromatic smells of the hot oil and spicy seasonings in the air. By the time I slid a pan of cornbread into the oven to bake, I was starting to feel like my old self.

While I got started on a spring spinach salad, I told the others what had happened at Dekes's mansion. How the vamp had known who I was thanks to McAllister and how Dekes had used Vanessa and Victoria as hostages against me and drugged me into submission. How I'd pretended to be dead and had found my way through the marsh over here to the other side of the island. The only things I skimmed over were the brutal details of the vamp's attack on me and that he'd almost torn my throat open in order to get every drop of magic he could out of my blood.

"So he's using the two women against each other," Finn said. "Vanessa can't leave or fight back because Dekes has Victoria as leverage."

"And he's draining the blood and their magic out of them again and again," I said. "That's probably why I didn't sense Vanessa's magic, because Dekes had recently fed off her. And Victoria was in really bad shape: thin, unconscious, and anemic. It won't be long before Dekes kills her. Then he'll do the same thing to Vanessa because he won't have her sister to keep her in line anymore. After that, he'll find some more elemental women, bring them to his mansion, and do the same thing to them. He's one sick bastard."

"Sick," Sophia rasped.

The sound of the Goth dwarf's hoarse, broken voice reminded me that I wasn't the only one here who'd been tortured. Many years ago, Sophia had been kidnapped by a man named Harley Grimes and had been forced to submit to all the unspeakable things Grimes had done to her, including making her breathe in elemental Fire, which had destroyed her vocal cords. Jo-Jo could have easily healed Sophia and made her voice whole once more, but the Goth dwarf had refused her sister's offer. I supposed Sophia felt the same way about her ruined vocal cords as I did about my spider rune scars. They were both reminders of what we'd gone through—of what we'd survived.

I looked at Sophia and saw the sadness that always glittered in her black eyes. My suffering at the hands of Dekes had been nothing to what she'd endured with Grimes. Somehow, the dwarf had found the strength to survive all the horrors Grimes had inflicted on her. She was one of the strongest people I knew, and she made me want to be just as tough as she was. I was going to be, I vowed. Because I'd be damned if I left Blue Marsh while Dekes was still alive.

"So what happened on your end?" I asked, turning the pieces of chicken over in the skillet so that the other sides could brown.

Finn shrugged. "We could all tell that Dekes's giants were getting a little too interested in us, especially after you left with the man himself. So I suggested to Bria and Owen that we make good our getaway. We slipped away from the pool, but two of the giants followed us. They chased us into another wing of the mansion, well away from the press conference."

"Did you have any trouble with them?" I asked.

"Not after I blasted the first one's brains out of his skull with the help of my new silencer," Finn said in a not-so-modest voice.

My foster brother might be a slick, polished investment banker, but he also could shoot the wings off a fly with any gun he picked up. Finn was even better with firearms than I was, and he always had one or two tucked away on his body somewhere, just like I did my knives.

I thought of my knives lying on the mantel in Dekes's library. That was something else the vampire was going to pay for—taking away my weapons.

"As you can imagine, the other guy got a little upset that his buddy's blood was all over his face," Finn continued. "Which gave Owen enough time to pick up a nearby candlestick and do his thing with it."

"It was solid silverstone," Owen said. "A couple of good whacks across the back of the head, and the second giant went down."

Not too long ago, I'd seen Owen take on a group of giants using a blacksmith's hammer, so I knew just how skilled a fighter he was. He could wield heavy, blunt weapons just as easily as I could knives.

"It was a thing of beauty, wasn't it, Owen?" Finn asked.

The two men exchanged a high five across the table. Bria rolled her eyes and shook her head at their antics.

"And while the boys were congratulating themselves on their awesomeness," Bria said, "I grabbed another candlestick and took care of a third giant who'd snuck up behind them and was about to squeeze Finn's head between his hands like it was an oversize lemon."

Finn draped his arm over my sister's shoulders and pulled her close. "Something that I will be forever grateful for, cupcake."

"If you don't stop calling me *cupcake*, I'll hit you with the candlestick next time," Bria groused, but she couldn't hide the smile on her face.

"Anyway," Owen said. "We came back here to the beach house to wait for you."

"But I didn't show up."

Owen's eyes met mine. "No, you didn't show up."

Nobody said anything, but I could see just how concerned the others had been about me. Just thinking about what Dekes had done to me last night made their faces tighten with worry—even Bria's.

Owen cleared his throat. "So we got some more guns and some more weapons, and we went back out to Dekes's mansion. But everything seemed normal there. None of the guards looked worried, and there was nothing to indicate that anything out of the ordinary had happened. It didn't even look like there was much of a fuss being made over the giants we'd killed earlier. We didn't know what to think, and we were about to storm the mansion when Finn got a call from Sophia, saying you'd come here to the house after all. We got back as quickly as we could."

I knew what had happened after that. Jo-Jo had healed me, and the others had tried to get some sleep while they waited for me to wake up.

By the time we all got caught up, the food was ready. Buttermilk fried chicken, hot, crusty cornbread, a baby spinach salad with diced tomatoes, shredded cheddar cheese, red onion, and crispy bacon crumbles, a roasted veggie medley of red potatoes, carrots, and zucchini. I even used the limes in a basket on the counter to make a tart, tangy limeade.

We fell silent as we ate, and I relished every single bite, enjoying the play of sweet and salty, hot and sour, on my tongue. I hadn't been kidding when I'd said I was starving, and I ate more than everyone else combined. But no matter how much I ate, it didn't quite fill in the hollow ache I felt deep down inside, in the place where my magic would normally be. Still, I stuffed myself, knowing I'd need the energy for the long night ahead—because Dekes wasn't living to see another sunrise.

Not when he had two women under his thumb and could kill them at any time. At first, I'd only wanted to protect Callie from the vamp, but Vanessa and Victoria needed my help as well. And after what had happened last night, things were personal between me and Dekes, and there was only one way they were going to end—with the vampire dead at my feet.

We'd just finished eating when a sharp rap sounded on the front door.

A second later, we were all in motion. Finn and Bria pulled guns out from against the smalls of their backs and took up positions close to the front door, while Owen and Sophia slipped into the rear of the house to see if there was anyone waiting to come in from that direction. Jo-Jo stood against a wall out of Finn's and Bria's lines of fire, her Air magic making her eyes glow a faint, milky white, ready to either attack or heal with her power. I grabbed a knife out of the butcher's block in the kitchen and stood at an angle behind the front door.

The rap sounded again, a little harder this time. Whoever was outside knew we were in here and wasn't going to take no for an answer. Worst mistake they'd ever made, even if they didn't know it yet.

Finn looked at me and raised his eyebrows in a silent question. I nodded back, telling him I was ready. Finn put his gun down by his leg and opened the door, ready to smile and send whoever was outside on their merry way if they'd knocked on our door by mistake—or raise up his weapon and blast them if it wasn't a mistake. And if Finn didn't finish the job, I'd step up with my knife and make sure that they got the point.

But instead of Dekes or his goons, Donovan stood outside on the porch. The detective glared at Finn a second before shoving his way into the beach house.

Finn shook his head. "Stand down!" he called out so that Sophia and Owen would hear him in the back of the house.

"Where the hell is Gin?" Donovan muttered, moving deeper into the hallway inside the front door. "I know she's here, since this is the address where Bria told Callie you all were staying at. I need to talk to Gin—right now."

I stepped out from behind the door. "Right here, Detective. Is there something I can help you with?"

Donovan whirled around in surprise. His eyes fell to the knife that I clutched in my hand, and his face hardened that much more.

"You're not as clever as you think you are," the detective said in a harsh voice. "You never are."

"What do you mean by that?" I asked.

"It means that Randall Dekes is still alive and well."

I shrugged. "So? If I remember correctly, you didn't want me to kill the vamp in the first place."

"I didn't then, but things have changed."

My eyes narrowed at his cold, angry, frustrated tone. "What happened?"

Donovan sighed and ran a hand through his black hair. "The bastard came to my house and took Callie."

❊ 20 ❊

Donovan pointed his finger at me, anger making his eyes glimmer like gold coins in his face. "Dekes took Callie, and it's your fault. He wasn't scared off by you at all. Instead, your little talk with him only made him that much more determined to get her restaurant no matter what, and the sooner the better."

Yeah, I'd fucked up and underestimated Dekes, but the detective's self-righteous tone still grated on my nerves. Donovan had no idea what I'd been through in the last few hours—and the horrors that were in store for Callie if we didn't get to her in time.

"Actually, Dekes and I didn't do much talking," I snapped. "Since he already knew who I was and that I was coming for him."

My sharp words penetrated some of Donovan's anger, making him frown. "What do you mean?"

"I mean that Dekes used my neck like it was his own personal blood bank last night," I said. "Jonah McAllister tipped him off that I was an assassin, that I was the Spider, so Dekes and his men were waiting for me. I barely got out of his mansion alive."

I didn't tell Donovan all the gory details about Dekes's frenzied attack on me. There was no point in it. The detective would secretly think I'd gotten exactly what I'd deserved, and it would only make him worry that much more about Callie. As convoluted as my feelings were for Donovan, Callie didn't deserve what was going to happen to her at Dekes's hands, and I wasn't going to paint the detective a picture just to get back at him for all the hurt he'd caused me. I might be a coldhearted bitch, but I tried to keep my pettiness in check. Most of the time, anyway.

"You know, Donovan, you look exceptionally well for a man whose fiancée was kidnapped," Owen drawled, walking over to stand by my side.

Sophia slipped into the room behind Owen, and Jo-Jo came in from the kitchen. The two dwarven sisters sat down on one of the couches while Finn and Bria moved to stand behind them, guns down by their sides.

"What the hell is that supposed to mean?" Donovan snapped.

"It means that you don't have a mark on you, Detective," Owen said in a soft voice. "Not a single scratch. Some of us fight back to protect the people that we love. But somehow, you never seem to."

The detective's face tightened until his lips were just a thin white slash against his bronze skin. Owen wasn't just talking about Callie, and we all knew it—especially Donovan.

"I wasn't there when it happened," Donovan ground out the words through clenched teeth. "I got called out on a case this morning. Vandalism and broken windows at an empty vacation home on the other side of the island. Now I know it was obviously a ruse to lure me away. When I came back, the front door was kicked in, the house was a mess, and Callie was gone. She wasn't in the house, she wasn't at the restaurant, and she wasn't answering her cell. One of the neighbors finally told me that she'd seen a couple of giants drag Callie out of the house kicking and screaming and shove her into the back of a black town car—and that Dekes got inside after her."

The detective's hands curled into fists, and he glared at Owen, daring him to say another word. Owen's violet eyes narrowed in response, and his lips quirked up into a hard smile, a clear indication that he was ready to rumble. I stepped in between the two men and held up my hands.

"Oh, cut the macho bullshit," I said. "Fighting among ourselves won't do a damn thing to help Callie, and we all know it. Rescuing her is what's really important, especially after what happened last night."

Donovan glared at Owen for several more tense seconds before turning his gaze to me. "And what was that? What did Dekes do to you?"

I shrugged. "The usual. Crowing about what a badass he was. Threats of torture. Some other assorted violence before I made good my escape."

My words were light, but Donovan must have realized there was more that I wasn't telling him. For a moment, I almost thought I saw a flicker of concern in his eyes, but his face hardened once more, smothering the soft emotion.

"Gin's right," Bria said. "Dekes has Callie. We should be focusing on how we're going to get her back, not wasting time pointing fingers at each other."

"*We're* not going to do anything," Donovan growled at her. "Callie's *my* fiancée. I'll get her back on my own terms. I don't need your help, and I especially don't want Gin's so-called help. You're a detective, Coolidge. You should man up and act like a real cop instead of just pretending to care about the law whenever it suits you."

Bria stiffened, and anger blazed in her blue eyes— more anger than I'd ever seen her show before, except maybe when she'd first realized that I was the Spider. Her hand tightened around the gun that she was still holding, and I got the distinct impression that my baby sister would love nothing more at that moment than to raise up the weapon, pull the trigger, and put a few bullets into Donovan's chest. Instead, she shoved her gun at Finn.

"Hold this," she growled.

Bria stalked around the couch and walked up until she was standing nose to chest with Donovan. The detective glared down at her, still spoiling for a fight.

"Callie might be your *fiancée*, but she's my *friend*," Bria spat out the words. "She's my best friend, and I love her like a sister. Now she's in the hands of a very bad man, and instead of asking us for our help to get her back, you're bitching at me about the fucking *law*. What the hell is wrong with you?"

For the first time since he'd stormed into the beach

house, uncertainty filled Donovan's features, and some of the anger in his eyes dimmed.

"You're a cop," he said. "You should understand where I'm coming from."

Bria drew in a breath, trying to get her temper under control. "I do understand, and most of the time, I'd agree with you. But Randall Dekes doesn't play by the rules, and he couldn't care less about the law. So I say we forget the rules and do whatever we have to in order to rescue Callie before Dekes kills her."

Donovan shook his head. "You know, you might pretend to be a cop, but deep down, you're no better than Gin is, always thinking that murdering someone is the only way to solve a problem."

"No," Bria snarled. "My sister's better than I am because she doesn't pretend to be anything other than what she is, and she always does exactly what she says she will. She's better than you are too, even if you're too much of a dumbass to realize it."

Surprised, I looked at my sister. Most of the time, Bria said the same things to me that Donovan had just spouted to her. That I was knife-happy and preferred to kill people rather than actually find another, less violent way to deal with them. Part of me knew that was true, that I did prefer to assassinate first and ask questions later. That's how Fletcher had trained me, and that's what had helped me survive so many bad situations over the years. But this was the first time I'd ever heard my sister defend me and my tactics, and I didn't quite know what to make of it.

Donovan bristled and opened his mouth to argue with Bria some more, but Sophia let out a loud, earsplitting whistle. Startled, we all looked at the Goth dwarf, who pointed her finger at Jo-Jo.

"Listen," Sophia rasped.

"*Enough*," Jo-Jo said, a hint of steel ringing in her soft voice. "That's enough. Every second that we waste arguing is another one that Callie spends with Dekes. And none of us want that, now, do we?"

The dwarf's clear eyes moved from face to face, and one by one, we all shook our heads.

"I didn't think so," Jo-Jo said. "Now, instead of arguing with each other, we are all going to sit down and talk about how we can rescue that poor girl, calmly and rationally, with no more snotty comments or accusations. Is that understood?"

We all murmured our agreement, except for Donovan. The detective glared at us all in turn before his gaze cut back to Jo-Jo. He gave her the evil eye as well, but the dwarf stared right back at him, her perfectly sculpted eyebrows raised in a silent question. Finally, Donovan sighed and gave in.

"Yes, ma'am," he said.

Jo-Jo nodded her head, graciously accepting his reluctant acquiescence. "Good. Now let's get started."

We all grumbled a little more, but thanks to Jo-Jo's chastising we sat down and got to work. Finn fetched his briefcase from one of the bedrooms and spread out all the information that he'd dug up on Dekes. Then he flipped on his laptop and started looking for anything that he'd missed or anything else that might help us rescue Callie.

I also explained to Donovan about Vanessa and Victoria and how we were going to save the two women as well. I told the detective how Dekes had been using the two sisters, feeding on their blood and the elemental magic that it contained. My intent wasn't to scare him or to get him to worry even more about Callie but instead to make him realize exactly what kind of monster we were going up against—and that killing Dekes was the only option now.

Donovan's features twisted with disgust when I finished. "So Dekes married Vanessa just so he could feed off her Fire magic? That's despicable."

"Yes, it is."

The detective's gaze fell to my neck. "Is that what Dekes did to you last night? Did he try to feed on your elemental power too? You have Ice and Stone magic, right? That's what all the rumors claim, anyway, the ones I heard after you killed Mab."

Once again, I saw that flash of concern in his eyes, and I wondered if maybe Owen was right after all—if Donovan still cared about or wanted me in some small fashion. If he did, he had a hell of a way of showing it.

"Yes, Dekes fed on me too," I said in a quiet voice. "It was . . . unpleasant."

I didn't say anything else, and Donovan didn't ask me any more questions. He didn't want to know anyway—not really. It would only make him feel guiltier about not being there to stop Dekes and his men from taking Callie. But my words had one positive affect—Donovan didn't raise any more objections about my killing the vampire.

"So Dekes has your Ice and Stone magic now, along with Vanessa's Fire and Victoria's Air magic? Fuck," Finn said.

"That's going to make it that much tougher for us to rescue the women and get out of the mansion, if not impossible."

The others murmured similar concerns, but I looked at Finn.

"Nothing's impossible. Remember Fletcher telling us that?"

Finn nodded.

"Besides, you know as well as I do that you don't need magic to kill someone. Don't you worry about Dekes. I'll take care of him."

I didn't tell the others that I had the same concerns they did about Dekes and that my own magic wasn't a hundred percent. There was no use worrying them. Besides, magic or no magic, I wasn't leaving the women to the vampire's mercy. I was getting them away from that bastard no matter what.

"How do we even know that Callie's still alive?" Owen asked. "According to what the detective said, Dekes has had her for at least two hours now. He could have killed her already."

I shook my head. "No, I don't think he's killed her yet. Dekes announced his casino yesterday, and he's getting ready to break ground on the project, remember? He can't afford any more delays. Callie has to sign over the restaurant to him first before he gets rids of her. Otherwise, the property would just pass to her next of kin, whoever that is, and be tied up that much longer."

Donovan shifted on the far end of the couch. "Actually, that would be me. Callie's parents died last year, and when we got engaged, she changed her will to make me her sole beneficiary."

Finn arched an eyebrow. "Well, how very nice for you, Detective."

Donovan's hands balled into fists in his lap, but he didn't respond to Finn's mocking taunt.

"So he gets Callie to sign over the restaurant to him; then what?" Bria asked.

I picked up one of the photos that Finn had shown us yesterday when we'd had brunch at the restaurant. This one showed an ashy husk of a man, burned to a crisp inside his own home. "Then, sometime later on tonight, Dekes and his men take Callie out to the restaurant, tie her up inside, and burn the Sea Breeze to the ground around her. Everyone will know what happened, but nobody will be brave enough to do anything about it, not even the cops. Dekes's stranglehold on the island will finally be complete, and all that will be left to do is clear away the charred rubble so the construction on the casino can start up. Two birds, one stone, and all that."

Donovan stared at the gruesome photo in my hands a second before looking away. "So how do we stop that from happening?"

"We slip into Dekes's mansion and grab her back," I said. "The vampire thinks I'm dead, and that Finn, Bria, and Owen are either in hiding or on the run. The bastard thinks he's already won. He might be wondering whether you're going to show up at his front door, flashing your badge and demanding to know where Callie is, but that's all. He's probably walking through his mansion right now, wondering what poor woman he can feed off next and admiring those creepy collections of his."

I'd told the others about the things that Dekes had shown me when we'd been touring the mansion last night. The dolls, the pirate treasure, the open lockets with their curls of hair, and all the other odd knickknacks the vamp had accumulated during his time here on earth—time that was rapidly drawing to a close.

Finn perked up. "What part of the mansion were the gold and jewels in again? I want to be sure to visit *that* particular room."

Donovan shot him an angry glare.

"After we've rescued Callie, of course," Finn added in a hasty tone.

We worked out a simple plan. Finn, Bria, and Sophia would cause a distraction in front of the house, drawing the giant guards in that direction, while Donovan, Owen, and I slipped into the back of the mansion. Jo-Jo would be outside the front gate and parked down the street in Finn's Escalade, waiting to pick everyone up and whisk us back to the beach house after we'd rescued Callie.

The others focused on where Dekes might have Callie stashed in the mansion, as well as where Vanessa and Victoria might be. I sat there and reviewed the blueprints that Finn had one of his contacts get for him, but my mind was already skipping ahead to what I would do about the vampire once I found him. Rescuing the three women was my first priority—that was the most important thing. I wanted them out of harm's way before anything else went down, but I had no intention of leaving the mansion until Dekes was dead.

The problem was that I just didn't know exactly how I was going to make that happen.

Dekes was a vampire who'd been sucking down blood for three hundred and some odd years. At the very least, that meant that he was physically stronger than me, his senses were sharper, and his reflexes were quicker, something he'd proved when he shot me with that dart gun last night. Then there was the small matter of the *kind* of blood that Dekes indulged in on a regular basis—elemental blood. I didn't know how long he'd been feeding off Vanessa and Victoria, but the vamp had used their Fire and Air magic last night with ease, like he'd been born an elemental himself—and now he had my Ice and Stone power running through his veins as well.

Any way you looked at it, Dekes would have the advantage. If he didn't kill me with his stolen elemental magic, he could always finish the job with his fists—or fangs.

Owen must have sensed some of what I was thinking because he leaned over and threaded his fingers through mine, his simple touch warming my whole body the way it always did.

"Don't worry," he whispered in a voice that only I could hear. "You'll get him, and I'll be right there to help you."

I nodded, not quite trusting myself to speak and voice all the doubts that were swirling through my mind, doubts about whether I could kill Randall Dekes—or if I'd end up being another one of the vampire's victims before the night was through.

❋ 21 ❋

Just before dusk that evening, I found myself in the marsh once more, staring at the back of Dekes's enormous estate. Jo-Jo had dropped Donovan, Owen, and me off about a mile away before getting into position closer to the front of the mansion. The three of us had left the road behind and made our way through the marsh, keeping to the high ground as much as possible. Now we huddled in a patch of swamp grass and cattails, watching a pair of giant guards walk a slow circuit around a patio on the back side of the mansion.

So far, I'd seen only the two men, but I knew there would be more inside the house, if only to keep an eye on Callie, Vanessa, and Victoria. The Fire elemental especially bore watching. Dekes might think he had Vanessa under control as long as he had Victoria for leverage, but I'd seen the hate that flashed in the Fire elemental's eyes whenever she looked at her dear husband. If Vanessa could have, she would have happily killed Dekes with her bare hands, then used her Fire magic to burn his corpse to cinders.

I wondered how much Fire power she had left, and if Dekes had weakened her as much as he had me. I had no idea how often the vamp fed from Vanessa, how much power he took when he did, or how long it took her magic to replenish itself. Hopefully, Vanessa would have enough juice left to be of some use to us.

"What are we waiting for?" Donovan muttered in the grass beside me, slapping at a mosquito that had landed on his arm. "Shouldn't Finn, Bria, and Sophia be in position already?"

My cell phone vibrated in my hand before I could tell him to be patient. I hit a button and held it up to my ear. "Talk to me, Finn."

"Looks like we've got three giant guards in the front of the house." Finn's voice was soft in my ear. "Two walking a route along the outer wall and one stationed by the front door. The gate is closed right now, but it won't be for long."

"You ready with the distraction?" I asked.

"Oh, yeah. The poor bastards will never know what hit 'em." I could hear the smug smile in his voice.

"All right. Get ready. As soon as you go, so will we. You guys search the ground floor and deal with any op-position there, and we'll take the third level and do the same. If we don't find the women there, we'll go down to the second floor and look there. Hopefully, we'll meet up somewhere in the middle."

"Got it."

Finn quit talking, but he didn't hang up. Neither did I. Instead, I kept the line open and slid the phone into one of the top pockets of my vest so I could get to it in a hurry if I needed to. Whichever group found the women first would signal the others.

I could feel Donovan's eyes on me, lingering on the vest that covered my chest. Zippered pockets stuffed with supplies covered the front of the vest, which also had a heavy layer of silverstone embedded in it. The vest was black, just like the rest of my clothes—boots, cargo pants, and a long-sleeved T-shirt. I'd pulled my hair back into a ponytail and smeared two stripes of mud under my eyes to break up the paleness of my skin.

I knew that it wasn't really the vest that got Donovan's attention but rather what it stood for. My wearing the vest meant I was creeping around in the shadows as the Spider once more, stalking my intended prey for the evening—and that he was right here beside me again, whether he wanted to be or not.

The detective sighed and looked away, checking his gun again. On the other side of me, Owen raised his eyebrows and shifted in the grass, running his fingers up and down the staff in his hands. He had shown me the long silverstone staff right before we left the beach house. Owen made weapons as a hobby, something that his elemental talent for metal helped him excel at, and the staff was his latest creation. He'd decided to bring it along when Finn called and said that Bria and I had gotten into trouble down here. Owen had put the same care into the weapon that he had the silverstone knives he'd made me, so I knew the staff would be more than adequate to help him cave in a few giants' skulls tonight.

Owen jerked his head at Donovan, but I just shrugged. I didn't care what kind of mood the detective was in as long as he helped us rescue Callie and the other two women.

As for me, Dekes might have taken my regular knives last night in the library, but that didn't mean I wasn't armed. I'd packed a couple of spare silverstone knives in my suitcase, just in case something unexpected came up while we were in Blue Marsh. One knife was in my hand, another was up my left sleeve, and the others rested in the pockets of my vest, just waiting for me to grab and use them.

Donovan let out another sigh and squirmed in the grass. "Any damn day now—"

In the distance, a sudden roar ripped through the air, and a flash of fire flared upward into the sunset sky before blooming into a black cloud of smoke. In addition to being rather handy with guns, Finn enjoyed making the occasional explosive in his spare time, and he'd just used his expertise to blast open the front gate. A few shouts rose up, followed by the sharp *crack-crack-crack* of a gun. Finn again, putting down the guards in the front of the house, along with some help from Bria. My baby sister wasn't quite as good a shot as Finn, but she could hit a giant's head at a hundred feet, which was all she needed to do tonight.

The two men guarding the back of the house froze at the sudden explosion of noise, fire, and smoke. They glanced at each other, then ran into the interior, heading for the front of the mansion to find out what the hell was going on. I waited a few seconds to see if any reinforcements would hurry outside and take up their positions, but none did.

"Let's go," I said, and slipped out of the swamp grass.

I took the lead, followed by Owen, then Donovan. The three of us sprinted around the edge of the pond that butted up against the back of the mansion and pounded up a set of stairs to the third floor. The giant guards had forgotten to lock the door to the patio in their haste to go help their friends, just like I'd hoped they would. I opened it, and we slipped inside.

We hurried down the hallway, keeping a lookout for any guards and peering into all the rooms we passed. Every single room, every single wall—hell, every single tabletop—featured some part of Dekes's collections, whether it was gleaming pirate treasure, stacks of classic albums, or other, weirder, creepier things.

"Never trust a vampire who collects dolls," Owen muttered as we passed that particular room.

We eventually came to a crossway with halls that branched off in four directions. I stopped, looking and listening, but I didn't hear anything. No footsteps, no shouts, no snaps of gunfire. I grabbed the cell phone out of my vest and held it up to my ear.

"What's your position?"

Some faint pops and crackles sounded through the phone before Finn picked up a second later. "Took out the first three guards in the front of the house, then another one who rushed out to join them. Bria, Sophia, and I are going in the front door now."

"We're on the third floor and about to start searching

the wings up here," I said. "There are probably at least two more guards coming your way. Be careful."

"Always."

I put the phone back into my vest pocket.

"Which way?" Donovan asked.

I thought back, trying to remember as much as I could from the tour Dekes had given me last night.

"Left," I said. "The library's down the right hall, and the one beside that leads down to the pool. I doubt that Callie's in either one of those places. Dekes would want her to be tucked away somewhere more secure and out of sight."

The three of us turned left and did the same procedure as before, walking quickly and quietly, weapons up and ready, keeping a watch out for any guards and peering into all the rooms that we passed. We reached another hallway, and I gestured for the others to hang back a second. I crept up to the edge of the wall, slid down until I was crouched on my knees, and slowly peered around to the other side.

Jackpot.

The hallway stretched out about thirty feet before coming to a dead end. The door at the end of the hall was shut, and a giant stood tall and stiff in front of it, a concerned look on his face and a cell phone in his left hand. That must be how he was communicating with the other guards. Judging from the loud squawks coming out of the phone, the news wasn't good.

I pulled back and got to my feet.

"I think we've found at least one of the women," I whispered to the others. "Callie most likely, since there's only one guard, a giant standing in front of what looks like a locked door. I'll deal with him. You two watch the other halls in case there are more of them lurking around."

Owen and Donovan nodded. I drew in a breath and grabbed another knife out of my vest. Neither one of the blades in my hand had my spider rune stamped into the hilt. The symbol wasn't much to look at, just a small circle surrounded by eight thin rays, but I still missed the feel of the rune pressing into the larger, matching scars on my palms. Maybe it was silly, but it comforted me to know that my knives bore my mark, my rune, my name. More than that, the weapons had been a gift from Owen, and I wasn't leaving here without them.

But I pushed those distracting thoughts away and concentrated on what I needed to do right now—kill the giant in front of me. There would be plenty of time to search for my knives once the women were free and Dekes and his men were dead.

So I tightened my grip on the blades, rounded the corner, and sprinted down the hall as fast as I could.

The giant had been murmuring something into his cell phone, but his head snapped up at the sound of my boots stomping against the stones. The giant's mouth fell open, and he blinked as if he couldn't quite believe that I was actually running at him instead of screaming, turning around, and going in the other direction. By the time his brain figured out that I was in fact real and not some weird trick of his imagination, it was too late. My knives flashed silver in the light before sinking into his chest. Three quick cuts, one to his heart, and two to his stomach, and the giant was down. Still, I leaned over and slit his throat, just to be sure.

"Clear!" I called out.

Donovan and Owen rounded the corner and hurried up behind me. Donovan rattled the door, which was locked, while Owen kept his eyes trained on the hall, watching our backs. I stooped to one knee beside the giant, ignoring the blood and guts still pouring out of his body, and started patting him down. I fished a key ring out of one of his jacket pockets and held it out to the detective.

"Here. Try one of these."

Donovan grabbed the metal ring. It took him three tries before he found the right key and the lock clicked open. Still holding his gun, Donovan grabbed the knob with his free hand. I took up a position on the opposite side and nodded at him. The detective nodded back. He threw open the door, and we both cautiously peered into the room, weapons up and ready, just in case there were more guards stationed inside.

But the room was empty—except for Callie.

She slumped on a bed in the far corner, right underneath a picture window covered with silverstone bars. She raised her head at the sound of the door opening. One of her eyes had started to blacken, and I noticed several cuts and bruises on her hands and arms, but other than that, she seemed to be in good shape. At least the skin on her neck and wrists was unbroken and not littered with bite marks like Vanessa's had been. No doubt she'd struggled with the giants who'd kidnapped her, and Dekes had probably smacked her around a little more to get her to sign over her property to him, but the vampire hadn't sunk his fangs into her.

Of course he hadn't. Callie wasn't an elemental, so she didn't have any magic he could steal. Dekes probably thought his palate far too sophisticated to sully it with mere *human* blood. It was a small favor that he hadn't bitten her, but I'd take what I could get.

"Callie!" Donovan cried out, and rushed over to her.

Callie's eyes widened at the sight of him, and she scrambled up off the bed. "Donovan! Oh, Donovan! I knew that you'd come for me! I just knew it!"

Tears streamed down her face, and she pressed her lips to his. Donovan hesitated a moment before wrapping his arms around her and pulling her close.

I wondered if the detective was thinking that he hadn't really come for his fiancée after all—I had. If Donovan could have had his way, he would have knocked on the front door and one of Dekes's giants probably would have put a bullet through his head a minute later.

But because I wasn't a total bitch, I let them kiss for a few seconds before I cleared my throat. The two of them broke apart and looked at me, Callie with fear and wariness, and Donovan with guilt.

"Come on," I said in a harsher voice than I would have liked. I wasn't jealous of Callie, not really, but the detective had never looked that relieved to see me before—something that still hurt, despite all this time. "The reunion's over. We've still got two more women to find and rescue."

Donovan nodded. He took Callie's hand and led her out of the room without a word. He didn't look at me when he passed. He didn't want to see the cold, mocking anger in my eyes.

Couldn't blame him for that.

✷22✷

We rejoined Owen in the hallway. While we'd been rescuing Callie, he'd grabbed the guard's cell phone and was listening to the crackles of conversation on the other end.

"Any sign of more guards?" I asked. "What are they saying?"

Owen shook his head. "Nothing much. I heard some footsteps and some shouts, but none of them seem to be headed in this direction. From the chatter on the phone, most of the guards are on the other side of the house, trying to figure out what's going on, who's in the mansion, and how they can stop them. I think that's where Dekes is too, although I can't be sure. They haven't said anything about Vanessa or Victoria."

"That's because the two women are probably somewhere secure already. I bet that Dekes keeps them under lock and key the whole time, except for when he needs Vanessa to make an appearance for his friends. After all, it just wouldn't do for Dekes to lose his elemental meal tickets," I said.

I pulled my own cell phone out of my vest. "Callie's secure," I said. "Repeat, Callie is secure."

"Roger that," Finn responded a second later. "Still searching the first floor. No sign of the other two women yet."

"Keep searching. We'll do the same up here."

I put the phone back in its slot on my vest, and we moved away from the door and the dead giant. We eased through the halls, looking and listening, but we didn't encounter any more guards. Finn and the others had killed four already, and I'd put another one down. That made five. I didn't know how many men Dekes had on his staff and how many might actually be in the mansion at the moment, but I was willing to bet that we'd put a good dent in their numbers.

We made it back to the crossway and started down the only other hall I hadn't explored yet. I led the way, followed by Donovan, then Callie, with Owen serving as the rear guard. We didn't pass any more of Dekes's men, but we started to hear faint shouts, screams, and scuffles. The hoarse sounds grew louder the farther we walked down the hall, peppered here and there with the sharp sting of gunfire.

Crack! Crack! Crack!

Looked like Finn, Bria, and Sophia had run into some more giants. The gunshots didn't bother me, though, because they told me that the three of them were still alive and fighting. I would have been more worried if I hadn't heard any noise at all. Besides, every once in a while,

Finn's triumphant shouts drifted out of the cell phone in the pocket of my vest, telling me that they were okay.

Eventually we reached another hallway that led to a dead end. I peered around the corner again, and just like before, I spotted a giant standing guard outside a door. Only this time he had two buddies with him. Jackpot.

I drew back before they saw me and looked at Owen. "Three of them, two of us. Care for a little tag-team action?"

Owen grinned and twirled his staff in his hands. "With you? Always."

I looked over at Donovan. "You stay here with Callie and watch our backs. We shouldn't be long."

The detective nodded and made Callie stand against the wall beside him.

I palmed a second knife and turned my attention back to Owen. "Same rush job as before, with me in the lead, drawing their gunfire. On three. One . . . two . . . three!"

We both sprinted out from around the corner and ran down the hall toward the giants. They were taken off guard just like their buddy had been before, but they recovered much quicker. One of them managed to get his gun out from under his suit jacket, raise it, and fire. I was in front of Owen, making me the target instead of him, just like I'd planned.

Crack! Crack!

Two bullets thunked into my chest, momentarily knocking me back, but the silverstone in my vest easily caught the bullets. The giant pulled the trigger again, but his buddy was also reaching for his gun at the same time and spoiled his aim. The third bullet plowed harmlessly into one of the walls.

Then Owen and I were on them, and it was far too late for guns.

Owen took the guy on the far right, bringing his staff down in a vicious arc on top of the giant's head. It wasn't enough to crack open his skull outright, but the snap of the metal was more than enough to daze him, and the giant's eyes rolled up into the back of his head. Owen brought the staff up, then swung it around, this time slamming the end of it into the guy's temple. That blow opened up a gushing wound, and the guy staggered back into the wall. Owen brought the staff around a third time, driving the end into the giant's throat. The giant immediately collapsed, choking and clawing at his crushed windpipe. Owen swung the staff a final time, snapping the giant's head to one side. The giant didn't move after that.

Meanwhile, I concentrated on the giant in the middle, the one with the gun, chopping at his hand with my knife. The blade sliced into his wrist, and he howled with pain. The gun clattered to the floor, and I used my foot to kick it behind me. The guy on the far left reached for me, but this time, his buddy stumbled into him, driving them both back against the opposite wall. After that, it was just a matter of keeping them penned in together while I went to work with my knives.

Slice-slice-slice-slice.

The blood spattered onto the wall, and they soon joined their dead friend on the floor. Once again, I leaned over and cut all their throats, just to be sure.

Never leave any enemies alive behind you. I could almost hear Fletcher whispering the words in my ear, and I was determined to follow the old man's edict tonight, when so many other lives besides mine depended on it.

Owen tried the door, but of course it was locked. I slid one of my knives up my sleeve, then dug through the giants' pockets with my free hand, but none of them had a key for the door. Not surprising. If I were Dekes and Vanessa was locked inside this room, I wouldn't be stupid enough to give the giants the key either. Because if they had a key, for whatever reason, sooner or later, one of them would be dumb enough to open the door at the wrong moment, and that's when Vanessa would strike. A couple of blasts of her Fire magic to the chest would be enough to put down a giant, and I was betting that the elemental had tried more than once to escape.

The door was made out of sturdy wood too heavy and solid to cut my way through with one of my knives, and it was reinforced with silverstone bars. Since the giants didn't have the key, that left only one way to open the door and see who was waiting on the other side.

So I tucked my other knife back up my sleeve and reached for my Ice magic—and was surprised once again at just how little there was of it. Once more, only a few silvery sparks flickered in the palm of my hand.

"Dekes," I cursed under my breath. "Randall fucking Dekes."

I'd hoped my magic might have replenished itself a bit while we'd been planning the attack on the mansion, but it didn't seem there was any more in my body than when I'd reached for it at the beach house this morning. I'd wanted at least a bit more power when I faced Dekes, but that wasn't going to happen. Since there was nothing

I could do about it, I reached for the scraps of Ice magic I had left.

This wasn't the first time that my power had been crippled. For years, I'd had problems using my Ice magic because of the silverstone that had been melted into my palms. The magic-hungry metal had simply absorbed my power instead of letting me easily release it through my hands the way other Ice elementals did theirs. I'd finally overcome the block when I fought Tobias Dawson, forcing my magic past the silverstone, and I'd been able to use it however I wanted to ever since. But thanks to Dekes sucking down my blood, I had only a small trickle of power right now, which made using it as hard as it had ever been—maybe even harder, since I was used to my magic being so much stronger.

I'd told Jo-Jo more than once that I didn't want to rely too much on my magic to get me out of trouble, but that's exactly what had happened since I killed Mab. I'd thought, with the Fire elemental dead and gone, things would be easier for me, that I'd never run into someone with that much raw elemental power ever again. As a result, I hadn't given much thought as to what I would do if my magic ever let me down or was somehow taken away from me. But I should have known by now that easy just wasn't meant to be—not for me.

For the first time in a long time, I had to struggle to bring enough magic to bear to do what I wanted. It took me a few concentrated tries, but finally I was able to form the simple shapes that I had in mind—two long, slender Ice picks.

"Are you okay?" Owen asked in a concerned voice, noticing the faint, weak sparks of my magic. "Normally, it takes you no time at all to make Ice picks."

"I'm fine," I said, not looking at him. "Just a little hic-cup with my magic. Nothing to worry about."

I slid the picks into the lock and started jiggling them around. I wasn't quite as masterful at this as Finn was, but a minute later, the tumblers slid into place, and the lock popped open. I threw the picks down on the floor to melt and got to my feet.

"Careful, now," I warned Owen as I twisted the knob. "Vanessa's probably expecting Dekes or his men."

He nodded and backed up against the wall so he wasn't directly in front of the opening. I threw open the door and did the same thing, leaping back against the opposite side of the hallway.

Good thing, since a ball of elemental Fire blasted out of the open doorway a second later.

I could feel the intense heat of the Fire as it streaked past my position, slicing down the hallway right between me and Owen. If we had been standing directly in its path, we would have been badly burned at the very least. Dekes must not have fed off Vanessa in the last few days— or maybe he just hadn't taken as much of her magic as he had mine, because it looked like she had plenty of elemental juice right now.

The ball of Fire kept going and going, seeming to grow larger and brighter as it sucked more and more oxygen into itself before finally slamming into a wooden door at the far end of the hallway. It exploded on impact, spewing red-hot flames everywhere. I heard Callie scream with fear and surprise, but since she and Donovan were around the corner, the elemental Fire had passed them by without touching or hurting them. The same couldn't be said for the other end of the hall, though. The flames quickly consumed the door and started spreading out along the walls, licking at the paintings, drapes, and furniture.

Yep, Vanessa was definitely in the room. The trick now was getting her to realize that we were friends, not foes.

I waited a few seconds, then leaned forward so that she could see my face.

Another ball of Fire immediately blasted out of the room.

I cursed and jerked back, barely managing to keep my eyebrows from being singed off. I *hated* having singed eyebrows. The flames once again slammed into the opposite end of the hall, adding more fuel and power to the ones already burning there. I'd wondered before if Vanessa would have enough elemental power to help us, but it looked like her magic had fully replenished itself. It made me feel a little better about my own power eventually coming back.

"Vanessa Suarez!" I called out. "We came here to rescue you, not be burned to a crisp! If you want to get you and your sister out of here, stop using your magic! Right now!"

No response.

I waited a few more seconds, then eased my head forward once again.

This time, nothing happened. I put my hands up in a placating gesture and tiptoed forward so that she could see me and I could see her.

Vanessa stood in the middle of a large bedroom, wearing a sleek black pantsuit and matching heels, along with her diamond-and-pearl choker and cuffs. Another ball of elemental Fire crackled in her hands. Even though I was twenty feet away from her, I could still feel the pulsing power of her magic. The feel of it lashed against my skin like a red-hot whip, making me grind my teeth in discomfort, and the spider rune scars embedded in my palms began to itch and burn, the way that they always did when I was exposed to Fire magic.

Two elements always complemented each other, like Air and Fire, and two elements always opposed each other, like Fire and Stone. Vanessa's magic was the antithesis of my own cool Ice and Stone power, hence my discomfort. But she wasn't my enemy, not like Mab had been, and I wanted to help her, not hurt her. Now the only question was whether I could convince her of that.

Vanessa's eyes narrowed at the sight of me. Surprise and wariness flashed across her face, while black fire burned in the depths of her gaze as she decided whether to go ahead and toss the ball of Fire at me and toast me where I stood. After a second, she frowned with recognition.

"You!"

"Me," I agreed. "Back from the dead again."

"You're the woman from the library last night. The one that Dekes said had Ice and Stone magic. How did you—" Her eyes narrowed a little more. "Wait a second. Cold skin, blue lips, Ice magic. You used your Ice power to make me think you were dead. Clever. Very clever."

"I do try."

"What the hell are you doing here?" she hissed.

I grinned at her. "Why, I'm here to kill your dear husband, of course."

Vanessa shook her head. "Wasn't one round with Randall enough for you?"

My grin widened. "What can I say? I'm a slow learner and a sucker for punishment. But before I track down your husband and ram my knife through his heart, I thought I'd swing by and see if you wanted some help getting out of here. Think of it as my good deed for the day. So are you coming or what?"

Vanessa didn't have to think twice about my offer. "Not without my sister. I'm not going anywhere without Victoria."

"Good answer," I said. "Because that's exactly what I would say."

I eased into the room, and Owen came with me. Vanessa eyed us and curled her fingers around the elemental Fire still burning in her hand, ready to unleash her deadly power if we made one wrong move.

Victoria lay on a bed in the corner, wearing a white silk negligee and robe and looking just as still and lifeless as she had in the library. She wasn't wearing the choker and cuffs, and I could see the puncture wounds and splotchy purple bruises from where Dekes had bitten her over and over again.

"That son of a bitch," Owen growled. "She can't be more than twenty, twenty-one. She's still a kid."

His violet eyes grew dark and stormy, and I knew he was thinking about his sister, Eva, who was around the same age.

Owen handed me his silverstone staff, then carefully scooped Victoria up off the bed, taking as much care with her as he would have if it had been Eva lying there. Vanessa watched him the whole time, but she could see the concern and anger in his face just as I could. She sighed, and the Fire burning in her hand flickered and went out. Owen nodded at her and stepped out of the room, carrying Victoria's still deadweight. I started to go after him, but Vanessa grabbed my arm. I could feel the heat of her fingers through my sleeve.

"You're really here to kill Randall?" she asked, her voice catching on the last two words.

Although she tried to hide it, one emotion flickered in her eyes now, overpowering all the others—hope. A small, tremulous hope that I really would be able to kill Dekes and end this nightmare that she and her sister had been trapped in for so long. In that moment, I knew I would have tried to save them even if the vamp hadn't attacked me. Hope. It was the one thing that kept suckering me in time after time, the one thing that always seemed to make everything I went through worthwhile in the end.

"You'd better believe it, sweetheart," I said. "I'm the Spider. If you haven't heard of me, well, you should know one thing—I never, ever go back on my word."

Vanessa nodded. That was good enough for her. She followed me out of the room, and I grabbed the cell phone out of my vest again.

"Vanessa and Victoria are secure," I said. "Let's meet up and get them out of here before I go after Dekes."

"Roger that," Finn said a few seconds later. "Let's regroup on the front lawn."

"See you there."

I put the phone away, and we moved down the hallway. Donovan and Callie were in the lead, followed by

Owen carrying Victoria, then Vanessa, then me. More shouts and screams filled the house now, along with growing clouds of black, billowing smoke. I could feel the heat of Vanessa's Fire magic still burning in the hallway behind me, gaining strength with every painting, carving, and piece of furniture it gobbled up. If Dekes didn't send some of his men to contain it, the flames could very well engulf the whole mansion and incinerate all the vamp's precious collections. What a shame that would be.

We came to another crossway. Donovan and Callie looked right, then left, before they both hurried across the open space to the hallway on the other side. Owen hefted Victoria in his arms and made it to the other side as well, along with Vanessa.

I'd just started to join them when three giants appeared at the end of the left hallway. They saw me standing there. For a moment they froze before all rushing at me at once.

Now I had a choice to make.

I could hurry and join the others, and we could try to outrun the giants and meet up with Finn, Bria, and Sophia. But I wasn't sure exactly where they were right now, and the giants knew the mansion far better than we did. Even with me acting as the rear guard, it would still put the others at risk, especially Callie and Victoria. All it took was one blow, one bullet, to end a person's life. No matter how hard I fought, the giants could always get lucky, and then someone would die.

I'd promised Bria I'd save Callie, and I'd promised Vanessa I'd get her and Victoria out of here. They'd all already suffered enough at the fangs of Randall Dekes, and I wasn't going to let the giants in front of me get their hands on the women—not now, when they were so close to being free of the vamp forever.

But even more than that, I'd made a promise to myself that Dekes would pay for what he'd done to me, and I wasn't leaving until the vamp was good and bloody and dead. I needed to kill him for my own peace of mind. If I didn't, I knew the tiny seed of fear and doubt Dekes had planted in me would grow and grow until it crippled me, until I wouldn't be able to think of anything else but my failure to kill him and take back the confidence he'd stolen, right along with my magic.

So that left option number two, which was me standing and fighting—alone—while the others escaped.

"Gin!" Donovan shouted. "Come on! We have to go. Now!"

I shook my head, and my eyes met Owen's across the distance. Gray on violet, with so many emotions crackling in the air between us. Love. Desire. Concern. But most of all, understanding.

Owen knew why I'd really come back here and what I had to do if I was going to overcome my fear and the ultimate pain of what Dekes had done to me. He hadn't said anything, but he knew I wouldn't be able to live with myself otherwise. That I wouldn't be able to be me, to be the Spider. Owen didn't like it, but he understood—he always understood me.

"Be careful," I thought he said, although I couldn't hear the words over the yells of the giants running toward me.

"Always," I replied, although I doubted he could hear me either.

My lover nodded, turned, and headed down the hallway with Victoria. A second later, Donovan let out a curse and started after him, holding Callie's hand.

Only Vanessa remained behind, frowning at me. Some emotion flared in the Fire elemental's eyes, but I couldn't tell what it was. Not with the three guards pounding toward me, getting closer with every second.

"Get out of here! Don't wait for me!" I yelled, waving my hand at her in a *go-go-go* motion.

Her tight, worried face was the last thing I saw before I turned again to face the giants.

✳ 23 ✳

Owen had given me his silverstone staff when he'd picked up Victoria, and I decided to put the weapon to good use. I tightened my grip on the staff and started twirling it in my hands, quickly getting a feel for the long weapon. Despite being made out of pure silverstone, it was surprisingly light.

The three giants rushed at me. Unlike their friends, they didn't bother going for the guns they wore under their suit jackets. No, they just wanted to get their hands on me and beat me to death, but I wasn't about to let that happen.

I stepped up to meet the first giant, slamming the staff into his chest, then pivoting and snapping it around and down, driving it into his left knee and making him lose his balance. He fell to the floor, and his two buddies stumbled over him before righting themselves and coming after me again.

Back and forth we fought. They charged at me again and again, pushing me farther and farther down the hallway with every step we took. I danced in between them, hitting first one, then another, then another with the staff. I opened up cuts and made bruises blossom on their heads, legs, and chests, but I just didn't have the upper body strength that Owen did, so my blows weren't quite as vicious as his. Still, I was grateful for the staff, as it kept the giants from immediately overwhelming me. I knew that if I let just one of the bastards put his hands on me I was dead, especially since I didn't have my Ice and Stone magic to fall back on—or at least not as much of it as I normally would have.

Finally, I managed to get one of the giants down on the floor again. I leaped forward and overturned a table, putting it between me and the other two men, then whipped around to the guy who was on the ground behind me. Before he could recover, I hopped up into a chair that was sitting along the wall and raised up my weapon. Using my weight and momentum, I drove the end of the staff into his head as hard as I could. I managed to hit the sweet spot at his right temple, and his face made a sick, squishing sound as that part of his skull caved in. The other two giants were still trying to get around the table, so I raised the staff and brought it down again in the same place. The left side of the giant's skull cracked against the stone floor, and blood started to gush out of the head wounds I'd inflicted. He wouldn't be getting up from those. Not quite dead, but close enough to it not to matter right now.

I stepped back, putting his body between me and the

other men, and twirled the staff once more. One down, two to go.

I got a lucky break when the second giant slipped and fell in the blood of his fallen buddy, and I drove the staff into his skull a couple of times just like I had with the first man.

But the last bastard just wouldn't die. Again and again, he came at me. He was quick for a giant and had good instincts, which was why he managed to sidestep my blows time after time. I was so busy fighting him that it took me a few seconds to realize he'd managed to force me all the way down the hallway and back into the library.

I risked a quick glance over my shoulder to make sure no more giants were waiting inside to sneak up on me from behind. A blur of books filled my vision before I focused on the danger in front of me once more.

"There's nowhere left to run, bitch," the giant snarled, bobbing and weaving like a boxer.

"You're the one who should think about running," I snapped back. "Seeing as how badly I've fucked up your two friends already. They'll both bleed out in another minute, two tops. And so will you."

The giant let out an angry roar and rushed toward me. *Swipe-swipe-swipe.*

I managed to duck his first two blows, but the third one connected with my chest. It felt like someone had slammed a telephone pole into my stomach. The blow forced all the air from my lungs, cracked the cell phone in my vest pocket, and threw me five feet across the library. I hit a table and rolled across it, dropping to the other side, and the silverstone staff slid out of my hand and clattered across the floor. But instead of immediately getting up, I stayed down. Partly because I was trying to suck precious oxygen back into my lungs, and partly because I was tired of whacking at the giant with the staff. It was time to put him down for good. So I palmed my silverstone knife and waited.

The giant laughed, delighted that he'd finally managed to hit me. He didn't waste any time stepping around the table. He thought he had an advantage, and he was determined to finish me as quickly as he could. I let him have his little victory. It would be the last thing he'd ever smile about.

The giant bent down, dug his fingers into my shoulder, and flipped me over onto my back. "Not so tough now, are you, bitch—"

I lunged up and drove my knife into his chest. I hit an empty spot between one of his ribs, and my blade slashed through his heart like it was made of warm butter. The giant screamed with pain, but I was already yanking my knife out of his chest and slashing it across his throat. Blood poured out of the wounds, the coppery heat of it splattering onto my face, hands, and clothes, but I didn't care. Maybe it was gruesome of me, but the familiar sensation told me one thing—that I was still alive and my enemy wasn't.

The giant fell forward onto me, his eyes already going glassy, and I wiggled out from underneath his heavy weight. I got to my feet and stood there, still breathing hard, a bloody knife in one hand and the other hand resting on the back of the table that I'd rolled over.

Behind me, someone started clapping.

I whirled around and found Randall Dekes waiting for me.

The vampire stood in front of the fireplace, still clapping. He wore another pair of dapper gray pants topped by a matching shirt. Once again, that palm tree diamond nestled in the exact center of his silk tie. He must have been working in some other part of the mansion, perhaps his office, because he wasn't wearing a jacket, and he'd rolled his shirtsleeves up to his elbows. No dart guns up his sleeves tonight. Good.

He'd cleaned the blood off his face since the last time I'd seen him, but he hadn't bothered to hide the elemental power glowing in his eyes. All that stolen magic made the vamp's gaze burn with emerald green fire—a fire that I was looking forward to snuffing out forever.

I hadn't seen Dekes before when I'd done a quick scan of the room, and a second later, I realized why. A door along the back wall was standing open, one I hadn't noticed before because it was hidden in one of the bookcases. The vamp had slipped into the library from some other part of the house while I'd been fighting the giant. I would have preferred to backstab Dekes from the shadows, but I supposed this saved me the trouble of looking for him.

"What is that? Some sort of secret passageway?" I asked, finally getting my breath back. "Isn't that a little cliché?"

Instead of being pissed that I was still alive and mocking him, the vampire's face split into a sinister smile.

"Ah, Gin. What a delightful surprise this is," Dekes practically purred. "I'm so very happy you're still alive. More so than you can possibly imagine."

I raised an eyebrow. "I doubt you'll be thinking it's so fucking *delightful* when you're choking on all that stolen elemental blood running through your veins."

Dekes let out a mocking laugh. "Ah, if only you'd known how many people have said something like that to me over the years."

Instead of responding to him, I tightened my grip on my knife and took a step forward. I was about twenty feet away from the vampire, which meant I was too far away to cut him with my knife, and, with his fast reflexes, he'd be quick enough to duck out of the way if I threw the weapon at him. And of course, I didn't have enough Ice magic to freeze him where he stood. No, I had to keep Dekes talking while I whittled down the distance between us and got him within arm's reach.

"I'm sure lots of people have wished you dead over the years, given what a sick, sadistic bastard you are," I said. "It's just a shame no one's been able to make it happen—until now."

Dekes gave me a small, patronizing smile, as if I were a child whom he was indulging in a temper tantrum.

"You don't have any hostages to hold over my head now," I continued, taking another step forward. "My friends have Callie, along with Vanessa and Victoria, and they're getting them out of the mansion as we speak. And I can tell you aren't packing your charming little tranquilizer gun up your sleeve tonight. So the way I see it, there's absolutely nothing to keep me from gutting you where you stand."

"Ah, but there is," Dekes said. "You, Gin. Specifically all that lovely, lovely magic I took from you yesterday."

The vampire held out his hand, and a silver light began to flicker over his palm. I recognized that light—it was the cool glow of my own Ice and Stone magic. Even across the room, I could feel my own power, my own stolen magic, calling out to me. It was one of the most bizarre sensations I'd ever felt, so twisted and wrong and utterly confusing that it put me off my game for one precious second.

A second that cost me dearly.

It was one thing to know that the vamp had my stolen magic running through his veins. It was another to come face-to-face with him—with *it*. Dekes smiled at the growing horror in my eyes. I rushed forward, trying to close the distance between us and stab him to death, but it was already too late. The silver light coalesced into a ball of power.

It took only a second for the vampire to rear back his hand back and throw my own magic at me.

✲24✲

I immediately reached for my Stone magic, trying to use it to make my skin as hard as marble, trying to protect myself from, well, myself.

But there wasn't any more Stone power in my body right now than there had been Ice magic before when I'd been trying to make the lockpicks. The ball of silvery magic slammed into my chest, right in the same spot where the giant had hit me earlier. I managed to summon up enough magic to blunt the full strength of the vampire's attack, but the force of it threw me back against the table, and I fell to the floor again. It felt like a concrete fist had hit me, and once again, I gasped for air.

"I'm not sure if you've figured it out yet, but I'm not going to kill you," Dekes murmured, stepping forward and leaning down, his shoes a foot away from my face. "That would be far too wasteful. Oh, no, Gin. I'm going to keep you alive for as long as I can. So I can dine on your delicious, magical blood for as long as I can. With your blood, with your Ice and Stone magic, I can become twice as powerful as I already am. I know about the void Mab Monroe's death has left in the underworld in Ashland. Perhaps I'll move up there and take over her operations. Wouldn't that be ironic? You killing Mab, and then me using you to pick up the pieces of her organization. It's quite poetic if you think about it."

It was one thing to want to kill me outright, to want to carve me up into bloody bits the way I'd done to so many other people. I could understand that. Hell, I could even respect it. But Dekes was suggesting keeping me around as his fucking *pet*, the way he had Vanessa, Victoria, and who knew how many other women. I'd already suffered once at his hands, and I had no desire to repeat the experience.

The vampire biting me over and over again, driving his teeth into my neck and wrists, and sucking the magic, power, and life out of me for years, maybe decades, on end. Just thinking about it made me want to vomit. To say that it would be my own personal hell was an understatement. It would be a waking nightmare—one that even I might not be able to endure or escape from.

Once again, I felt cold, cold fear pressing down on me, smothering me, paralyzing me, but I ruthlessly pushed the feeling aside, squashing it under my own rage. Fear was a useless emotion. Fletcher had taught me that with our trip to Bone Mountain so long ago. He'd left me there in the woods and forced me to rely on myself that day so I'd be prepared for moments like this. So that I'd have the strength and the will to overcome my fear and take down anyone who was stupid enough to mess with me.

I drew in a breath and surged up, trying to drive my knife into Dekes's black heart the same way that I had the giant moments before. Trying to end this—now.

But the vampire was expecting the move. He held out his hand and blasted me back down to the floor with the Air magic he'd stolen from Victoria when he'd taken her blood. I tried to get up, but Dekes held out his hand, keeping the force of the Air magic steady across my chest and arms like an invisible lead weight pinning me down. No matter how I strained, cursed, and struggled, I just didn't have enough magic to push back his Air power and free myself.

"And now I'm going to suffocate you," Dekes murmured in a silky voice. "But only until you lose consciousness. After that, I'll have my giants make the necessary arrangements to keep you safe and secure. Oh, Gin. We're going to have so much fun together."

Once again, I reached for my Ice and Stone magic, trying to bring enough of it to bear to block his attack, but my reserves were even more depleted than before. I managed to hold him off for maybe five seconds before I felt the air being sucked out of my lungs. Struggling would only use up my oxygen that much faster, so I forced myself to lie still and try and think of some way to fight back or at least get the vampire to release his hold on his stolen Air magic. Because if I blacked out, this fight was over, and I knew that I wouldn't want to wake up to whatever accommodations Dekes had in mind for me.

But there was nothing I could do. My own magic was too weak to counter Dekes's power, and now I didn't even have the energy or freedom to try to raise the knife in my hand and drive it into the vampire's foot. White, then gray, then black spots began to flash before my eyes, warning of danger, doom, and death. If I could have, I would have howled with rage at Randall Dekes getting the better of me not once but twice now—

A ball of Fire streaked through the air and slammed into the vampire's chest.

Since Dekes had been holding on to his stolen Air magic, the Fire didn't immediately erupt and engulf him the way it would have if he hadn't had any elemental power at his disposal. But the shock of the unexpected flames shattered his concentration, making the invisible, airless bubble around me pop open. I rasped in a gasp of air, and cold tears streamed out of the corners of my eyes at how good it felt to be able to simply *breathe* again.

But Dekes quickly regained his composure. He curled his hand into a fist, and I felt the invisible power stream out of his clenched fingers. Now, instead of using his Air magic to smother me, the vamp was using it to douse the sparks that had singed his perfect gray shirt.

"Leave her alone," a voice called out.

A second later, Vanessa stepped into view. She stood there facing Dekes, another ball of elemental Fire in her hand. The flares and flickers perfectly matched the hate burning in her black eyes.

Dekes brushed the last of the red-hot sparks off his shirt and gave her the same mocking look that he had given me just moments ago. "What do you think you're doing, Vanessa?"

"Killing you," she snarled. "Finally, finally killing you for everything you've done to me and my sister."

On the floor between them, I sucked down breath after breath, trying to get enough oxygen into my lungs to get back into the fight. My fingers trembled, twitched, and then finally tightened around the hilt of my silverstone knife.

Dekes let out another light, mocking laugh. "Please. As if your puny Fire magic could compare with the Ice and Stone power that I've taken from Gin. You should have gotten out of the mansion while you could have, Vanessa. I admit I would have had fun tracking down you and dear Victoria, but now you're not even going to get the chance to run. I'm going to kill you where you stand and find a stronger Fire elemental to take your place. You know that I don't tolerate insolence."

The elemental Fire flashing in the other woman's hand burned a little brighter and a little hotter at his smug tone. Doubt and fear flickered in Vanessa's eyes, right along with the rage, but she'd gone too far to back down now. This was her moment to finally stand up to Dekes, to finally get payback for the horrible, horrible way that he'd used her, her sister, and their magic. Her spine stiffened, and the flames in her hands intensified.

Dekes responded to her silent challenge by holding out his palm. Once again, a ball of silvery magic glowed in his hand—pure Ice power this time. Vanessa's face tightened, and she couldn't stop the tremor that shook her body. She could feel the power Dekes was wielding just like I could, and she finally realized exactly how strong my blood had made him.

Dekes smiled at her, relishing her shock and increasing fear. "Good-bye, Vanessa."

He drew back his hand to hurl the ball of Ice at her—and that's when I drove my knife through his right foot.

Since I was still lying on the floor, I didn't have the best angle in the world, and I was still too weak and light-headed to put as much force behind the blow as I would have liked, much less reach up and sever his femoral artery as I really wanted to do. But the vampire's howl of pain and surprise still made me *smile*.

I ripped the knife out of his foot and drove it into the side of his calf, twisting it in as hard and deep as I could.

"How do you like that, you sick son of a bitch?" I snarled.

Dekes staggered away from me, my knife still stuck in his leg, and the ball of Ice magic in his hand flew over his head and back into the fireplace. The magic—my magic—slammed into the stone there, freezing it in places, shattering it in others, and causing jagged cracks to zip out from the center of the blast. The force of the blow also rattled the mantel above the fireplace and the five items that had been arranged there in a perfect row—my knives. The ones that Dekes had made me put down before he'd savaged my neck last night. The ones I'd vowed not to leave the mansion without.

But instead of freezing or shattering like the stone around them, the knives lit up with the silvery glow of my Ice magic, burning so cold and bright that I could see the spider runes stamped into every one of the hilts. The symbols glowed like tiny stars for a second. Then, just as quickly, the magic winked out, and the runes and the knives were a dull silver once more.

My eyes narrowed, and a knowing smile curved across my face. I couldn't beat Dekes, not when he was using my own magic against me, and I was still so weak from the loss of it in the first place. But I didn't need magic to kill the vampire. He bled, just like the rest of us did. I just needed something to keep his power from immobilizing me while I went in for the kill shot.

I got to my feet, blinking away the last of the spots and sucking down another deep breath for good measure. But instead of palming another knife and charging after Dekes, I picked up the staff that had fallen to the floor and slowly started twirling it around and around. Vanessa started to step in front of me and hurl her ball of Fire at Dekes, but I held out one hand, stopping her.

"Save your magic," I muttered out of the side of my mouth. "He has all three of our powers, plus your sister's Air magic, which makes him stronger than us right now. We've got to get him to drain off some of that excess magic first before you throw another ball of elemental Fire at him. Wait for my signal and stay out of the way. Because if this doesn't work, or if he manages to take me down, then you are going to want to run, and run fast."

Maybe it was all that stolen elemental magic pumping through his veins, but Dekes recovered quickly. He tugged the knife out of his leg and held it up, studying the crimson drops sliding off the end. I wondered how long it had been since he'd seen his own blood and not what he'd taken from his victims. My hands tightened around the staff. I hope he enjoyed the sight, because the bastard was about to see a whole lot more of it.

Dekes's upper lip curled with disgust underneath his mustache, and he threw away the knife and glared at me. "That's going to cost you, Gin. *Severely*."

"Bring it on, you psycho," I snarled, still twirling the staff.

Surprise flashed in his eyes. Apparently, he'd been so used to being obeyed for so long that it never crossed his mind that someone would stand up to him—that *I* would stand up to him, especially after the way he'd mauled me almost to death.

"Surrender to me now, and your punishment won't be quite as severe. Keep fighting, and I will make you wish that you had never been born," Dekes warned.

"Ah, if only you'd known how many people have said something like that to me over the years," I said, mocking him with his own words, then let him see just how cold, hard, and unyielding my eyes really were. "Like I told you the other night, I don't just lie down and die, and I always come back to finish what I started."

"Suit yourself, then," Dekes said, shrugging. "After all, I don't really need that pretty face of yours intact. Just your heart pumping out all that delicious blood."

The vampire smiled and reached for his magic—my magic—again. Once more, a ball of Ice power filled the palm of his hand before he threw it at us. Behind me, Vanessa gasped in surprise, but I was already shoving us both out of the way. We slammed into one of the bookcases against the wall, knocking several of Dekes's precious first editions off the shelves. Vanessa started to scramble up, but I put my hand on her shoulder and pushed her back down.

"Stay down," I whispered to her. "This is my fight now. You've done your part."

She bit her lip and nodded, her black eyes full of fear. Still holding the staff, I got back up on my feet and turned to face the vampire again. "Is that all you've got, Randy? How disappointing. And look at that, you've ruined some of your most prized books."

I pointed to the front wall of the library. Instead of skewering me, the elemental Ice had punched into the case, the shards turning all the books on five shelves into very expensive pincushions. Dekes's eyes followed my finger, and his mouth fell open a little when he realized what he'd done.

"All those books in your collection—ruined. What a pity. I know how much you valued them."

I *cluck-cluck-clucked* my tongue, and the vampire's face contorted with rage. He reared back and threw another blast of Ice magic at me, but once again I ducked out of the way at the last minute.

"Is that all you've got?" I asked.

Another ball of elemental Ice came my way in reply.

Again and again I taunted Dekes, and again and again he threw his magic—my magic—at me. I retaliated by tossing a few of my knives at him, along with all the books I could pull off the shelves. Of course, Dekes used his stolen Air magic to fling my makeshift weapons away before they so much as ruffled his hair, or incinerated them outright with his Fire power, but that was just fine with me. I didn't really expect to hit him, and I didn't really need to anyway.

From her spot on the floor, Vanessa looked at me like I was crazy, antagonizing the vampire so. She didn't realize that Dekes was doing exactly what I wanted him to, exactly what I *needed* him to do.

Finally, though, I ended up back in front of Vanessa.

This time, I couldn't stop her from getting to her feet and standing behind me as I turned to face Dekes for the last time.

By this point, the library looked like an Ice bomb had gone off inside. Long, jagged icicles stuck out of the walls, the books, and even the green leather couch in front of the fireplace. The temperature had dropped ten degrees, and just about every surface had an inch of elemental Ice on it now. I'd give Dekes credit. He could fling my magic around just as well as I could.

"What's wrong, Gin?" the vampire snarled, spittle flying out of his lips. "Did you finally run out of room? No matter, I'm tired of playing this game with you. This ends right now."

"You're damn right it does," I muttered.

Dekes reared back a final time, and once more, a ball of elemental Ice formed in between his hands. The vamp studied the silvery magic shimmering between his fingers, looking at it with undisguised glee and hunger, before raising his eyes and giving me a sneering smile. Then he threw both hands forward and shoved the raw, pulsing ball of power at us.

Vanessa gasped again. Behind me, I felt her take a step back, even though it was already too late for either of us to get out of the path of the magic roaring toward us. We wouldn't escape it—not this time. Dekes had meant it when he'd said that he didn't care what kind of shape I was in as long as I was still alive, because he'd put every last bit of power he had into this final blast. It wasn't a kill shot, but it was meant to cripple in the most brutal, painful way possible.

The magic streaked through the library, seeming to gain more force and more power with every molecule of space it gobbled up between us, just like Vanessa's elemental Fire had earlier in the hallway. At the very last second, I stopped twirling the silverstone staff that I'd been holding on to this whole time and held it out in front of me like a spear.

A moment later, the Ice magic hit the end of the staff—and stopped cold.

No, *stopped* wasn't the right word. The staff didn't really *stop* the Ice magic from hitting me and Vanessa—the silverstone that it was made out of did.

Elementals had rings, necklaces, watches, and more made out of the magical metal to hold bits and pieces of their power, but the shapes didn't matter at all—it was the metal itself that made the difference. That's what I'd realized when I saw my silverstone knives on the fireplace mantel soaking up Dekes's earlier ball of Ice magic—that the staff in my hands could do the exact same thing, only on a bigger scale.

All I had to do in the meantime was level the playing field between me and the vampire by getting him to waste as much of his magic—my magic—as possible. That's why I'd been flinging myself across the library and ducking Ice blasts for the better part of three minutes now. I'd had to get Dekes to fritter away most of his stolen magic so that the staff could soak up the rest.

Randall Dekes had spent three hundred and some years stealing blood and magic from elementals. To him, there was an endless supply of both, and when he used up one elemental, he simply tossed her aside like trash and found another to take her place. But even the strongest elementals could completely exhaust their magic in a fight, something that I'd learned when I'd killed Mab, something I'd realized again tonight when I had to struggle to make two simple Ice picks.

Something I'd just made Dekes do without even realizing it.

In a second, it was over. Instead of skewering me and Vanessa with icicles, the silverstone staff soaked up every bit of the Ice magic that Dekes had thrown our way. Now the long metal rod hummed with cold power. My power, my magic, back in my hands, right where it belonged.

Surprise and confusion filled Dekes's face before melting into anger once more. He reared back his hand again, but this time, only a few silver sparks filled his palm, instead of the pulsing orb of power he expected. The vamp stared down at his hand like he couldn't believe he didn't have any more magic left. Arrogance will get you, every single time.

"But how—and why—"

I cut off his sputtering. "Didn't I tell you? This staff is made out of pure silverstone. You know about silverstone, don't you, Dekes? How it stores and absorbs magic? All forms of elemental magic? I'm sure you have a piece or two of it in your collections somewhere. Now this staff is full of all that lovely Ice magic that you just threw at us. *My* Ice magic. And unless I'm mistaken, you're all out of juice, Randy. And out of time too."

The vampire's eyes widened with understanding, but I didn't give him a chance to do anything but die.

"Now, Vanessa!" I screamed.

She didn't hesitate. Vanessa stepped out from behind me and threw every scrap of Fire magic that she had left at Dekes. The vamp wasn't expecting such a quick coun-terattack, and there was nothing he could have done to stop it anyway. Not now, with all his stolen magic gone. He raised his hands, but it was already too late. Vanessa's flames slammed into his chest, and this time, Dekes was the one who flew back against the fireplace and thumped to the floor, flames licking at his clothes and skin.

I didn't give him a chance to get back up.

I raced over to the vampire and cracked him across the skull with the silverstone staff, forcing him to roll over onto his back. The movement smothered most of the flames siz-zling on his body, but I didn't care. I was more than happy to finish the job they'd started myself. I raised up my boot and stomped down on his chest, feeling his ribs crack under the sharp, heavy blow. Dekes groaned, but I didn't stop. I slammed my foot into the stab wound on his calf, then put my boot over his face and crunched down as hard as I could, like he was a bloodsucking tick that I was squishing into the ground. In a way, I supposed he was.

In another second, I was in as much of a frenzy as Dekes had been last night, when he'd gone crazy at the amount of raw elemental power in my blood. I could have stood there and kicked and punched and beaten the vamp all night long, letting out all of my rage, frustration, and fear, but I forced myself to come back from the edge and finish the job.

Breathing hard, I dropped to one knee beside him, grabbed another one of my silverstone knives from a pocket on my vest, and shoved it into his heart as hard as I could.

Randall Dekes threw back his head and screamed—and he didn't stop. He drew in a breath, and I clamped my hand down over his mouth. As much as I enjoyed the sound of his pain-filled cries, I wanted him to hear my last words to him—the last words he would ever hear. The vampire looked at me with wide, panicked eyes. I just tightened my grip.

"You know what, Randy? You forgot one thing. No matter how much stolen blood you have running through your veins, no matter how many elementals you drink from, no matter how powerful you think you are, there's not a fucking thing you can do about a knife in your heart," I said. "Especially when the Spider is the one who put it there."

I used my free hand to twist the blade in deeper.

Dekes arched his back, trying to get away from the knife, trying to get away from the pain, trying to get away from *me*.

I didn't let him.

Blood covered both of us by that point, pumping out of his heart with every slow twist of my knife. Finally, when I'd pushed the blade all the way down to the hilt in his chest, I ripped it out just as brutally as I'd stabbed it in. I drew my hand away from Dekes's mouth, letting the vampire scream as much as he wanted to now, even though his voice was already dying down to a raspy whimper and his green eyes were glazing over.

Then I leaned down and cut the bastard's throat, just to be sure.

❋ 25 ❋

I climbed to my feet, stood there, and watched Randall Dekes bleed out. It didn't take long, considering the vicious wounds I'd inflicted on him, but it was immensely satisfying all the same. Vanessa came to stand beside me. The diamonds and pearls in the choker around her neck and the ones in the matching cuffs on her wrists gleamed like teardrops underneath the library's lights. They matched the glitter of the elemental Ice on the books and walls.

"You killed him," she whispered in an awed voice. "You did it. You really killed him."

"I told you that I would," I said, giving her a crooked grin. "I always like to keep my promises. And don't sell yourself short. You helped—a lot. A whole hell of a lot. You saved me from him, Vanessa."

She nodded, although I didn't think she'd really heard my words. Her lips pressed together in a thin line, and she kept staring at Dekes with wide, unblinking eyes, as if she couldn't quite believe he was gone and that she was finally free of him.

Another popular myth about vampires was that they could come back from the dead or that they were even dead, or undead, to start with. But I'd killed enough folks over the years to know that nobody could get up from that last, fatal slice I'd made across Dekes's throat—vampire or not.

Still, despite what Dekes had done to her and her sister, I thought Vanessa would be okay in the end. After all, the Fire elemental had been strong enough to stand up to the vampire when it had really counted. Instead of leaving the mansion with Owen, Victoria, and the others, Vanessa had come looking for me instead—and Dekes.

She'd had to face him the same way I'd had to, and the Fire elemental was the reason that I was still standing and the vamp wasn't. If she hadn't come in and distracted Dekes with her magic when she did, I would have woken up bound, gagged, and at the vamp's mercy—at the very least. I owed Vanessa for that, whether she realized it or not, and I was going to do whatever I could to help her.

I let the Fire elemental stare at Dekes's cooling body while I went around the library and picked up all my various knives. I put the extra weapons into the pockets of my vest, but the knives that Owen had crafted for me went into their usual slots. My five-point arsenal, back where it belonged.

I also grabbed Owen's staff, which still hummed with my Ice magic, just like all my knives did. Of course, the knives had soaked up my power during my final fight with Mab all those weeks ago, but now they contained even more of my magic. I wasn't quite sure what I'd do with the power that was stored in the weapons, but I was certain I'd find some use for it sooner or later.

When we were both sure that Dekes was rotting in hell where he belonged, Vanessa and I left the library and stepped out into the hallway. I went first, keeping an eye out for any giants who might be left in the mansion, but the men's hoarse shouts and the sounds of their heavy footsteps had vanished from the house like they'd never even been here. I didn't know if it was because Finn and the others had killed all the guards or if maybe some of the giants had gotten smart and slipped out of the mansion. Didn't much matter. If one of them popped up and tried to stop us, I'd put him down just like I had his boss.

While we'd been fighting Dekes in the library, something else had happened—Vanessa's elemental Fire had spread through the mansion, leaping from one hallway to the next. The flames burned through the structure unchecked, and most of the west wing was already fully engulfed, with the rest of the house soon to follow. We headed toward the main staircase to go out the front door but had to turn back because of the smoke and intense heat.

Vanessa stood there, watching the flames lick at the walls in front of us. The fire had already engulfed the rooms on either side of the hallway, the ones that housed all the things Dekes had collected over the years. The models, the lockets, the antique dolls. The bright glow matched the fierce emotion in her eyes.

"Burn, baby, burn," she muttered in a hard, satisfied voice.

I cleared my throat. "As much as I hate to interrupt the supreme satisfaction you're taking in watching the mansion blaze to the ground, I'd really like to get out of here before the whole house collapses on top of us."

Vanessa gave me a chagrined smile. "This way," she said, leading me down another hallway.

The flames seemed to chase us through the house, moving almost as fast as we did, and we were coughing and choking on smoke by the time we finally stumbled out of one of the side doors. We stood there a moment, getting our breath back and letting the night air clear our lungs, before walking around to the front of the mansion. My cell phone had been broken during my fights with the last giant and Dekes, but I knew that the others would be there waiting for me, just as I would have been for them.

My friends, my family, stood on the front lawn, a safe distance back from the burning mansion. Owen, Finn, Bria, Sophia. They stared up at the flames, waiting for me to walk out of them, waiting for me to come back to them the way I always did—the way I hoped I always would.

Nearby, Jo-Jo was using her Air magic to tend to Callie and Victoria, who were both on the grass even farther back from the roaring flames. Jo-Jo had already healed Callie's minor injuries, and Callie watched while the dwarf worked her Air magic on Victoria. The dwarf had the girl's head cradled in her lap and was slowly stroking her hair, whispering to her, even though Victoria was still unconscious. I could see the power glimmering in Jo-Jo's eyes all the way across the massive lawn, and I knew that

Victoria would be alert and awake by the time the dwarf got done with her.

A few of Dekes's men who'd escaped our hunting party and the fire milled around on the grass and stared up at the burning house as if they couldn't believe what they were seeing. I wondered if they were waiting for their boss to stroll out of the dancing flames. If so, they'd be waiting a long, long time. If there was any justice in the great beyond, Randall Dekes was already getting ripe and toasty in hell.

Vanessa spotted Jo-Jo and Victoria and ran across the lawn to them. The others were turned the wrong way, so they didn't see me step out of the shadows behind the Fire elemental.

But Donovan did.

The detective had noticed Vanessa running out of the corner of his eye. He turned his head to follow her movements—and that's when he saw me. His eyes widened, and he did a double take, just like he had that night in the Sea Breeze when we'd first seen each other again.

His mouth dropped open, and he blinked and blinked, as if his eyes were playing tricks on him, as if he couldn't believe that I'd somehow survived the giants, Dekes, and the fire. He should have known by now that I always came back—no matter what.

I braced myself for what I knew was coming next, for that old, familiar, bitter disgust to fill Donovan's face at the knowledge that I was still alive and kicking and that I hadn't met the messy demise I so richly deserved. But instead of looking conflicted and disappointed as he had when I'd shown up on the hill above Tobias Dawson's coal mine, relief filled Donovan's face, and he did a most unexpected thing—he smiled.

He actually *smiled* at me.

It was a wide, welcoming, beautiful smile, full of relief, warmth, concern, and other, deeper things that shocked the hell out of me. It was the smile I'd expected to see that day outside the coal mine; it was the smile I'd hoped to see a dozen times before. It was all that and so much more—it was everything I'd ever wanted from Donovan.

The others were standing behind him, so I headed in that direction. Donovan hesitated, then took a few steps toward me, then a few more, then a few more still, until he'd walked halfway across the lawn—meeting me in the middle. He didn't say anything, and neither did I.

I stood there a moment, my eyes trailing over him, starting with his black hair and bronze skin and working my way down his strong, lean body. Despite the smoke that boiled up into the dark, humid night, I could somehow still smell his clean, soapy scent, the one that used to appeal to me so very much. Finally, I raised my eyes to his, so that our gazes locked, gray on gold.

Desire glimmered in Donovan's gaze, more desire than I'd ever seen him show before—desire for *me*. For the first time since I'd been in Blue Marsh, he let me see just how much he wanted me, maybe just how much he'd always wanted me. Desire, heat, raw, naked longing. They were all tangled together in the sharp planes of his face, along with other, softer emotions. I stood there and just stared into his eyes, looking at all the things I'd hoped to see, all the things I'd thought he'd never feel for me—ever.

Finally, Donovan held out his hand to me, palm up in supplication and a silent, agonizing question. I knew that if I took his hand, if I wrapped my fingers in his, he'd kiss me and pull me close, even though his fiancée was less than a hundred feet away.

I stared at his outstretched hand. Once upon a time, I would have given just about anything to have Donovan look at me like he was doing now, to reach out to me like he was doing now. The old feelings rose up in my heart then, all the electricity that had sparked and hummed between us, all the desire we'd felt toward each other, all the delicious things we'd done to each other the few times we'd been together.

I stood there, and I remembered all that.

And then I walked right on past him.

I saw surprise fill his face, but I kept on going, heading toward the others, heading toward Owen.

"Gin?" Donovan called out behind me. "Gin?"

I kept walking, and I didn't look back.

A few seconds later, Bria spotted me. My sister let out a shriek of glee and pointed me out to the others. They all ran in my direction, but Owen was the fastest.

My love caught me in a fierce embrace, lifting me up off my feet and spinning me around and around. I laughed at the dizzying feel of it, and the rush of emotions that tightened my chest to the breaking point. Owen put me back on my feet and rained kisses down on my cheeks, nose, and forehead before finally capturing my lips with his. I wrapped my arms around his neck and kissed him back twice as hard.

I didn't look at Donovan, and I didn't give him another thought. Not once. I didn't need to. Not now, not ever.

Dekes's massive mansion continued to burn well into the night. The island's fire department was eventually called out, but the house was too far gone by the time they arrived. There was nothing the firefighters could do but stand there with the rest of us and watch the mansion disintegrate.

"Burn, baby, burn," I said, echoing Vanessa's words and encouraging the flames with a smile.

The Blue Marsh Police Department arrived as well. Donovan stood off to one side of the yard, talking with several men in suits and spinning some story about what had happened, while Bria stood behind him, listening and occasionally adding to the conversation. The higher-ups in the department had already come out in full force to make sure that all the i's were dotted and all the t's were crossed, since Dekes had been one of Blue Marsh's leading citizens. Of course, the po-po didn't know about the *had been* part yet, but they would when the ashes cooled and they found whatever was left of Dekes's body in the library.

While we waited for things to calm down, I filled the others in on my battle with the vampire and how Vanessa had helped me defeat him. Vanessa crouched down on the lawn a few feet away, her arms wrapped around Victoria, who was now awake and sitting up. Both sisters stared at the burning mansion with grim, satisfied expressions on their faces. I got the impression that if they could have, they would have blasted the structure again and again with their Fire and Air magic to make it burn that much hotter and faster.

Finally, Bria broke away from the group of cops and came over to where I was standing with Owen, Finn, Sophia, and Jo-Jo.

"So what's Donovan telling them?" I asked.

Bria shrugged. "Some lame story about a gas leak getting out of control, exploding, and causing the fire with the added unfortunate consequences of Dekes and several of his men being trapped and burned alive by the flames."

"And what's he going to say about the busted gate and all the bodies with bullets in them?" Owen asked. "Especially the ones outside?"

He jerked his head. The giants that Finn, Bria, and Sophia had killed on their way inside the mansion lay strewn about the lawn like oversize garden gnomes that had been toppled over onto their sides.

Bria shrugged again. "Donovan's claiming that he came to rescue Callie from Dekes and that the giants wouldn't stand down and forced him to fire on them. Apparently, he's going to hang the four bodies Gin and I left in the pool at the Blue Sands on the vampire and his men as well. I heard Donovan say something about infighting among Dekes's men, some feud that got out of hand."

Well, that was a rather convenient way for Donovan to clear his case, but I wasn't going to complain, since it would keep the cops from looking at Bria and me in connection with those deaths. For once, the detective was actually doing me a favor. Maybe I wasn't the only one who was mellowing.

"I don't think anyone will be too concerned about Dekes, his men, or how they really died," Bria added. "The folks the vamp threatened will just be glad that he's gone. So will the other power players on the island, since his death will let them grab a little more of his empire for themselves. Pretty soon, it will be business as usual again."

Eventually, Vanessa helped Victoria up to her feet, and the two sisters drifted over to us. Victoria still looked frail, weak, and ashen, but Jo-Jo had claimed she'd be all right in a few weeks now that Dekes wasn't around to continually suck out her blood and magic anymore.

Vanessa walked toward me, her arm around her sister's slim shoulders. "I just wanted to thank you. For coming back for us. If I could have spared you what Dekes did to you in the library last night and again today, I would have. I hope you know that."

I waved my hand, dismissing her concerns. "You tried to warn me about him during the press conferece. It was my own fault that I didn't listen to you. But I think things turned out okay in the end, since the bastard is burning in hell right now. The question is where will you two go? What will you do now that you're free of him?"

Vanessa shook her head. "Honestly, I haven't thought that far ahead. I'm just trying to figure out how I can put clothes on our backs and find us someplace to stay while everything gets sorted out. Even though I hate this place with every bone in my body, I almost wished that the mansion hadn't burned. At least then I'd have something to start with to help us get back on our feet."

I pointed at the diamond and pearl choker and cuffs that she still wore. "Those baubles you have on will be a good start. The diamonds are especially exquisite."

"Really?" Vanessa asked, looking down at the cuffs on her wrists. "I thought they were glass, fakes, just as fake and twisted as Dekes was."

"Oh, no," I said. "I know a thing or two about gemstones, and those are the real deal. You won't have any problem hocking those for cold, hard cash—quite a bit of cash, actually."

Bria cleared her throat. "Speaking of cash . . ."

Her voice trailed off, and she looked at Finn, who winced.

"Aw, come on. Do I have to?" Finn grumbled.

Bria cleared her throat again and gave him a little shove forward.

Finn sighed. "All right, all right. You know you were talking about cash, Gin? Well, these might help too."

He reached into his pants pocket and came out with a fistful of gold doubloons. I recognized the gleaming coins as being part of Dekes's collection of pirate treasure. Bria cleared her throat a final time, and Finn stuck his hand in his other pocket, drawing out a lovely ruby necklace, three bracelets, and several rings. He stared down at the jewel-crusted booty in his hands before sighing again and handing everything over to Vanessa.

"Finnegan Lane," I drawled. "You should be ashamed of yourself. When did you have time to stop and raid one of Dekes's treasure rooms? Some of us were fighting to stay alive, you know."

Finn shifted on his feet. "It was right after you said that you guys had found Vanessa and Victoria. We were retreating out of the mansion, and we passed one of Dekes's pirate rooms. I knew that if you had your way Dekes wouldn't be missing it, so I stopped long enough to slip a few items in my pockets."

We all looked at him.

"What?" he muttered. "You can't blame a guy for looking out for himself."

I laughed, leaned over, and rumpled his hair. "No, you certainly can't do that."

26

"You know," I murmured a few days later. "I think I'm finally starting to get the hang of this vacation thing."

"Really?" Owen said, pressing a soft kiss to the hollow of my throat. "It certainly took you long enough."

It was early Wednesday morning. Owen and I had left the others sleeping in the beach house and had slipped out to the cove so we could have a little privacy. The sun had just come up over the eastern horizon, and we were lying on a couple of blankets, protected once again by the striped umbrella over us.

And once again, we were completely, blissfully naked.

We'd already made love and were basking in the warm, soft afterglow, watching the rest of the world wake up around us. The seagulls were once again flying their usual circles above, while the heat of the day had already started to shimmer up in waves from the golden sand. The ocean rolled in and out of the shore on its endless journey, the sparkling water looking just as bright and blue as the cloudless sky above.

"I can't believe we're going home this afternoon," I said, snuggling a little closer to Owen.

"Don't tell me these past few days have turned you into a beach bum," he teased.

"No, but it has been nice to just relax. As much as I hate to admit it, Finn was right. I needed a vacation."

And I'd finally gotten one these past few days. We'd all decided to play hooky from work and stay in Blue Marsh a little while longer to help sort out the consequences of Dekes's oh-so-timely demise. Really, though, Donovan had done most of the heavy lifting, dealing with the police and their questions and keeping the rest of us out of things. I didn't know exactly why the detective was being so helpful, but I wasn't going to question his motives too closely, since his handling of the investigation had left the rest of us free to while away the hours as we pleased.

Jo-Jo had spent her days by the beach at the Blue Sands hotel, sipping tropical drinks and flirting with the cute cabana boys and lifeguards. More often than not, Sophia joined her older sister, although the Goth dwarf was more interested in swimming and relaxing than flirting. Finn also frequented the hotel to get his long-awaited massages and other lavish pampering, along with Bria.

My sister had also spent quite a bit of time with Callie, helping the other woman come to terms with everything that had happened. Callie had been more than a little shaken up after being kidnapped and smacked around by Dekes, and Bria was helping her friend deal with things as best she could. I thought that hanging out with Callie was good for Bria too, and that it might get her to face her own lingering demons about being tortured by Mab. I hoped so anyway.

As for me and Owen, we'd taken more than one long, clichéd walk on the beach to the cove. In between walks, we'd gone out and explored Blue Marsh, from the downtown shops and restaurants to the island's nature preserves and parks. We didn't talk much, but just being with Owen soothed me and made my own nightmares about Dekes and his attack on me a little easier to bear. I would never forget what the vampire had done to me, how he'd stolen my blood and my magic and had almost killed me, but that was all right. I'd add the hard lessons that the vamp had taught me to all the other painful ones I'd learned over the years.

"So what are you going to say to Donovan when you see him this afternoon?" Owen asked, cutting into my thoughts.

Callie was throwing a good-bye luncheon for us at the Sea Breeze before we headed back to Ashland. I knew as well as Owen did that Donovan would be there. I hadn't seen the detective much these past few days, but I'd told Owen how Donovan had reached out to me when he'd seen me outside Dekes's burning mansion. Needless to say, Owen hadn't liked that one little bit.

"I don't think there's anything to say," I replied. "Donovan made his choice back in Ashland, and I made mine the other night. Actually, I made it a long time ago, even if I didn't know it yet."

"Really? What choice would that be?" Owen asked.

I tapped my index finger on his nose. "Why, you, silly."

"Oh. That."

I rolled my eyes and punched him in the shoulder. Owen just laughed, his deep, rumbling chuckles washing over me like the waves crashing into the shore.

"Well, I still think that I should kick Donovan's ass for hurting you. Hell, just on general principles," Owen said. "The man's an idiot."

"Oh, quit being such a guy. I am perfectly capable of defending my honor and whatnot. Besides, kicking Donovan's ass might be satisfying, but in the end it's not worth the effort of washing the blood out of my clothes."

"But I thought you womenfolk liked it when your guy acts all rough and tough and alpha male. When we take charge of things."

"Maybe," I admitted. "It depends on what you think you're taking charge of."

Owen drew me into his arms, and his hands started sliding down my body once more in slow, deliberate, delicious way. I drew in a breath and arched my back, leaning into him.

"Just maybe?" he whispered, his violet eyes shimmering with heat.

"Definitely," I whispered back, before pulling his lips down to mine once more.

Owen and I made love again and then lounged on the beach for most of the morning before putting our clothes back on and heading to the beach house. We took a shower, threw on some fresh clothes, and packed up our belongings. Jo-Jo, Sophia, Finn, and Bria came back from their various excursions and did the same, chattering on about all the things they'd done and seen. Then we all headed over to the Sea Breeze for our last vacation hurrah.

Callie had decided to close down the restaurant for the afternoon to give us a private good-bye luncheon—and what a luncheon it was. Grilled chicken smothered with a sweet mango salsa, sticky cilantro rice mixed with chunks of pineapple, smoky mesquite-marinated steaks, lobster tails dripping with butter, blackened shrimp, fresh-baked bread, baskets of deep-fried hush puppies, crispy sweet potato fries, gallons of pomegranate lemonade, even a couple of key lime pies for dessert. Callie had pulled out all the stops, and we all dug into the scrumptious meal, sitting at a series of tables that had been pushed together in the center of the restaurant.

"I couldn't have made it better myself," I told Callie after I'd stuffed myself with two pieces of pie.

Callie smiled. I hadn't spent as much time with her as Bria had these past few days, but we'd gotten to know each other a little better. I'd told her all about the Pork Pit and the food I cooked up there, and she told me how her family had started the Sea Breeze decades ago. I wouldn't say that Callie and I were friends now, but we weren't enemies either. I'd even apologized to her for the bitchy way I'd acted the first time we'd met. It was important to me to be friendly with Callie for Bria's sake, and I found that I wasn't jealous of their close relationship anymore. We were both part of Bria's life, and we each had our place in my sister's heart. What exactly those places were was up to Bria to decide, and I was going to respect her wishes—whatever they might be.

"So do you have any idea what you're going to do now?" Bria asked her friend.

Callie's smile widened. "Just keep on keeping on right here at the restaurant. You don't know what a relief it is, not to have to worry about Dekes or his men bothering me anymore."

She didn't have to say the words—I could see the difference in her for myself. The worried purple smudges were gone from under her eyes, and her whole body was utterly relaxed. Her gray-green eyes were that much brighter in her pretty face, and there was a lightness in her step that hadn't been there before. A weight had definitely been lifted off Callie's shoulders, and seeing how relaxed and happy she was made me glad that I'd been able to help her.

"In fact," Callie added, "I'm thinking about expanding the Sea Breeze with the help of my new business partners."

Callie looked down the table where Vanessa and Victoria were sitting next to Finn. As was usual whenever he was around anyone with money, my foster brother was telling them all about the wonderful things he could do with the cash that the sisters had made hocking the treasure he'd swiped from the mansion before the fire. Victoria's eyes glazed over as Finn started talking about tax shelters, but Vanessa had a shrewd, calculating expression on her face. I thought that the Fire elemental was going to be a force to be reckoned with in Blue Marsh someday very soon.

Callie, Vanessa, and Victoria had become fast friends, bonded together by what they'd suffered because of the vampire. The sisters had been staying at the beach house with the rest of us these past few days. I'd thought that they would leave Blue Marsh immediately, but apparently, despite the bad memories, they liked it here and felt it would be a good place to settle down. Besides, someone had to stay around to oversee Dekes's many business interests on the island. The vampire had died without leaving a will, so everything he owned now belonged to his wife, Vanessa. Vamps. They all thought they were going to live forever.

Vanessa had already hit the ground running. Finn had helped her get started, and she'd already scrapped the casino project and planned to return all of the property that Dekes had bought to their rightful owners—with a little something extra for their time, trouble, and suffering at the vampire's hands. It would be a lot of work, erasing Dekes and his legacy from the island, but I thought Vanessa was up to the task.

"I'm glad you're going to be here for a long time to come," Bria said, squeezing Callie's hand. "And the restaurant too. Blue Marsh wouldn't be the same without either one."

Her friend squeezed back. "Me too. And it's all thanks to you."

Bria shook her head. "Thank Gin. Not me."

"I already have," Callie said. "Many times. I even offered to pay her what I could for doing her . . . ah . . ."

Her voice trailed off, and she winced. Callie still wasn't completely comfortable with the knowledge that I was an assassin, but I couldn't blame her for that. I was just glad she'd accepted me as much as she had for Bria's sake.

I didn't want things to be awkward between the two of them—not because of me.

"Pro bono work," I said in a helpful voice.

"Right. Pro bono work," Callie finished. "But she wouldn't hear of it."

"Keep your money," I said, waving my hand. "Taking care of a scumbag like Dekes was its own reward. Trust me on that."

Callie bit her lip and nodded. Then she turned back to Bria.

"Anyway, I have a question for you. Back before all this started, I was going to ask you if you wanted to be my maid of honor. The wedding's not too far away. Besides, you know how much I've always wanted to make you wear a horrible bridesmaid's dress," she joked. "Something with bows and lace and in a totally ridiculous color that will look hideous on you."

Bria's blue eyes flicked to me and then farther down the table to Donovan, who was talking to Jo-Jo. I hadn't told Bria what had happened between Donovan and me, but my sister was a cop. She was good at reading people and sniffing out secrets. She knew there was something going on with me and the detective—she just didn't know what it was. I also hoped she knew that I would never do anything to purposely hurt her friend.

"I'd love to be your maid of honor, Callie," Bria finally said. "You know that."

The two of them put their heads together and started talking about dresses, color schemes, and hairstyles. I sat back and let their cheerful words wash over me before looking up and down the table at my friends and family.

It was calm, quiet, happy moments like this that made what I'd suffered because of Dekes and all the other bad guys like him worthwhile, and I was determined to savor it, to tuck it into my heart so that I would always remember and appreciate it.

We talked, laughed, and joked for the better part of two hours. But eventually, all of the food was eaten, and the conversations wound down. One by one, we got to our feet and drifted toward the door. Jo-Jo and Sophia were the first ones to leave, with Jo-Jo saying that she had to have the salon open in the morning or her regular customers would be beating down her front door with axes to get inside and have their hair and nails done. Jo-Jo hugged everyone a final time, then followed Sophia out the door. A minute later, I heard the Goth dwarf's convertible start up and zoom out of the sandy lot.

Vanessa and Victoria said their good-byes as well, adding they were headed back to the beach house. I'd managed to get the rental on the property extended through the end of the summer, which would give them plenty of time to find a place of their own if the two women didn't just go ahead and move into the lavish penthouse suite at the Blue Sands hotel. Finn was all for that idea and for coming back down soon for another weekend of pampering—on the house, of course.

"Is he always so shamelessly greedy?" Vanessa whispered to me at one point.

"Yes," I said. "But the man can do magical things with money. Trust me. You won't find anyone better than Finn to help you get a handle on Dekes's business interests."

Once Vanessa and Victoria stepped outside, that left Finn, Bria, Callie, Donovan, Owen, and me in the restaurant to say our good-byes. The others headed for the front door, but the detective grabbed my arm and pulled me aside.

"Gin?" Donovan asked in a low voice. "Can I talk to you a minute?"

Donovan had been a few seats down from me on the opposite side of the table. The detective hadn't spoken much during lunch, although he'd laughed and joked at the appropriate times. Mostly, though, he'd been sneaking glances at me.

I stared at the detective, then looked over my shoulder at the others. My gaze locked with Owen's, and once again, I wondered at the love that I saw there for me—the love and the trust and how I'd ever been lucky enough to earn either one of them. I nodded at Owen, and he nodded back. He knew I needed to talk to Donovan one last time, that I needed to say some things to the detective that were a long time coming, and he was enough of a man to let me do that without interfering.

Owen stepped outside, but he wasn't the only one who'd noticed that the detective had drawn me aside—so had Bria. My sister raised her eyebrows and jerked her head at the door.

"Gin?" she asked, a warning tone creeping into her voice. "Aren't you ready to leave yet? I thought that you wanted to get back home before dark."

"Y'all go on ahead," I said. "There's one more thing that I need to wrap up with Donovan. It won't take but a minute. I promise."

Bria shot me a worried glance. She knew just how much damage could be done in a minute, especially between old lovers. But Callie looped her arm through my sister's and pulled them both outside, either oblivious or unconcerned about the looming drama. The screen door banged shut behind them, and their voices faded away as they walked out into the parking lot.

I turned back around to stare at Donovan. "You wanted to talk, so talk."

The detective looked at me, an agonized expression on his face, his fingers curling and uncurling into fists by his sides, his whole body tight and rigid with tension—but still he didn't move. Our eyes locked together, and I saw all these conflicting emotions shimmering in his bright gaze. Heat, need, desire, guilt—but still he didn't move.

The seconds ticked by. Ten . . . twenty . . . thirty . . . forty-five . . .

Finally, Donovan jerked forward, pulled me into his arms, and crushed his lips to mine.

27

Donovan wrapped his arms around me and pulled me even closer, grinding our bodies together. His soapy scent filled my nose, and his tongue flicked against my lips, trying to get me to open up to him.

"Gin," Donovan rasped against my mouth, his arms tightening around me that much more, as if he could somehow drag me inside his own body. "Oh, Gin. You have no idea how much I want you."

"Oh, I think I have a pretty good idea," I said in a wry tone, feeling his erection pressing against my thigh.

Donovan didn't seem to notice the sarcasm in my voice. Instead, he pressed another feverish kiss to my mouth and ran his hands up and down my back. There was no denying that the detective was an attractive man, and back before he'd dumped me, I would have been happy to go along with things just like he wanted me to. Hell, I probably would have already suggested that we see just how sturdy the table closest to us really was. I wasn't shy about getting what I wanted, and for a long time, that had been Donovan Caine.

But for the first time, his touch left me completely cold. I didn't feel anything when he kissed me, and his lean, strong body failed to stir any sort of warmth or desire in me. Even his clean scent seemed to have taken on a sour, bitter note.

"You have no idea how I want you now," he repeated. "How I've always wanted you. I know that it's wrong, I know what you are, I know that you're an assassin, but I'll be damned if I can keep from wanting you. Just looking at you drives me crazy. I've replayed the nights that we were together a thousand times in my mind, remembering the way you felt against me, the way I felt when I was holding you. I just can't stay away from you, no matter how hard I try. And you know what? I don't want to try anymore. I just want you, Gin."

He drew back, his golden eyes bright and earnest in his face. He obviously expected me to say something along the lines of how much I'd always wanted him too and how we could pick right back up where we'd left off. But the detective was about to be seriously disappointed—in all sorts of ways.

"Is that all you have to say?" I asked.

His black eyebrows knit together in confusion. "Isn't that enough? I want you. What more *is* there to say?"

He reached for me again, and I drove my fist into his stomach as hard as I could.

Donovan gasped and stumbled back, grabbing one of the tables for support. He looked at me with a surprised expression on his face, and I knew it had never occurred to him that I would turn him down, that I would say no to him, that I'd fucking gotten *over* him. But that had always been the problem with Donovan—he thought he was so much better than I was. Maybe he was, but now I realized he didn't have a right to look down on me either. Owen had taught me that by accepting me for who and what I was—knives, blood, and all.

"Gin?" Donovan asked in an uncertain voice.

I stared at him with cold, dispassionate eyes. "First of all, nobody, and I mean *no damn body*, touches me without my permission, much less tries to stick his tongue down my throat without my consent and express invitation. And second, what you're feeling right now? The sharp ache in your chest? The trouble breathing? That's exactly what I felt when you turned your back on me outside Dawson's mine. Do you remember that, Donovan? Because I certainly do. I didn't expect you to turn cartwheels that day, but it would have been nice if you hadn't been so fucking *disappointed* that I was still alive and around to tempt you with my wicked, wicked wiles. And then, to add insult to injury, you came to the Pork Pit later on and spelled out exactly how much you didn't want to be with me. How do you think all that made me feel? I'll give you a clue—not good. Not good at all. Now, instead of offering me some sort of apology for the shitty way that you treated me, you expect me to be just as happy to play grab-ass as you are, as though nothing bad ever happened between us."

Donovan rubbed his chest and slowly straightened up. "You're angry, and you have every right to be. I was a fool to act the way I did toward you. I'm sorry for that. Sorrier than you'll ever know. I thought about calling you a dozen times after I left Ashland, but I just couldn't. I knew that if I heard your voice again, I'd be tempted to go back to the city—to go back to you. Now I'm sorry that I didn't call you, that I didn't go back."

I shook my head. "That's where you're right—and wrong too. Yes, you were a fool to walk away from me, but your doing that was the best thing that ever happened to me because it let me find Owen."

Donovan frowned. "Grayson? But you just took up with him because I left town. We all know that."

I raised an eyebrow. "And what? You think that I'm just going to forget about Owen and happily fall back into your arms now because you've finally gotten off your high horse and decided that you want me? Or at least want to fuck me again? Are you really that arrogant, Detective?"

He winced, but he stubbornly lifted his chin. He wasn't going to take back his words because we both knew they were partially true.

"Tell me that I'm wrong," he challenged. "Tell me that you didn't start sleeping with Grayson just because he was there."

"Well, I do have slightly higher standards than that. But yeah, maybe that's how it started out with me and Owen," I said. "Maybe I was lonely and hurting because of you and how shitty you made me feel about myself and what I do. But I love Owen, and he loves me. What we have is real—the forever kind of real. More than that, Owen accepts me for who and what I am. He knows that

I'm an assassin, but he's not hung up on it like you always were. Like you still are."

Donovan stared at me, guilt flickering in his eyes, along with just a touch of shame. Yeah, he still wanted me, but he still wanted to keep his conscience clean too, and that just wasn't going to happen. Even if I wanted to, there was no way I could ever stop being the Spider— not now, not after killing Mab. The Ashland underworld was in major turmoil, and probably would be for some time to come, which meant the bad guys were going to keep coming after me. Donovan would just never understand this need that I had to take them on and to try to help all the innocent people I could. He would just never understand that sometimes my way was the only way to help folks—folks like Callie who didn't have the money or darkness inside them to go toe-to-toe with the people threatening them.

It wasn't wrong of Donovan to believe in truth and justice and to want to follow the law and do things by the book. But it wasn't right of him to always condemn me out of hand either, or more importantly, want me to change to suit his ideals so he could feel better about being with me.

Still, for the first time, I didn't feel any anger or rancor toward the detective. Instead, I just felt sorry for him. Donovan was a good guy who wanted the thrill of being with a bad girl. It was up to him to come to terms with that. I wasn't apologizing for myself anymore, especially not to him.

"You have a good thing going with Callie," I said in a soft voice. "She really does love you, Donovan. You should try to make it work with her, but if you can't love her wholeheartedly like she loves you, like she deserves to be loved, like everyone deserves to be loved, then you need to let her go. That's what good guys do, Donovan. They think of people other than themselves and what they want. So you need to man up and walk the walk that you always spout to others."

He didn't say anything, but I could see the conflict, guilt, and shame in his face. He cared about Callie, maybe he even loved her, but here he was, kissing another woman inside his fiancée's restaurant with her standing just outside the door. That wasn't exactly the kind of good, upstanding, honorable guy Donovan wanted to be, but that was his problem now—not mine.

Not anymore.

"Whatever you decide about Callie, I hope that you have a good life, Donovan," I said. "Because I certainly intend to—with Owen."

I stared at the detective a second longer, looking at the planes of his face, remembering everything he'd made me feel, remembering everything he'd once meant to me. Then I put those feelings and memories away forever— finally severing the last thread that had tied me to him for so long.

I turned my back to Donovan the way he'd once done to me and walked away. I didn't look back. I didn't have to. There was nothing for me here.

My future was waiting outside—with Owen.

☀ 28 ☀

I opened the screen door, stepped outside, and rejoined the others. Callie and Bria were standing in the lot, still talking about bridesmaids' dresses and when Bria might be able to come back to Blue Marsh for a fitting, while Finn and Owen were sitting on top of one of the electric blue picnic tables, sunglasses on and faces turned up to enjoy the sun. I walked over to the two of them.

"So how did it go?" Finn asked, looking at me over the tops of his sunglasses. "Did Donovan tearfully proclaim his undying love?"

"Something like that," I said in a mild voice, making sure that Callie couldn't hear us.

"And then what?" Finn asked, his green eyes gleaming. "I want all the juicy details."

"You're such a gossip." I spoke to Finn, but I looked at Owen, who hadn't said a word. "And then I punched the smug bastard in the stomach and told him that I loved Owen. That's what."

Finn grinned. "That's my girl. Always resorting to violence."

I shrugged. "You stick with what works."

Owen got off the table and gently brushed a piece of hair back off my face. "I'll second that."

He leaned down and kissed me, and I felt everything with him that I'd been missing with Donovan—everything I'd always been missing with the detective. Understanding. Concern. Caring. Love.

A minute later, Donovan stepped out of the Sea Breeze, his face carefully calm and blank, the earlier turmoil in his eyes gone, although perhaps not forgotten. He looked at me standing next to Owen, and his face tightened. For a moment, I thought I saw a flash of regret in his eyes. Whatever it was, the detective quickly pushed the emotion aside. He went over to Callie's side and slid his arm around her waist. He didn't look at me again. Good. I didn't want him to.

Callie and Bria finally wrapped up their conversation, and Owen, Finn, and I walked over to where they were standing. Once again, my sister's eyes drifted from me over to Donovan and back again.

"Is everything okay?" Bria asked in a cautious voice. "Are you ready to go now, Gin?"

That wasn't what she was really asking me, and we both knew it. But I had been ready to let go of Donovan for a long time, even if I hadn't realized it.

"Yeah, I'm ready."

She looked at me and nodded. "Good. I'm glad to hear it."

We all fell silent for a moment before Finn let out a long, tired, I'm-so-put-upon sigh.

"Well, I suppose that it's time for me to hand these over again," he muttered.

Finn pulled his car keys out of his pocket and dangled them in front of Bria. "Do me a favor. Try not to get my car smashed up on the way back home, okay?"

That was another reason that we'd decided to stay in Blue Marsh a few more days—so Finn could get his car fixed. The mechanic had finally returned the Aston Martin this morning in what Finn had reluctantly deemed appropriate shape, meaning that everything had been replaced and that he couldn't find any real fault with the car. He had perked up considerably though when he handed me the bill for the repairs. Finn always enjoyed passing the buck like that.

So we were leaving the same way that we'd come down to Blue Marsh. Bria and I were driving the convertible back to Ashland, while Owen was riding with Finn in the Escalade.

"Oh, shut up and give me those already." Bria snatched the keys out of Finn's hand.

Instead of being intimidated by her slightly cross tone, he took the opportunity to draw her close, bend her over, and plant a long, sound kiss on her lips just like he had in the restaurant a few days ago. Finn always liked to be grandiose, no matter how large or small his audience was. After a moment, Bria let out a sigh, wrapped her arms around his neck, and melted into his embrace.

I just smiled.

After Finn and Bria came up for air, the guys said their final good-byes to Callie. Then Finn and Owen got into the Escalade and pulled out of the parking lot. A minute later, they were gone, headed back to Ashland, although I'd see them again before we reached the city. We'd already made plans to hook up at a rest stop between here and there in an hour or so and follow each other back home.

That left me standing outside the restaurant with Callie, Bria, and Donovan. The detective shook hands with Bria, then turned and finally looked at me. His eyes were dark and a little sad too, but I also saw relief mixed in with the other emotions. Donovan might have wanted me, but deep down, he hadn't wanted to wreck his new life with Callie either. Sooner or later, he'd realize that, if he hadn't already.

"Good-bye, Gin," Donovan said in a low, rough voice.

He hesitated, then stuck out his hand, like we were just two casual acquaintances going our separate ways instead of a couple who'd once had an intense affair. Maybe acquaintances were all that we were now. Hell, maybe that's all we had ever really been to start with.

I wrapped my fingers around his and gave his hand a firm, final shake. "Good-bye, Donovan."

The detective's fingers tightened around mine for the briefest instant before I dropped his hand and stepped back. And that was that—Donovan Caine was out of my life once again. But this time, it was by my choosing and on my terms.

Donovan stared at me another second before going back inside the restaurant. I didn't watch him go. I didn't need to. Not anymore.

Bria gave Callie a final hug, and the two women made all sorts of promises about visiting each other and staying in touch, trying to make the moment last just a little while longer. Then Callie turned to me. I was surprised when the other woman held out her arms and hugged me as well.

"Thank you for everything, Gin," she whispered in my ear. "Especially for Donovan and letting him go."

My eyebrows shot up in surprise. Perhaps Callie hadn't been as oblivious about the detective as I'd thought. I wondered what she would say to him after I left and where they would go from here. But that was up to them now, and I was out of things—for good.

"You're welcome," I whispered back.

We broke apart. Callie waved at us a final time and then went back inside the restaurant, getting ready to open up for the supper crowd. The familiarity made me smile and miss the Pork Pit. Vacations were all well and good, but I was looking forward to going home and getting back into the swing of things.

And then there were two of us—Bria and I standing outside in the sandy lot where this whole thing had started last week. My sister's eyes traced over the neon blue clamshell sign, the one that spelled out the words *The Sea Breeze*, and a wistful look filled her pretty face. I walked over to stand beside her.

"I'd understand if you wanted to stay here in Blue Marsh," I said in a soft voice. "I know that it was your home once and that it could be again. That you have a lot of good memories here and that part of you wants to go back into the restaurant and tell Callie you're leaving Ashland and moving back down here for good."

Bria tried to smile, but it didn't come off so well. "Is it that obvious?"

I nodded and drew in a breath, bracing myself. Now came the hard part. Because there was something else I wanted to say to my sister before we left Blue Marsh, something I needed to say, something I'd been thinking about ever since I'd had those dreams about Fletcher leaving me on the mountain so long ago. The old man had taught me a lesson that day, one that I'd half forgotten, but that was still important—maybe the most important thing he'd ever made me realize about myself and what I did.

"You know, ever since I killed Mab, I've been waiting for the other shoe to drop with you," I said.

Bria frowned. "What do you mean?"

"I mean that Mab's dead. She can't hurt us anymore, she can't hurt *you* anymore. The threat she posed to you is over. Done. Finished. You're free to live your life however you want to—wherever you want to. Don't tell me you haven't thought about it, that you haven't thought about leaving Ashland for good."

Her face tightened with guilt, but I wasn't finished yet. I had to get the words out. I had to know where we stood. I had to let her know that she was free from everything now—including me.

"I know how much Mab hurt you, how horribly she tortured you. We both know that none of that probably would have happened if I hadn't been the Spider and so determined to kill Mab for murdering our family. Like it or not, I'm the reason that you got hurt."

Memories of that horrible night flashed in Bria's eyes, along with the emotions that went with them—rage, fear, helplessness, pain. So much pain that it took my breath away, but I kept talking.

"So every day since then, I've been waiting for you to tell me you've had enough. That you're tired of having an assassin for a sister and that you want to go back to your old Gin- and Spider-free life. It wasn't so bad in Ashland because of all the distractions, all the folks gunning for me. But then we came down here, and everything changed. I saw how happy being back here made you, and it only made me that much more insecure because of my fear that you'll someday leave me behind and never look back. That was one of the reasons I was such a bitch to Callie that first night in the restaurant. I was jealous of her and her relationship with you. I was jealous of how much you loved her, when you don't seem to feel the same way about me."

Bria opened her mouth to protest that it wasn't true, that she was just fine with my being an assassin, that she wasn't thinking about getting while the getting was good, but I held up a hand, cutting her off.

"It's okay," I said. "I understand how hard this has been for you. It's why Donovan and I didn't work out. Because he couldn't accept who and what I was and that I was okay with being an assassin, that I'm okay with being the bad guy."

I drew in a final breath. "But I've been tiptoeing around you because you're my sister, and I just can't do that anymore. Like it or not, I'm the Spider. I'm always going to want to kill first and ask questions later. It's just who I am, who Fletcher raised and trained me to be, just like your foster dad raised you to be a cop and follow the law. I'm your sister, and I love you, Bria. More than you'll ever know. But if you want to stay here in Blue Marsh and pretend you never discovered that I was still alive, I'll understand. It's your choice, just like being an assassin is mine. But I'm not going to apologize for what I do anymore, and I'm not going to be afraid of losing your love or approval."

The words hung in the air between us for a moment, before the wind whipped them away and carried them out across the ocean. But I'd said the words, finally voiced my worrisome thoughts, and there was no taking them back. In a way, it was like a burden had been lifted off my shoulders, just as it had been that day when Fletcher had left me in the woods. Sure, the old man had dumped me out there, but he'd also shown me that I could keep going—no matter who abandoned me or the hardships I had to face as a result of that.

Maybe I wouldn't like what Bria would say. Maybe she'd want nothing more to do with me. Maybe she'd break my heart with harsh words. But now, at least I'd know one way or the other how she felt, and I could get on with my life accordingly.

And most of all, I could quit being afraid.

Bria stared at me for a long, long time, feelings flashing in her eyes one after another like stones skipping across the surface of a still lake. Guilt. Regret. Love. Wariness. Shame. The last emotion surprised me. What would Bria have to feel ashamed about? I was the one who killed people, not her.

"I do love you," she finally whispered. "But you're right. It's been hard for me these past few months in Ashland, knowing what you are, watching what you do. It goes against everything that I know about being a cop and upholding the law. I know it wasn't your fault that Mab tortured me, but part of me was still angry at you because it happened. So angry. Like you should have killed her before you did, even though you almost died trying to do that at her mansion before I was ever kidnapped."

Her words hurt, like a dozen knives twisting into my heart all at once, but they weren't unexpected. In fact, they were far kinder than what I'd thought they'd be, but I still braced myself for what was to come. I might be willing to let Bria go, but it was going to hurt all the same—maybe even more than losing her in the first place had.

This time, Bria sucked in a breath. "I'll admit that with Mab gone I've thought about moving back down here and picking up my old life again. But I'm not the same person I was when I left Blue Marsh. Not after everything that's happened to me and to you too. I might not like what you do, but you're not going to lose me, Gin."

"Why not?" I said, forcing the words out through the lump of emotion that clogged my throat. "What's changed?"

Bria looked at me. "Because we came down here, and I saw how Donovan treated you. How he thought he was so much better than you, so much more righteous, and I realize that it's the same way I've been treating you for months now, when you've done nothing but save my life over and over again. With no question, no hesitation, and nothing asked in return. Not one damn thing."

Tears streaked down her cheeks, and her blue eyes were agonizingly bright in her face. "The truth is that I'm ashamed of myself for acting like him and most especially for taking you for granted. When we found out that Callie was in trouble, you were the first one to do anything about it. You immediately stepped up and offered to help her. If it wasn't for you, Callie would be dead now and probably Donovan along with her. You saved her not because I asked you to and not even because she was my friend but because you saw someone who was in trouble and you realized you could help her. Maybe you *are* an assassin, maybe you *are* one of the bad guys, but you know what? I don't give a damn anymore. You're my sister first, and that's all that matters to me."

I blinked and was surprised to find hot tears sliding down my own cheeks, one after another in a torrent that I couldn't control. She . . . she . . . *understood*. She actually understood who and what I was and that I would probably never change or give up being the Spider. She knew it all, and she was still here with me. All sorts of emotions surged through my heart then, but there was one that drowned out all the others—relief. Pure, sweet relief that she wasn't going to walk out of my life, that she was going to stick with me through the good and the bad and whatever else the world threw at us.

I reached forward and wrapped my arms around Bria, and she did the same to me. We stood like that for several minutes, still and quiet, with silent sobs shaking both of our bodies. Just letting out all the fear and anger and guilt that had crept up on us both and had created this gulf between us. But we'd overcome those emotions, and I'd be damned if we'd ever grow apart like this again.

Finally, we both drew back and wiped the tears from our faces, both of us pretending not to notice that we'd been crying in the first place.

"So," I said when I could finally speak again. "What do you say we hop into Finn's fancy convertible and drive back to Ashland?"

Bria smiled and held out her hand to me. "Let's go home."

I threaded my fingers through hers and, hand in hand, we headed for the car.

❖ 29 ❖

Two weeks later, it was business as usual at the Pork Pit.

Sophia wearing her Goth gear and baking bread for the day's sandwiches. The smells of grease and sugar flavoring the air as burgers and more sizzled on the grill. Waitresses grabbing plates and handing out food as fast as Sophia and I could dish it up. Finn, Bria, Owen, and all my other friends and family dropping by for meals. Me reading my latest book behind the counter in between lulls in the action.

Customers wondering whether or not I'd kill them for merely looking at me.

Things hadn't changed much since I'd come back from Blue Marsh. Actually, things hadn't changed at all. People still flocked to the Pork Pit to get a glimpse of the notorious Gin Blanco, the woman who might or might not be the Spider and who might or might not have killed Mab Monroe. Whispered rumors still followed me from one side of the restaurant to the other, and everyone froze every single time I picked up a knife of any sort to peel potatoes or slice tomatoes.

But my time in Blue Marsh had given me a different perspective on things, and now the obvious stares, rumors, and whispers didn't bother me as much as they had before. People would think what they wanted to about me, and there was nothing I could do to stop or change their rampant speculations. Eventually, some other scandal would pop up in Ashland, and everyone would turn their attention to it instead of me. Gin Blanco and the infamy surrounding her would die down and slowly be forgotten, and I'd be relegated to an urban legend, a myth, if folks bothered to remember me at all. But I was okay with that. In fact, it couldn't happen soon enough for me, and I looked forward to the day when I was back in the shadows once more. In the meantime, I'd survive—just the way I always did.

The folks in Ashland might not have changed while I'd been gone, but I found that I had—at least a little bit. I might have almost died fighting Dekes, and I'd never forget the vampire's vicious attack on me, but I'd made peace with some of the things in my life, mainly my fears about Bria.

She was my baby sister, and I'd saved her from Mab. I'd kept that promise to her, and her life was her own now. I'd always love Bria whether she chose to stay in Ashland or decided to spread her wings and live somewhere else someday. But I didn't think my sister would be going anywhere anytime soon. We were getting along better than ever, now that everything was out in the open between us, and I thought that Finn and Bria were on the verge of something serious too.

As if she'd heard my thoughts, the bell over the front door chimed, and my sister stepped into the restaurant. It was warm outside today, as spring was finally in full force in Ashland, and Bria had left her long coat at home. She wore a pair of dark jeans, along with a crisp white button-down shirt and a pair of comfortable but stylish black boots. As always, she was on the job, and her gun gleamed on her black leather belt right next to her gold detective's badge.

It was late in the day, almost closing time, and only a few folks sat at the blue and pink vinyl booths in front of the windows, chowing down on their food. Bria came over and slid onto a stool right next to the cash register.

"Hey there, baby sister," I said, using one of the day's credit card receipts to mark my place in the copy of *Watership Down* by Richard Adams that I was reading. "What can I get you?"

"Just an iced sweet tea," she said. "I'm parched."

I filled a glass with the sweet, sugary tea, then wrapped my hand around it and reached for my Ice magic. Elemental Ice crystals spread across the glass, immediately frosting it, and I held my palm up and created a couple of Ice cubes and dropped them into the tea as well, just for good measure. It had taken several days for my body to replenish the magic that Dekes had stolen from me. I was back up to full strength now, and I couldn't help but test my power every so often to make sure that it was still there. Maybe it was paranoid, but I wasn't going to take my magic for granted—not anymore.

I added a couple of slices of lemon to the tea before passing it over to Bria. She took a few long drinks before setting the glass aside, reaching into the back pocket of her jeans, and coming up with a small square cream-colored envelope. She put the envelope down on the counter and carefully slid it over to me.

"Callie sent me a wedding invitation," Bria said in a quiet voice. "I just got it today. I thought you might want to see it. She put a note in there, inviting you to come to the wedding if you wanted to."

I'd thought about Callie a lot over the past two weeks and even more about Donovan. I'd wondered if the detective would go through with the wedding, but given the invitation, it looked like he intended to after all. I knew that in his own way, Donovan had made a promise to Callie when he'd given her that engagement ring, and he wanted to keep it. He wouldn't want to embarrass her by backing out now, no matter how he really felt about her—or me.

Still, I thought they'd be happy together. Callie adored the detective, and she was just the kind of woman Donovan really wanted to be with, deep down. Smart, sweet, pretty, charming, and a great cook. They'd find a way to make it work. Whatever lingering feelings Donovan might have for me would fade in time, and he'd eventually be glad I'd turned him down in the Sea Breeze, because he'd have exactly the kind of life that he wanted—and so would I.

"I don't need to see the invitation," I said, pushing the envelope back across the counter to her. "But you can tell Callie that I hope that she has a great life with Donovan. I really mean that."

"I know you do."

Bria slipped the invitation back into her pocket. She sat at the counter and sipped her tea, and the two of us talked back and forth while I wiped down the counter.

"You want to head over to Northern Aggression and get a drink after I close up the restaurant for the night?" I asked. "Just the two of us?"

She shook her head. "Sorry, but I can't. I'm supposed to meet Finn for an early supper over at Underwood's. But how about a rain check? Maybe tomorrow night?"

"I'd like that."

Bria smiled. "Me too."

My sister's smiles came easier and lasted longer these days. The tension and anger in her had eased as well, and her eyes weren't quite as dark and haunted as they had been before. She was slowly getting over the torture she'd suffered because of Mab, just like I was coping with what Dekes had done to me. Together, we were helping each other heal and move on with our lives.

That isn't to say it was all smooth sailing. After all, I was still an assassin, and Bria was still a cop. The push and pull between our two chosen professions would always be there, but there was more to us than that now. There was more to our relationship than that now. We were starting to become real friends, in addition to being sisters.

Still, I knew that no matter what happened in the future, no matter what challenges we faced, we would do so together.

And that was all that really mattered.

Eventually, Bria polished off the rest of her sweet tea and headed out to meet Finn for dinner, promising to call me tomorrow. Thirty minutes passed with no new customers coming in the door, so Sophia and I started closing down the Pork Pit for the night while we waited for the few folks left inside to finish up their meals and leave. After we turned off all the appliances, I grabbed the last of the day's trash bags and stepped out into the alley behind the restaurant.

The darkness greeted me like an old friend, as did the rest of the sights. The oil and grease on the pavement, the crack in the wall opposite the Pork Pit, the soft, slow murmurs of the bricks.

The two guys in the shadows waiting to get the jump on me.

Nope, things hadn't changed much since I'd been back in Ashland. The underworld was still in turmoil, which meant that the lowlifes were still gunning for me, still coming around the restaurant in hopes of taking out the Spider. I'd seen a few of them hanging around the Pit, looking at me with cold, calculating eyes, but no one had tried to kill me—until now. I was mildly surprised that it had taken them this long to start up again.

I threw the trash bags into one of the Dumpsters, then turned to see exactly who was lurking around tonight.

"Y'all might as well come on out," I said. "I know you're there. I can smell you."

"Smell me? But I just took a shower this morning!" an indignant voice drifted out of the shadows.

There was a loud sound, like someone was getting smacked upside the head. Then another voice let out a low mutter.

"Shut up, idiot."

My thoughts exactly.

But the two men knew their cover was blown, so they stepped out from behind the Dumpster at the far end of the alley. I recognized them immediately, and it was déjà vu all over again.

It was Billy and Bobby, the giant and the Fire elemental who'd jumped me the night Finn had said I needed a vacation. Apparently they hadn't learned anything from the previous ass-kicking I'd given them. Some people just never did, like Jonah McAllister.

Through the grapevine and his many spies, Finn had heard that the slick lawyer was deeply, deeply disappointed that I'd made it back to Ashland in one piece. Apparently, after he'd attacked me that first night in his library, Dekes had called McAllister to brag about how easily he'd killed me. That had gotten Jonah's hopes up— hopes that I'd dashed as soon as he'd learned Dekes was really dead instead of me. I had no doubt that McAllister was already cooking up another scheme he hoped would lead to my death, but it was the lawyer's days that were numbered—not mine.

The two guys stepped forward and cracked their knuckles, evil grins spreading across their faces. Nope, looked like they hadn't learned a thing last time—or they wouldn't be stupid enough to be standing in the alley with me right now.

"Surrender now, Spider," Billy the giant said. "And we might just go easy on you."

"Yeah," Bobby the Fire elemental chimed in. "We won't hurt you—much."

The two men chuckled at their seeming cleverness. I rolled my eyes. The only people these two were really hurting were themselves.

"Didn't y'all learn your lesson the first time?" I said. "You should be grateful you're still breathing. Now, run along like good little boys before I lose my temper and kill you."

Bobby's face twisted, and a murderous glint shimmered in his eyes along with his Fire magic. "Nobody talks to us like that, bitch."

The Fire elemental sucked in a breath and went on a long, rambling rant then, talking about how he and his buddy were going to make me wish I'd never been born. Typical talk in the shadows of Ashland. It amused the hell out of me, and I found myself leaning against the wall of the Pork Pit and just letting him talk—because that's all these guys were.

"What are you smiling at?" Bobby growled, finally noticing that I wasn't the least bit scared of him, his magic, or his giant friend.

"Nothing much," I drawled. "I was just thinking that there's no place like home."

The two men looked at each other, obviously confused. Then they charged at me, the way I knew they would. This time I didn't bother picking up one of the dented trash can lids. Instead, I palmed the silverstone knives tucked up my sleeves and stepped up to meet them.

Magic and blood arced through the air and splattered onto the alley floor and walls, punctuated by sharp, pain-filled screams that quickly died off to choking gurgles.

Then . . . silence.

I got to my feet and wiped my bloody knives off on the clothes of my latest victims. Billy and Bobby stared up at the black sky, eyes and mouths wide open in shock and fear. It was far too late for them to agree with me. It was far too late for them to do anything at all.

Oh, I knew that it wouldn't end with these two. More Billys and Bobbys would seek me out in the coming days, trying to cash in and build their street cred at the Spider's expense. Not to mention McAllister and whom he might decide to send after me next.

But I'd be right here at the Pork Pit waiting for all of them, serving up the best barbecue in Ashland and helping those who couldn't help themselves after-hours in my own special way. With Owen, Bria, Finn, the Deveraux sisters, and all my other friends right by my side.

Yep, the Spider was definitely back.

Still smiling, I slid my bloody knives up my sleeves and headed inside the restaurant to ask Sophia to come and help me get rid of the blood and the bodies.

Turn the page for a sneak peek at the next book
in the Elemental Assassin series,

WIDOW'S WEB

Jennifer Estep

Coming soon from Pocket Books

❊ 1 ❊

Breaking into the building was easy.

Too easy for an assassin like me.

Hell, I didn't even have to break in—I could have walked right through the front door, waved at the guard stationed behind the reception desk in the lobby, and taken the elevator up to the appropriate floor. Stroll into an office building holding a vase of flowers, an oversize teddy bear, or a couple of pizza boxes smelling of grease, pepperoni, and melted mozzarella, and no one looks too closely at you. Except to wish that they were the ones who'd thought to order pizza for dinner.

The delivery ruse was one that I'd used countless times before, and I would have done it again today—except he knew that I was coming for him. He was on his guard, and everyone coming into the building was being checked and double-checked for weapons and to see if they even had the right to be there in the first place.

Besides, I preferred to be subtle about these things—to creep around in the shadows, leap out, take down my target when he least expected it, and then vanish back into the darkness once more. As the assassin the Spider, I had a reputation to uphold—that I could get to anyone, anywhere, anytime.

Something that I planned on proving once again this evening—no matter how tight my target's security was.

It had taken me the better part of a week to scout out various locations where the hit might go down. Home, office, the route in between, restaurants he liked to frequent for lunch and dinner, even Northern Aggression, Ashland's most decadent nightclub, where he spent a fair amount of time after-hours. I'd eventually decided to do the job in his office, which was housed in one of the city's downtown skyscrapers. He probably thought he was safe there, given the amount of security, but he was going to learn exactly how wrong he was.

It had taken another week and been a bit more difficult than I'd expected, getting my hands on the building's blueprints and figuring out a way to get close to my target, but I'd managed. I always managed. I wouldn't have been the Spider otherwise. Besides, I always enjoyed a challenge.

Now I was into the third week of the operation, and it was finally time to put my plan into action, since the job had to be done before the end of the month. Normally that wouldn't be a problem, but the target knew about the looming deadline and that I was gunning for him. Every day that passed meant that security got that much tighter and my job that much more difficult.

Two hours ago, I'd strolled into a downtown parking garage wearing a black pantsuit and matching heels. I'd pulled my dark, chocolate brown hair up into a high, sleek ponytail, while black glasses with clear lenses covered my cold gray eyes. I looked like just another corporate office drone, right down to the enormous black handbag that I carried.

The garage lay on the opposite side of the block from the front entrance to the skyscraper, but thanks to the blueprints I'd looked at, I discovered that the two were connected by a series of maintenance corridors, which meant I didn't have to go anywhere near the skyscraper lobby to actually get inside the building.

Always take the most unexpected route. That was something my mentor, Fletcher Lane, had told me more than once, and I expected it to work just as well tonight as it had so many other times in the past.

Still, I'd thought that my target might have a few guards stationed in the garage, hence my business attire, but I didn't see anyone as I walked down the ramp from the street to the basement level. A few security cameras swiveled around in slow loops on the walls, their red lights blinking like malevolent eyes, but it was easy enough for me to walk through their blind spots. Sloppy of him not to make sure the entire garage was covered by the cameras, even if it was on the other side of the block.

My heels cracked against the concrete as I headed toward the elevator, the harsh sound bouncing around like a Ping-Pong ball someone had tossed into the middle of the garage. Despite the fact that I was in the downtown business district, muggings weren't unheard-of here, and my eyes scanned the shadows, just in case there was any-one lurking around who shouldn't be. Assassin or not, I had no desire to get blood on my clothes before I'd gotten close to my target. I was the only one getting away with any violence tonight.

As a final precaution, I reached out with my magic and listened to the stone around me.

People leave behind emotional vibrations in their sur-roundings, in the places where they spend their time, in the houses, apartments, and offices where they live, love, laugh, work, and die. All those feelings, all those emo-tions, especially sink into stone, whether it's a concrete foundation of a house, the gravel that constantly crunches under the tires of a new convertible, or even an expensive marble sculpture prettily perched in a living room.

As a Stone elemental, I can hear those vibrations and pick up on those emotions as clearly as if the person who had put them there was standing right next to me, tell-ing me all about how he'd used that marble sculpture to bash in his wife's brains just so he could collect on her life insurance policy.

I reached out with my magic, and the usual sharp, worried murmurs echoed back to me. Nobody much cares for parking garages, and the low mutters told me just how many folks had fearfully clutched their bags and briefcases to their chests as they hurried to unlock their cars—and the ones who hadn't made it before they'd been beaten, robbed, and left for dead.

Still, there were no recent disturbances in the stone, and no indication that someone had set his sights on me. Satisfied, I shut the murmurs out of my mind, rounded the corner, and reached the elevator that led from the garage up into the office building on this side of the block.

A man wearing a suit and carrying a silverstone briefcase waited in front of the elevator, watching the numbers light up as it slowly descended to our level. I gave him a polite nod, then pulled my cell phone out of my bag and started tapping the buttons on it, sending a message to no one.

The elevator arrived a minute later, and the man stepped inside, holding the door open for me.

"Going up?" he asked.

I waved him off. "I need to finish this text first. My reception always gets cut off in there."

He nodded and let the doors slide shut. I hit a few more buttons on my phone, just in case there was anyone else behind me heading toward the elevator, but no one appeared. When I was sure that I was alone, I put the phone away and headed to the far end of the corridor and a door marked MAINTENANCE ONLY.

I looped my bag across my shoulder so that my hands would be free, held my palm up, and reached for my magic again—but not my Stone power. Most elementals are only gifted in one area—Air, Fire, Ice, or Stone—but I was among the rarest of elementals in that I could tap into two different areas. So now, instead of using my Stone magic, I grabbed hold of my Ice power and used it to form a very specific, familiar shape—one that would help me get through this locked door.

A cold silver light flickered in my palm, centered on the scar there, one that was shaped like a small circle surrounded by eight thin rays. A matching scar was embedded in my other palm. The marks were spider runes, the symbol for patience. My assassin name and so many other things to me.

A second later, the light faded, and I clutched two slender Ice picks in my fingers. Still keeping an eye and ear out for anyone else walking through the garage, I went to work on the door. I wasn't as good at jimmying locks as Finnegan Lane, my foster brother, was, but I got the job done in under a minute. I threw the Ice picks down on the concrete where they would soon melt away and slid through the opening, letting the door close behind me.

I stood in a long, narrow hallway set with flickering bulbs that gave everything an ugly, sallow tint. I paused a moment, listening for the footsteps of the maintenance workers who used these corridors. I didn't hear any scuffles or other whispers of movement, so I started walking. Even if I ran into someone down here, I'd just claim to be a lost office drone, desperately trying to find my way back to the hive.

But for once, my luck held, and I didn't see anyone as I hurried through the hallways. Eventually I wound up in the basement of the skyscraper where my target's office was. After that, it was just a matter of taking the service elevator up to the second floor, above the guards in the lobby. Then I leisurely walked the rest of the way up the emergency stairs until I reached the top floor.

I cracked open the stairway door and found myself looking out over a sea of cubicles divided by clear plastic walls. I'd gotten here right at quitting time, and everyone was trying to wrap up their work for the day so they could be out the door by five sharp to get their kids, get dinner, and get home. Everyone hunched over their phones and computers, sending out a few last messages for the day, and no one noticed me slip out of the stairway, softly pull the door shut behind me, and stroll into their midst.

I kept to the edge of the cubicle area and walked down a hallway until I came to a corner office that I knew was being used to store supplies. The office door was open, and I stepped inside like I had every right in the world to be there. I looked over my shoulder through the window, but no one so much as glanced in my direction, so I went into the private bathroom that was attached to the office and closed the door behind me.

I stood there behind the door, counted off the seconds in my head, and waited to see if anyone had noticed me and had alerted security. Ten . . . twenty . . . thirty . . . forty-five . . . After the three-minute mark, I felt safe enough to move on to the next part of my plan. Now that I was in the building and on the appropriate floor, all that was left to do was get to exactly where I wanted to be.

I removed a small electric screwdriver from my bag, climbed up onto the marble bathroom counter, and used the tool to open one of the air duct vents high up on the wall. Once that was done, I climbed back down, stripped off my suit and glasses, and reached into my bag and put on my real clothes for the evening—cargo pants, a long-sleeved T-shirt, a vest, and boots. All in black, of course. Yeah, wearing head-to-toe black might be a little cliché for an assassin, but you went with what worked—and hid the bloodstains.

I looped my bag around my chest, got back up onto the counter, and hoisted myself up and into the air duct, making sure to close up the vent opening behind me. Like many buildings in Ashland, the ducts here were made slightly oversize, in deference to the city's giant population, so I didn't have any problems sliding inside. I slowly, carefully, quietly crawled through the air ducts until I reached the office that I wanted. Then I eased up to the vent and peered through the slats to the other side.

The duct opened up into an office that was both impressive and elegant. A large desk made out of polished ebony stood in the back of the room. Pens, paper, a monitor, two phones. The usual office detritus covered the surface, while two black leather chairs crouched in front of the desk. Even from here, I could see how rich and supple the fabric was. Matching furniture in varying shades of black and gray filled the rest of the room, along with elaborate metal sculptures, while a fully stocked wet bar took up the better part of one wall. Behind the desk, floor-to-ceiling windows offered an impressive view of downtown Ashland and the green-gray smudges of the Appalachian Mountains that ringed the city.

The office was empty, just like I'd planned for it to be right now, so I didn't have to be quite as quiet as I used my screwdriver to undo the grate on the duct and put the loose screws in my vest pocket. I practiced removing the grate from its frame until I was sure that I could do it without making any noise, then I slid it back into place. I also reached into my bag and drew out my weapon of choice this evening—a small gun made out of plastic.

Normally I carried five silverstone knives on me at all times—one up either sleeve, one against the small of my back, and two tucked into the sides of my boots. I liked my knives, and those were the weapons I used on the majority of my jobs. But my target had an elemental talent for metal, which meant that he could sense whenever the element was near, just like I could hear the stone around me, no matter what form it took. In fact, metal was an offshoot of Stone, just like water was an offshoot of Ice magic and electricity was one of Air power.

Since I didn't want to give my target any hint that I was here, I'd decided to leave my knives at home. I wasn't as good with a gun as I was with a blade, but the plastic device I'd brought along tonight would get the job done in the office's close quarters.

As a final touch, I reached into my bag and pulled on a pair of black gloves, making sure that the leather covered the spider rune scars embedded in my palms. The scars were really silverstone that had been melted into my flesh years ago by a particularly vicious Fire elemental. I didn't think that my target would be able to sense the metal in my palms—not through the duct—but the gloves offered another small bit of protection, and I wasn't going to take any chances tonight.

With the grate and my gun in position, all that was left to do was settle down and wait for my target to arrive.

I'd been in position inside the air duct for almost an hour when the office door opened, and two men carrying briefcases stepped inside. Both wore expensive tailored suits and shiny wing tips, marking them as the movers and shakers they were. My target was having an after-hours meeting with his moneyman to go over company financials and various other things. Too bad it was a meeting that neither one of them would live through.

Through the grate, I watched a third man step into the office—a giant who was almost seven feet tall. He also wore a suit, although his wasn't quite as nice as those of the other two men.

The two businessmen hung back while the giant did a sweep of the office, peering behind the desk and wet bar, then going into the private bathroom and repeating the process by glancing into the shower. A moment later, the giant stepped back out into the office.

"All clear, sir," the giant said. "The rest of the floor has been swept and is empty as well."

My target nodded his thanks, and the giant left, closing the door behind him.

The second man didn't even wait until the door had been shut before he moved over to the bar, grabbed a bottle of expensive Scotch, and poured himself a healthy amount into a cut-crystal tumbler. He took a long swallow of the amber-colored liquor and nodded his head in approval. Then he turned his attention to his friend.

"Any sign of her today?" the drinker asked.

The other man, my target, shook his head. "Nothing so far."

The drinker grinned. "Well, since the Spider hasn't come to call yet and it looks like you get to live another day, let's get down to business. I happen to have someone waiting up for me tonight. I'm sure you know what I mean."

My target smiled a little at that, and the two men opened their briefcases. They spread the papers inside over a table in front of the wet bar, then sank down into the chairs on either side and got to work.

"Now," the drinker began, "as you can see from these latest tax and earnings figures . . ."

I waited until the two men were thoroughly engrossed in their conversation before I slowly, carefully, quietly removed the grate from the air duct opening. I paused, waiting to see if they'd noticed the slight, furtive movement above their heads, but of course they hadn't. Few people bothered to look up—even those being hunted by a notorious assassin like me.

I put the grate to one side of the duct and made sure the gun was within easy reach in its proper slot on the front of my vest. Then I drew in a breath and slowly wiggled forward until I was at the edge of the opening. I drew in a final breath, let it out, and slid forward.

I let my weight and gravity pull me down before grabbing the edge of the duct, flipping over, letting go, and landing on my feet, facing the two men. They'd barely had time to blink, much less get to their feet, before the gun was in my hand and trained on my target.

Puff-puff.

I double-tapped my target in the chest, and he dropped to the expensive carpet without a sound. I trained my gun on the second man, who immediately leaped to his feet, put up his hands in a placating gesture, and started backing away.

"You don't have to do this," he said, pleading with me. "You've proven your point already. I'll pay you whatever you want to put the gun down now and walk away, you know that."

"I do know that." A cold, cruel smile curved my lips. "But walking away is not nearly as much fun as this. You know that as well as I do."

"No, please, don't—"

I pulled the trigger twice, cutting off his protests, and he joined the first man on the floor.

Silence.

Then the protestor, the drinker, the second man I'd shot, let out a loud, unhappy sigh and climbed to his feet.

"Really, Gin, did you have to ruin my suit?" Finn said. "This was a Fiona Fine original."

He stared down at the bright red paint splattered across the black fabric of his suit jacket and white shirt. Then Finn raised his head and glared at me, his green eyes as bright as polished glass in his ruddy face. I didn't bother pointing out that the red paint from the gun had also splashed onto his face and up into his walnut-colored locks. My foster brother was just as obsessive about his hair as he was about his suits, and it just wouldn't *do* for Finnegan Lane to ever look anything less than perfect.

"I have to say I agree with Finn," the first man rumbled and sat up. "I didn't think our little experiment would get quite so messy."

Owen Grayson got to his feet, his chest covered in just as much red paint as Finn's was. Still, despite his ruined suit, my eyes traced over him, from his blue-black hair to his intense violet eyes to his strong, muscled body. All the paint in the world couldn't dampen Owen's rugged appeal or the way he had of making me feel like I was the most important person in the world to him.

I walked over, leaned against the desk, and pointed my paintball gun at Owen. "You were the one who agreed to let me test your security," I told my lover. "And Finn was the one who bet me dinner at Underwood's that I couldn't kill you both by the end of the month. So you have only yourselves to blame."

Finn sniffed his displeasure again. "I still say that you didn't have to ruin my suit."

"No," I agreed. "I didn't *have* to ruin it. That was just an added bonus."

Finn narrowed his eyes at me, but I just gave him my most innocent, gracious, beatific Southern smile.

"Well, it's getting late, and I'm supposed to head over to Bria's," Finn said. "And I obviously can't go looking like *this*."

I rolled my eyes at his put-upon tone, but Owen just laughed.

"Go," Owen said. "Get cleaned up. We can finish our business tomorrow."

"Say hi to Bria for me," I added in a sugary-sweet voice.

Finn grumbled something under his breath about what I could do with various parts of my anatomy before packing up his papers and briefcase and leaving the office.

"Well," Owen said after Finn had shut the door a little harder than necessary. "You got us both, just like you said you would."

I grinned. "That's what people pay me for. Or used to pay me for."

Owen raised an eyebrow. "Good to know that retirement hasn't lessened your skills any."

I shrugged. We both knew that I couldn't afford to let myself get rusty. Not now, when so many folks in Ashland and beyond would love nothing more than to see me dead. Back in the winter, I'd finally managed to kill Mab Monroe, the Fire elemental who'd been the head of the Ashland underworld for years. Mab had murdered my mother and sister when I was thirteen, and her death had been about revenge to me more than anything else. But the Fire elemental's demise had left a power vacuum in the city, and now, every lowlife and not-so-lowlife was clawing for position, power, and prestige. Some of them thought the best way to do that was by killing me, Gin Blanco, the semiretired assassin known as the Spider.

So far, I'd put all the challengers in the ground right next to Mab, but they just kept coming at me. A few weeks ago, I'd decided to test and update the security at all the places I frequented, including Owen's home and office. There was no point in making things *easy* for my would-be murderers. Then Finn had piped up and suggested that we make it into a contest—with him and Owen trying to outwit me. Of course, that hadn't turned out exactly like Finn had planned, but I was happy with the outcome. I always liked to win, no matter what game I was playing.

"So give me the rundown," Owen said. "Exactly how did you get into that air duct?"

I recapped my wanderings through the parking garage, maintenance halls, stairwell, office, and air duct.

"Overall, your security's sound," I said. "All we have to do is fix a few holes here and there, and no one will be able to get to you, me, or anyone else in here short of bringing down the whole building."

His eyes were fixed on mine, but there was a blank look on his face, as though he were only politely listening to my words with half an ear. I know it wasn't the most romantic talk, detailing how I'd just paintballed my lover, but this wasn't the first time he'd spaced out on me in the last few days. Something was on Owen's mind, and I didn't know what it was. That worried me more than I would have liked, especially since I'd given him plenty of openings to tell me what was bothering him—openings that he hadn't taken.

"Owen?" I asked.

Something flashed in his eyes then, something that almost looked like worry, but it was gone too quickly for me to pinpoint exactly what it was. He shook his head and focused on me once more.

"Sorry," he said. "What were you saying?"

Owen shrugged out of his suit jacket, the muscles in his arms and chest rolling with the motion. Suddenly I was interested in playing something else besides a war game. Something that would be far more entertaining and pleasurable—for both of us. Not to mention keep my lover firmly in the here and now with me. I didn't like playing second fiddle any more than the next woman did.

Owen started to loosen his tie, but I put the paintball gun down on the desk and strolled over to him. He stopped what he was doing and watched me as I put an extra roll of my hips into my step. Heat sparked in Owen's eyes—heat that matched the warmth that was quickly flaring up inside me as well.

"Let me," I said.

Owen watched with dark, hooded eyes as I carefully unknotted his silk tie and let it fall to the floor. Then I ran my hands across his chest, marveling at the warm muscles there before reaching up and undoing the top two buttons of his shirt. I pushed the fabric aside, leaned forward, and pressed a soft kiss to the hollow of his throat. Owen's arms snaked around me, pulling me close to his chest, and his fingers began pressing into my back, urging me even closer. I definitely had his full attention now.

"Why don't I help you get out of that ruined suit?" I murmured. "In addition to killing people, this assassin also happens to be very good at cleanup."

A sexy grin slowly spread across Owen's rugged face, softening the scar that slashed underneath his chin. "Really? That's something I'd be very interested in seeing."

I led Owen into the bathroom. The door didn't even shut behind us before my lips were on his, and I forgot about everything but the pleasure we could give each other. There would be time enough to figure out what had Owen so concerned—later.

Much, much later.